MODI
Common Man's PM

MODI
Common Man's PM

Kishor Makwana

PRABHAT PRAKASHAN

ISO 9001: 2008 Publishers

Published by
PRABHAT PRAKASHAN
4/19 Asaf Ali Road,
New Delhi-110 002 (INDIA)
Tele : +91-11-23289777
e-mail: prabhatbooks@gmail.com

ISBN 978-93-5048-979-6
MODI: COMMON MAN'S PM
by Kishor Makwana

Translated into English by
A.K. Gandhi

Edited by
Dr. Radhika Nagrath

Paperback Edition
First, 2015

Price
₹ 250.00 (Rupees Two Hundred Fifty only)

Printed at
R-Tech Offset Printers, Delhi

Dedicated to the Indians

Languages numerous – sentiment one.
States numerous – nation one.
Faiths numerous – goal one.
Languages numerous – voice one.
Communities numerous – India one.
Traditions numerous – culture one.
Schemes numerous – goal one.
Tasks numerous – resolve one.
Paths numerous – destination one.
Dresses numerous – talent one.
Faces numerous – smile one.
Colours numerous – Tricolour one.

—Narendra Modi

A thought...

The well-known weekly American magazine, *Time* had stated in its issue dated March 26, 2013: "If Modi succeeded to reach national politics, it would necessarily change the picture and essence of India." Today, more than a year later, this truth has been realized. The entire India has got this great national leader as its PM.

India, a land of 125 crore people, a land of great heritage, is going through terrible times, so a lay man is looking forward to just one personality in a bid to have a change. He is the man who draws crowds wherever he goes. The people thronging his public rallies number in millions; he has even superseded the rallies conducted by prominent leaders in 1977 or in the pre independence period from 1942-47. He continues to be the most favourite face amongst people of the country. The youths can find in him a confluence of development, opportunity and modernity. People get elated to see him. Their eyes light up when they get glance of their hero. When they hear him, their hearts are moved with vigour and vitality, as if they all were waiting for such a leader for a long time in whom they could take pride and who could lead the nation in full capacity. He is none else, but just one man, one personality; there is no alternative of him, no substitute of him, he is Modi...Modi...Narendra Modi.

At present, Narendra Modi is the strongest leader in the country's politics, who has led Gujarat to the numero uno position and is now leading the greatest democracy of the World—India. He has superseded even the American President in individual popularity, and most people in the world wish to know more about him. He is the one who has shown the resolve and courage to address the rally at Patna despite bomb explosions. He can challenge the extremists in their own houses. Giving him a visa is major news for countries like America and England; Pakistan is just shivering at his name; he is at the target of the terrorists, yet he has moved the entire country with his uproar. He has neither any personal property, nor land, nor bank balance. His image is untarnished by the demon of corruption.

When he speaks, the entire country feels that he is raising their souls' voice. His present is the riot-free and developed state of Gujarat, and his aspiration is a strong India. Latest technology and modernization are his means, and preservation of Indian culture his duty; to make India the leading nation in global competition is his goal, and to realize it is his resolve through participation of the people. The nation too is looking its future in Narendra Modi. The renowned American journalist Robert D. Copland says: "I have met both Presidents – Jimmy Carter and Bill Clinton, but I am yet to see Modi's charisma in any one."

Narendra Modi is leader of the long struggle of the common Indians. His childhood passed in anti-untouchability movement, rendering help to the poor and in service to the troops during the 1962 India-China War; his adolescence passed in Gauraksha movement (protection and conservation of cows), and his youth passed in opposing corruption in Gujarat, reconstruction movement and struggle against Indira Gandhi's autocracy during the Emergency. He inherited fondness for spirituality which made him renounce everything, and the national ideology made him a *Karmayogi*. With his joining of the Bharatiya Janata Party, we can find a persona of a skilled strategist and successful executor.

After he became Gujarat's Chief Minister, he became a synonym for development. Gujarat had been known for riots for the past 300 years. The first riot in Ahmedabad took place as far back as in 1713; in the past 35 years there have been 979 riots. In his 12 years as the Chief Minister, Narendra Modi has put Gujarat on the path of development and has created a golden chapter in the history of the state which had tasted the sour fruits of riots over ages. Today, Gujarat is fully free from riots.

Narendra Modi became the Chief Minister for the third time. Finally, the court of law has ridiculed all allegations against Modi and accepted that he played no direct or indirect role in the riots.

Despite mental torture of more than a decade, he has dedicated every moment of his life for Gujarat. He was sworn in for the first time on October 7, 2001. At that time, Gujarat was passing through the deadly consequences of the earthquake and other natural calamities. Thousands of people had been killed; towns and villages had been devastated. The Gujarat Government, to the amazement of the world, constructed 8,76,618 houses in just five hundred days. When Surat got devastated from the flood, Modi himself took over the relief operations. A rickshaw-puller in Surat said: "I have seen many leaders touring the flood-affected areas, but I have seen for the first time a Chief Minister has stepped down in the mud and worked." When a natural calamity hit the state of Uttarakhand, Modi immediately reached there. The readiness he showed for the protection and relief of the victimized devotees is now well known to the nation.

Due to his profound interest in science and technology, Narendra Modi has transformed Gujarat into an e-governed state, and has encouraged several schemes. The Swagat Online and Tele Fariyad are such initiatives, on account of which e-transparency has occurred, and now a common man can contact the highest office directly. He listens to the complaints of the common man carefully and ensures that the problems are resolved in a given time frame. Narendra Modi has focussed his attention on the social sector in an adequate manner in order to achieve complete socio-economic development, and he worked to reform the imbalances prevailing there. He has conceptualized a five-point strategy – Panchamrit Yojana – for the all-round development of the state. Today, Gujarat is marching ahead in a number of fields such as e-governance, capital investment, poverty eradication, electricity, SEZ, road construction, financial management and other fields. His mantra of 'Sabka Sath – Sabka Vikas' and maxim of 'pro-people pro-active good governance' together with development projects in Gujarat have led to people's active participation. Despite several barriers, he was resolved to take the height of the Narmada to 121.9 metres. He even undertook the fast against those who stood against this project.

Achievements and prosperity of Gujarat are being talked about not only because of development in economic and agricultural fields, but also because of the work accomplished in social, educational, health fields, as well as augmenting the people's confidence. The people of Gujarat are full to the brim with pride and self-confidence. All this has come about due to Narendra Modi's hard work and transparent governance. Narendra Modi has executed a large number of such schemes which had not been heard before. There are a number of such programmes and schemes like Samras Gaon, Pavan Gaon, Tirthgram, Vanche Gujarat (Study Gujarat), Patang Utsav, Vibrant Summit, Jyotigram, Krishi Mahotsav, E-gram Vishwa Gram, Statue of Unity and the likes. As soon as he came to power, he gave a new doctrine of Panchamrit for all-round development of Gujarat, this comprised the power of knowledge, power of people, power of water, power of security and power of energy; this resulted into Gujarat's development in every field. Narendra Modi auctioned the gifts he received and donated the money from them for girl education.

The E-gram Vishwa Gram scheme is executed through the satellite technique, by which the villages are connected to the world, and the computer network facilitates to provide quick government service. The government also issued Vidyalakshmi Bonds for poor girls and rural women were motivated for savings through the Sakhi Mandals. The landless labourers were given insurance cover. Today, Gujarat leads the country in education.

Admission to school is one hundred percent in Gujarat through movements like Kanya Shiksha and Shala Praveshotsava. There are a number of latest projects for all-round development of the tribals and the Dalits. The organisation of poor welfare fairs for development of urban and rural poor people is unprecedented. The roads in Gujarat are worth emulating for the whole country.

The Sujalam-Sufalam project is working to create several grids of water sources in order to initiate a wonderful programme in water conservation and its proper utilization. The initiation of Soil Health Card and Roaming Ration Card are such tasks which display his concern for the extremely ordinary man of the state. Gujarat has received all-round development through schemes like Krishi Mahotsav, Chiranjivi scheme, Matra Vandana, Beti Bachao Abhiyan, Jyotigram scheme and Karmayogi scheme, E-mamta, M Power, SCOPE, I-Create and other extraordinary schemes.

Gujarat has also obtained a number of honours and awards. It has received the Sasakava award from the UN for its disaster management, CAPM (Commonwealth Association for Public Administration and Management) and UNESCO for creative and active administration, CSI award for e-governance and others. In a survey, Narendra Modi has the honour of being the best Chief Minister for three consecutive years. The Chiranjivi scheme was given the Asian Innovation award by the *Financial Express* for reducing the delivery time, child and mother mortality rate. Gujarat has been honoured with more than 250 national and international awards.

Narendra Modi had not been just the Chief Minister of Gujarat, he is also a ray of hope for 125 crore Indians. People have been impressed by him, right from the ordinary farmer to the industrialist and students. People have joined his campaign for corruption-free, dearness-free, capable and united India. He has presented himself as a game changer. He has not inherited power, rather he has won the hearts of the millions by his resolve to development despite numerous barriers, hurdles and struggles. He has succeeded in bringing out the government from the air-conditioned offices to the common man's threshold.

Narendra Modi realizes what he says. He is an excellent seer and is the architect of Gujarat's reconstruction. His sole goal is to reform and rejuvenate India in order to establish her as the superpower in the twenty-first century, to make her the *Jagadguru*.

The whole India is looking to this great national leader with hope and optimism. In such a time, this book on the personality of Narendra Modi is a humble tribute, which will allow you to look into the life, works, personality and thought of Narendra Modi, as a whole.

I must thank the Journalist writer Dr. Radhika Nagrath of Haridwar, for the invaluable help which she has given by contributing the major achievements of Shri Narendra Modi as PM, his foreign trips and country-wide campaigns, collected from various authentic sources like news agencies and news dailies in the concluding chapter. But for these materials, the biography of this towering personality would not have been complete.

Radhika Nagrath is an investigative journalist for Hindustan Times. She is the awarded author, most recently of *The carnival of Peace-Kumbh Teertham Haridwaram* and *Vivekananda-The known philosopher the unknown poet. She appeared as historian journalist in a documentary shot by Discovery channel on Kumbh Mela.*

We acknowledge heartfelt thanks to the media agencies and reporters across the world, especially of US, Japan and China who covered the visits of the Indian PM in their countries.

—Kishor Makwana

Premise

This book is not the life sketch of Narendra Modi, rather it is a minuscule effort to underline his personality and creativity. The life of Narendra Modi is like a story. A child forsakes his house with a goal to become a *Sanyasi (renunciant)*, but the fate takes him to the assignment of the ruler. He has devoted everything of his life to the service of Mother India through the Rashtriya Swayamsevak Sangh.

In 1984, Narendra Modi had an intellectual talk at Dholaka's Kuberji Temple (in district Ahmedabad) where a camp was organised by the Rashtriya Swayamsevak Sangh on the occasion of Makar Sankranti festival. He spoke from his heart: "Social science is behind each festival of India. Makar Sankranti festival weaves the entire society into a fabric; it cultivates an atmosphere of goodwill, harmony, coordination and affectionate environment in the society. Our festivals cultivate the spirit of social development and progress within us."

When we heard of his talk on this occasion, we were quite young, studying in class 12 but his speech had an inerasable impact on our minds. His intimate conduct with everybody draws people to him. He is talented and influential, yet natural and simple. Just one introduction with him and, he will call you by name whenever he meets you next; this shows his sharp memory and his close relation with each person. We have examined him from close quarters right since 1984, we have seen his personality very closely. His face glows all the time with vigour and vitality, and these are the marks of his personality. He remains calm and keeps his poise under any given situation, and his line of thought is very succinct.

When we studied his life, we felt that Narendra Modi has no distinction between his thinking and doing, deed and speech. This book took shape during the course of our endeavour to know and understand him.

Narendra Modi is called a strict ruler, but he possesses a soft heart. His heart goes out for the poor, the exploited, the deprived, and he feels restless as well as active for the welfare of these people. He possesses qualities of an able administrator, organizer, impressive speaker, poet-writer-thinker and visioner. When I joined the *Sadhana*, a weekly, he wrote on the national news in a column called 'Akshar Upavan' by the pseudonym 'Aniket'. He wrote this column for about four years. Later, he became the Chief Minister, and continued to write on several topics.

I have witnessed his entire journey right from the time when he was a dedicated *Pracharak* of the Sangh to his becoming the Chief Minister. During this course, he has carried out every responsibility assigned to him, and he has worked hard for it. The marks of his personality are complete devotion to his work, self-confidence, higher goals, discipline towards work and achievement.

This book discusses the important stopovers of his life, his personality, his patriotism, his working efficiency and vision – these are the five points. Besides, the most important part of this book is a detailed interview focussing his life and personality. This is perhaps the first interview that people would feel as if they are talking to Narendra Modi face-to-face. He has responded to many a question of his life, right from his childhood, becoming a *Sanyasi*, life as *Pracharak*, likes and dislikes, becoming the Chief Minister, his views, ideas and doctrines, dreams and aspirations, and he has responded to all these without any hitch or reservation. This book in itself is a detailed account of the fine personality of Narendra Modi.

—Kishor Makwana

Sakshi Bhav

Sakshi Bhav, penned by Narendra Modi, is a journey of his inner-self. It is not a literary creation, rather a flow of emotions collected from his diary which he had written about twenty-five years ago, when he was doing social service in the capacity of a Sangh *Pracharak*, Narendra Modi used to write the diary addressing the Supreme Mother. Most of the pages had been burnt down by him about that time, but some pages still remained. *Sakshi Bhav* are those leftover pages. These were written around 1968, and express his sentiments. Narendra Modi writes: "I am an ordinary human, just like you. I keep thinking continuously how I can effect my personality development." And the nectar that was produced from this thinking has been written down for the readers. Here, we present an extract from *Sakshi Bhav*. This extract seems to belong to the time when he was sent from the Sangh to the Bharatiya Janata Party; however, his sentiments, expressed about 28 years ago, appear to be relevant even today.

Inspiration for New Life

Mother
I bow to thy feet.

The final day of the camp.
Until yesterday
There was rush and work and urge for whose construction
Now inclines towards dispersal all that arrangement
These short-term arrangements
Are like the symbols of human life!
This world too is like this!
Who doesn't know it is an illusion?

But why then human mind
Get emancipated from it?
All this is meaningless.
This sorrow, this pleasure, this bliss,
This satisfaction, this tendency, this aspiration,
This desire – all that are transient.
Perhaps satisfaction gives a fleeting bliss,
Maybe mental resolution will be achieved,
Maybe there will be contentment to conquer the others,
But this satisfaction too is transient.
As it is, the joy of attainment in the mortal world is especially
transient.
Still, Mother, everybody including me
Is after achievement.
Why so? In fact, in human heart
Where is expected to cultivate culture
Why does there arises
A tempest of such transient tendencies?
This is the tempest that raises human
From his base life
To throw far.
Mother…as a human I too
Will be a victim as natural.
Eternal desires, eternal satisfaction,
Awakening of eternal desires,
Is there no way out?
Perhaps the eternal desires will enlighten
The path of eternally contented life.
The discovery of that path is
The greatest introspection of human life.
I have experienced the bliss of introvert life.
There is contentment of fulfilment.
Extrovert life may be impressive,
But not inspiring.
Extrovert life will focus on the aura,
But introvert life will manifest inner-self.
Inner life has no noise,
It is replete with silent peace.
A quiet stream flows continuously.

This stream may not be able to fertilise
The whole land, but this quiet stream
Certainly infuses life into barren land.
It too has unique bliss.
The stream creates a true, quiet dialogue,
In which melody of music jingles
And then human tingles with it.
How short-lived is the flow.
No sound, no noise, no mass like a lake,
No tempest like an ocean, no flow like a river,
Still the stream is self-contented!
Tiny strength of it even
Marks multitude within it.
Yes, this all is grateful to introvert abidance.
So its area of influence
Sharpness of its impact – is not all despite size,
How sharp is its motivation?
It is the outcome of that discontinuous flow without a desire.
My eternal flow of inner-self is linked to it inseparably.
No destination, no rest is possible.
This liveliness of its becomes fragrant,
Inspires for new life.
Mother...all this is true yet
I am going against it.
Free from quiet, healthy mind,
I am seeking noise.
No confusion exists in the mind.
Mother...I am aware.
Now this body has to ascend a new theatre.
I have to adorn it as per the new theatre.
I have to transform as per the new theatre
All my organs of the body –
Mind, intellect, heart.
Mother...it will occur with your blessings,
You will have to make feel liveliness there,
But I am after the soul, the inner soul
Now I shall be with you by this inner soul.
How I appear before the world
Has no significance in my heart.

20

The eternal flow of my inner-self
Is inseparably connected to you.
No goal, no rest is possible.
Perhaps this devotion of mine
Will preserve me in this inner-outer situation.

Date: 9 December 1986

Contents

The Village, The People

The life story of Narendra Modi, the Prime Minister of India, is no inferior to a fancy tale. Today, everybody appears to be curious to know more about him. He was born in a small town called Vadnagar and the economic status of the family was quite ordinary. He studied in the government primary school, and with the advent of youth, he renounced his home in order to devote himself to the service of Maa Bharati, the Motherland. Narendra Modi ascended the stairs of success on the basis of his perseverance and capability. Man can achieve success by deed, and not birth, and the entire life of Narendra Modi has been cast from deed.

Vadnagar is an ancient town, 34 kilometres from Mahesana and 112 kilometres from Ahmedabad. It finds mention in the *Skanda Purana* too. Basically, Vadnagar is very ancient; it took several different names during the passage of time – Skandhpur, Kanakpur, Chamatkarpur, Arkasthali, Anartpur, Anandpur, Vriddhanagar and finally Vadnagar. This town is also known as the 'town of temples and ponds'. The *Skanda Purana* mentions a place of pilgrimage – Hatkesh Tirtha. There is a magnificent temple of Hatkesh here, and the Shiv Linga (Phallus of Lord Shiva) has originated of Itself. The ashram (hermitage) of Sage Yajnavalkya was located on the bank of the Kapila River, now extinct. In the ancient past, it has also been a centre of pilgrimage for the Jain and Buddhist faiths. In Jainism, it was considered to be Talhati of Palitana. The *Kalpasutra* was first recited here. About 640 CE, the popular Chinese traveller Huen Tsang had visited Vadnagar. In his travelogue, he has admired the culture and wisdom of the people of Vadnagar. There was a time when over one thousand Buddhist monks resided in the Buddhist monastery here and the sound of 'Buddham Sharanam Gachchhami' (I seek the refuge of

Buddha) used to resound here. Vadnagar continues to hold the ancient pride even today. Its glorious gates are world famous and worth seeing; these gates are the specific identity of Gujarat.

Two sisters from Vadnagar – Tana-Riri – learnt fine music traditions and underwent penance. There is a legend that Akbar, the Mughal Emperor, asked Tansen, the court singer, to sing the Deepak Raga. When he did, his body was engulfed in fire, and he could be saved from this heat only when somebody sang the Raga Malhar. Tansen set out in search of a singer who could sing Raga Malhar, and when he came to know about the proficiency of Tana-Riri of Vadnagar in Gujarat, he arrived there. It was at this time that there lived three hundred Sarangi-players in Vadnagar.

Tana and Riri, at this time, were away at the Sharmishtha pond for fetching water. When they heard of the arrival of legendry Tansen in Vadnagar, they rushed back. They set down to sing Raga Malhar, as a result of which the heat of Tansen's body was pacified and he was infused with a new life. When Akbar came to know of this, he summoned the two sisters to appear before him in Delhi to sing the Raga Malhar, but the two proud and dignified sisters refused to appear in the Mughal court. When compelled to do so, the two sisters sacrificed themselves. There is a Dehri (a small temple) in Vadnagar dedicated to the two sisters. Even today, the tale of two sisters' devotion and pride in music continues to be sung. It was on such a cultural and dignified land that Narendra Modi took birth on 17 September 1950.

Narendra Modi's siblings include his two elder brothers – Sombhai and Amritbhai, a younger sister Vasantiben, and two younger brothers – Prahladbhai and Pankajbhai. Pankajbhai studied journalism and joined the Information Department of the Gujarat Government. Sombhai has retired and is engaged in community service and abides by the family bindings strictly and devotedly. Today, we find family-relations and favouritism assuming the level of traditions in politics, but we don't find any trace of Narendra Modi's family anywhere in public life. It is natural that this is a matter of pride for Narendra Modi, and stands out as an inspiration for all those engaged in public life.

The *Time*, a renowned periodical published from America, published the cover story on Narendra Modi, and asserted that he has kept away his private life from public life; not only this, none of his brothers or sisters or any other family member has ever met him in the Chief Minister's office. In addition, his younger brother, Pankaj is employed in the Information and Broadcasting Department of the State Government, yet he has never stepped into the court of his elder brother. Today, we can find evident manifestation of favouritism based on relations and family, but here we have an instance, inspiring and imitable, where all brothers and sisters of Narendra Modi live an ordinary life. The limits of the family life are adhered to strictly in this family.

Due to poor financial condition of the family, none of the six siblings could get higher education. The paternal home at Vadnagar was made from mud and brick, 40 feet long and 12 feet wide, and it was in this small house that all siblings lived together with parents, Damodardas and Heera Ba.

Damodardas Modi and Heera Ba were cultured and disciplined, they loved to serve guests and people. They infused these qualities in their offspring too.

Narendra Modi obtained in heredity such traits as kindness, spirituality, mutual love and curiosity, as if in the form of divine blessings. He had his unique viewpoint to look at things. His viewpoint is guided, not by intelligence, but by traits and sensitivity. Besides, we can see in him acute eagerness and desire to achieve the aim of life. He got his primary education from the government school and secondary education from B.N. High School at Vadnagar.

Narendra Modi has been made from the fragrant soil of Mother India and has a rich personality. He never shies away from emphasizing that he once sold tea in the railway compartments, rather he prides in the fact that he helped his father and family in childhood. According to him, Vadnagar was an important trade centre from the time of Gaekwad state and the railway infrastructure has existed there for several years. Narendra Modi's father ran a small tea stall near Vadnagar railway station. The school in which Narendra Modi studied was not far off. As soon as he was free from school, he would straightaway make to his father's stall and help him in work. If needed, he would serve tea to customers and would go about the railway platform whenever there was a train coming.

This remains true that Narendra Modi was no extraordinary student, but has always possessed a different viewpoint to look at things in all situations and contexts. He spoke rarely but meaningfully. Sometimes his talk was replete with the typical sense of humour. His consciousness has always guided him towards acquiring the best. He has grown loving books. He spent much of his time in the public library at Vadnagar, as if it was his abode. He was much interested in reading the biographies of great people. It was here that he read through the life stories of Vivekananda, Shivaji and others.

Despite his hesitant nature, Narendra Modi took part in debates during his school life. His Sanskrit teacher says that he was a determined student and possessed a clear view on all topics. Even his mates admired him for this quality. He possessed an intense understanding to make good from bad. One day, his Sanskrit teacher assigned the students to write the forms of *Nadi* (river), and they were asked to show the homework to the class monitor. Narendra Modi refused to do so claiming that the teacher was the only eligible person to do so as the monitor himself was a student.

Once during the days of terrible heat, all school students attended the NCC camp. You might well know the discipline maintained at such camps. The coach and science teacher, Goverdhanbhai Patel noticed that Narendra Modi had climbed up a pole. He raged in fury; however, when he saw that he was on a rescue mission to save a hapless bird, his rage pacified and he admired him for his deed. Narendra Modi, right from childhood, was full to the brim with mercy for living beings and attachment with nature. It is perhaps due to this proclivity that he has implemented the projects as 'Pashu Arogya Melas' (Animal Health Fairs) to this day.

Rasbehari Maniyar, the then professor of Vadnagar Bhagwatacharya Narayanacharya High School, says about him: "Narendra Modi was very service-oriented and sensitive from childhood itself. He actively took part in NCC activities. His basic traits included discipline, punctuality and help to others. Despite ordinary condition of his family, his face always glowed in self-respect. He took active part in extra-curricular activities in addition to physical exercise. His strong points have been oratory, reading and sharp memory. He was wont to resolve any problem in no time."

He further recollects that this student of eighth standard participated in drama too. It shows that he had deep understanding of social injustice and how to present it. Right from small age, the underlying seeds in his personality are being manifested in the form of administrative leadership and social harmony. Revealing this social problem in school life, he once undertook mono-acting titled *Peeloo Fool* (Yellow Flower). The dramatization was unique, especially because it was he himself who had written, directed and acted it. The story of the drama revolved round a Dalit (oppressed) family of a village. The mother has a son who falls ill. The poor mother seeks the cooperation of the *vaidya, hakim* (medicine men) as well as *tantric* (sorcerer), but none of them agree to treat him. The illness worsens, and then somebody advises her to offer yellow flowers at the temple and touch those flowers to the ill child. In hope, she rushes to the temple, but she is forbidden from entering it. The poor mother begs for the life of her child. In the end, the priest takes pity on her and gives him the yellow flower. Unfortunately, when she reaches back home, she finds that her lovely child is no more. It was at the eighth standard that Narendra Modi had used this play to pass the message that everybody has the right over God's flowers.

Narendra Modi had a specific viewpoint to look at the society. His thought-process revolves and manifests itself desiring to see the common man happy. The focal point of his viewpoint is to make the common man happy. We find his views and ideology being put into practice in his daily life, behaviour, conduct and working methodology. The source of this system is woven into him right since childhood. This is the reason that, in his student life itself, Narendra Modi passed, through his plays, the messages such as 'Untouchability is a sin' and 'All are equal before God'. His personality in childhood had started to show the traces of intelligence, cleverness, organisational capability, strategy formation and such traits.

We can recall another instance of his organisational capability. Once at Vadnagar, there was an inter-school kabaddi competition. Narendra Modi's team – Kumar Shala-1 – was the team of junior students. As compared to this team, the players in the Kumar Shala-

2 team were seniors, and Captain Umedji was a fine kabaddi player and never lost a point in it. He used to enter from the right and ran along the end point. Narendra Modi had observed minutely how he entered and played, and he accordingly formed his strategy to make the opponent team taste defeat, not once, but on three occasions. On such success, his teacher Kanubhai Bhavsar had exclaimed, "Look how cleverness and organisational capability have overtaken power!"

Dr. Sudhir Joshi, childhood friend of Narendra Modi and a well-known doctor of Vadnagar, states recalling his student life: "Narendra Modi was replete with self-confidence, he was afraid of none. He confronted all problems head on and found out their solutions. He had a wonderful power of logic. He was a determined, fearless and courageous fellow. He was a motivated participant in leadership conferences. Once in the school elections, he had defeated a stronger candidate on the basis of his tact. Whatever work he took in his hands, he was committed to its accomplishment to the full. What we see of Narendra Modi today is a reflection of his childhood nature."

It was the silver jubilee celebration of the school when he was at high school. There was no boundary wall round the school and the school management lacked funds for its construction. Narendra Modi was of the view that students should contribute some funds to the school. He sought their cooperation in this task. He convinced them as to make them feel that they had contributed in this task to some extent. He had interest in dramatization, and he made use of this talent in himself. In cooperation with his friends, he played a drama *Jogi Das Khuman*, in which he himself played the lead role of the king of Bhavnagar. This charity show helped to collect a good amount which was utilised to build the boundary wall of the school.

The financial condition at home did not allow him to buy shoes. His uncle bought him a pair of white canvas shoes. Being light in colour, it was natural for the shoes to be stained, but he had no money to buy polish. Motivated to maintain cleanliness, he found a solution to this problem too. At the end of school, when all students were racing towards their homes, Narendra Modi gathered the chalk pieces that were scattered under the blackboard.

He carried them home, ground them into fine powder and then applied it to his shoes wet. When dry, the shoes shone like new.

Discipline has been devoted to disciple and service in his daily life. He never overlooked any of the commands of his parents. One day, Narendra Modi went to Sharmishtha pond with his childhood friend, and carried back home a small tortoise. Looking at it, his mother Heera Ba said to him in all affection, "It is not good to bring a tortoise home, it is painful to separate a kid from mother. Son, will you feel sad if you are separated from your mother? How does one feel when separated from one's mother? We ought not separate this kid from its mother, should we? Run and deliver it where you brought it from." Listening to his mother's command, Narendra Modi rushed back to release the tortoise in the pond.

From childhood itself, Narendra Modi shared responsibility in his father's business and mother's domestic duties. He engaged himself in kitchen, dish-washing, cleaning, much of time. Whenever his mother was ill, he would cook and wash clothes at the pond too. His father had a great attachment with the cow, so he reared one at home. Narendra Modi looked after the cow and milked it too. Growing in an ordinary family, he did never have more than two pairs of clothes. He kept these clothes clean – he washed them himself, ironed them himself, often he folded them and kept under his pillow which were pressed until the morning. Sometimes, he placed hot charcoal in a metal tumbler to iron his clothes.

There is a village near Vadnagar called Kesimpa. It was from here that Abbas Bhai Momin travelled to Vadnagar to study at B.N. High School. His father was a farmer and often visited Vadnagar in connection with his work at Ganj Bazar. Whenever he visited, the Modi tea stall was his favourite spot to stay. Narendra Modi's father and he sat and talked together for long. Thus, they had a lasting friendship. Abbas Bhai was in the seventh standard when his father breathed his last. He says: "When I got into the tenth standard, it was quite painful to travel between the village and Vadnagar, and at this time, I talked to my uncle, Damodardas, and he made arrangements for me to stay at his home. He had instructed all family members to ensure that I faced no problem at any stage. The whole family looked after me in all care for one whole year. It was due to his blessing that I could get higher education. I lived in the Modi family for one year and it was during this sojourn that the qualities of service, harmony and goodwill were inculcated in me."

There was a close friend of Narendra Modi in school life, named Jasudkhan Pathan. They both studied together in the eleventh standard, they shared the same bench, their colonies were adjacent. Jasudkhan recalls his old days and says: "I can't remember a day when there was a discord between us, nor did we ever talk any communal issue. We all lived together and took part in the other's ceremonies. We all had goodwill, nobody felt any discrimination for anybody else."

Narendra Modi inherited the traits of service and goodwill from his father. His mother possessed knowledge of native medicinal herbs; it was like God's blessing. She used to provide free medication to the patients who visited her. A large number of people thronged the house right from early morning at five o'clock. To help his mother, Narendra Modi too rose early and engaged himself in the service of the sick. Narendra Modi has said himself: "My mother was not literate, but she had been blessed by God with the knowledge of native herbs."

The Quit India Movement was surging ahead in the whole of the country. During this period, the work of the Rashtriya Swayamsevak Sangh was started at Vadnagar. Dr. Keshav Baliram Hedgewar established the Sangh at Nagpur. He was of the opinion that the nation is his mother and he, her son; and everybody who thought so was his own brethren. Dr. Hedgewar had not presented any new concept or doctrine. Our national concept has revolved round *Mata Prithivi, Putroaham Prithivyam* (The Earth is my mother and I am the Earth's son) since earliest times. Dr. Hedgewar carried forward this doctrine to set up the Rashtriya Swayamsevak Sangh in 1925 on the pious day of Vijayadashami, and thus laid the foundation for the establishment of a capable, powerful, united and magnificent India. Narendra Modi is just one of those millions of volunteers who work for the reconstruction of India.

As soon as the doctrine of this Hindu nation was formulated in his mind, he undertook an earnest effort to explain to the contemporary leaders that 'Hinduism is nationalism'. His mass contact was extensive and nobody doubted his credentials so far as patriotism was concerned. His character was clean and intention clear, and all leaders held a uniform opinion about him. Another inference drawn from his thought was that he should initiate the work with those children who are yet to be infused with the traits of right and wrong, and who have not yet crossed the mouldable age. Initiating this project, the purpose was to prepare those volunteers who were ready to give their lifetime for the national cause. A young and adolescent mind is naturally inclined towards sacrificing himself to embrace martyrdom with a smile on the lips; and this concept was to be cultivated in the children of this age. It could be on their strength that this self-effacing society could be guided towards a desirable direction, and the Hindu community could be once again infused with the lasting sentiments for the nation, to the peril of their lives. This doctrine started to take root in his mind.

He himself contributed in revolutionary tasks. He came to feel that martyrdom is like walking on the edge of a sword. Climbing the gallows with a broad smile on the face requires infinite patience. He was sure that only martyrdom could not lead to eternal awakening among the people. Martyrdom is certainly illuminating, it stimulates the people, but this proves like a lamp which goes out after some time; it takes to lethargy after some time, and then falls into dormant state. People are wont to offer flowers on the birth or death anniversaries, but they are seldom ready to follow the same path. He often said, "Shivaji was a great man – the society would utter this innumerous times and bow before him, but would never wish to make their son a Shivaji."

Thus, it was here that he took a decision that he would set up an organisation comprising volunteers who would sacrifice their lives by deed, by speech and by heart to the nation. For this purpose, he gathered children in the age group of ten to fifteen years for games. A sound mind resides in a sound body, so he motivated these children to take physical exercise with a view to 'make their bodies the means to undertake their duties'. There was no dearth of *akharas* (arenas) and *vyayamshalas* (gymnasiums), there were a number of games institutions too; there were many arenas where wrestlers were trained; and there were institutions which trained in cane-charge, sword-fighting, lance-fighting, as well as other prevalent arms those days. However, among this throng of institutions, what was absent was an institution which could cultivate traits in the children so that they could be dedicated to the nation.

In order to cultivate spotless character in the children, Dr. Keshav Baliram Hedgawar gathered a few children in the ruined premises of Salubhai Mohite Bara in Nagpur, so that on their basis, a Sangh could be created which would comprise the youth who would be fully motivated for the pious patriotic work, and this great work was initiated on the day of Vijayadashami in 1925. It was how the Sangh was born. It was on the basis of those few children that the Rashtriya Swayamsevak Sangh has reached every nook and corner of the nation, and it occurred nine decades ago.

Dr. Hedgewar wished to establish a massive voluntary organisation which spread through the length and breadth of the country. He did not want it to be associated with any particular individual, institution or party. His sole wish was to dedicate the organisation to the national service by deed, by speech and by heart. He dreamt to establish an organisation infused with the spirit of 'do what is for national good'.

His sole purpose was to bring into existence a countrywide organisation, united by self-inspiration, inclined on the path of continuous thought for national well-being; it was the reason that he named the organisation as Rashtriya Swayamsevak Sangh. The Sangh could not afford even an office, where then could its signboard be put? However, the scope of the Sangh continued to expand. In the beginning, Dr. Hedgewar's effort was termed childish, and he was often jeered at as unsocial, musician and several other degrading nomenclatures. However, the Sangh continued to tread its path to glory at a constant rate, and today, it has touched its glorious peak.

Samarth Guru Ramdas said that the capability for movement and fortune are quite essential for the success of an organisation. He meant that five factors are responsible for the success of any task – initiative, effort, resources, diversity of efforts and luck. Of these, initiative is the foremost; this fact was revealed to us by the *Geeta* and Guru Ramdas repeated this fact.

Dr. Hedgewar had well assimilated this fact, so he provided the Sangh a solid ideological initiative. If we wished to make our country free and majestic, we would first have to locate the factors due to which it reached the present levels of poverty and penury; how it came to be enslaved. He set out to find answers to these queries. His search led him to the inference that due to coming of various castes and tribes to the fore, and due to several social communities, the spirit of 'all are Hindus' went missing, and this is precisely the cause of its fall. In the absence of this spirit, our country came to be shackled by the native and foreign aggressors and invaders. When the basic concept of 'The nation is our mother and we, its children', weakened from our social life, and people became selfish, it led to destruction of social integration. If the society has to be led back to its glorious peak, the spirit of integration has to be re awakened in order to unite the society, and this remains the sole path. It was the foundation or initiative of the ideology of the founder of the Sangh.

The *Shakha* (branch) of the Rashtriya Swayamsevak Sangh started at Vadnagar from 1944. It was started by Babubhai Naik, a primary schoolteacher. Babubhai attended the *Shakha* at Yukudpura in Baroda from 1942 to 1944. The work of the Rashtriya Swayamsevak Sangh had begun in Gujarat from Baroda. Babubhai arrived at Vadnagar in 1944 and started its work. India possessed a great desire to see the country free. Every Indian wished that the shackles of slavery were broken down. It was natural that this environment had an influence over the *Shakha*. The youth infused with the spirit of patriotism thronged the *Shakha*. The work of inculcating patriotism, nationalism in children, adolescents and youths was thus started.

Chandrakant Dave, the Hindi teacher at Bhagavatacharya High School, conducted the *Shakha* at Vadnagar. It was at this time that Narendra Modi came into his contact and was thus infused with nationalism and sociality. Several *Pracharaks* (full-time workers) often visited Vadnagar in connection with the Sangh work, and during one such sojourn, the *Prant Pracharak,* Vakil Saheb, too visited and he chaired a meeting there in which Narendra Modi too was present. It was for the first time that he was introduced to Vakil Saheb. In the same manner, Kashinath Bagvade, another Sangh *Pracharak,* who had provided momentum to the Sangh work in Mahesana district too visited Vadnagar quite often, and Narendra Modi kept himself in contact with these *Pracharaks*.

After Dashahra festival, there was organised a Sangh programme in which about forty volunteers attended; its venue was the Daneshwar Temple at Vadnagar. All volunteers had brought food from their homes; however, the mother of Ramesh Ojha had made no special dish, rather she had cooked *kulhar* (made from bajra, a coarse grain, *ghee* and *gur*) with all the affection in her heart. All the volunteers joined the group with the dishes they had brought, but Ramesh was hesitant thinking how they would find *kulhar* when faced with such delicious dishes. He felt hesitation as well as anger; he just said to his companions that he was not feeling well and did not want to eat anything.

Bharat Dave took Ramesh Ojha's bag from near the tree and showed it to others. Two volunteers got up to their feet. Haresh picked up the tiffin, and the other volunteer took it from Haresh with an amazing look. This volunteer was none other than Narendra Modi. He opened the tiffin, tasted *kulhar*, and served it to all the volunteers partaking food there, and remarked at this occasion, "Brother, a dish as delicious as Sudama's rice is never kept hidden away."

It was at this that Ramesh Ojha's hesitation disappeared into thin air. A volunteer had infused attachment in another. Harmony, attachment, brotherhood, like members of a family, all these traits were cultivated in Narendra Modi during his attending the Sangh *Shakha* in childhood.

Narendra Modi has possessed sympathy for the suffering, the troubled, the suppressed, the exploited, the deprived and the victimized people right from the beginning. His heart is very sensitive for these classes of people. When he was a student of ninth standard at Vadnagar, heavy rains during the monsoon had caused floods in different parts of the country. The Tapi River, near Surat in Gujarat, too overflowed its banks in order to devastate a number of villages. The delicate heart of Narendra Modi was pained greatly at this suffering. He had attachment for his countrymen from a tender age. However, what could a fourteen-fifteen-year-old adolescent do, especially when his financial condition was not at all good?

At Gauri Kund, Vadnagar was organised a fair every year in the month of *Savan* (July-August), which was attended by people in large numbers from local and adjoining villages. His father gave him one rupee when he was to visit this fair. He had in his heart a suppressed desire to assist the flood victims, but this small sum of one rupee could not provide any succour to anybody. An idea flashed in his mind, that was to unite his friends. He consulted them for the purpose, and decided that they would set up a tea stall in the fair, and the income from it would be donated for the help of the flood victims. All friends put together their one-rupee coins. Narendra Modi brought stove and utensils from his house and thus a stall was set up. The income from the stall was dedicated to the flood victims. Not only this, he accompanied Dr. Vasant Parekh, a saintly social worker, to go out of Vadnagar to tour south Gujarat where he served the victims.

Indo-China war was fought in 1962. The entire country was moved with the spirit of patriotism. At that time, the railway passing Mahesana, near Vadnagar, was the place from where the trains carrying troops often passed. Narendra Modi was just twelve years old then, but he had a desire to do something for the troops even at that stage. When he came to know that some people of Vadnagar were going to Mahesana to serve the troops, he sought his parents' permission and accompanied them. There at the railway station, he served the troops with food packets and tea cups with indomitable spirit. He devoted himself to the task without caring for his own rest or food; he made every effort to ensure that no troop went without his service. He used to keep awake late into the night, and when fully fatigued, he would have a nap or two in one corner, only to come back and resume his duties. The young men were recruiting themselves to fight the enemy on the borders, and in the service of such troops, he found infinite solace.

Narendra Modi was fond of swimming right from his childhood days. He was a skilled swimmer. Those days, he used to visit Sharmishtha pond at Vadnagar. The pond was the home to tortoises too, but the enterprising Narendra Modi was hardly frightened of them. Every year in the second of the *Ashad* month (June-July), the townspeople gathered and swam across the pond to hoist a flag at the *Chhatra* (umbrella) located in the centre of the pond. Narendra Modi too swam to the Chhatra from the bank near the public library. The rainwater was released into the pond during this month, so this effort involved risk in addition to the danger posed by the tortoises. Narendra Modi was wont to take any risks. Once he jumped into the pond with his friends – Mahendra and Bachu. The people on the bank drummed hard to keep the tortoises away. Narendra Modi swam to the Chhatra with his mates and replaced the flag. They were warmly welcomed by the people at this adventure.

The traits of patriotism and social service were obtained by Narendra Modi from his mother and Sangh *Shakha*. So, he nursed an ambition to get admission to the Sainik School at Balachari in Jamnagar. He found out the details and informed his father about it. But his father explained that his financial condition did not allow him for that. It was due to poor financial condition that Narendra Modi could not be admitted to the Sainik School, so he continued with his education in the secondary school.

We can find a trace of religious leaning in Narendra Modi right from childhood. He had interest in it, it was innate to him. His personality showcased the glimpses of harmony and goodwill among different faiths. A little distance away from his home was located a Mahadev Temple, which he visited daily to offer his prayers to Lord Shiva. Having finished his morning chores, he would set off for the temple, would go round it, offer his prayers, and then sat down at one place for chanting and meditation. His regularity and punctuality at the temple were often cited as an example. The pious image of the adolescent Narendra Modi could be seen in the temple complex. It was the outcome of the traits that he had inherited from his parents and their blessings. Narendra Modi felt it good to serve and be in the company of saints and sages. Once a wedding ceremony at his uncle's place was planned in which all family members had to go. Any child loves to be at his uncle's place as it is so joyful, but Narendra Modi refused to go with them because a saint was present at Vadnagar at that time, this saint had grown plants all over his body and palms, only his face was free of them. As he was unable to eat by himself, Narendra Modi had taken upon himself the responsibility to feed him at the required hours, and he did this duty in all vitality and bliss. It was in this state of joy that he refused to go to his uncle's place. This left his family members worried if he could become a saint.

An incident from his life when he was only sixteen years old: It would not be reasonable to evaluate those times in accordance with the exalted dignity and post he holds now. However, it is essential to mention that incident that is of his marriage. Right since childhood, Narendra Modi attended the Rashtriya Swayamsevak Sangh's *Shakha*. He was greatly influenced by the life and thought of Lord Buddha and Vivekananda. He derived joy from serving the saints and seers. It was in his nature to serve the nation and the society. As soon as he entered youth, he had firmed up his mind to devote his life to the service of the nation and the society and renounce the home. However, his family was financially weak. Influenced by the prevalent orthodox and evil practices of the time, the Modi family forced marriage on Narendra Modi at a tender age of only sixteen years. Narendra Modi never wanted to marry. Still, he was forced into the marital alliance. Narendra Modi had devoted all his life to Mother India, far from the worldly attachments; he was not at all inclined to be bound into marital limitations. Somabhai Modi, the elder brother of Narendra Modi, painfully recalls that incident that occurred 45-50 years ago:

"About 45-50 years ago, our family, comprising my parents, five brothers and a sister, was a very ordinary and poor family. At that time, we were socially, educationally and economically backward, we were the offspring of the family that was bound in backward and orthodox practices. Education was next to nil in our family marred by backwardness and poverty. Our family lived a life amongst the evil orthodox practices. Of all brothers and sisters, the daily routine, interests, attitudes, aptitudes and hobbies of Narendra Modi were quite distinct from the rest of us. The family was quite aware of his inclination towards the service of the nation, but none of us was aware of the acute desire that he possessed in his heart. He was influenced by the renunciation of Lord Buddha and Vivekananda. Our parents were somewhat literate; therefore, Narendra Modi was like any other ordinary child in the family. At that time, they brought us up as they thought fit keeping in view the prevailing situations. It was in such a perspective that our parents got Narendra Modi married at a tender age."

Somabhai flows in emotions when he says: "The only virtue or duty for Narendra Modi was the service of the nation. He renounced the home giving up all the material comfort and convenience. The formal marriage held with Jasodaben Chimanbhai Modi was reduced to only a formality because Narendra Modi had renounced the home just those very days. Even 45-50 years after that incident, Narendra Modi remains completely detached from the whole family. Jasodaben too passed her life with her parents working in the educational field. Narendra Modi continues to live a life of meditation and penance. We will have to accept that the people of the country know him better than we do. We would request, with folded hands, that this incident should be seen in the context of the prevailing circumstances of a poor and orthodox family."

Narendra Modi was thirteen and the year was 1963. Saints and sages often visited Vadnagar. One day, a saint visited the town, and the tradition of the village entailed that he was fed at someone's home. One day, a saint visited Narendra Modi's house for food. After the meals, he asked for Narendra Modi's horoscope. Heera Ba handed him over the horoscopes of Sombhai and Narendra Modi which she had with her at that time. Looking at Som's zodiac, the saint declared that he would live a normal life, though he could be jailed. Later he looked at Narendra Modi's zodiac and his eyes dilated in astonishment. He asked his mother, "Whose zodiac is it?" Heera Ba said that it was that of her third son, Narendra. The saint predicted, "Mother, this zodiac is very impressive. If this boy joined politics, he would spread his influence all round, and if he became a hermit, he was bound to assume the high post like that of a Shankaracharya." With the passage of time, Som had to be behind bars because he was the chairman of the workers union and he had undertaken a movement. When the government imposed the Section 144, which he violated, he was put behind bars. As for Narendra Modi, his life is unfolding right before our eyes.

At the age of seventeen years, Narendra Modi gave up home and study, and set out to the Himalayas to attain spiritual wisdom. This decision of his was a great hurt to his family members, but he was resolved, while his parents were quite indecisive. Finally, they decided that he should be allowed to go if he wanted so. On an auspicious day, the mother put a piece of sweet in his mouth and daubed his forehead with vermillion. Narendra Modi bowed down to touch the feet of all elders and sought their blessing, and then he stepped out of the four walls of his home in search of divinity.

Wandering from place to place and meeting sages and saints on the way, Narendra Modi reached the hilly Himalayas. He had no money when he left home. He enquired of different people about human nature and it expanded his learning, but after some time, he arrived at a conclusion that wandering thus could lead to no purpose. Narendra Modi states: "I wanted to do something, but I was confused what I should."

Wandering purposelessly for over two years, he decided to go back home. Nobody knew about him during this period. At first, he reached the Ramkrishna Mission at Rajkot. Impressed by his devotion, the head offered him a place to live at the Mission, but he did not stay there for more than a week; in fact, his curiosity had not been satisfied there.

Narendra Modi returned to Vadnagar. Recalling this incident, his mother Heera Ba says with wet eyes, "We got no news from him for two years, I was just despaired and hopeless, and then one day, he emerged before me suddenly. He held a bag in his hand. I was in the kitchen and my daughter Vasanti was standing outside. She started to shout, 'Brother has come, Brother has come.' I wept bitterly on seeing Narendra. I asked him where he had been, what he ate. He said that he had been to the Himalayas. I asked him about meals. I informed him that there was bread and vegetable and I would cook some sweet dish, he calmly said at this that he would partake of these and there was no need to cook anything else.' At that time, there was no other person at home other than myself, my daughter Vasanti and Narendra. After his meals, he went out to the village. Out of curiosity, I opened her bag, which had a pair of clothes, a saffron shawl and a photograph of mine at the bottom. I am not aware from where he took it, he had never told me about it. He stayed at home for one day and one night, and then he said that he was going once again."

It was from this hour that Narendra Modi has not visited Vadnagar again.

□

Devoted to National Service

Narendra Modi arrived at Ahmedabad, but he had no purpose as where to go and what to do. Sometimes he visited his friends, visited his uncle's canteen at Geeta Mandir State Transport Bus Station in Ahmedabad, and sometimes took part in the social, government and religious programmes and conferences. Perhaps he was on the lookout for a purpose. He was then ten years old when he attended the Rashtriya Swayamsevak Sangh *Shakha* at Vadnagar, and his contact with the *Shakha* had as good as been severed; here in Ahmedabad, this contact was revived. He wandered about and visited the Sangh office and met the *Prant Pracharak*, Lakshmanrao Inamdar (Vakil Saheb). He talked to him for hours, and it was from this stage that another turn took place in Narendra Modi's life. Now he dedicated his entire life to the Sangh as a *Pracharak*, and from here on, he engaged himself in the worship of Motherland full time. A wandering being had ultimately found a passage to his purpose.

At the age of 21 years in 1971, Narendra Modi did Sangh work staying at the Sangh office. In addition, he looked after sundry matters there. Vakil Saheb continued to be his guiding light, and Sangh work became his sole purpose in life. He took part in the Sangh training camps which were organised in every summer. As a Sangh *Pracharak*, he dedicated everything of his to the Rashtriya Swayamsevak Sangh. In 1973, he completed his first year course – Sangh *Shiksha Varg* – in 1973 at Nadiad. Just before the Emergency was declared in 1975, he attended the second year Sangh *Shiksha Varg* at Bajwa (district Baroda), and undertook his third year at Nagpur in 1978. He worked with complete effort and sentiment for the expansion and development of the Sangh. Now, the Sangh office – Dr. Hedgewar Bhavan – had become his abode.

Some time later, a movement was held at Delhi to protest against the atrocities on and massacre of the Muslims and Hindus of East Bengal at the hands of the Pakistani army. Narendra Modi took part in this movement to demonstrate his loyalty and spirit of service. He was arrested and sent to jail, but he was released soon. In 1972, he put on the garb of Sangh *Pracharak* on a full-time basis, and he abandoned his uncle for this work.

In this connection, Narendra Modi has stated: "I visited Vakil Saheb and talked to him. He agreed to keep me with him. I was working at the Sangh office those days. When Vakil Saheb invited me to stay with him, there were a dozen of other people too staying there. My daily routine revolved round rising early at five o'clock, fetch milk, awake other people, attend the morning assembly, make tea, offer it to everybody, clean the utensils and serve breakfast and then go to attend the *Shakha*. On return from there at about nine, I cooked and served breakfast, clean the building comprising eight-nine chambers, wipe the floor and wash clothes for myself and Vakil Saheb. He did not want me to wash his clothes, but when I said that I loved this job, he agreed for it. For the lunch, I visited Swayamsevaks – one a day in turn. On return from there, I made tea for all people. It was my daily routine for close to one year."

In the meantime, he was handed over the additional charge of correspondence of the state office. Narendra Modi had to devote more time to it. It continued for another year. After this, he was assigned the work of attending the families of Sangh volunteers that visited Ahmedabad from Gujarat and outside in connection with medical treatment.

Narendra Modi carried out his duties devotedly. Whenever his assistance was sought, he would make himself available for it. He had a friend who had returned from America with his sister after his sister's husband had died there. Narendra Modi welcomed them and assisted them in every possible way. This gentleman states: "Narendra Modi, together with Keshavrao Deshmukh and Lakshmanrao Inamdar, called on us at this hour of bereavement. He often visited us and supported us morally." Several such touching anecdotes are revealed by his friends.

Looking at his perseverance, he was once assigned the duty of reserving seats in buses and trains for the travelling officials of the Sangh. This brought him in touch with the transport and railway officers, and this evolved into friendship over a period of time, and this begot him working experience in this field.

Another chapter unfolded when the Vishwa Hindu Parishad, under the guidance of Dr. Vanikar, held its Gujarat conference at Siddhapur. The arrangement and management of the conference was assigned to Narendra Modi, which he did with perfection, and thus displayed his organizing capability.

Narendra Modi enriched his experience through working in diverse fields, and he accumulated his experiences into a large treasure. It helped him study the human nature. He was ever ready to take up any new responsibility, the only condition was that it ought to be challenging. He loves to work, keep in touch with people and make others' life comfortable.

Cooking food, washing clothes, sanitizing toilets and serving his comrades in every possible way, Narendra Modi never recalled to his mind the forecast that the sage had once made, he had said that he would rise to glory as a sage or as a ruler. The time proved amply that the element of a *Sanyasi* is devoid of attachment and it can culminate into the essence of a *Samrat* (emperor).

Recalling the arrival of Narendra Modi in the Sangh office, one of his friends said that this decision of his proved to be a better course; because it gave him an identity and he found his purpose in life. He was not alone there, he was part of a huge family, and this transformation evolved in him a new personality, a new image; which manifested the innate ability and personality; and it would not be out of course to appreciate the ability of Vakil Saheb who recognized such talent and promise in a young man. An insight into Vakil Saheb would help us understand Narendra Modi's personality better.

Lakshmanrao Inamdar, better known as Vakil Saheb in the Sangh, occupied a unique place in the Sangh tradition in Gujarat. His public life was devoted to the Sangh, and when Narendra Modi came into his contact, the purposeless life found a springboard; and this brought him into the Sangh office and transformed him into a full-time Sangh *Pracharak*.

Vakil Saheb was born on 21 September 1917 at Khatao village in Satara district (Maharashtra). According to the Indian calendar, it was the Bhadon Sudi Panchami or Rishi Panchami. Vakil Saheb was the third among his seven brothers and two sisters. His father was Madhavrao and his caste was Khatavkar, which later came to be known as Inamdar.

Those days, a child was admitted to school at the age of seven, so his education started as such. In 1923, his father was transferred to village Dudhondi, near Kirloskarvadi. He was admitted to a school there, and he attended school there for two years before returning to his grandfather at Khatao. His elder brother, Rambhau was already there.

Vakil Saheb attended school at Khatao until the fourth standard, and when it came to further education, his father rented a house at Satara. His one sister was already there, so he too joined school there. In 1929, he was admitted to the New English School at Satara. His elder brother, Rambhau too had come there a year before.

Vakil Saheb started his public life from Satara. He joined his peer group during exercise, as he loved physical exercise right from childhood, but he had not aimed to become a wrestler. His purpose was to set up groups or organisations through which the games of kabaddi and kho-kho could be organised. He had been the team leader on several occasions and had won several awards in games. The government rewards had all vanished, but he won the games rewards on the basis of his hard work, and thus gave a meaning to his caste Inamdar (its literal meaning is the one that possesses reward).

His life sketch at Satara is also delineated by Gopalbhai Gujar, who worked as a *Pracharak* in Gujarat for ten years. He says: "We set out in the morning to run across the Ajinkya Tara hill and undertook different types of exercises in order to strengthen the body; we also played different types of games in order to cultivate the spirit of unity. Our child sports association was the leader among all associations in Satara, while Savarkar, the freedom fighter, and several others were living a life of hell in Andaman's Circular Jail, undergoing every possible torture there. The tales of Aurobindo and Barindra of Bengal, Chandrashekhar Azad and Khudiram Bose saddened our hearts; it was hard to imagine how they underwent the atrocities inflicted by the British Government, and how they could have borne all those with purpose, devotion and determination. The tale of Yatindranath was sung in every home who sacrificed himself after fasting for 53 days at a stretch.

Our role models were Bhagat Singh, Rajguru and Batukeshwar Dutt who held the *Geeta* in one hand and hailed the Motherland before kissing the knot at the gallows. At that time, the martial law was imposed at Solapur, in which Mallaya Shetty and three others were hanged. All this shook us completely and we were of the opinion that something had to be done to tackle this. Many thoughts and ideas stormed our minds, but we could not find a direction to proceed to."

Gopalrao further writes: "Gradually, Lakshmanrao passed the seventh standard (today termed as matric or tenth standard) and went to Poona for college education. Amongst four of us, Govindrao Gajendra Gadkar went to Ahmedabad for service. After our examinations, we came to Satara during summer vacation. Lakshmanrao was, at that time, preparing for the entrance test for matric. One night, Lakshmanrao and his elder brother Appa called on me. I accompanied them to the house of Dada Saheb Karandikar, a renowned lawyer. There, about 20-25 youths had gathered who worked in a group devoted to the cause of Hinduism. It was for the first time that we came across Dr. Hedgewar. It was the month of March in 1935. Having started *Shakhas* in Vidarbha at several places, he had come to visit western Maharashtra. The Sangh *Shakha* was first started at Poona. He wore a high black cap, coat, white shirt and a scarf round his neck – it was the simple dress that he wore."

"He held a cane much like a military officer. At the knob of his cane was embossed the image of a lion with a raised tail, and on it was written 'Swayamev Mrigendrata' (That conquers deer automatically). Dr. Saheb himself was a divine being. He was simple, earnest but impressive; the words coming out of his mouth were inspiring us all. His speech centred round the view that uniting the Hindu society would lead to make our nation integrated and free. He had repleted his statement with illustrations from history and contemporary incidents, each of his word expressed his inner pain."

"The respected doctor, before commencing his speech, introduced himself and sought others' introduction. He talked to all people for long before and after his speech. We came to know of his clean heart, liberality and wonderful ability to win others' hearts. After that, he discussed how to start the Sangh *Shakha* at

Satara and how one could become a *Swayamsevak* or volunteer. He made some people take a vow too. However, Lakshmanrao possessed a little medical inclination, so he never accepted anything without having trust in it, and he never approved of anything in a hurry. Therefore, the meeting was set for the following day. The whole night, he thought over what the doctor had told him, and then he went back to the doctor, took a vow and became a *Swayamsevak*. The sacred saffron flag was swaying in the light wind which signified vitality and renunciation. In its evidence, Dr. Hedgewar spoke in his earnest and clear voice each statement of the vow, and we all repeated in matching earnestness:

'To protect the Hindu faith, Hindu culture and Hindu society...'

'To protect the Hindu faith, Hindu culture and Hindu society...'

'To free the Hindu nation I have joined the Rashtriya Swayamsevak Sangh...'

'To free the Hindu nation I have joined the Rashtriya Swayamsevak Sangh...'

'I will undertake the Sangh work with authenticity, selflessly and with body, mind and wealth...'

And in the end, the doctor pronounced in the final statement:

'I will abide by this vow the whole life.'

We too repeated it after him, 'I will abide by this vow the whole life.'

After the formal vow, we felt in ourselves a tempest taking place, as it subsided, the clear direction became manifest before us and then we repeated to ourselves in our mind and soul: 'I will undertake the Sangh work with authenticity, selflessly and with body, mind and wealth, and I will abide by this vow the whole life.'"

Having completed high school, Vakil Saheb headed for Poona. He had already decided not to join the government service, because it was transferable in which a government servant was required to visit villages, he had felt this pain in his father who was a government servant. The second fact, a more important one, was that he did not want to serve for the foreign masters; his pride did not allow this. After his vow with the Rashtriya Swayamsevak Sangh, this view strengthened further. Therefore, he decided to be a lawyer, and took admission in the law department. This profession allowed him simplicity and freedom; it allowed him to work both in his profession and in the Sangh.

The financial condition of the family was much like before. Living at a city like Poona was quite burdensome when it came to boarding, food and other educational expenses. It was by chance that some friends of his sports association at Satara were there in Poona for practice, and he started to live with them, and this led to their finding a way out by which they fed four people with three tiffins. After their arrival in Poona, they continued with the Sangh work as before. They were assigned the duty of holding *Shakhas* in the remote areas; they had to travel 6-8 kilometres for this purpose, and it was not possible for them to have a vehicle for each. Therefore, they shared the bicycle or walked the distance if it was not so far. Thus, they used the bicycle in turn, and it was a source of immense joy to them. One could reach the destination if he is willing to work for it. Under such difficult situations, Vakil Saheb moved towards his goal. He had to divide his time between his practice and Sangh work. Having passed the intermediate with art stream, he took admission to the LLB course and passed the first year. In the meantime, a *Satyagraha* was started at Bhaganagar (Hyderabad) in 1939. Vakil Saheb took part in this movement; it was to protest against the atrocious rule of the Nizam.

Vakil Saheb abandoned his LLB midway and joined the *Satyagraha* team body and soul. As the *Satyagraha* gained momentum, the Nizam abandoned truth, justice and policy, and started to inflict atrocities on the Hindu people still more severely.

The protestors were jailed and were subjected to inhuman treatment. Vakil Saheb had to be in prison for close to seven years before his release. A chapter of his life's goal had been accomplished which had tested positive on the criterion of body, mind and soul.

Vakil Saheb had taken part in the Bhaganagar *Satyagraha* without his father's permission. It could not have been possible for his father to allow him to abandon his studies midway and join the *Satyagraha*, especially in the prevailing financial condition of the family; therefore, he joined without his permission. His father was unhappy about it, it was natural too; but a streak of fear that surrounded his mind if he would ever be released from the Nizam's prison. Thus, fear and anger existed in him side by side.

Finally, Vakil Saheb reached back home. His father thought that enough was enough and he would not get back to his education and he would resume his normal life. Thinking this, his father did not express his anger about the *Satyagraha*.

Inamdar passed the second year of LLB and fulfilled his father's wish; however, his wish for him to take to normal way of life deviated from its course, as the path that he chose was that of the Sangh.

The entire country was engulfed in despair and pessimism. When Dr. Hedgewar breathed his last in 1940, there was a massive hurdle to cross. The independence was round the corner, his word was about to come true. However, he was well aware of the British policy of revenge, he knew that they would not leave the country united behind them. The doctor had already anticipated it, so he had urged the youth in all villages and towns to enroll in the *Shakha*, and goal was to increase the attendance to three percent in towns and one percent in villages. The challenge and warning of the doctor enthused Vakil Saheb and other Sangh workers. After the death of the doctor, Guruji came to the helm and he set down to undertake a rapid tour of the nation for expansion of the Sangh work.

In the psyche of Vakil Saheb resounded the vow that he had taken before the respectable doctor that he had joined the Rashtriya Swayamsevak Sangh in order to protect the Hindu faith, Hindu society and Hindu culture and to free the Hindu nation.

He had seen in the life of the doctor what the significance of this vow was. He had abandoned his village to tour other states. He had seen a number of dedicated and respected members before him. Vasantrao had gone to Delhi, Rajabhau Paturkar to Lahore, Bhaurao Devras to Kanpur, Dadarao Paramarth to Madras, Gopalrao Verkunthavar to Andhra and Balasaheb Devras to Bengal. Gopalbhai Gujar, one of Vakil Saheb's comarades, had gone to Ahmedabad after his education in 1940. Two other people – Manohar Khadke and Tribankrao Chitnis had attended the Nagpur education camp in 1942, and had become the full-time *Pracharaks* direct from there. The late Bagrao Bhide from Maharashtra was the *Prant Pracharak* of Gujarat. For expansion of the Sangh work, he formulated a scheme 'Prant Swayamsevak Yojana', under which each of them had planned to work as *Pracharak* for one year at the least. It spread through the influence of the Sangh everywhere. As if a competition was in the air, people were being initiated as *Pracharaks* in good numbers; how could Vakil Saheb restrain himself in such a scenario? He arrived at Navsari in Gujarat in 1942 to join in this scheme.

In the Sangh, there is a little charming song which says that it is easier to take a vow than to abide by it. This remains the complete thinking of a *Pracharak,* his thinking revolves round it, its abidance requires renunciation, sacrifice, dedication, devotion, and this entails a difficult situation. Vakil Saheb had lived with difficulties right since beginning, so such a challenge was nothing new to him. He had just crossed one page of his life's book, and keeping the further events of history in Gujarat, it would not be out of place to claim that the new chapter deserves to be written in golden letters. A new chapter had begun. Vakil Saheb was a dexterous organizer; he possessed direct experience of the Sangh work at Satara and Poona, and this worked wonders for him.

Vakil Saheb arrived at Navsari, where a small *Shakha* had been initiated a few years before. The Sangh work that had begun on a small scale at Baroda in 1938 had now expanded to 25-30 small and big towns. The Sangh *Shakhas* used to be focal point of the youths in those days when the freedom struggle was at its peak. Under the guidance of *Prant Pracharak,* Madhukarrao Bhavatji, the Sangh work was touching new glory. Vakil Saheb arrived in Gujarat with a young team of *Pracharaks.* Pledged to the cause of the Motherland, these young *Pracharaks* started to expand the work in about half the districts of the state. The Sangh became perceptible in Saurashtra, Kutch and other places. To undertake the increasing responsibility, the Sangh *Pracharaks* were fully devoted; the young generation was coming into the Sangh's fold. Vakil Saheb was the fountain of inspiration; he had sowed the seeds of patriotism in them. In the brief period of eight years, forty-five young men had stepped out of their homes to become full-time *Pracharaks,* dedicated in body and soul, for the cause of the Motherland. The work of culturisation started in over two hundred Gujarat villages through daily *Shakhas,* and this gained further momentum with time.

In 1947, two *shivirs* (camps) were organised for the volunteers of Gujarat and Saurashtra, in which 4,000 full-dressed volunteers took part. The Sangh work was expanding in Gujarat at such a massive scale that one-month-long camps were organised in 1943, 1945, 1946 and 1947. During these years, the volunteers from Sindh, Malwa, central India and Punjab had attended the camps for training. Prior to 1947, the Sangh work was proceeding ahead without any obstacle, and it was becoming a popular movement too. However, after the assassination of Mahatma Gandhi, the Sangh suffered due to hostile propaganda of the Congress. It was a difficult period for the Rashtriya Swayamsevak Sangh.

After the ban, the discriminatory Congress policy continued to have adverse impact on the Sangh for the period until the eighties. The Sangh had to be erected again after the ban was removed. The invigorated volunteers were ready to launch themselves and pass through this tough test. Their progress was of course slow, but it was certain. After Bhagwat, Rajpal Puri became the *Prant Pracharak* for a brief period. In 1942, the young Vakil Saheb took over the reigns of the Sangh there. It was no easy task to expand the scope of Sangh after such a long ban. Several *Pracharaks* had to go back to their occupations in order to mitigate their financial difficulties, and the number of volunteers had nose-dived to twenty; everything seemed to have undergone a change after independence. It was our own government, the mass opinion had been formulated into narrow bonds, and to take forward the Sangh work in such a hostile environment was no easy task. The young Vakil Saheb worked with patience and insight. These qualities of his helped to prosper the Sangh work and in a period of just three-four years, the Sangh *Shakhas* started to function at over 150 places as before. The Shiksha Vargas, held annually, were participated by 150-200 young volunteers. The number of volunteers gradually rose and with this, the number of *Pracharaks* too augmented.

In the sixties, the Gauraksha Abhiyan (the movement for protection of the cow) attained success due to their efforts, and the programmes held in the honour of Guruji witnessed spectacular success. As per Vakil Saheb: "Two events of those days had augmented the self-confidence of the volunteers like never before." Vakil Saheb kept in touch with the training camps, big and small. His work over eight years helped to put forward a very optimistic picture. His scheme for recruiting students was appreciated. The youth went to different places for training as per the plan, and this helped to expand the scope. After the Chinese aggression in 1962, 1200 volunteers took part in a state camp, and this number rose to 1700 in the camp in 1968. Until then, the Sangh office was functioning from a small room in the third storey at Manik Chowk (Ahmedabad), which had been the centre of activities of Vakil Saheb. The increasing workload led to the construction of a state office in Ahmedabad. The number of *Shakhas* reached 200. The volunteers, trained in *Shakhas*, were now working on high posts.

Vakil Saheb was carrying out the responsibility of the entire state work. He had formed a team of selected workers. Several other dedicated workers started to look after different departments of the state. The basis of success for a Sangh worker was not the amount of work one could do, but how many workers he could recruit. The working methodology of Vakil Saheb was quite successful from this viewpoint. In 1973, he was assigned the responsibility of the Kshetra Pracharak, at this time, the number of *Shakhas* was 250, with 30 *Pracharaks*. He had deployed a series of responsible workers in each district. As a *Prant Pracharak*, now Keshavrao Deshmukh was working under the guidance of Vakil Saheb. In 1974, the struggle for public values was held in Gujarat. In fact, after independence, the people who talked of morality, ethics and values, had now descended to running an autocratic rule. They had breached all limitations of corrupt conduct. This mass movement started in protest against this corruption. The public had now noticed these jackals that left no stone unturned to vitiate the name of the Sangh. In this indirect mass movement, several thoughtful citizens had raised several mind-boggling questions. This situation motivated them to find an alternative path.

Naturally, the people looked towards non-political powers, and in such a scenario, the Sangh illuminated their minds with a ray of hope. It was the time when the Sangh could have expanded and developed at a massive scale, when the calamity of Emergency befell the nation. The Sangh dealt with this calamity. Not only this, it secured for itself greater respect, and in the eighties, the number of *Shakhas* crossed 450. The team of workers had engaged itself in enrolling students and expanding the scope. As the Sangh expanded, the result of the unimaginable patience of Vakil Saheb started to manifest fruits. 'This is a divine effort,' thought Vakil

Saheb as he gave further momentum to this fine work. In this stream, he served the nation devotedly for 40 years at a stretch.

After Narendra Modi was initiated as a Sangh *Pracharak*, Vakil Saheb had once said to him: "Almighty has bestowed upon you such intellectual vitality; you must now get back to your studies." Later, Vakil Saheb himself gathered prospectus for admission. Narendra Modi appeared as an external student of Delhi University and became a graduate. Later he attained his postgraduate degree from Gujarat University as an external student. Professor Pravin Sheth, the guide of Narendra Modi during his studentship in Gujarat University, says: "Narendra Modi practised neo-politics in my class. He was a Sangh *Pracharak*, so he was quite busy. Whenever he came, I gave him the subject file, he would take it with him and come back with complete preparation. It is quite amazing that he secured a first place despite being an external student when compared with regular students."

After he became a *Pracharak*, he engaged himself in the task of expansion and propagation of Sangh work, body and soul. His habit to talk on diverse subjects, sense of humour, helping nature, sharp memory – all these factors made him a favourite of the Swayamsevaks. Despite his busy schedule in social life, his inner heart was always busy in spirituality.

The state office of the Rashtriya Swayamsevak Sangh, Dr. Hedgewar Bhavan, was the refuge of Narendra Modi, and he stayed there to guide the Sangh work further.

□

Movement Against Corruption

In 1971, Narendra Modi dedicated his entire life as the Sangh *Pracharak*. At that time, the political environment in Gujarat was explosive and the whole of it was burning in a flame of discontentment.

Narendra Modi watched the entire occurrence closely. The Congress had come to power with mere 32 percent votes. During this period, the Congress government across the states proved to be very unpopular. A belief was strengthened in the people's mind that they had been born to rule the country. In sum, they had not been able to control the support and encouragement of even this 32 percent people. Common people were noticing the lack of virtue and logic in their conduct. When somebody has trust in us, our responsibility is increased still higher, but this basic tenet of service had been completely neglected by the rulers.

It is evident that the country would not have witnessed such a decline had the then rulers used their power for the welfare of the common people. The power-hungry Congressmen had already distanced themselves from the Gandhists, and now in the arena were left only a few skilled musclemen who were trying every trick to hold power at their will. As a result, this epidemic spread through all Congress leaders, big and small. The infection of power infected from high to low, just like the flow of water. It was misfortune for the nation that these power-hungry Congress politicians were able to control the power as a strong opposition was nowhere in sight.

It was natural for corruption to rise in such a selfish administrative and political system. Corruption had better of all the officials, right from the village headmen to the highest post in the country. Corruption had become much like an organ of the administration. No paper or file could move further if it was not made weighty with an expected amount of money. Offering a favour to the peon before a meeting with the minister or officer had become an unwritten rule, rather a part of normal etiquette. Due to all these causes, the administration thought it better to overlook good functioning of the government.

The rulers lacked necessary energy to check corruption in the administration, because they themselves were fully absorbed in political corruption. The corrupt government had no time to care for the needs of the common man, resulting into rising costs. The sky-rocketing prices of everyday commodities had made the life of people miserable. The very people who had been returned to power on the slogan of 'Garibi Hatao' (remove poverty), had inflicted upon people the very thing shattering the hopes and aspirations of common people.

The people of Gujarat were in the vicious cycle of rising costs. The hoarders had no control over them. One member of a family was required to stand in queue waiting for their turn in order to buy essential commodities, still there was no certainty that they would ever get the goods.

While the rising costs were having the better of common people, the leaders were having the time of their lives at the cost of the hapless people, and such people were now least liked by people. The people of Gujarat are never wont to tolerate such people for long, so it was natural for them to raise their voice in protest.

Closing their eyes to the problems of the people, the ministers were all busy in political exploitation. Due to internal factionalism, the Gujarat Vidhan Sabha Congress had to impose a leader from outside. The leadership of Ghanshyam Bhai Ojha further invited dissatisfaction within the Congress. Ghanshyam Bhai had no control over the government machinery, he was not being cooperated by his comrades; still he managed the state affairs for some time.

However, his immature and half-hearted decisions continued to make matters worse for the administration and people. Consequently, people were now raising their voices. When the people were suffering like never before, the power-hungry Congress factions were fighting with each other, and they competed in July 1972 to seize power by hook or by crook. The legislators were being bid for favour. Ghanshyam Ojha, nominated by the Congress high command could not control Gujarat Congress or its government there; finally, his government collapsed.

This incident was like rubbing salt to injury of the Gujarat people. The Congress factions there spent money in order to come to power, and finally, Chimanbhai Patel was able to form the government after his tricky show of strength; as it is, he is better known for his tricks and exploitation. Despite his administrative skills, he did nothing to rescue the people from a difficult situation, and practised politics replete in inimical inclination, and he had to taste the fruit of such action too. Once again, the divide between people and administration started to widen.

In protest against such things, now truthful and pious efforts had started by small and big groups and organisations. There was an increasing number of people claiming that they did not support such things, and these type of views were openly expressed in public. Due to their evil conduct, the Congress leaders were quite often criticized.

The street meetings held here and there raised the voice that the very leaders were inflicting harm to their morals and ethics, and exploitation of democratic values had become a plaything for them. Gradually, people became restless, the surrounding environment had been vitiated due to the political, social leaders and power-hungry hounds. Now people were becoming gradually more vocal. By the end of 1973, this grief started to transform into anger.

Narendra Modi states: "It was not possible for Gujarat to remain a silent spectator to these anti-nationalistic activities despite its peaceful nature. Besides, there were historical factors behind this awakening of Gujarat. Gujarat has been the land of activity for several proponents and great people who have illuminated the light of democracy. The national movement and national leaders were closely related with Gujarat. Gujarat has always been in the forefront before and after independence. It has contributed to the solution of every small and big, national or social problem."

Looking at this historical backdrop, Gujarat was now turning within. Towards the end of December 1973, the students of the engineering hostel at Morbi were forced to undertake a protest against the raised food bill. This protest reached the premises of

L.D. Engineering College hostels. The then education minister, Smt. Ayesha Begum Sheikh remained inactive like her government. She was seeing a Jansangh hand behind this protest.

The students had stepped out in the open against this corruption. The Akhil Bharatiya Vidyarthi Parishad (ABVP) put its complete force behind this movement. Narendra Modi was in an active role in this crusade. As the demand was raised to remove the causes behind corruption, the government started to suppress them anyhow. When it became evident that the root causes of corruption were the Congress and its leaders, the students were resolved to remove them from the power. Not only in Gujarat, but in the whole country, the Gujarati student shone like a star on the political horizon.

Due to several supplementary factors and dissatisfaction, the reconstruction movement gained gradual momentum. Due to different reasons, the people of all classes contributed to this movement. Internal factionalism of the Congress too contributed in it. Now, this movement was no more restricted to students alone, rather it had become a mass movement. The people had started to confront the government high-handedness openly.

After twenty-five years of independence, people were moved with a strong sense of dissatisfaction, and this anger was aimed against the Congress Government. For their neglect of the mass opinion, the leaders were now being taught a lesson. Some farsighted Congress leaders were worried at this development.

An unfortunate outcome of this movement was that it had no leader or organisation as yet. As a result, this got divided into several fronts. The incidences of counter-violence started to take place, while the government overlooked its responsibility and started to violently suppress the people. The government was not at all hesitant to suppress the youths in Gujarat in all cruel manifestations.

Despite repressive measures on the part of the government, the people kept struggling for their demands. Even Jaiprakash Narayan (JP) was impressed by the commitment of the Gujaratis against corruption. He offered his moral support to this value-based movement. Impressed with it, he went to Bihar. Consequently, the Central Government had to withdraw Chimanbhai Patel from the state in order to stop the movement from acquiring national connotations. After this information too, people continued to struggle and several priceless young lives were sacrificed in the process. Several innocent youths were killed; the land of Gujarat had, as if, acquired the furious form of Goddess Chandi. A situation of bloody struggle had come about there. Looking at the gravity of the situation, Chimanbhai Patel had to finally resign. With his resignation, the people had once again started to believe in their power, it was for the first time in twenty-five years after independence.

This self-confidence in the common people motivated them to proceed further. They were not content with the resignation of Chimanbhai Patel, they were still angry with the legislators they had sent to the assembly. Therefore, now the demand for dissolution of the Vidhan Sabha was raised. Troubled and angered by one defeat, the Central Government was not at all ready to suffer another defeat in such a short span of time. It rejected the demand for dissolution outright. Its bowing down could lead to several problems for it. However, the rising vigour and vitality and self-confidence of the people provided further momentum to the movement. On the other hand, the government repression grew bad to worse, from cruel to crueler. Consequently, Gujarat needed able guidance, the services of an able guide was immediately desired.

It was at this time that Morarji Desai was given the charge of guiding Gujarat. Supporting and terming the demand for dissolution of the Vidhan Sabha, he started the *Amaran Anshan* or fast unto death. His *Anshan* invigorated this movement greatly and it became a prestigious movement now. Now, the government had no way out but to dissolve the legislative assembly. It was how the people of Gujarat acquired their second victory. This victory had, of course, claimed the lives of about one hundred youths.

Narendra Modi, in the book *Apatkal Mein Gujarat*, states: "Both these victories on the part of Gujarati people became a guiding factor for the entire country. The success of these mass movements made the common people aware of the effect of these movements. JP was fully able and capable to lead such movements taking place in other parts of the country, and it was fortunate for the country, that he accepted this role for himself."

'Imitation to Gujarat', these words was becoming the source of inspiration for the countrymen those days, though for the rulers, these very words were like bad dreams, so they were wont to repeat every time that the events of Gujarat would not be allowed to recur anywhere.

However, the movement under the leadership of JP progressed far more systematically towards its goal. This movement was evidently the outcome of the inspiration provided by Gujarat. The demand for dissolution of Bihar assembly grew strong, so the then Prime Minister Indira Gandhi had said in a statement: "I have committed a grave mistake to accept the demand for dissolution of Gujarat assembly."

After the resignation of the Chief Minister and dissolution of the assembly in Gujarat, the people were ready to elect their new representatives; however, the Congress Government was in no mood to see the face of imminent defeat. It wanted to postpone elections until the movement for reconstruction was weakened, but it was not acceptable to the people.

The demand for elections caught momentum. During these days, the Gujarat Lok Sangharsh Samiti (a forum for public struggle) was set up. Overcoming the mutual differences, the efforts of K.D. Desai and other personalities were significant in this effort. All parties came together in Gujarat to strengthen the demand for fresh elections, and thus challenged the Central Government.

Once again, Morarji took over the reigns of leadership in the movement. He started his *Amaran Anshan* at Delhi for his demand for elections. Obstinate not to accept the defeat, the Central Government was forced to accept the demand and kneel down before the popular opinion, and thus the elections for the legislative assembly were announced. It was the third victory for Gujarati people in a row. In the fight between individual and democracy, the democratic Gujarat was feeling pride on its third consecutive success.

The government had used its entire means to suppress the mass movements, it had applied all possible tricks in its diary, but the government could not face up to the people. Its reputation had been extensively blotted. The Congress Governments were deep in the marsh of their sins; they were now confronted with two enormous challenges in the form of elections in Gujarat and Bihar movement at its peak then.

The mass movement in Gujarat had greatly helped to bring together the scattered opposition leaders. The people, troubled by the Congress rulers, too were looking for a capable alternative. On March 22-23, 1975 was held a two-day political conclave at Ahmedabad. It discussed that all opposition parties should come together to contest elections from the common platform; and finally, an organisation was formed called Lok Sangharsh Samiti.

The election in Uttar Pradesh had proved beyond doubt that it was mandatory for all opposition parties to come united in order to taste victory. The people of Gujarat were determined to motivate the opposition leaders to unite themselves. The All India Executive Council of the Jansangh, in its Jammu session, confessed the need for such a front, and gradually, it united all the parties under the banner of Janata Morcha.

It was for the first time after independence that bipolar elections were fought, and the credit for this goes to Gujarat. Indira Gandhi could look into this challenge and its gravity, and a defeat in this election could put into jeopardy her very political existence, and she was well aware of it. She put in all her efforts to win this election. She addressed over one hundred rallies in different parts of the state, working day and night, in a bid to draw the people towards her; however, her effort did not bear fruit. Even the fascination of 'Gujarat Ki Bahu' could not have any impact on the people.

The people of Gujarat evaded any insight into them, and causing a massive fourth consecutive defeat to Indira Gandhi, elected the Janata Morcha. It was now that on 12 June 1975, Indian democracy found a new direction from Gujarat.

Indira Gandhi and her comrades had applied every trick in the book to suppress the Gujarati movements and anger, but they met with failure, and people emerged victorious on every occasion. As if all these failures were not much significant, Allahabad High Court inflicted mother blow to her wavering boat. The Gujarat results and the judgement of Allahabad High Court had caused a great internal storm in the Congress.

The entire imaginary fancy world of Indira Gandhi had been devastated. The power-hungry Indira Gandhi was not ready to renounce the power. She was worried how to stay in power. On the other hand, the demand for her resignation was resounding the skies at the national level. Even her associates were of this opinion. To protect herself from these calamities, she required a new strategy, and this fear psychosis led to the birth of Emergency. It is proven from different facts that she had formed the idea for Emergency much before 26 June and all preparations had been made much in advance.

While plans were afoot in Delhi to shackle India's freedom, the Janata Morcha was then embracing to establish a democratic rule in Gujarat in true sense of the term. On 19 June, the government was formed in Gujarat under the leadership of Babubhai Patel. However, the seven-day-old government had been reduced to the condition of a helpless child.

Narendra Modi says that Gujarat was about to take to rest after a one-year-long struggle, and the leaders too were feeling at rest after the Janata Government had been formed. Suddenly in the final hours of the summer, precisely on 25 June, 1975, the telephones of the Gujarat leaders started to ring ferociously, intimating the onslaught of an occurrence which was far from imagination. Nobody had ever dreamt that the government could take such a harsh step. The whole night, the telephones continued to communicate with Delhi. JP had been arrested, Morarji was under arrest, the Sangh office had been seized by the police, the offices of political parties had been raided, no contact could be made with newspaper offices, at some places the telephones were being received by the police, the office of the Rashtriya Swayamsevak Sangh had been vacated, important files and papers were shifted to secure places, the important workers of the Delhi RSS had been put in prison…

The telephones continued to divulge this type of information:

Inform Delhi as soon as there is information about Nagpur. Evade arrest until the situation is clear. Inform everybody concerned. Atal, Advani are in Bangalore, no information should be passed to unknown numbers.

Before the autocratic Indira Gandhi could broadcast her first address to the nation in her new capacity, all these types of information and messages had been passed around.

The regional office of the Rashtriya Swayamsevak Sangh at Kankaria-Maninagar in Ahmedabad was alive with activity. The Sangh *Pracharak* and state Jansangh minister Nathabhai Jhagda had passed the whole night giving and taking messages. Narendra Modi and others busied themselves to put everything 'in order' in the office.

Until the morning, all important people of all political parties had been informed. The gravity of the situation had been understood by everybody. The government in Gujarat, being that of Janata Morcha, the people were yet to suffer the direct onslaught which had been happening in other states. Due to this advantage, Ahmedabad had become the centre of exchanging information at all-India level from the first night of the Emergency. Right from wee hours of the following day, the entire city and Gujarat were aware of the invasion on democracy. This resulted into agitation in the atmosphere.

As the news of Emergency spread, its opposition too scaled up. The markets were closed down soon after they were opened. Students boycotted schools and colleges. All offices in Ahmedabad, including those of the High Court, remained close. The lawyers took out a procession in protest against the Emergency, and a public meeting was organized, criticizing Indira Gandhi for her undemocratic conduct.

The Janata Sangharsh Samiti was formed in Baroda. On 26 June, a vow was taken to re-establish democracy in a meeting chaired by Mar.ubhai Patel.

The strikes conducted in every small and big villages proved success. Mass meetings were organised in Surat, Valsad, Bharuch, Vadodara, Nadiad, Mahesana, Bhuj, Jamnagar, Rajkot, Junagarh, Bhavnagar and other important cities.

A mass meeting was organised in Ahmedabad under the chairmanship of B.K. Majumdar. A large number of people participated in the anxious environment. The whole day, rumours floated in the air about the arrest of Babubhai Jashbhai Patel. Vasantbhai Gajendra Gadkar, the state general secretary of the Janasangh, and Dineshbhai Shah addressed the meeting. They transmitted information from other states. Accepting the challenge that Indira Gandhi had given to the people of India, he exhorted the people to protest peacefully. Due to democratic government of the Morcha there, Gujarat had the moral responsibility to lead the nation; therefore, a decision was taken in this regard.

Most of the national leaders had been put behind bars. Despite efforts, no national leader could be contacted right late into the night of 26 June. The contact between the Gujarat Lok Sangharsh Samiti and the Kendriya Lok Sangharsh Samiti could not be made. It was difficult to predict when and what could befall Gujarat. Looking at the national scenario, Gujarat appeared to be a lagoon isolated from all other places. Owing to the action being taken by the government in order to expand the impact of Emergency, there was every chance that the Rashtriya Swayamsevak Sangh could be attacked at any time.

The *Prant Pracharak* of the Gujarat Rashtriya Swayamsevak Sangh, Keshavrao Deshmukh was on a tour of Jamnagar district when the Emergency was declared. He cut short his visit and returned to Ahmedabad. Narendra Modi and other prominent workers of the Sangh congregated to estimate the prevailing situation on the basis of available information. It was written on the wall that the Sangh would be banned in all probability.

Before the ban could be imposed, a decision was taken to strengthen the communication system of the organisation. The volunteers proceeded to different districts with necessary information of the new system. The new system had been created between new places of the state before 30 June. The Sangh offices were shifted to secret places. And then on 30 June came the news of the arrest of Balasaheb Devras, the *Sarsanghchalak*, or the chief of the Rashtriya Swayamsevak Sangh. Now it was certain that a ban would be imposed on the Sangh.

Right from 26 June, Nanaji Deshmukh, the office bearer of the underground Kendriya Lok Sangharsh Samiti and the remnant central leaders were busy to establish contact with all states, but it was not possible while being at a remote place in Delhi. It was not possible to contact the underground leaders in Delhi. How far Gujarat could fill this void was the question, and to judge this, Rambhau Godbole, an underground worker, arrived in Ahmedabad. He possessed detailed information of the situation in Delhi. He met all important leaders in Gujarat and discussed the changed situation and how the favourable situation in Gujarat could be utilized. His arrival also facilitated a contact with Nanaji Deshmukh who was in Delhi then.

Commenting on this calamity, Narendra Modi says: "The changed situation was considered and to formulate a new strategy, a meeting was organised of the state workers of the Gujarat Jansangh. In this meeting, everybody was of the uniform opinion that Indira Gandhi would never dare to dissolve the Gujarat Government which could amount to step on the tail of a hibernating snake. The second opinion that came to the fore was that she would rather like to defeat the State Government after her situation became stronger. Despite these views, a decision was taken to be ready to embrace any situation that might be confronted."

Now Gujarat was faced with the state of Emergency in two different ways. One was to keep the protest ability active, and the other was to keep contact with the underground movements and workers in other states, in order to infuse vitality in them. The Gujarat Lok Sangharsh Samiti was quite active in it, but there was need to make special arrangements for establishing contact with the centre and other states. To keep contact and exchange information with all states required a large organisation. This work was quite simple for the Rashtriya Swayamsevak Sangh and the Jansangh. Narendra Modi was only 25 years then. The young Narendra Modi played the role of a fighter on the forefront in the struggle for democracy. He took over the responsibility of keeping in touch with protests in Gujarat as well as other states.

The initial stimulation had been manifested, and now the time had come when every care had to be taken to move ahead. The Kendriya Lok Sangharsh Samiti announced the programmes of individual *Satyagraha*.

A meeting of the Gujarat Sarvodaya Mandal was held at Ahmedabad, in which the undemocratic ways of Indira Gandhi were opposed, and a decision was taken to create awareness among common people and to protest using the non-violent means as shown by Mahatma Gandhi.

Due to the Morcha Government in Gujarat, no ban was imposed on meetings and rallies. On the evening of 29 June, a march was organised for Raj Bhavan in Ahmedabad. This march was led by Km. Manibahen Patel, the daughter of Sardar Vallabhbhai Patel and Bhogibhai Gandhia led this march and it was attended by five thousand citizens. A memorandum was handed over to the Governor, K.K. Vishwanathan, a representative of the Central Government, in which it was demanded that the emergency should be lifted and democracy should be established once again. The Governor was requested to pass the sentiments of the people of Gujarat to the Central Government.

A senior social worker, Ravishankar Maharaj sent a telegram to Indira Gandhi and expressed his sentiments. He too demanded for the establishment of democracy in the interest of the nation and Indira Gandhi, both. Besides, several well-known people of Gujarat expressed their protest.

Those days, danger hovered over the Gujarat Government, and any slight rising of head on the part of the government could lead to inviting debacles. In such a disastrous situation, the government decided to protest. The Gujarat Government refused to impose the MISA and ban on public meetings as instructed by the Central Government. As the first effort against the Emergency, a proposal was passed by the ruling party of the Janata Morcha in the legislative assembly, it was done on 30 June. This proposal also appreciated the people for their peaceful protest and declared its active support for the peaceful and non-violent movement for establishment of democracy.

It was during the stint of the Morcha Government, the citizens of Gujarat were spared of the cruel impact of the Emergency. Their civil rights were secure only until then. However, the propaganda being carried out on radio and television was a sore in the eye. In its protest, the Lok Sangharsh Samiti staged *dharnas* outside the Akashvani centres in Ahmedabad, Vadodara, Rajkot and Bhuj. Hundreds of youths participated in these programmes. In front of the Ahmedabad Akashvani centre, a symbolic 'Janvani' programme was organised in which special news bulletin was read out.

The calamity that had befallen the nation and the martyrdom of the reconstruction movement of Gujarat were closely related. The sacrifices that the martyrs had made fighting against evils and atrocities, the Emergency had been imposed precisely to re-impose the same things. The Gujarat Lok Sangharsh Samiti organised a sentimental programme in this connection. It was decided that the people should go to the memorials of the martyrs and take a vow to protest against the Emergency and support the establishment of democracy.

In over one hundred memorials dedicated to martyrs spread over towns and villages, people went in thousands and took a vow that they would not allow to go waste their martyrdom. They even took a vow to sacrifice if needed for the freedom and integrity of the nation and for the protection of their civil rights.

The citizens of Vadodara took out a massive silent march on 28 June, in which people wore black ribbons to protest against the atrocious ways of the Central Government. The procession offered floral tribute at the Shahid Smarak and took a resolve to sacrifice them for the sake of truth.

□

Sentinels of Democracy

After the arrest of Balasaheb Devras, the *Sarsanghchalak* of the Rashtriya Swayamsevak Sangh on 30 June 1975, it was as good as certain that the Sangh would be banned.

To confront the imminent situation, about fifty important workers of the Gujarat state met in Ahmedabad. Narendra Modi, a Sangh *Pracharak,* too attended this meeting. To attend this meeting, Lakshmanraoji Inamdar, the *Kshetra Pracharak* of the Sangh, had flown especially from Nagpur to Ahmedabad. Rambhau Godbole, the underground leader from Delhi, too attended it.

Several topics were touched in the meeting. It could not be possible to work openly in case a ban was imposed on the Sangh, so it was decided that the important workers should continue their work remaining underground or evading arrest wherever possible.

During an underground sojourn, it is essential that the places of stay and meetings, the addresses for correspondence and telephone communication have all to be chosen very carefully. The large organizational machinery of the Sangh had enabled to provide such facilities quite easily. The formalities about the false names and other systems had been completed the same day.

Vakil Saheb from Nagpur intimated news from Maharashtra and Nagpur. It would not be proper for Gujarat to think of itself under the changed circumstances. Its focus had to be to think out ways how it could act more effectively for the entire nation.

It was decided that Ahmedabad would function as the link between four contact centres in the country, which were Ahmedabad, Bangalore, Bombay and Delhi. This responsibility was given to a little known Swayamsevak. It was also decided that he would tour these centres by air every ten days, and meet the important functionaries there at the predetermined places. This execution required great care and courage. He had to carry important documents with him. The security system on the airports, especially during the initial phase of the Emergency, was quite alert, so he had to be on guard for the safety of the secret documents.

In this meeting was also decided that on the third day after the imposition of the ban, all *Vibhag Pracharaks* (the in-charge of a division of two-three districts in the organisation chart of the Sangh) will gather at one place with all available information with them. With this decision, all of them proceeded to their respective destinations.

To take stock of the situation in Saurashtra, Vakil Saheb made for Rajkot. On the evening of 3rd, a telephonic message was delivered from Bombay which was for Keshavraoji Deshmukh which said that an individual was arriving at Ahmedabad in the morning with all information. Deshmukh was waiting for the arrival of this messenger on the next day morning. Narendra Modi and Nathabhai Jhagda, the general secretary of the Jansangh, were out of the place for making arrangements for a new address.

It was 12 at noon. Narendra Modi and Nathabhai Jhagda returned by scooter after having settled the task at their hand. Narendra Modi was riding it. When they reached near the office, they spotted a police van there. A glimpse from the distance told them that the *Prant Pracharak* had been lodged in the police van and the entire office had been seized by the police force. At this time, some repair work was underway in the office, and all labourers could be seen standing outside. It was clear that the office was now under the charge of the police. It was not out of danger for Narendra Modi and Nathabhai to be there anymore. Narendra Modi accelerated and passed by, without attracting any attention of the busy policemen. Having reached a secure place, they concealed their scooter in the house of an acquaintance. Then he took an autorickshaw to visit a worker. They were in the dark about the arrests that were being made in the state of Gujarat at this hour.

When Narendra Modi enquired on telephone, he came to know that the Sangh as well as other 25 institutions had been banned. He passed this information to each district. By the evening, there was news of the arrest of several other volunteers.

When Narendra Modi remembered that Keshavraoji Deshmukh must be in possession of secret documents which had been delivered to him by a Sangh official, he planned something dramatic to secure them.

A sister of Maninagar was sent to Maninagar police station with breakfast to meet Deshmukhji who was under arrest there. In the bag were also sent newspapers, books and other things. The sister was also informed what she was supposed to do there. Very stealthily, she replaced all the papers from the handbag of Deshmukhji with the things she had brought and concealed them in the books and newspapers that she had brought with her, and this was how the secret documents had been secured by Narendra Modi.

These papers were quite important, which included the underground operations of the Sangh as well as movements of the Sangh volunteers, and a letter that had been written by the *Sarsanghchalak* before he was put under arrest. In this letter, Devrasji had appealed to all *Swayamsevaks* for the protest and had asked them to run the movement keeping themselves underground.

By the evening, it became clear that the workers of the banned organisations had been arrested under the DIR and their bail could be secured. It was decided to bail out all Sangh workers in Gujarat in order to carry forward the work. Most of the workers had been released in two-three days.

Now the condition of the Morcha State Government was quite shaky in Gujarat. Therefore, the *Pracharaks* had been asked to be cautious against arrest, even under DIR. While the Morcha government was still in power, arrest warrants had been issued under the DIR, so about 29 Sangh workers decided to go underground, Narendra Modi being one of them. There were many other workers who were unknown to the administration, so their arrest warrants were not yet issued.

As predetermined, on the third day of the imposition of the ban, the *Vibhag Pracharaks* of the Sangh met in the evening of 7 July at Ahmedabad.

The term '*Pracharak*' is quite well-known in the Sangh circles, but other people know little about it. In the Sangh, an individual who renounces his family and house and devotes himself full-time to the Sangh work is called a *Pracharak*. The network of *Pracharaks* is spread throughout India. Even Morarji Desai was greatly impressed by the role played by underground *Pracharaks* and how stealthily they executed their responsibilities. It was the first meeting of such devoted *Pracharaks*.

Despite the democratically elected government of the Morcha, the police was overawed by the Emergency provisions. Because the Sangh was now a banned organisation, a meeting by its members could attract imprisonment up to seven years. Keeping these possibilities in view, all precautions were taken in its organisation. Narendra Modi too was present in the meeting.

Date: 7 July.

Time: Half past eight in the evening.

Venue: A worker's residence at Maninagar.

All doors were secured, the lights were put out. A sister of the family sat outside in the dark corner. The visitors would reveal their secret code word in a hushed voice, and the sister would guide them to go in using the backdoor. By the specified time, all members had gathered there. All of them were the *Pracharaks* whose names appeared in the DIR list. They had camouflaged themselves so as to evade identification by family members and police. The radio on the window was put on so that their voices could not breach the four walls of the chamber. After having examined all the necessary precautions and assured of them, the meeting started.

Such occasions require that maximum work should be finished within the minimum time. One after another, the information from different states was exchanged. The district level Sangh volunteers had been arrested in important cities of Gujarat and the police was on the lookout for other *Pracharaks*. The police had raided over 22 offices all over the state and a total of 168 workers had been arrested under DIR, of which 141 belonged to the Sangh.

The other important banned organisations included the Anand Marg, Protestant Block and Jamat-e-Islami. The workers of Anand Marg had been arrested mainly from Himmatnagar, Surat, Bhuj and Ahmedabad; while those of Jamat-e-Islami from Ahmedabad, Vadodara and Dholaka.

At several places, the offices were searched in the presence of the arrested members, and the government handed over the seized documents to the courts. Several of the arrested volunteers had not been released on bail until 7 July. The information that filtered out later revealed that the application for bail had not been accepted for as long as 15 days. Thus, this meeting helped to pass information between the state and the centre.

Discussions were held on what should be done under the changed situation. An important decision was taken that all Sangh *Swayamsevaks* would function as the workers of the Lok Sangharsh Samiti and would actively support its activities. The other decisions, in addition, included the following:

- Despite the ban, the Sangh work should be kept alive by starting clubs, musical assemblies and service associations in different names so as to carry out the daily and routine programmes.
- People should be kept in contact regularly and necessary information should be passed to them. The *Swayamsevaks* should act fearlessly so that the community could be made fearless.
- A worker from each *Vibhag* should visit Ahmedabad with the entire information regarding the work being done, and should carry back the literature and information required to be disseminated at the local level.
- The place for exchange of information in Ahmedabad would be the office of an industrialist.
- A code word was specified for the visitors at the contact place. Mahendrabhai Bhatt alias Batukbhai, a Sangh *Pracharak*, was assigned the duty of attending the new office regularly.
- Secret places should be specified in each *Vibhag* where information from all over the district should be gathered.
- False names should be assigned to the underground workers and other workers assisting them.

Thus, the meeting concluded after finalization of even minute points and arrangements. Everybody was satisfied that the first meeting had been completed without any obstacle. Later, all of them became habituated of such meetings, and Narendra Modi continued to be one of them.

On behalf of the Kendriya Lok Sangharsh Samiti, its coordinator Nanaji Deshmukh had exhorted people in the massive historical rally in Delhi on 25 June, to start a nationwide *Satyagraha* from 29 June, but the same night, the whole nation had been transformed into a large prison. Consequently, the massive *Satyagraha* was no more possible; however, he emphasised that small-scale *Satyagraha* should continue to take place in different states at regular intervals. The Gujarat Lok Sangharsh Samiti decided to put this suggestion into practice effectively. In accordance with it, daily *Satyagrahas* were planned by five members each in all district centres of Gujarat between 15-26 July.

To further extend the scope of the *Satyagraha* and to make it an effective tool, several meetings and rallies were conducted at different places. South Gujarat was in the forefront for the implementation of these programmes. In Navsari, students and workers joined together to organize rallies in streets and colonies. In Surat, a large rally was organised on 7 July by the Yuva Morcha and Lok Sangharsh Samiti. This rally was attended by rural people in large numbers. The people vowed to peacefully protest standing before the image of Sardar Patel. Large meetings were also held in Vadodara and Nadiad.

In Ahmedabad on 11 July, a silent rally was taken out by about 250 workers with the image of locks on the face as a symbolic protest against Emergency. On the following day, the preamble of the Constitution of India was pasted on the vehicles running on roads. Besides, in the evening, a programme for public reading out the Preamble of the Constitution of India was held near Rupali theatre and Raipur Chakla. A student rally was taken out in Sardar Bagh near Lal Darwaja. On the eve of the *Satyagraha* to be held from 15 July, the programme of ringing of bells was held successfully in the whole city.

It was quite simple to disseminate the information of all these programmes to the active volunteers, the Sangh volunteers were in the forefront to deliver such information to the common man. The noticeboard in each ward was regularly annotated with the new news and programmes to be held.

Saurashtra did not lag behind in taking up this cause of mass awakening. A large rally was taken out with black flags in a small village like Rapar in Kutch. A large rally and meeting were held in Rajkot too. After these programmes, the public training programmes were held through secret meetings at different places. In a small village like Vadnagar, Dr. Vasant Parekh addressed a large assembly.

Thus, the *Satyagraha* which commenced from 15 July, started to warm up the environment in each Gujarat village. As there was no ban on the rallies and meetings in Gujarat, it was thought better to formulate the *Satyagraha* in a specific style. The *Satyagraha* could achieve its purpose only when the Censorship Law was violated. Therefore, programmes were held all over Gujarat in which the censored periodicals and books were publicly read out as a mark of expression for the *Satyagraha*. The *Satyagraha* was represented by people of all classes. It ran for eleven days and over 400 people took part in it in the whole of Gujarat.

There were several complications when it came to punish the people participating in the *Satyagraha*. At several places, these people were kept under trial for up to fifteen days, and at others, they were awarded an imprisonment from fifteen days to one month. The courts in Ahmedabad also gave historical verdicts in which the *Satyagraha* was considered complementary to democracy and an essential element, therefore, the people taking part in it were set free.

The people being set free by the court were warmly hailed by the people. To bid farewell to the protesters going to jail and to welcome them on their return – these occurrences showed acute courage and fearlessness of the people.

The Sangh offices were the places of residence for the *Pracharaks*. The Sangh was banned on 4 July, and the Sangh offices were seized by the government. Therefore, Narendra Modi and Keshavrao Deshmukh, the *Prant Pracharak*, stayed at the residence of Vasantbhai Gajendra Gadkar.

A morning walk was an inseparable part of Narendra Modi's daily routine. He used to go to Parimal Garden at Ambabadi, Ahmedabad for it. This place was also visited on a morning walk by Prabhudas Patwari, the former Governor of Tamil Nadu. These two became known to each other in the first week of July itself. Due to the underground system that had been created, Narendra Modi possessed information pertaining to different areas of the country. Narendra Modi used to acquaint Prabhudas with these pieces of information. He knew it well that Narendra Modi was a Sangh *Pracharak*.

During the concluding days of July, he invited Narendra Modi to his house who reached there right at half past ten. Prabhudas was waiting for him. There was none else at home at that time. He seated Narendra Modi near him and said in a very soft voice: "George Fernandes is about to arrive here in ten minutes' time, I have called you here so that you could meet him."

The two were discussing some issues when a yellow Fiat car pulled up before the door. From it came out a large-bodied George Fernandes wearing a mutilated kurta, a green cloth on the head, printed *tahmad* (loin cloth) and a golden wristwatch and a stub, much looking like a Muslim faqir and being addressed as Baba.

It was quite joyful to meet the people connected with the struggle. Narendra Modi and George Fernandes hugged each other and appreciated each other for their contribution to fight against oppression.

Narendra Modi passed to him the information that he possessed about Gujarat and other states. He was extremely happy to know that Nanaji Deshmukh, an office-bearer of the Kendriya Lok Sangharsh Samiti, was yet to be arrested. They also touched the points about the watch that the government had on the Sangh volunteers; they were worried and concerned about it. Discussions were held on the desired anticipations from the Sangh in view of its abilities under the changed circumstances.

George was in agreement with him that Indira Gandhi would not give up her obstinacy. He was of the opinion that armed rebellion was the only measure to counter the Emergency. He said that the Sangh should commence this type of activities right away. However, the Sangh was assured of its role under the most terrible situations even. The Sangh was not in favour of adopting any violent means; it fully believed in democratic methods; and this was all that Narendra Modi intimated him about.

After this incident, George stayed in Gujarat for the most time until the Morcha Government was in power there. Living there, he continued to publish some magazines with the cooperation of his socialist friends in Bombay in which opposition was expressed against the acts of the Central Government. Of course, it should be admitted that the extent of confidentiality about George's movements, stay and who met him and when, and other details was not maintained. Some meetings discussed about him quite openly. It appears that he could evade arrest only due to the Morcha Government in power.

The government had not succeeded in arresting Nanaji Deshmukh, the office-bearer of the Kendriya Lok Sangharsh Samiti. Indira Gandhi regularly connived to arrest him, but he evaded successfully. On the other hand, Nanaji kept meeting important workers and planning the underground movement. In the beginning he was in Delhi, still the government could not track him. In the first week of August, he met workers in different states. In this series, he visited Rajasthan and Haryana and now he was in Gujarat.

Nanaji had changed his make-up so much that even a *Pracharak* like Narendra Modi could not identify him. In dhoti-kurta, the grey-haired Nanaji looked quite different and distinct. Nobody could say that the man on the bicycle was not a clerk in some government office. He adopted this dress out of compulsion.

He breathed in the free air of Gujarat for three days. He finished his scheduled tasks and appointments and then proceeded to Maharashtra. During his tour in Gujarat, he met several people. Narendra Modi had an opportunity to be with him during these meetings.

George was in constant touch with Narendra Modi, and he arranged his meeting with Nanaji. The two great entities, the source of terror for Indira Gandhi and her government, who were being chased about in the whole country, were now meeting in the first week of August. In this meeting were conversed in detail the prevalent situations of the country and future course of action.

One thing that became quite clear in this meeting was that the Lok Sangharsh Samiti was in favour of adopting only Gandhist methods of protest. Nanaji was an ardent follower of Gandhism. On the other hand, George was in the favour of adopting any means to root out the Emergency and its proponents. An arrangement was made for a meeting between Nanaji and Gujarat's legislators; Narendra Modi was present at this meeting held in Ahmedabad. In his discussion with the legislators, he said that the continuation of the Morcha Government in Gujarat was like a source of optimism for the people of the country and was a symbol of democracy in the country. He also stressed the need for expanding the impact of the struggle and to establish the Morcha Government as a symbol of democracy for protection of the people's interests, and this task required great work. Nanaji was in possession of information from around the country. He also knew who all had been arrested and where they had been kept. All this information was made available to him in such a short span of time; this clearly showed the strength of his system even while he had to be underground.

Some time had now passed with the ban on the Sangh, still its work continued in different forms. The Sangh had to carry out the responsibility of struggle so that democracy could be re-established in the country. For this task, special training was required to be given to workers. Arrangement was made for training of 20-25 volunteers in each district on full-day basis. Though some freedom was available to the Sangh in Gujarat, yet being a banned organisation, all care was taken in the conduct of these training sessions.

These sessions were held at 20 places in Gujarat. Vakil Saheb too arrived there to guide the volunteers. He was being chased out by Maharashtra and Madhya Pradesh police with the MISA warrants. Therefore, he had given up his regular garb of dhoti-kurta, and had adopted the prevalent dress of pant-shirt. During this period, he was called by an alias name 'Bhai'.

These twenty-one-day camps were attended by about 500 selected volunteers. The agenda in these camps included – how the Sangh could contribute in the new circumstances; what role should volunteers play; how to contact different political parties, social organisations and talented people during the course of Emergency; how to locate the Congress' dissatisfied leaders and contact them; how to make proper use of the media; how to disseminate information in different parts of the state; what type of system and network should be created to deal with the situation; and so on. Vakil Saheb stressed in these camps that it was a war of nerves. The volunteers who did their duties patiently were sure to taste success in the times to come.

The presence of the Morcha Government, the mass awareness programmes among common people – these two factors contributed towards raising the level of democratic values in Gujarat, and due to this, this state was like an island in the stormy ocean inflicted with undemocratic waves. The underground contact system in Gujarat during the initial days of the struggle rose to become an important factor in the nationwide movement. Narendra

Modi was an important part of this struggle, and it was resulting into the evolution of his personality too.

A number of programmes were held in Gujarat in protest against the Emergency. The common people supported in full measure. Most of these programmes were held under the aegis of the Lok Sangharsh Samiti. Under its banner, the contributing parties, Rashtriya Swayamsevak Sangh, supporters of JP, independent people and others made all efforts to make the programmes successful. Besides, they were assisted by college professors, teachers, advocates, journalists and others who supported the struggle for democracy.

At that time, Gujarat was like an island of democracy. The whole of nation was looking forward to Gujarat, because democracy had been squeezed out of the whole country, while the Morcha Government in Gujarat had preserved the light of democracy. Due to these factors, Gujarat continued to be a place where democracy workers of other states met and presented their views fearlessly. Ahmedabad courageously welcomed these people. A number of conferences were held here which challenged the Emergency. Thus, the land of Gujarat played a special role in uniting the strugglers.

After the meeting of Sarvodaya Mandal held in Ahmedabad on 29 June, the Gujarat Vidhan Sabha Janata Paksh and other small and big organisations passed resolutions against the Emergency. The Sardar Patel University Kshetra Adhyapak Mandal of Vidyanagar passed a resolution in a general body meeting on 29 July 1975 regretting the circumstances prevailing in the country. In this meeting, the government was urged to release the arrested leaders without any condition, remove the autocratic laws like pre-censorship to enable democracy to work.

In the attendance of ten thousand representatives, the massive state-level Janata Morcha rally was held in Ahmedabad on 16 November 1975, Sunday. This rally, held under the chairmanship of D.K. Majumdar, was participated by Nana Saheb, Gore, S.M. Joshi, Shantibhushan and Mohan Dharia and other national leaders. The presence of Karpuri Thakur, an underground leader in the rally was a subject of joy for all workers. While the rest of the country had been transformed into a massive jail, the land of Gujarat was raising its voice against autocracy.

In this rally, the successfully working Janata Morcha Government and the institutional unit of the Morcha becoming increasingly stronger were considered to be the worthy points of the changing times. This rally brought a new ray of hope for national politics which was being suppressed under the harsh measures of dictatorship.

This rally of the Janata Morcha vowed to fight in full measure against the anti-democracy powers. Different resolutions were passed in it which supported the re-establishment of the Emergency, release of leaders, removal of ban on different organisations and striking down of the pre-censorship laws. Yet another resolution revolved round the formation of the Janata Morcha at the national level which could further evolve the experiences earned in Gujarat.

During this rally, a magazine the *Satyagraha Samachar* had specifically drawn the attention of people; this magazine was distributed openly. Its main cause was the fearlessness of the distributors, and secondly, it published the news of each state concerning the nationwide *Satyagraha* beginning from 14 November. People wondered at this endeavour that the news was being published and disseminated even while a situation of blackout was imposed over news media.

Protest to the Emergency was becoming more vocal with the passage of time. Big and small conferences, meetings and rallies were being held to manifest this protest, due to which, the opposition leaders of the Morcha Government had to rush to Delhi quite often. Thus, Gujarat was becoming an eyesore in the eyes of the Central Government, which was now aiming to suppress it somehow. However, Gujarat did not care for this. Perhaps, a *shayar* (poet) must have said this *sher* (couplet) in the context of Gujarat:

Kaho na khuda se langar utha de,
Ham tufan ki jid dekhana chahate hain.

(Let us go into the ocean despite difficulties, we would like to see how adamant the tempest is.)

Gujarat continued with its struggle against the Central Government. Now the state-level conferences and rallies were not considered enough, so the national-level conferences too were being held here.

On 12 October, the Janatantrik Nagrik Samiti of Ahmedabad convened an all-India conference which discussed freedom of citizenship, it was a historical conference in the context of the Emergency.

The well-known thinker and legal expert, Chandrakant Daru and Vasant Gajendra Gadkar had made specific effort behind the organisation of this conference. The conference was inaugurated by M.C. Chhagla, former judge of Bombay High Court, and it was chaired by J.C. Shah, former Chief Justice of India. This conference was guided by the talks by V.M. Tarkunde, Minu Masani, S.M. Joshi and Mohan Dharia and other thinkers supporting the system of justice and politics. Over 400 representatives from all over the country participated in it.

In his speech, Chhagla expressed regret over the calamity that had befallen the nation. He struck at the government's dictatorship in harsh words. In his speech, he stated: "No conspiracy had ever been hatched by any opposition member; in fact, this conspiracy was mooted by the Prime Minister. I would like to re-stress that the Prime Minister is involved in the conspiracy in which the opposition leaders have been lodged in jails, newspapers have been censored and Fundamental Rights of the people have been snatched away."

Supporting the *Satyagraha*, he further said: "The *Satyagraha* is no violation of any law. The very term denotes non-violence and truth; this is a contribution of Mahatma Gandhi to the world dictionary, but we need not go back to the times of Gandhiji to look for the context of this word, we can well refer to the recent judgement of the Supreme Court in which it has explained this term well." Referring to the Constitution, he rued over the undemocratic ways and stated: "The worst deformed form of dictatorship could be nothing else but this type of constitutional dictatorship. According to me, whatever Indira Gandhi is doing, if it were correct constitutionally, then it would be better to throw away the Constitution rather than endorse this sentiment or remain in doubt."

The big and small leaders of the Jansangh had been put behind bars due to the Emergency. However, some leaders had gone underground. To discuss this national situation under such circumstances, it was not possible to hold an all-India meeting, because it was feared that the remaining leaders could well be arrested too. As Gujarat was somewhat safer, an underground meeting was held in Ahmedabad.

There was a specific purpose behind this meeting. Most of the members taking part in it were active in carrying out underground activities and the government had aimed to arrest them all and was making all possible efforts for this purpose. There were some members for whom the warrants had not been issued, yet they were quite well-known for their activities. If these two types of workers meet together at one meeting, there could be quite terrible repercussions. Besides, the police was alertly watching the leaders who were not yet underground, their activities were being closely monitored, and the government was kept informed about their movements every hour. It could be possible to mislead the police for a couple of hours, but doing so over a few days could alert the government, which could result into worse problems.

Narendra Modi states: "Observing all these difficulties, the Gujarat Jansangh leaders formulated a to-the-point plan, according to which, the workers against whom arrest warrants had been issued were sent invitations for the Akhil Hind Nagrik Svantrya Parishad to be held in Ahmedabad on 12 October, and it was made to feel as if they were to arrive in Ahmedabad to attend this council."

"On the other hand, information was given to the underground workers to arrive at Ahmedabad two days in advance if possible. The visitors coming from Delhi hạd to get off at Sabarmati railway station and those coming from Bombay had to get off at Maninagar railway station. Though the leaders were well-known in Gujarat, yet it was possible due to their changed appearance that they might not be identified. Therefore, it was planned that each of the underground worker would carry a copy of the *Illustrated Weekly* in their hands. Besides, it was also decided that the workers welcoming the guests would hold white handkerchiefs in their hands, so that the guests could make them out. All this information was passed to all the workers.

As per the scheduled programme, the workers from all over the country proceeded towards Ahmedabad. It was not considered appropriate for the well-known workers to fetch guests from the railway station, so little known workers and sisters were assigned this task. Before 12th, several underground leaders such as Sundar Singh Bhandari, Swami, Madanlal Khurana, Dhanraj Ojha, Jagdish Prasad Mathur, Rajen Sharma and others reached Ahmedabad and they were lodged in secure places.

Special precaution was exercised about their places of stay. Not more than two underground workers were lodged at any one place, so that collective arrest could be evaded. The workers who were not underground were lodged at places with due precaution.

The venue for the meeting too was chosen with due care so that the people in the vicinity could not know about this. The non-underground workers were sent to the Nagrik Parishad, then being convened in the auditorium of HK College, so that the officials of the Intelligence Department, then in Ahmedabad, could be assured of the presence of the workers there, and no chance of any suspicion could arise to them. These workers had to be in the meeting for some time, and from there, they had to proceed with the specified local workers to different places, before finally arriving at the meeting venue. It was somewhat simpler to bring the underground workers direct to the meeting venue as it was not necessary to show them up to the authorities. The entire task of bringing the workers to the meeting place was accomplished without any obstacle.

Despite all these precautions, no meeting was held for over three hours at any one place. The morning session of the meeting was held at one place, after which they went back to their places of stay, and the next session used to be held at another place. Thus, arrangement was made to hold different sessions of the meeting at different venues.

Those days the Central Government was of the firm opinion that all underground leaders were in Gujarat. Consequently, all paths leading to Gujarat were under alert watch. Besides, there were a large number of intelligence officials camping in Ahmedabad in order to collect information about the members attending the Akhil Hind Nagrik Svantrya Parishad. These intelligence officials belonged to the state intelligence as well as Central Bureau of Intelligence. Despite all this watch, the underground meeting of the executive council of the Jansangh was held successfully in which over thirty national-level leaders participated.

In the first week of January, a meeting of the ABVP workers was held in Ahmedabad. Indira Gandhi was already unhappy with the ABVP, consequently, several big and small workers of the Parishad were arrested, while many of them evaded arrest and went underground. These underground student workers endeavoured to propagate among students the essence and purpose of the nationwide campaign and to urge them to unite fearlessly for struggle. These struggling workers of the ABVP were held in equal secrecy as was the case with those of the Jansangh.

In this meeting, about fifty workers arrived in Ahmedabad from all over India. It was very likely that the people of intelligence department would keep a close watch on all student movements; therefore, Gujarat had taken upon itself the responsibility to deliver each worker back to his place safely after the meeting. The entire arrangement and management of this underground meeting was borne by the workers of the Gujarat chapter of the ABVP.

This meeting discussed how to make students more active, and it was also decided that effort should be made to enable students to become more vocal in support of their demands. It was also planned to publish and distribute underground magazines which would highlight the students' activities as well as the atrocities being inflicted upon students in the name of Emergency.

In the meanwhile, an underground meeting of the national leaders belonging to the Lok Sangharsh Samiti was also held in Ahmedabad.

Towards the end of October, a large conference of the parliamentary representatives of the Commonwealth countries was held in Delhi. There was every possibility that the autocratic Central Government would make all efforts to save its image before the world, though it was curtailing the freedoms by bringing new ordinances day in and day out. Everybody was aware that it would leave no stone unturned to bring a bad name to the opposition and JP, and it was what was done there. Indira Gandhi's Government made this forum its tool to justify all its actions. It displayed everything that could show it the greatest protector of democracy.

The opposition was already aware of this type of possibilities. Therefore, the leaders of the Lok Sangharsh Samiti gathered in Ahmedabad in September-October, and they planned to check this false propaganda and bring out the truth before the world.

According to the plan, it was decided to get small booklets published in English which would revolve round topics like political summary of the Emergency, repressive measures of the government, viewpoint of the opposition dedicated to democracy and the like. These booklets had to be distributed among the foreign representatives. Preparing such literature in a large measure amounted to great peril and risk. The Kendriya Lok Sangharsh Samiti assigned this responsibility to the Sangh workers in Gujarat. Narendra Modi was assigned the responsibility of getting these booklets published and delivered at Delhi.

In this series, five booklets had got to be prepared:

1. Indian Press Gagged.
2. Facts (Nail Indira's Lies).
3. 20 Lies of Mrs. Indira Gandhi.
4. When Disobedience to Law is a Duty – Mahatma Gandhi.
5. A decade of Economic Chaos.

Despite the Morcha Government in power in Gujarat, the printing presses were often raided in search for any underground literature. Even under such a situation, some printing presses got ready to print these booklets despite the conjoined risk and peril.

The challenge before Narendra Modi and his team was that, after publication, it was no easy task to deliver so many of these booklets to Delhi. This challenge was met by some enterprising and active workers who were sent to Delhi by train. The booklets were concealed in their luggage. These booklets had to be utilized not only in the Commonwealth Conference, but also in the Congress session being held at Chandigarh.

After these booklets arrived in Delhi, the toughest task was to get these booklets delivered to the representatives attending the conference. The government was on the alert. The task of this distribution was given to a representative of the Gujarat Vidhan Sabha. Taking courage, he delivered this literature to all the representatives attending the conference which could disclose false propaganda of the government. The entire work had been accomplished before the government could find out what was happening. The government could do nothing in the matter. Thus, a plan chalked out in Gujarat had been accomplished successfully.

Another plan that Narendra Modi had sketched was following the plan to have the Commonwealth representatives go around

India on a tour. He planned that at every destination these representatives visited, a protest demonstration should be held in which the oppressive measures of the Emergency would be highlighted. This programme was quite successfully accomplished in Gujarat, but the workers taking part in it in other states were badly thrashed.

On the day of Bhai Dooj, the Sangh volunteers had made a plan to welcome the conference representatives with placards and slogans against anti-democracy measures of the government. For it, the Sangh volunteers reached the airport; however, overlooking the instructions of the Morcha Government, the police commissioner of Ahmedabad arrested all these volunteers.

The government had by now succeeded to arrest Nanaji Deshmukh, the in-charge of the Lok Sangharsh Samiti. His arrest led to certain hurdles in the struggle. During his sojourn underground, Nanaji had felt the people's power and situation and had estimated how the *Satyagraha* could be carried out at every level in each state. Before he could implement the scheme, he was arrested.

One day early in the morning under such a situation, Ravindra Varma arrived at Ahmedabad. Immediately on arrival, he telephoned to the place where Narendra Modi stayed. He called Narendra Modi by the name Prakash. He wished to meet Keshavrao Deshmukh, the *Prant Pracharak* of the Sangh. His speech indicated urgency and importance of the matter. He seemed to be in a bit of hurry.

Dejected, the news of Nanaji's arrest was conveyed. He felt terribly hurt due to the arrest that would slow down the movement. This news was quite stunning. There were chances that the information about the underground centres could reach the government. Now, the Sangh had to intimate all the concerned people not to use the old contact centres, and new system had to be created immediately afresh.

Another cause of turbulence for Varma was his increased responsibility which was divulged later. Now, the entire responsibility of running the Lok Sangharsh Samiti rested on his shoulders. Leading so many struggling workers all over the country needed massive effort. He felt pressed down by this sudden responsibility; at least it appeared from his demeanour. During this meeting in which Narendra Modi and other leaders were present, they discussed about the actions that had to be taken during the course of *Satyagraha* in future.

To review the situation after the arrest of Nanaji, Narendra Modi and other workers gathered together to take stock of the situation. The messages of the cancellation of the previous network had been delivered to all the contact centres in Ahmedabad. By now, all care was taken to remove all literature or other material from these places.

A few days later, Varma arrived at Ahmedabad again. As it was decided in the previous meeting, these people had to discuss the *Satyagraha* in detail. Therefore, this meeting was held at the residence of Dr. Vanikar, a Sangh worker. For this, a total of five people gathered – Vasantbhai Gajendra Gadkar, Ravindra Varma, Radhakrishnaji of Gandhi Shanti Pratishthan, Keshavraoji Deshmukh and Narendra Modi.

The meeting discussed in detail different aspects of the *Satyagraha* such as favourable days for the *Satyagraha*, number of places where favourable atmosphere could be created, delivery of the *Satyagraha* magazine to maximum number of people, effect of the *Satyagraha* on the elections to be held in Gujarat, possibilities of workers participating in the *Satyagraha*, estimated number of participants, attitude of the Morcha Government towards the participants, etc.

Besides, the points of discussion included about what type of assistance could be sought from the neighbouring states. There was every possibility that the government would take pre-emptive action by arresting the people connected with the *Satyagraha* in order to neutralise it fully. Publication of *Satyagraha* and mass awakening literature on a large scale and its distribution was a mammoth problem, because it was definite that the government was going to have a watch over the printing presses. Under such situations, the meeting discussed how Maharashtra, Rajasthan and Madhya Pradesh could assist in the execution of this programme.

Elections were scheduled in Gujarat during the course of the *Satyagraha*; therefore, the most of political workers were busy. The Morcha considered these elections as part of the struggle and decided to take part in them.

A large part of responsibility for the *Satyagraha* rested on the shoulders of the Sangh Swayamsevaks. The meeting also discussed how the teams of volunteers would reach different districts as per the scheduled programme; how non-violently the programme had to be carried out, if a false charge sheet were presented against a worker, a panel of lawyers would be kept ready to counter this effort, and such other matters.

An underground meeting of the Lok Sangharsh Samiti was held in Delhi to decide upon the first day of *Satyagraha*, its form and duration. After much discussion, it was decided that the *Satyagraha* should be commenced from 14 November. This day has been an important day in the Indian society after independence. From the birthday of Jawaharlal Nehru, who supported democratic values all his life, would be launched the *Satyagraha* against the very daughter, Indira Gandhi, who had violated all norms of democracy, so that she could be forced to re-install the democratic values.

All care was taken so that this decision could be kept a secret from the government; else several workers could be arrested under the MISA before the launch of the *Satyagraha* itself. The Lok Sangharsh Samiti passed this information to all state centres that they ought to wait for a special message on 4 November. The code word for the fixing of the *Satyagraha* was 'Wedding has been settled'.

Narendra Modi was at Ahmedabad and was eagerly awaiting the telephone call from Delhi. The message he had been waiting since morning, finally came late into the night. After exchange of necessary messages, it was informed that 'Wedding has been settled for 14 November'.

With the information, the Sangh activated itself in full strength to join the *Satyagraha* movement to be held under the leadership of the Lok Sangharsh Samiti. All the concerned busied themselves in making relevant literature, magazines, posters, banners and other things.

The underground *Pracharak* of Sangh, Kishan Bhaiya arrived from Rajasthan to Ahmedabad to get the literature published. To get two lakh magazines published in Hindi and get it delivered to Rajasthan was no trivial challenge either. Narendra Modi and the general secretary of the Jansangh, Nathabhai Jhagda set out in search of an adequate press for this purpose. To publish Hindi literature in such a large quantity was quite a difficult task at least in Gujarat. Besides, it would be a still tougher challenging task to make the printer agree to print it too. It was also compulsory that all workers in the press were reliable and the entire work was done completely secretly. Their two-day-long search culminated with a printing press owner, and with this Narendra Modi heaved a great sigh of relief. He decided that he would deal with the matter of its delivery once the literature was published. The magazines were now raised in a heap.

These magazines were kept at four different places in Ahmedabad with all care. Now, a plan was chalked out with Kishan Bhaiya on how to deliver the literature to Rajasthan. Information was passed to different districts of Rajasthan to send two workers with empty holdalls to Ahmedabad. These workers arrived at the prescribed places on prescribed days. Each worker was given literature as much as was necessary in their respective districts. The literature had to be stored in the holdalls such that nothing could be made out from outside. After this, they all had to leave for their respective places in the teams of two each. They were instructed to behave with each other as if they were stranger to each other. It was also instructed that in case anyone of them was caught, the other would pass the information at the required place.

Thus, all workers were bid adieu after due arrangement of security. It was quite fortunate that nothing untoward occurred in this exercise, undertaken at such a massive scale. The literature had been delivered in each district and village of Rajasthan well before 14 November. When the literature was distributed among people, only then the Rajasthan police was shaken out of its slumber, and a number of raids were conducted at different printing presses all over Rajasthan.

The *Satyagraha* literature for Maharashtra and Madhya Pradesh too was printed in Gujarat. Literature was also written for Gujarat, and it was prepared at four centres and then delivered to each village in the state. The posters related to the *Satyagraha* were printed and pasted at public places. The propaganda for the *Satyagraha* beginning 14 November was started with slogans writing on the walls from 10 November onwards. The Sangh workers pasted wallpapers all over Gujarat, down to villages.

Like the *Satyagraha*, a nationwide system was thought out. According to this, the volunteers in each district had to conduct the *Satyagraha* at their district headquarters. For it, the people had to be brought from small villages to the district headquarters, to make arrangement for their stay and food, to specify the route of their march, to inform the police as per the existing rules, and undertake all other necessary steps which could facilitate the working of these strugglers.

Due to the Morcha Government in Gujarat, all these facilities could be made rather easily, while in other states, all information regarding the *Satyagraha* had to be guarded secretly until the very last moment. Not only this, different teams of strugglers were made to conduct the *Satyagraha* in case the first team was arrested by the police. The Sangh volunteers left no stone unturned to accomplish these tasks despite all the adversities.

The favourable atmosphere had started to be created in Gujarat even before the commencement of the *Satyagraha*. People had been urged for it in the meetings conducted at different places. Magazines, posters, banners and wallpapers greatly helped to create a wave of awareness among people. It was quite hoped that fearless people would come forward in large numbers. The youths started to rouse in sentiments even before the specified date.

On 14 November, the district headquarters all over Gujarat echoed with sloganeering. Meetings were held at different places and strugglers were honoured. Thousands of people gathered in a farewell meeting at Manik Chowk in Ahmedabad. The strugglers were garlanded in order to express their commitment to democracy.

All the strugglers marched to the Akashvani centre in a large rally. The statue of Mahatma Gandhi was offered a cotton garland and the *Janata Bulletin* was read out. After politely violating the law, the strugglers offered themselves for arrest voluntarily with the heartrending slogans of 'Bharat Mata ki Jai' (Hail Mother India), 'Tanashahi Murdabad' (Down with Dictatorship) and 'Loktantra Zindabad' (Long Live Democracy).

From the first day of the *Satyagraha* movement, protests were held in all eighteen districts of Gujarat barring Gandhinagar, in which a total of 170 volunteers took part. Such protests were held all over the country. The news about these protests was received from all parts of the country by noon the following day. For propagation of this news, the Janata Morcha utilised the first state conference held during those days. Ten thousand copies of the magazine called *Satyagraha Samachar* were distributed among the workers attending the conference from different places.

On 26 November, the autocratic government of Indira Gandhi was about to complete its five months in power. On this day, the women from the whole of Gujarat decided to take part in the *Satyagraha*. A team of men and women volunteers started for *Satyagraha* from Raipur area of Ahmedabad. This team comprised thirty-three women and twenty-one men.

The Sangh played a vital role in making the *Satyagraha* successful all over the country including Gujarat. The Sangh volunteers had contributed massively in all tasks right from forming the teams for *Satyagraha* to the propaganda.

It had been decided that in the conference to be held at Pavnar on 25 December, in the presence of Vinobaji, that the volunteers of the Lok Sangharsh Samiti would apprise the representatives taking part in this conference about the actual conditions prevailing in the country, so that the decisions could be formulated in favour of democracy. The task to keep these representatives informed about this all was assigned to the Sangh workers in Gujarat. Besides, the Kendriya Lok Sangharsh Samiti had prepared literature in a large quantity for the Pavnar conference, and it had to be printed and distributed by Narendra Modi and his team. This literature was given to Narendra Modi by Dattopantji before leaving for Delhi. Now, this task had to be accomplished by Narendra Modi.

To carry out the responsibilities given to the Sangh, a meeting was held in Ahmedabad in which were present Bhaskarrao Damle, the *Vibhag Pracharak*, Deshmukhji, the *Prant Pracharak* and Narendra Modi. Literature had been printed by now, and different types of literature had to be delivered to Pavnar, numbering 5000 copies. Small booklets had been prepared dealing with different topics such as the incidences of repressive measures by the government, the details of people dying in jails, the condition of their families, the government propaganda and its response, nationwide *Satyagraha* and other matters.

This literature had to be delivered to Pavnar which is located 36-hour away. Besides, there were several discussions taking place about the relevance and significance of this conference at Pavnar, due to which the government and people had focussed their attention towards it. The government was making all efforts to turn the atmosphere in its favour; therefore, there was abundance of government machinery there. This delivery had to be made by evading the government machinery, which required acute courage as well as caution.

After due consideration, Narendra Modi came to the decision that this responsibility would have to be carried out by a sister, she wouldn't be a point of suspicion and the job could be accomplished quite easily. If the services of a Marathi sister were made available, it would be still easier and better. Narendra Modi decided that Subhaga, a sister from Ahmedabad belonging to a Sangh family, would be sent to Pavnar. When she was asked about it, she readily agreed to accept the challenge.

After her consent, Narendra Modi contacted Nagpur and passed the message about the 'goods' accompanying the visiting sister. Subhaga was instructed to get off at Ajni station just before Nagpur. She had been told of the code word of the individual who would receive her. Besides, she was told to be cautious throughout her journey from Ahmedabad to Nagpur. The security of Subhaga was ensured by the visits of Sangh volunteers who visited her compartment during the course of journey in different garbs such as the pen vendors or newspaper vendors who stayed with her for couple of hours before leaving and the next taking over the charge. These volunteers also scanned the compartment for any possible threat to Subhaga.

After she got off at Ajni, Subhaga was welcomed by a family there. This family comprised of little children too. A scene was presented as if a family was there on the station to receive a guest. The entire process was carried out so spontaneously that any onlooker would not doubt anything about it. It was how the 'goods' were delivered to Nagpur in the company of Subhaga. The work of distributing the literature was carried out by the *Swayamsevaks* in Nagpur.

Narrating this incident, Narendra Modi has written in his book *Sangharsh Mein Gujarat*: "The day Subhaga left for Nagpur was a memorable day. Her courage was worth admiring. Despite all the threats like arrest on the way, indefiniteness of release, harsh enquiry by the police and such other things, she showed no signs of fright; rather she was happy that she had been chosen to do her duty. I had gone to meet her before she left. I was happy to see her vigour. I talked to her in all vitality. I displayed artificial signs of courage, but in my heart resided a cause of anxiety. I was one of those who were bent upon sending this woman to count the lion's teeth. Had anything untoward happened to her, her entire family would be shattered; this thought sank my heart. At the same time, I was feeling proud at the traits that had been cultivated in the Sangh workers. Such families have been the source of power who could lay down their lives on one call of the Sangh. Our source of trust in our victory lay in such families that could sacrifice everything of theirs."

After the meeting of Members of Parliament on 29-30 December, an all-India meeting was to be held of the Lok Sangharsh Samiti in Ahmedabad, but its information was available with few people. About thirty-five of the leaders of the Lok Sangharsh Samiti had to visit Gujarat for the first time. About one-half of the Lok Sangharsh Samiti leaders were such who had arrest warrants on their names. The remaining leaders had no arrest warrants against them, but a strict watch was kept on them. The purpose behind the holding of the meeting soon after that of the parliamentarians was to deceive the government agencies. The movements of the leaders under watch to Gujarat, made the government assume that they were going to attend the meeting of parliamentarians there.

There was need to exercise extreme care in the management of the meeting. With the cooperation of Nathalal Jhagda, general secretary of the Jansangh, Narendra Modi and other volunteers had chalked out a plan. According to it, all leaders on 29-30 December were made to stay at the places of different volunteers. Besides, some leaders were lodged at Gandhinagar and others at the Sangh office in Ahmedabad. As per the plan, they had to be together until the evening. All underground leaders were taken to the meeting venue quite easily, but those under watch had to be cared about greatly.

Besides, an underground leader of the Lok Sangharsh Samiti intimated Narendra Modi which augmented his anxiety. According to this information, unexpected and amazing, was that some people attending the conference were suspicious, and it could be possible that they passed the information to please Indira Gandhi and the government. Therefore, they should be told nothing about where they were going and why they were going. This information made Narendra Modi feel that even a minor slip could lead to a major disaster, which could prove a blot on Gujarat.

Looking at the gravity of the situation, Narendra Modi reconsidered his plan once again. A new plan was chalked out, and when it was considered to be foolproof, it was put into implementation.

A special feature of the old city of Ahmedabad is its wide network of streets. The houses in these streets are so joined together that one could go from one end to the other without taking to the road anywhere. Narendra Modi immediately listed the Sangh volunteers who lived in those streets and had houses on the edges and had two entrances. As per the plan, the leaders were taken to the houses of these volunteers, and from there, the leaders were boarded into cars for taking them to the venue. This helped to check the security personnel who kept a close watch on the leaders. This was how the plan was successfully accomplished. After all leaders reached the venue safely, Narendra Modi and his team breathed a sigh of relief.

The meeting had, at length, discussed the matter of violent and non-violent protest. This discussion finally led to urge people to protest as per the Gandhian values and disapproval was expressed for violent means.

The meeting lasted the whole day and a number of important decisions were taken in it. It also discussed the effect of the *Satyagraha* on the society, government and the arrested people. By now, the *Satyagraha* was one and a half month old, and more protestors were ready to go to jail than was assumed by the government. This caused wonderment to the government and this point was mentioned in the meeting too. The committee expressed satisfaction over the impact of *Satyagraha*.

This type of protest activities against dictatorship kept occurring in Gujarat. Despite the Morcha Government in power, all care was taken that no information reached the Central Government. This was the reason that no underground leader ever faced any trouble. A strong and vital link of this struggle was the 25-year-old Narendra Modi.

A landslide victory of the Morcha in four metropolitan elections, and expanding scope of the Morcha in small and big villages just prior to the Zila Panchayat elections was a cause of acute worry for the Congress. Moreover, the movement of *Satyagraha* was gradually spreading across every district of Gujarat, further causing anxiety among the Congress leaders. These leaders made every effort to bring bad name to the Morcha Government, which they had continued right from the time of awareness movement; in their hearts they wished to teach the people of Gujarat a lesson in vengeance. Like Tamil Nadu, they were too restless, and wanted to bring down the Gujarat Government anyhow. Because the Central Government knew it well that the methods adopted in Tamil Nadu could prove costly if repeated in Gujarat, so it asked its leaders in the state to make some Morcha leaders defect to its side, and promised its leaders to make all resources available for the purpose.

The Congressmen in Gujarat, under the leadership of Hitendrabhai Desai, were now ready to bring down the Gujarat Government at any cost. The State Government was already shaky, an atmosphere of its possible fall at any time was in the air. And in this atmosphere, the Rajya Sabha elections approached. The name of Lal Krishna Advani was put forward. He was the all-India President of the Jansangh, and was at this time, cooling his heels in the Bangalore jail, and this amounted to poking the Central Government. The State Government in Bangalore too tried to impede the nomination of Advani anyhow.

The then housing minister of Gujarat, Makrandbhai Desai was sent to Bangalore, accompanied by Amar Zariwala, a Jansangh worker of Bombay. They tried to contact Advani, but the home minister there clearly refused to permit them to meet Advani. Therefore, as soon as the courts of law opened in the morning, the well-known lawyer Santosh Hegde filed a writ petition for a parole so that Advani could file his nomination. In a few days, another writ petition was filed for permission of a meeting with Advani in connection with the election. This was how the entire matter reached the court of law.

On the other hand, Babubhai Patel, the Chief Minister, called on K. Brahmananda Reddy and stressed the need for making available all facilities and assistance so that Advani could take part in the election. The court too acted favourably on the writ petitions and accepted the demand for releasing Advani on parole. However, now Advani himself protested against autocratic ways of the government and refused to go out on parole. Thus, in this moral contest, the government was badly defeated while Advani tasted victory.

Advani was brought to Ahmedabad from Bangalore by air under the police confinement. He was lodged in a guest house in Gandhinagar. It was here that all formalities regarding his nomination were completed. Thus, Advani was elected to the Rajya Sabha facing all the adverse challenges that existed at that time.

The Congressmen increasingly believed that the State Government would fall sooner or later. The Morcha Government wanted to ensure that Gujarat continued to be in peace even when the State Government was brought down, while the Congressmen wished to bring a bad name to it through different means, as charges of corruption. They took the help of defectors in order to produce a picture that the Morcha Government was coming down under its own weight due to underlying differences among its ranks. They also propagated that the state Government was indulging in undemocratic ways and encouraging violence, and so on. The efforts in this direction became stronger with every passing day, which were all aimed at to bring a bad name. In addition to these efforts, the 'tunnel issue' was raised in order to raise another controversy in all-out effort to strike the hardest. Some Congressmen and a parliamentarian of Gujarat informed the Central Government and the CBI about the tunnel matter.

Finally, the Congress succeeded in its scheme. The Morcha legislators defected the party, some did out of selfish interests, others did for power, while others were scared of the MISA, and this was how a democratically elected government in Gujarat was brought down. The number of Morcha legislators decreased day by day, and finally on 12 March, it was reduced to minority. Babubhai Patel submitted the resignation to the governor on behalf of the Morcha Government.

As soon as the fall of the government was decided, the Lok Sangharsh Samiti conducted a meeting on 11 March. The members made for the unknown places with a fear of being confined and improper medical treatment in the jail. Narendra Modi too was present in this vital meeting.

The members present in the meeting discussed the new situation. Narendra Modi and others talked on different matters. They were doubtful if they would ever meet again. It was sure that all the members would be in jail in some time. This meeting was more like a farewell party. Everybody hugged everybody else with a promise that they would meet again in a new India, and thus good wishes were exchanged.

In the meeting of the Lok Sangharsh Samiti, the members like Narendra Modi were of the opinion that it would be better to evade arrest, rather than go to jail, in order to keep the flame of protest burning. Therefore, all people expressed good wishes for people, especially Narendra Modi, who wished to protest while being underground. All members, other than a few, had to be ready to go to jail, while Narendra Modi and a few others were ready to challenge the MISA too, they had to plan to go underground.

Keshavrao Deshmukh, *Prant Pracharak* of the Rashtriya Swayamsevak Sangh, called an emergency meeting of the Gujarat state workers and took necessary decisions regarding the new situation. Everybody was at his post. The second round of underground life was now about to begin for people like Narendra Modi. Now, they were being confronted with the massive challenge to MISA, and it was like walking on the edge of a sword.

The Morcha Government submitted its resignation. The common people were opposed to this development; still there was no violent protest against it. The people lived a normal life; still a large number of people were arrested at will.

Arrests were made right from midnight and this process occurred all over Gujarat. Like other states, the workers of the Sangh, Jansangh and ABVP were targeted in Gujarat. Besides, some Sarvodaya workers too were arrested. The news floated about the arrest of different people. People were disturbed from their sleep in order to trace the underground workers. The Ahmedabad police could not find even a single Sangh worker. All of them were in their secure hideouts while keeping an eye on the development. When even a single Sangh worker could not be arrested, the government grew puzzled and restless, and now it started to threaten the family members, raiding all possible places to trace them. Searches were conducted in the houses of workers against whom there were no arrest warrants even.

The police continued to raid at Sangh workers for over a week; the entire state was terrorized due to this police action. Despite all this hard work, the police failed to arrest even one underground worker, nor could it find any other trace about them.

Right from the initial days of the struggle, the leaders of the underground movement, including Keshavrao Deshmukh, Nathalal Jhagda and Narendra Modi, kept meeting regularly in order to discuss the situation on daily basis.

These sudden arrests despaired many families. The very thought of indefinite imprisonment under the MISA was sufficient to shake even the courageous families. Therefore, several political workers had deviated from their path in order to protect themselves from the harsh measures under the MISA, and thus had submitted themselves. The newspapers carried in large number the advertisements declaring the resignation of workers from their posts. Some of them undertook shameful acts by sending copy of their resignation to the police station and Congress leaders in order to save their skin anyhow. These pieces of news were used by the Congressmen for their selfish interests. A number of so-called leaders, who had emerged from the reconstruction movement, now wore round their necks the placards admiring the twenty-point programme. Not only this, they submitted to the Congressmen senseless application to secure the arrest of underground Sangh workers.

Despite all the efforts, the government machinery had fully failed to secure the arrest of underground workers; they were far from success in any measure. In just one week after the fall of the Gujarat Government, the government had taken in its clutches every link that might relate to the underground movement. This success on the part of government proved quite amazing, it put barriers for the execution of a successful movement. An important link of the underground workers, Navinbhai Bhavsar was arrested. His house was raided as soon as some important literature reached his home by post. The information relating to the underground centres reaching the police was like a shock for Narendra Modi. He also feared that the government might have traced the information regarding other important places and contact centres.

Navinbhai was already arrested, and this process was followed by the arrest of Parindu Bhagat (Kaku), Govindrao Gajendra Gadkar and Vinod Gajendra Gadkar. All of them were put through tough examination. The name of the sender on letters was Prakash. (Let us tell you that this was the false name of Narendra Modi during the underground state.) The government now knew who Prakash in fact was. Now different arrested people were threatened to divulge details about Narendra Modi.

Now Narendra Modi and other underground leaders set themselves upon the task to disseminate information to other underground centres across the country about cessation of contact with Ahmedabad. The MISA prisoners had been lodged in nine jails – Sabarmati, Vadodara, Bhavnagar, Rajkot, Jamnagar, Bhuj, Surendranagar, Palanpur and Mahesana. Most of the arrested people belonged to Sangh, Jansangh, Socialist Party and ABVP.

The fall of the Morcha Government and the misuse of the MISA resulting into terror among the people were anyhow borne by the people of Gujarat. This state was now once again ready to launch its protest. Babubhai Patel and other former ministers of the Morcha Government kept communicating their messages to the workers and people quite fearlessly. The government had banned big rallies, but there was no ban on small conferences and meetings. Therefore, small meetings were used to create awareness among people.

On the first anniversary of the declaration of Emergency, 26 June 1976, a massive rally was planned to be held by Gujarat Janata Morcha in Ahmedabad, and it resolved to continue to fight against the Emergency and resultant oppressive measures. The government and administration were scared that the waves of awareness rising from this rally would not allow common people to remain silent; therefore they were bent upon preventing this rally at any cost. The police vans went round the streets to announce the prohibition on the rallies and meetings. The newspapers were ordered not to publish any news regarding the rally. The policemen stood guard near the noticeboards located in different streets of the town. Despite all these efforts on the part of the government, the workers in Gujarat were determined to sacrifice everything of their own; groups and groups of workers arrived in the premises of Sardar Congress Bhavan. A massive police force was present there as if a large battle had to be fought out.

Kripalani, Mahinder Kaur and Ashok Mehta, who were recently released from jail, too arrived in this rally. Besides them, the massive gathering was addressed by Babubhai Patel, R.K. Ameen, Manubhai Patel and Brahmakumar Bhatt and others. After the rally, the legislators, parliamentarians and members of the state executive of the Gujarat Morcha marched to the Raj Bhavan under the leadership of Babubhai Patel; however, they were stopped on the way. Amongst the loud applaud of thousands of people, sixty-two leaders offered themselves for arrest.

The news regarding the success of this programme had reached towns and villages through the underground contact centres. Besides, the entire state was instructed about putting up posters in opposition to the Emergency and dictatorship. The same night, posters appeared on the walls in towns and villages all over Gujarat. On 26 June, on the occasion of the black day, Jai Prakash sent across a message to the citizens of India. More than 50,000 copies were distributed among the people. Despite the police force being alert, this task was successfully accomplished by the underground workers in Gujarat.

Despite all restrictions and atrocities, the Sangh workers displayed their courage and determination and organised a protest on 26 June as planned. On that day, the prisoners arrested under the MISA in Gujarat jails fasted and offered tributes to the martyrs of this freedom struggle.

On 21 November was held in Ahmedabad a unique conference of the Gujarati youths. Invitation was sent to Piloo Modi and Babubhai Patel too who had been recently released from jail. However, in the wee hours of 21 November itself, a ban was imposed on the conference. The organizers immediately thought a way out, and decided to conduct the conference at Barejadi, a place out of the prohibited territory. The youths arriving for the conference were secretly intimated to reach Barejadi before they could be confronted with the police. Gradually, this information campaign led to the attendance of over 500 youths at Barejadi.

Babubhai, Piloo Modi and K.D. Desai too evaded the police watch to arrive at Barejadi secretly. The youths there displayed exalted vigour. Babubhai and Piloo Modi addressed the gathering. In this meeting of the youths, a message sent by Narendra Modi too was read in the capacity of the representative of the struggling youths. Despite the presence of a massive police force, the Sangh workers distributed the copies of the message among the youths; this message to the youths remains relevant even today. It exhorts the youths to stand erect in the face of corruption, immorality and autocratic rule. It goes thus:

"Young men!

"You are the affectionate sons of Mother India, you are the sprouts of optimism of future India. O sons of the invincible Mother India, just think to which direction we are being pushed. What will happen of your future? If you do not awake at this hour, you will have to think about the circumstances that would befall in the times to come.

"You are the future of India, because today's youth is the leader of tomorrow's society and country. Then, the responsibility of resolving today's problems naturally rests with the youth – it is obviously yours.

"Today the country has been rendered speechless – dumb, and you will have to face this helplessness in the times to come, yes, you will have to face it. Today's poverty, unemployment, illiteracy, immorality, corruption and excessive repression will trouble whom? You, of course! Today, democracy is being trampled down to enlighten the path of dictatorship, and who would be compelled to tread the given path like goats and sheep? Naturally, you! If you did not contribute in the freedom struggle of this second phase, whom would the future history blame? None else but you! Whose name will the historians include in the list who could not understand the value of precious blood of the martyrs who sacrificed themselves for liberty? Certainly, yours!

"Young men! Never forget that this role could not be played by the writers or readers of history – this role rests with you – the history makers. A great man annotates the words of future history through his deeds, and the present remains future's history. What the time would note down in history depends on you.

"Who will decide whether our future history will be a narration of events written in ink, or a chapter written in blood of Indian men and vermillion of women? Again it is you.

"We are only a step away from the victory of democracy and defeat of dictatorship. Whose responsibility to traverse this step and kiss victory? Yours!

"Whose duty it is to emancipate Mother India now shackled like a helpless woman? Yours, no doubt! Despite all these troubles, helplessness and challenges, O young men of India, you are the artists who have to forge the golden period of the future!

"You have to make the effort, that is, you have to resolve and determine. You have to identify the opponent, and you will have to raise the arms. Young men! If you did not come forward, the Indian revolution would lose its direction. If you did not accept the challenge, the coming tomorrow would refuse to acknowledge you as the youth, because a true youth fights against atrocities, and it has been a true manifestation over ages. The youth have never knelt down before the panorama of atrocities around them; they have never felt obstructed or fatigued.

"Why is the youth silent today? A golden opportunity is waiting to knock at the door in order to keep up with the glorious traditions of history. Rise! Awake! Devote yourself in the second phase of the freedom struggle of Mother India.

"Friends, we are all the offspring who took birth after independence. Come, let us make it known that dying in slavery is not acceptable to us, we know how to blow up the shackles of slavery. This is what we call youth.

Yours,
A young underground friend"

In this second phase of the struggle after the *Satyagraha*, special emphasis was laid on training of people and infusing fearlessness in them. It was essential that open protests were held on these matters. For this purpose, different methods were adopted to undertake the extensive work of this public struggle.

The workers, then in jails, continued to struggle for people's welfare. The relatives and friends of the prisoners thronged the jails on every occasion, whether it was Rakshabandhan or Diwali, Janmashtami or Vijaya Dashami. Such occasions looked more like fairs. All those present in the crowd were related to the struggle somehow; therefore, everybody felt a pang of flame within. The courage shown by these relatives and friends was the only source to keep the inmates motivated, the protestors were well aware of this fact. Therefore, some dedicated workers were sent in the garb of these relatives. These workers used to talk to them in order to infuse the waves of courage, devotion and trust, in order to awaken new consciousness in them, and thus made the entire environment replete with optimism and vigour. This plan of the Sangh to infuse optimism among the people and inmates could never be traced by the government at any time.

After the Gujarat Government fell, this motivation was a part of the underground movement. All plans were chalked out from underground locations, but they were acted upon in the open. The planners were underground, but those who carried out the plan walked in the open among common people. Of the public programmes being held in different ways, some of them were such which were being carried in a much camouflaged manner.

Not only here, efforts for the protection of Indian democracy were being made in other countries too. Gujarat had been in touch with tendencies coming to the fore abroad. The initial phase of the Emergency was somewhat less complex. The people abroad who struggled against the Emergency included a large number of Gujaratis. Looking at their contribution, it had become essential that a representative of Gujarat went abroad to conduct a meeting with these people. This scheme had been made right before the fall of the State Government. It was planned that Makarandbhai Desai had to go abroad evading arrest. He was a Morcha leader as well as a good worker of the Jansangh. As soon as a message was passed to him, he readily accepted this. He was instructed that he would have to go abroad in case the Gujarat Government fell. As was assumed, the fall of the government was likely anytime. This plan was known to only a few selected workers of Gujarat, including the wife of Makarandbhai. Therefore, as soon as the government fell, then Makarandbhai rang up his house and said very briefly, "I am coming as per the plan." He was welcomed by the fearless reply, "Okay, best of luck!"

On 26 April, Makarandbhai appeared in the first international council of Friends of India Society International in the capacity of special guest; he urged all Indians abroad to get united. He was then selected the general secretary of the FISI.

Under the editorship of Makarandbhai, two fortnightly periodicals were started, the first in England and then in America titled *Satyavani*. A Gujarati person inaugurated his printing press there by printing the first issue of *Satyavani*.

The news material for the *Satyavani* was sent from India, and hundreds of its copies were delivered in India. Besides, the newspapers all over the world published news about Indian struggle, the copies of these newspapers were made available in India. A few days later, Makarandbhai made America his centre of activities. Now, the *Satyavani* was published from America.

The Gujaratis living in other countries did not lag behind too. Anil Poth of Hong Kong bore the responsibility of the FISI as the vice president. Babubhai Patel of Tanzania contributed significantly. Thus, the Indians living abroad had played an active role in this revolutionary struggle. Despite their distance from the country, they served the Motherland in all earnestness.

The important role played by Narendra Modi could be gauged from a letter sent by Makarand Desai from England. It reads:

"Brother Sri Narendra,

I was extremely glad to read your letter, keep writing in the same spirit. If we keep in touch, our activities could become simpler. The information of important news and events should be disseminated, especially those which are related to our struggle. Continue to send all news about the failure of Emergency in particular, so that we can publish them in the *Satyavani*.

On the coming 26 June, we have organised a worldwide programme, the detailed information of which will be sent to you later.

Please send more and more addresses to which we can send the *Satyavani*. Please keep in touch with my home at Vadodara. Reply if you happen to get this letter.

Compliments from Makarandbhai"

In another letter of 16 July, 1976, Makarand Desai writes to Narendra Modi:

"Brother Sri Narendra,

We continue to get news through your letters. Your arrangement and management are good. The information got from you is published in the newspapers here; these pieces of news are also included by the BBC in its broadcast. Therefore, it is important that all pieces of news are sent to us on urgent basis.

Sri Seth, the transferred judge has filed an appeal in Gujarat High Court which will come up for hearing on the coming 26th, please let us know the news about this hearing.

Rising costs are presenting terrible problems before people; this news remains important. If correct news is sent, it would be easier for us to get it published in newspapers. We are facing some problems in getting news published, but they eagerly wait upon any correct news."

In another letter, Makarand Desai writes to Narendra Modi:

"Brother Sri Narendra,

Several false doubts have been eradicated by your letter. I was worried if all you friends were now arrested. Now, I have gone through the information, it is acceptable. Initially, after coming here, we were facing some problems in starting a newspaper, but now it will be published regularly. The addresses sent by you have been received. Your request for sending a larger number of copies is acceptable.

Our effort is focussed on delivering our newspapers to all those people who matter. Please keep sending the lists of addresses, without any hesitation. The thing to worry is that we are not able to get any addresses from outside Gujarat. Will you be able to manage them?

Please keep in touch with your comrades and keep guiding me. Sometimes it appears that I should even go to jail to know more about the Emergency in its manifest form. Please discuss with senior workers, volunteers and officials and pass on the news.

It appears now that people have changed opinion about the Emergency. They are of the view that this step has been taken by the Government of India out of selfish interests which would prove detrimental to India in the times to come. Consequently, our propaganda is becoming stronger by the day; at least it appears to be so. In particular, our friends are proving to be quite useful. Generally, the Indian people are not coming into the open lest the government should take any steps against them, but they are all assisting us in due measure.

Compliments from Makarandbhai"

In broader perspective, it is no big thing to pass days without doing anything while being underground. Such a situation entails that one has to save himself from the police; however, those who choose this path of going underground in order to hide themselves from the police and take forward the struggle, they are certainly doing a tough task, much like walking on a two-edged sword. There were a large number of underground volunteers in Gujarat. Most of them belonged to the Rashtriya Swayamsevak Sangh, Jansangh and ABVP. Of these, many have been taken prisoners and many others had to surrender before the police due to varied causes. Thus, by the end of the struggle, only 35 volunteers have been able to be active. These workers were those against whom the MISA warrants had been issued. Besides them, there were many workers who were undertaking their task as planned. They had to remain underground in order that the government or society did not suspect them. These underground volunteers had to work very cautiously all the time so as to conceal their real identity. Generally, the Sangh *Pracharaks* wore dhoti-kurta, but now they had to adorn themselves in different modern robes and change their names.

The family members of these volunteers too exercised every care that they should talk nothing about these people, especially before any outsider. They always talked about them with terms like Dada, Mama, Bada Bhai, Chhote Chacha or Bade Chacha. On the other hand, the volunteers had assumed several aliases for identification among them such as Dixit, Dr. Umesh, Ajit, Swamiji, Chaudhary, Anand, Navin, Lalaji, Prakash, Ranjit, Batuk, Timir, etc. As the number of underground workers was large, the managers of the struggle at the state level had to take every care as well as remember the false names of all central and state volunteers. The changed robes were quite strange in a few cases. They were now dressed as Vohraji, Mullaji, sardarji, Parsi baba, LIC agent, swamiji, professor, doctor, agarbatti vendor, journalist, astrologer and so on, and they had to wear the clothes accordingly as well as behave themselves accordingly.

These workers changed their garbs so efficiently that even those who knew them for years failed to identify them without introduction. A worker who became an astrologer had to do forecasts, which of courses were false. Narendra Modi wore saffron clothes. He was staying at a worker's house when an *Acharya* of the Swaminarayan faith happened to visit. The family members introduced Narendra Modi as a swami who had come from Udaipur. Now after formalities, the debate started between a true *Sanyasi* and a Swami who had adorned this garb out of compulsion. The Swami had no way out but to save his skin anyhow in that hour-long *Shastrartha*. The *Acharya* never came to find out that all this was pure drama. The LIC agent had to teach himself to answer queries about the insurance policies. The worker who became a Pandit was once travelling by bus, when an acquainted person looked at him. It was a point of danger, so he tried to evade him, but he approached and asked him, "I am sure you are ....Bhai. We have met before, haven't we?" and such likes were raised to these garbed fellas.

The Pandit kept negating everything, but the gentleman was bent upon raining down his queries, "What do you do? Do you own a factory? Do you make oil engine? What are the prices?" and so on and so forth.

Finally the Pandit had to retort, "My factory produces knives. Do you want them?"

Only then did the gentleman keep quiet.

Mahendrabhai alias Batukbhai, who contributed significantly in underground correspondence, communication, etc., was better known as the compounder of Dr. Dave. He had come to Ahmedabad when he first became the *Pracharak*. Therefore, his stay had been arranged with Jyotindra, a nephew of Dr. Dave.

The underground struggle had several aspects. Efforts were made to create mass awareness as well as utilize each opportunity to oppose the government. Constant contact was kept with the jails, and the inmates were passed regular information about events, programmes and schemes in order to keep them motivated. It was to alleviate any doubts in their minds that nothing was happening outside the four walls of the prison. This entire struggle required to take risks quite often.

Once it became inevitable to get in touch with a Jansangh leader who was lodged in Bhavnagar jail in connection with an important matter. This purpose could not be attained by secret correspondence. Therefore, it was decided that Narendra Modi should go personally and discuss it with him. For an underground worker to go anywhere near the jail was like committing suicide. With due preparation, Narendra Modi arrived at Bhavnagar in September 1976. He proceeded to the jail along with a sister from Bhavnagar to meet the leader. The 'Swamiji' was finally permitted to meet his disciple. He stayed there for one hour and conducted free '*Satsang*' with his disciple before coming out safely.

After the Gujarat Government was pulled down, the Central Government did its best to arrest the underground workers, but when it miserably failed in its bid, it declared them absconders and much publicized about it through newspapers and radio. This propaganda by the government was responded by publishing an underground magazine from Kheda district. It said: "We are those who sacrifice themselves for the purpose of re-establishment of life values. We shall live under the shadow of injustice, but would work to eradicate it at any cost. We offer you a challenge to catch us if you could." This magazine was delivered to a number of government officials too, besides pasting it on walls at different places.

Underground literature was of three types. The magazines like *Mukhpatra* were published to deliver news to people. A magazine called *Muktavani* was published in Gujarat, its editing work was looked after by Narendra Modi. After all the material was collected, three to five manuscripts were prepared. Each issue was printed in some new press. Sometimes, the printers had to be given higher costs in order to make them agree to print the magazine. After printing, these magazines were delivered to underground centres in specified numbers. This magazine was also sent to Maharashtra for delivering to the Gujaratis living there. These magazines were carried by the Sangh workers. To keep the police in dark, the publishing date of the magazines was kept indefinite, and the entire work regarding a magazine was completed in a matter of two days. Sometimes the police sniffed through the underground literature and raided the printing press. Once when the *Muktavani* was being printed in a printing press, a policeman came there in private clothes and showed the printer an old issue of *Muktavani* and said that he was a member of the Lok Sangharsh Samiti and he wanted to get more copies of the magazine printed. The printer was alert. He rebuked the policeman and showed himself to be the greatest devotee and supporter of the government and threatened him to get arrested if he did not leave from there. The police spy returned with a good opinion of the printer. Those days, the *Muktavani* had become a source of news for people. This magazine continued to be published right through the end of the struggle and thus the flame of mass awareness was kept lighted.

The second type of underground literature was the books dealing with the Emergency and analysis of democracy. Efforts were made to deliver these books to the learned and thinkers of Gujarat. Magazines were also published to bring out the facts about the exaggerating claims on the economic front by the government.

Some of the important books were: *Twenty Point Deception, Emergency X-rayed, Proposed Constitutional Reforms, Review of a Decade, When Disobedience to Law is a Duty, Form of Fascism* (in Gujarati), *Forty-fourth Constitutional Amendment* (in Gujarati), *Indian Press Gagged, Saga of Struggle, Why Emergency, Anatomy of Fascism, Twenty Lies* (in Gujarati), *Facts – Nail India's Lies* and others.

The government continued with its anti-Sangh propaganda during the period of Emergency. The government revenue was much wasted on spreading lies against it in radio, newspapers and other government publications. The focus of all these activities was the Sangh. Therefore, the Sangh too decided to let people know the truth, and it published small underground booklets which presented the Sangh in true light. Some of the booklets in this series were *Who is Fascist – We or They?, Sangh and Violence, Why Atrocities on Sangh in the Name of Emergency, Rashtriya Swayamsevak Sangh Casteism and Untouchability, Financial Assistance of Sangh, Do Away Injustice from Sangh, Why Ban on Sangh, Sangh, Democracy and Support Strength*, and others. Thousands of copies were distributed among the people.

A system of underground circular papers was created to bring out the true news from all over the country. The news-magazines were based on these circulars. These were published in English and Hindi, and dealt with political scenario of the state, internal activities of the Congress, psychological condition of people, news from jails, protest programmes and so on. The circulars were delivered to different underground centres through inter-state messengers. True news from India was in great demand abroad. Therefore, a plan was chalked out for this purpose. These magazines and circulars were also delivered to other countries through secret channels. In order to include news from even tiny villages of Gujarat, a system was created at the state level. This system coordinated with such systems in other states in order to compile and deliver news to different countries.

The success of the plans chalked for the underground movement depended on the truthfulness of the news thus attained. It was due to the massive and disciplined organisation of the Sangh that all types of true information reached different centres, and further plans were chalked out on the basis of this information. The plans thus made were passed on to the concerned individuals. This system was also used to deliver guidance of the leaders to the volunteers spread across the country. The information system of the Sangh proved far more effective than that of the government.

Moropantji Pingle, the all-India chief of all-India information system and underground leader, arrived in Gujarat on a tour for this purpose. He met over one hundred and fifty volunteers in different Gujarat regions over a couple of days. They discussed in detail what could be done to win the elections despite all the bans imposed by the government.

The Sangh volunteers had no experience in conducting elections; therefore, there was need to make arrangements for their training so that they could make adequate response to the possible candidates favouring them, possible candidates of the Congress, the attitude of internal factions within the Congress, possibilities of maximum utilization of thinking youths and women, needs for vehicles during elections, system of election funds (it was difficult to manage funds those days), provision of a large number of booklets if censorship continued, contact with big and small newspapers, contact with prestigious people and institutions of the community, etc. Different individuals were assigned specific responsibilities. One individual was made the in-charge of a parliamentary constituency. All this system had been created right before November. This plan had not yet taken into consideration the people who could join them on their release from jail. Their release would certainly add to their numbers. Every care was taken that such preparation was not divulged to the government. As guessed, the elections were declared. The plans were already in place. As the elections were to be held in a free atmosphere, the confidence of the volunteers peaked to the maximum.

Narendra Modi and other Sangh workers used to conduct meetings in a house located in the deep interiors in a residential colony. These meetings were used to exchange information and messages. One day, the police raided the colony. The entire colony was seized and each house was being searched. The family that had given the house for use was quite anxious, especially for the security of the strugglers. This house too was searched. That day, Nathalal too was there, however, he had just left a few minutes before the raid. Later, it was revealed that the raid, in fact, was for a gambling house being run in another house of the same colony. This incident taught Narendra Modi another lesson in safety and caution; now he took care to enquire about the houses in the vicinity before finally selecting a place for the struggle work.

Some extraordinary things had become quite ordinary during the course of their struggle, like change of meeting venues at the eleventh hour, running around for making alternative arrangements anytime, and so on. Once, Deshmukhji was in a meeting with some underground workers as well as other normal workers. Just about this time, a team of the LIB reached there. Now, there was no other way out but to flee from there. Some of them kept the LIB people busy while the others escaped one by one.

It was also a part of their routine to conceal themselves in houses for hours. One day, it was raining heavily. Thinking that the weather was favourable as no one would notice her, a worker – Shanta Bahen – set out for the residence of Gajendra Gadkar. Hardly had they talked for some time when the police van pulled up before the house. The family members were out of their wits as it seemed quite imminent that the guest would be taken into arrest. The policemen made their way to the upper storey room where they had seated themselves. Finding the police in the house together with Keshubhai Patel and Arvindbhai Maniyar, the guest worker made to the adjoining room and removed all the papers safely, so that no secret information was leaked to the government even if she was arrested. Later it was found out that Keshubhai and Arvindbhai had been arrested from Rajkot and the police had brought them here with some other purpose. However, the guest worker kept hiding in the adjoining room until the police remained there, and they left soon after the police had left.

The socialist workers, involved in the underground movement, had to stay in the houses of Sangh workers. During this period, they were impressed with the courage, style of thinking, purity of conduct and high-grade patriotism.

Towards the close of 1976, several meetings were held in Gujarat; therefore, most of the leaders were in the state those days. Early morning on 1 January 1976, Narendra Modi had to go to meet Ravindra Varma, who was waiting for him at Ramlal Parekh's residence. As soon as Narendra Modi entered, he wished them saying 'Happy New Year'.

Varma replied, "Narendraji, I was about to wish you Happy New Year, but you are a Hinduist, thinking so I didn't wish you lest you might feel bad about it. But you yourself..."

Narendra Modi intervened and said, "The greatness of Hinduism lies in this very fact that it does not compel its followers to tread a narrow path."

There were a number of such small incidents, discussions, expressions and talks that brought different workers close together.

The capabilities of the Sangh had been used to the greatest extent in order to undertake the daily routine tasks, due to a number of factors. The Sangh workers were closely related at the family level with one another; moreover, they had the courage to work without an iota of desire to come to fame. Above all, the structure of the organisation proved to be the greatest advantage. There was a system of hierarchy of the Sangh officials, but the execution of tasks did not require being fully dependent on them. This was precisely the reason that the Sangh work continued unabated despite a large number of Sangh workers being in jail under the MISA; what normally happens in other organisations when the leaders are arrested. Troops are seen to disperse when they find their commanders absent from amongst them, but nothing like that had happened with the Sangh. This was due to those very grass-root workers whom the *Sarsanghchalak* himself had called 'Dev durlabh' (or, who are rare to gods even). These workers had accomplished the tasks of their own.

It was on the basis of continuous work, sacrifice and faith that these workers conquered this second phase of the freedom struggle. Of all factors that helped to secure victory included the most important one, that was none else but the citizens of India, the voters of India. The sentiments prevailing in the people for change could be materialized successfully; to ensure it steps were taken. Let us see one of them.

Narendra Modi was on a tour in connection with the elections. In a small village of northeastern district Sabarkantha, a sixty-five-year-old woman was travelling in the bus. She appeared to belong to a financially famished family. The conductor demanded her ticket, to which she remarked, "How much money do you want? I am illiterate, can you get me? Take this note and refund the balance."

The conductor gave her the ticket and the balance money, which also comprised two notes of one rupee each.

She said, "O dear, change this note."

The conductor retorted, "Mother, what is there in this note? It is okay."

The old woman said, "Yes, I know it is okay, but I want a new note because I have to give it to Babubhai Patel who is about to arrive in our village. It was for this purpose that I came to work here."

If curiosity is expressed by an individual located at the lowest ebb of the community, if the poor person of the smallest of villages shows this curiosity towards change, nothing could be a higher achievement than this.

* * *

These twenty-one months of the Emergency proved very significant as far as Narendra Modi was concerned. The struggle against Emergency carved out his personality and organisational capability. Several of his capabilities came to the fore in the eyes of the Sangh. After the emergency was lifted, Narendra Modi remained very busy. He lived in the Hedgewar Bhavan, which was the headquarters of the Rashtriya Swayamsevak Sangh, where national leaders often visited. Narendra Modi used to communicate with them on intellectual and conceptual levels. Two of such leaders were Dattopant Thengadi and Eknath Ranade. Dattopant Thengdi had founded the Bharatiya Mazdoor Sangh and the Bharatiya Kisan Sangh. The only offspring of his parents, Dattopant had dedicated his life to the Sangh as a full-time *Pracharak* from 1938. Eknath Ramade had been the Sangh *Sahkaryavah*. He had been given the responsibility of constructing a majestic monument at Kanyakumari, the place where Swami Vivekananda had sat in meditation to witness the nobility of Mother India. It was to be done to mark the birth centenary of Swami Vivekananda.

Eknath Ranade wished to devote his life at Kanyakumari's Vivekananda Centre, but the fate wished something else. Both Dattopant Thengdi and Eknath Ranade had close attachment with Narendra Modi, it could be spiritual or intellectual. Narendra Modi could talk to them on any topic. Narendra Modi states: "My relation with these two gentlemen can be termed spiritual or intellectual; both of them had attachment with me." In 1978, Narendra Modi was assigned the responsibility of *Vibhag Pracharak*; his *Vibhag* comprised six districts of rural Vadodara, Panchmahal, Dahod, Anand, Kheda and Vadodara city. His ability and capability as an organiser were coming to the fore. As a Sangh *Pracharak*, Narendra Modi was quite popular among the *Swayamsevaks* and their families. He mixed up with them quite easily. He was promoted as *Sambhag Pracharak* within two years. His field of work extended from central-south district of Kheda to Umargaon of Valasad. The Sangh office at Baroda was his residence. He toured different places from there.

11 August, 1978, 4 p.m. The Machchu Dam of Morvi town was destroyed in minutes; it took hardly any time when the entire area was flooded in water, as high as 20 feet. The entire area around Morvi was devastated together with numerous villages around it. This terrible calamity claimed over one lakh casualties. The first group to reach the site for rescue and evacuation work was a team of 50 *Swayamsevaks*.

Narendra Modi was one of the *Pracharaks* who reached there. He stayed there for several days and guided the *Swayamsevaks* in the service. Narendra Modi is very skilled in planning and its execution. The Swyamsevaks from all over Gujarat carried the deformed dead bodies and undertook their final rites. The Flood Assistance Commission formed by the Sangh started the rescue and evacuation work right from the first day. The three main tasks given to them were: 1. To rescue the people who were struck up in the flooded area. 2. To conduct final rites of the dead bodies which were lying all over in ruined houses, in fields and hanging on poles. 3. To sanitise and clean the places of living by removing garbage. In addition, they took over the responsibility to offer medical aid for the victims suffering from different ailments and to run the shelter camps for those whose houses had been destroyed or rendered beyond use. The *Swayamsevaks* undertook the rescue work not only in Morvi town, but also in the villages affected in the tehsils of Morvi and Bankaner. Some of the localities in Morvi were strewn with a large number of dead bodies in the mud, and it had become a challenging task even for the government disaster management teams. The Sangh workers disposed of the dead bodies and cleaned up the area of garbage which was sent out in about 200 trucks. The Sangh also ran an information centre along side rescue and evacuation work.

The then chairman of Morvi municipality had remarked to the journalists once: "Without the assistance of the Sangh *Swayamsevaks*, Morvi would have been inflicted by another calamity; it could have been struck by cholera." Ghulam Mohammad, the chairman of the Gujarat Muslim Majlis, inspected the relief camps being organised by the Sangh and appreciated them for the relief work. He also contributed an amount of ₹ 1001 to the fund. The Bishop of Karnavati church too visited these centres and appreciated the rescue efforts.

Those were the days of the fast (of Ramzan). There were about 4000 Muslims in a relief camp in Rajkot. The *Swayamsevaks* provided them necessary facilities so that they could carry out their religious work, without any impediment on any occasion. The food for their early morning diet was cooked and distributed as required by the religious norms. Later when Atal Bihari Vajpayee visited these camps, he was told by the Muslims: "We would not have survived but for the assistance of the Rashtriya Swayamsevak Sangh."

A number of special correspondents of different newspapers too arrived at Morvi. The *Tughlaq* of Madras wrote: "The people of Morvi consider the *Swayamsevaks* equal to gods." The *Hindustan Times* of Delhi wrote in its editorial on 25 August, 1978: "While some opposition parties are trying to take political advantage of the calamity, the Rashtriya Swayamsevak Sangh has presented before us an illustration and has shown to the world what a volunteer organisation can do in such times of crisis. The *Swayamsevaks* devoted their time and energy in numerous relief centres, and assisted the victims until their safe return to their homes. Besides, they removed the dead bodies and undertook final rites in all respects; it could not have been done by anybody else. It is service to humanity, and there is no place of party-politics in it. The political leaders, who visit the site like a storm, can at least create such an environment that these *Swayamsevaks* are allowed to work without any obstacle; at least they could not criticize these people who are devoted to the rescue work." M.V. Kamat, the then editor of the *Illustrated Weekly* remarked: "You might say anything about the Rashtriya Swayamsevak Sangh, but when it comes to service to the countrymen, they immediately roll up their sleeves and get working happily, and they expect nothing in return."

After the relief and rescue work, the second phase was started, that was to rehabilitate the flood victims. The Flood Assistance Commission resolved to gather funds and construct 500 cemented houses for the homeless people.

Within eight months of the *Bhumi Pujas*, on 14 September 1980, on the day of Rishi Panchami, the Third Sarsanghchalak Balasaheb Devras dedicated to the nation the Jankalyan Nagar in which the Sangh had built 400 houses. The chief guest in this programme was the then Chief Minister Babubhai Patel.

In this programme, Balasaheb addressed the people. He said: "The Sangh undertakes the service work, it is admired and appreciated, and it is a source of joy. The significant point is that all this does not occur all of a sudden, it is a natural process, the way the Sangh works, and its culmination is right before your eyes. Wherefrom has this natural tendency and outcome appeared from? It is the outcome of the hard work that the Sangh has done in the last fifty-five years."

Babubhai addressed: "The work undertaken by the Sangh at Morvi is second to none. It was no easy task to remove the stinking and deformed dead bodies, touching which meant breaking away of the body parts, but the *Swayamsevaks* did all this work and offered adequate final rites to the dead. The Sangh Swayamsevaks have added glory to their names by working in the disastrous calamity at Morvi."

The rescue and relief work, including the reconstruction work, were undertaken by the Sangh Swayamsevaks, the chief amongst them being Narendra Modi. After this calamity, Narendra Modi returned to the organisation work of the Sangh as usual.

Keshavrao Deshmukh, the *Prant Pracharak*, breathed his last on 2 March 1981. The state headquarters of Gujarat was then at Ahmedabad. Now, Narendra Modi was given the responsibility of *Prant Sahvyavastha Pramukh*, or the vice state chief of the Sangh.

The collective conversion at Minakshipuram in 1981 took the

entire Hindu community by surprise. The Virat Ekatmata Yatra was undertaken. This was accomplished by the untiring efforts of the *Swayamsevaks* in Gujarat. Over 4000 villages were contacted in which about one crore people participated. The entire Gujarat echoed with the slogans for Mother Ganga and Mother India. In the increasing work of the Sangh, a camp of 5,000 *Swayamsevaks* was accomplished at Ghodasar in Karnavati in 1984. In the arrangement of this camp lot was done by Narendra Modi, then *Pracharak* of Ahmedabad *Vibhag*. This camp displayed the massive Sangh's might to the society.

On the 60th anniversary of the Rashtriya Swayamsevak Sangh, the *Swayamsevaks* undertook a contact programme in which they visited each house of the region. A small booklet bringing out the chronological evolution of the Sangh became quite popular among the readers.

In the second year of the contact programme, Gujarat suffered from acute drought. It had not rained for three years, and now people were shifting to other places; cattle were dying of hunger. The Sangh formulated the Dushkal Peedit Sahayata Samiti in order to render relief to the victims. The *Swayamsevaks* distributed grain at several places, they also organised relief camps and grass centres, in order to enable people to face up the natural calamity with courage.

After some time, Narendra Modi was assigned the responsibility of Sabarkantha *Vibhag Pracharak* in addition to the charge of *Prant Sahvyavastha Pramukh*. This new responsibility entailed the work in rural Ahmedabad, Sabarkantha and Gandhinagar (district).

Narendra Modi was giving momentum to the Sangh work in all devotion. About this time, on 15 July 1985, Vakil Saheb succumbed to cancer in Poona. He had devoted his life continuously for attainment of the goals. Narendra Modi remarked at this: "The sage has gone, the impact is still there." A few months after the demise of Vakil Saheb, a new and most important turn came about in the life of Narendra Modi, it was towards the close of 1986. Narendra Modi states: "I was a Sangh *Pracharak*, I was busy in Sangh work. Our senior *Pracharak*, Nathabhai Sagda was the organisation in-charge of the Sangh for years, later he became the general secretary of the Bharatiya Janata Party. Everybody was of the view that the Bharatiya Janata Party was in need of a young man, who could work hard and run about, and dedicate himself to the cause. It was thus that I was sent to the Bharatiya Janata Party." Thus, a decision was taken to send Narendra Modi to the BJP, and this decision was taken by none else but Balasaheb Devras, the then *Sarsanghchalak*.

□

Devotion to Literature

Saraswati, the Goddess of Learning, is undoubtedly pleased on Narendra Modi. When he speaks, Mother Sharada resides right on his tongue and when he writes, She resides on his fingertips. There are few lucky people who are the focus of all attention when they speak. He has written not only moral articles but also short stories. He has penned down on a range of topics including people, festivals, culture, religion, society, and politics, among others. He is also a poet and lyricist. A CD has been made of his songs too.

Few people knew Narendra Modi when he was not a general secretary. His books were popular among people. They became bestsellers. In 1975, when he was mere 25 years, he wrote a book titled *Sangharsh Mein Gujarat* (*Gujarat in Struggle*). Its second print came out within a month. It has been written in such a fascinating and interesting style that one could not leave it without having finished in one sitting. The famous litterateur of Gujarat, Chandrakant Bakshi, had listed two of his most favourite books, one of which was this book of Narendra Modi. During the 70s, his stories and short novels were published in a Gujarati magazine called *Chandani*.

In 1975, precisely on 25 June, Indira Gandhi, the then President of the Congress and Prime Minister of India, had imposed the Emergency, squeezing life out of democracy. This book deals with the underground tendencies and work during such trying times of the Emergency, and can be presented as an authentic historical document of these activities. Much has been written about the circumstances prevailing during the Emergency, but there is hardly any literature about what was being done to preserve democracy. This book enumerates the struggle that was undertaken for the protection of democracy in the country, and the types of feats that were accomplished in this connection. All this was a planned struggle which was fought on several fronts with great enterprise and courage. This struggle did not lag behind the freedom struggle. Narendra Modi has presented this struggle in realistic terms in this book.

This book has been written by Narendra Modi, not in the capacity of a writer, but as if he was a soldier – a fighter. He says: "During the Emergency, I fully depended on my memory to write. I had only paper and pen, and no reference material. I completed this book in 23 days. My memory is somewhat strange. I don't make notes or note down points anywhere." He tells that he chose to confront the troubles for meeting his purpose. He had devoted all his life in the service of Mother India. Due to his obstinacy, motivation and duty, he became a guide and protector of thousands of workers in Gujarat. This book by Narendra Modi was published with Rajabhai Nene as the co-author. He was a *Pracharak* of the Rashtriya Swayamsevak Sangh. This book has also been translated into Hindi. It continues to be a guide to the volunteers. In the words of Narendra Modi himself: "This is the outcome of penance – hard work and perseverance, so it touches the heart."

Narendra Modi has been studious right from childhood. When he studied in school at Vadnagar, it was said that he could be found in the library most of the time. Vadnagar was a tiny village, but its library was well-equipped and rich. There is a book by Vaman Mukadam on the life and times of Chhatrapati Shivaji, running over 600-700 pages. Eleven years is too delicate a stage to lift the book of this size, but Narendra Modi carried this book home and read it in all concentration. He had finished reading the *Mahabharata* and *Ramayana* at a tender age of 13-14 years. He found reading the books very interesting which coordinated thoughts and language. When Narendra Modi was in the eighth standard, he wrote a play called *Peela Phool* (Yellow Flower), which was played at school. At that time, he was merely 13 years of age. This play was written on a sensitive topic like untouchability, which explained that untouchability is a great sin.

His aptitude in reading gave perfection to his writing too; his writing became fresh and lively. During his days as a *Pracharak*, he wrote his diary in the memory of his mother. To illustrate: "O Mother, I bow to thee, I committed this mistake...I ought not have committed it...and so on." He kept writing for about eighteen months and he derived a great pleasure in this work. He burnt down all these pages, a few of them were saved, and these have appeared now to produce evidence of such sentiments.

During the Emergency, he also edited a magazine named *Satyavani*, with a purpose to create mass awakening. In a weekly magazine called *Sadhna*, he wrote a column *"Akshar Upavan"* under a pseudonym Aniket for three years. He also used his pen to write on different topics covering politics, society, personalities, culture, etc. We have already discussed him as a story-writer. A collection of his stories is the *Prem Tirth*. The focal point in his sensitive stories is motherhood. These stories exhort the readers to take a dip into motherhood. These stories are profoundly linked with social concerns which were written in different conditions in 1975. Gunwant Shah, a popular writer-thinker of the Gujarati language, states about these stories: "If you asked me about the special feature of these stories, I would reply it in one word - that is motherhood." This is the sentiment of the sensitive mind of Narendra Modi. These stories divulge an urge for relations and attachment. The unique stream of attachment flowing among different relations would compel the readers to take a deeper dip. When a conscious and capable manager acquires the post of Chief Minister on the basis of ability and working efficiency, the wonderful joy of taking a dip into his sensitive heart can easily be felt.

The exalted point from which Narendra Modi creates a story, the same spontaneity continues when he sketches a person on paper. His book titled *Jyotipunj* is its evidence enough. Narendra Modi has got an opportunity to be in proximity of a number of extraordinary people in his life, and to understand them. Love, affection and attachment with these personalities have been the light-poles on the journey of his life. He has also worked with many of them shoulder to shoulder. However, when he pens down his views about them, he continues to be objective in his expression. He has commented on different personas in the book in an amazing and interesting manner. This would acquaint you with such *Karmyogis* or people who were devoted to deeds fully, these people devoted their lives in the feet of Mother India selflessly and without any desire for anything in return; they invested each moment of their lives in the cause. Perhaps no one else has ever mentioned these great people, but the fragrance of life continues to spread due to their efforts. A memory of these people gives us a new wave of inspiration. Therefore, Narendra Modi has written that this effort begets ultimate bliss. The book *Jyotipunj* enumerates the life stories of different people and would make the readers experience devotion and commitment to the society. This book by the patriotic writer will infuse the readers with traditional and cultural values as well as sentiments of devotion and loyalty.

Narendra Modi has created independent original works. Two books *Sikhe Vata Shikshan* and *Samajik Samarasata* are collections of his speeches. The first book deals with his educational views, while the other is connected with social harmony. A total of 45 speeches have been collected in these. He has dealt in these books with the topics right from Dr. Baba Saheb Ambedkar to Samras village and from Rakshabandhan to collective marriages, giving expression to his well-thought out views.

Narendra Modi is a sensitive personality. We can find its glimpse in his poetry. He creates stories, and with equal spontaneity, he creates poetry. He expresses his sentiments and attachment majestically in his poems.

His collection of poems goes by the name of *Ankh Yah Dhanya Hai*. The poet Narendra Modi can be revealed before you, body and soul, if you read his poems. His poems present man and his nature in an extremely meaningful manner. He writes:

Safal hue to irshya bhajan
Vifal hue to daya patra
Chhoo na sake kayarata mujhko,
Pamarata ki kya parvah?

(Success brings jealousy and failure pity, but I am far from cowardice, what do I care for the outcome?)

Narendra Modi gathers nature in life and life in nature, and thus reveals the mystery of being happy even under all types of difficulties and catastrophes. He says:

Jindagi ke yaar hain hum
Aur chhalakata alhad pyar hain hum.
Man chahe to udate hain ya
Dariya mein doob lagate hum
Apani marji ke darbar hain hum.

(We are the comrades of life, we are the unbounded love, we

fly in the air or dive in the river when we wish to, and we do what we like best.)

Gujarat, together with the water of Narmada, finds manifestation in his creations. His poetry is replete with the sentiments of patriotism. Look at the first page of this collection:

Mere Gujarat ko prem karen
Wah meri aatma.

(Love my Gujarat, it is my soul.)

And on the last page, he notes:

Mere desh se prem karen
Wah mera Paramatma.

(Love my country, it is my God.)

Bent upon sacrificing everything at the altar of Motherland, Narendra Modi has written about Vande Mataram. He says:

Yah shabd nahin, yah mantra hai hamara
Ajhahi ki urja ki dhadkan hai haari.
Vikas ka yah rajpath hai,
Rashtrajivan ka sankalpit yah mahamarg.

(This is no word, it is a mantra for us. It is the pulsation of energy within us, it is the highway to development, it is the determined highway to national life.)

He says that determination or resolve is the highway of life. In this poem, he expresses his aspiration to realize his dream. His love for the Motherland too is well known:

Main to kaleje ki kothari mein baitha hoon Maa
Maa mujhase kahna tu 'khamma-khamma'.
Mujhe daivan dena
Mujhe kuvvat dena
Mujho dena tu sat.

(I reside in thy heart, O Mother; say me one who tries; give me spirituality, give me ability and give me truth.)

This poet states with purpose and resolve. He says that he is not an eagle that eats up others, nor has he any helplessness in his blood. Discussing his true nature, he says:

Prarabdha ko kaun puchhata hai yahan?
Main chunotiyan jhelanewala manushya hoon.
Main udhar ka tej nahin leta
Main swayam jalata fanoos hoon.

(Who cares for destiny here? I am the man who confronts

challenges. I don't borrow glory from others, I myself am the lighted chandelier.)

The Indian masses look forward to an individual who could emancipate the country of all sufferings and all eclipses. Pointing to this, Narendra Modi had said in a poem several years ago:

Raat parajay ki doob gai
Aaj uga hai vijaya-prabhat.
Prabhat ko utsav bana lo aaj
Ujala hai aanewala kal hamara.
Timir ki toot gai buland deewar
Aaj uga hai shaurya prabhat.

(The night of defeat has gone by, now rises the morning of victory. Let us celebrate the morning, the light is about to dawn tomorrow. The strong wall of darkness has been broken down, today has risen the morning of courage.)

A fine leader, a first grade Chief Minister, Able, understanding and effective administrator, Skilled organizer, Shining thinker and a Fascinating speaker - Narendra Modi is full to the brim with several of such qualities, and with the pen in his hand, he makes us feel a person who is a majestic orator of words. The extensive reading right from childhood and pulsation of the society while being in touch during the course of his work; all these find manifestation in his words. He is a thinker, so naturally, he can create sentiments and views on the paper like none other can do.

□

Attachment with Workers – A Panorama of Workers

Bharatiya Janata Party: History

In 1986, Narendra Modi was assigned the responsibility of a party which had been founded with a certain purpose, dream and goal.

The Bharatiya Janata Party (BJP) is a nationalist political party, which is resolved to make India strong, prosperous and powerful having its due place in the international arena. This party had been founded on 6 April 1980 at Kotla Maidan, New Delhi in the executive session, with a purpose to make India a capable nation. Atal Bihari Vajpayee was elected as the first President of the party. With its foundation, the BJP expressed its views on international, national and popular topics, and thus manifested its active and powerful participation in Indian democracy, and went on to add various dimensions to it. Until then, the unipolar political system, reined by the Congress, was transformed into a bipolar system, and played a leading role in the alliance politics. Development-based politics too was laid down in the country by this party. After having come to power in different states, it set its goal as the central rule by the BJP-led National Democratic Alliance or NDA. In the past two decades, the Bharatiya Janata Party has come to the fore as a powerful political party and has earned recognition.

Background

Though the Bharatiya Janata Party was founded on 6 April 1980, yet, its past history is linked with the Bharatiya Jansangh. With independence and partition of the country, a new political situation was confronted. After the assassination of Mahatma

Gandhi, a ban was imposed on the Rashtriya Swayamsevak Sangh under a new political conspiracy. After the demise of Sardar Patel, Nehru became all-powerful in the Congress. What he said became the rule. In the absence of both Gandhi and Patel, the Congress was now under the complete impact of Nehruvism; with it came to the fore such topics which troubled the nationalists like never before, like minority appeasement, licence-permit-quota system, carelessness towards national security, kneeling down on national issues like Kashmir, negligence of national interests in international matters, and the like. Troubled and angered by Nehruvism and India's silence on atrocities on Hindu minorities in West Pakistan and East Pakistan (now Bangladesh), Dr. Shyama Prasad Mukherjee resigned from the Nehru Cabinet. On the other hand, while reeling under the ban on the Rashtriya Swayamsevak Sangh, some *Swayamsevaks* felt that they had been isolated from the political spectrum of the nation because they had kept themselves aloof from politics, and that the Sangh was being targeted for political reasons. In such a situation, a need for a nationalist political party was felt in the country. Consequently, the Bharatiya Jansangh was founded on 21 October 1951, under the chairmanship of Dr. Shyama Prasad Mukherjee. This ceremony took place at Radhomal Arya Kanya High School, Delhi.

Under the leadership of Dr. Shyama Prasad Mukherjee, the Bharatiya Jansangh started a movement on Kashmir and national integration, and opposed to give any special rights to Kashmir. Due to autocratic ways of Nehru, Dr. Shyama Prasad Mukherjee was put in prison in Kashmir, where he died under suspicious circumstances. Now, Pandit Deen Dayal Upadhyay was assigned the responsibility of strengthening the new party. The Bharatiya Jansangh played a vital role during the Indo-China War, and opposed the Nehruvian policies on national security. For the first time after independence, it was in 1967 that the sole right of Congress over Indian politics was snatched, the Congress tasted defeat in many states' assemblies before the Bharatiya Jansangh that fought under the leadership of Pandit Deen Dayal Upadhyay.

In the seventies, Indira Gandhi, the then Prime Minister, was becoming autocratic. People grew restless against the Congress Government. With the reconstruction movement in Gujarat, the student movement started in Bihar too. The Congress chose to repress these movements. At this, Loknayak Jai Prakash Narayan consented to lead the movement, and with this, people rose in opposition against the Congress rule. In 1971, external Emergency was imposed on the country in the context of Indo-Pak War and revolt in Bangladesh, which continued to exist long after the war ceased. A sharp voice was raised to remove this. Troubled by the mass movements, Indira Gandhi's Congress Government tried to suppress the people's voice. The internal Emergency was imposed on 26 June 1975, under Article 352 of the Constitution of India, second time in history. All major national leaders had been detained or put in prison. A ban was imposed on the Rashtriya Swayamsevak Sangh and several other organisations. Thousands of workers had been arrested under the MISA and put in jail. There was a real threat to Indian democracy now. Mass struggle was started, underground activities were undertaken. Troubled by the mass movements, Indira Gandhi dissolved the Lok Sabha on 18 January 1977 and declared elections for the new popular verdict. On the urge of Jai Prakash Narayan, a new national party, Janata Party was constituted. In a bid to make the entire opposition fight election from a common platform, this party had been formed, but due to lack of time, its constitution had not been achieved as a full-fledged political party. The Congress was badly defeated in the general elections, and the Janata Party and other opposition parties came to power with a huge majority. As announced before, the Bharatiya Jansangh joined the Janata Party in a session on 1 May 1977. It was attended by over 500 representatives of the party.

Unfortunately, the experiment of the Janata Party did not bear fruit for long. In about two and a half years, internal conflict came to the fore. The Congress too played its cards in a bid to play its game of politics. The matter of double membership of the representatives who had come from the Jansangh too was raised. It was said that the members of the Rashtriya Swayamsevak Sangh could not become the members of the Janata Party. On 4 April 1980, the national executive council of the Janata Party banned the members of the Rashtriya Swayamsevak Sangh from becoming the members of the party. The members pertaining to the former Jansangh opposed this decision, and they formed a new party by the name of Bharatiya Janata Party on 6 April 1980. It was how the Bharatiya Janata Party came into being.

The Bharatiya Janata Party is making continuous efforts towards making a strong, powerful, prosperous, capable and self-dependent India since then. The party has aimed to establish a democratic nation which does not discriminate between any castes, communities, or sexes and endeavours to provide all citizens political, social and economic justice, equal opportunities and freedom to religious belief and expression.

The party has embraced the ideological philosophy of Ekatma-Manavavaad (Philosophy of One Humanism), as laid down by Pandit Deen Dayal Upadhyay. Besides, the party is also specifically active in the emancipation of the suppressed classes, good administration, cultural nationalism, development and security too. The party has also expressed its loyalty towards five main principles, which are called Panch-Nishtha (Five Resolves).

These five principles are:

- Democracy,
- Nationalism and national integration,
- Positive secularism (harmony of all religions),
- Gandhist socialism (establishment of a harmonious society free from exploitation), and
- Value-based politics.

Atal Bihari Vajpayee was elected the first President of the Bharatiya Janata Party. With its foundation, the party became active in national politics. The non-Congress parties came to one forum on the issues of Bofors and corruption, and Rajiv Gandhi-led Congress had to face huge defeat in the 1989 general elections. The Rashtriya Morcha Government, under the leadership of V.P. Singh, was given outside support by the BJP. In the meanwhile, the Ram Mandir movement was started. The then BJP President, Lal Krishna Advani started the Rath Yatra from Somnath to Ayodhya. The Rath Yatra was obstructed midway by the government because of the massive popular support and increasing popularity of the Bharatiya Janata Party. Therefore, the BJP pulled back its support from the government, resulting into the decline of the V.P. Government, and now Chandreshekhar became the Prime Minister riding on Congress support. The popular support to the Bharatiya Janata Party continued to go up in the elections to come. In the meanwhile, Narsimha Rao-led Congress and the Congress-supported Samyukta Morcha ruled the country. This period also witnessed newer records of inaction, corruption, unruliness, maladministration, favouritism and dynastic politics.

In the general elections of 1996, the Bharatiya Janata Party secured 161 seats. It had secured 85 Lok Sabha seats in 1989 and 120 in 1991, and now it had reached up to 161. The popular support to Bharatiya Janata Party continued to rise. For the first time in 1996, the Bharatiya Janata Party Government, under Atal Bihari Vajpayee, was sworn in; however, this government could last just 13 days in the absence of enough support. In 1998, the Bharatiya Janata Party secured 182 seats.

The National Democratic Alliance Government, led by Atal Bihari Vajpayee, was sworn in. After Jayalalita-led Anna Drumak pulled back its support, the government fell because it failed to secure majority by just one vote. It was due to the immoral conduct of Girdhar Gomang of the Congress, who had not resigned from his Lok Sabha seat despite being the Chief Minister of Odisha, and voted against the confidence motion. The country had to face fresh elections due to this illegal and immoral conduct of the Congress. In 1999, the Bharatiya Janata Party secured victory on 182 seats while the National Democratic Alliance secured a total of 306 seats. Once again, Atal Bihari Vajpayee was sworn in as the leader of the NDA.

The BJP-led NDA Government, under Atal Bihari Vajpayee, set up new records in development. Its successes included the Pokharan explosion, Agni missile launch, Kargil victory and others, which raised its status in the international arena; India now attained honour and dignity; America and European countries looked up to India with hope and awe. The construction of national highways, reform of public distribution system, new initiatives and experiments in education and health, rapid development in agriculture, science and industrial fields, as well as the stable costs were a number of achievements which go to the credit of this government.

Several effective steps were also taken to improve India-Pak relations, resolve internal problems such as Naxalism, terrorism, separation of Jammu and Kashmir and northeast, among others. Several decisive steps were taken to focus on national integrity and unity, good administration, security, prosperity and related matters. Under the leadership of Atal Bihari Vajpayee and Lal

Krishna Advani, the NDA Government initiated a new era of development in the country.

Today, the Bharatiya Janata Party has risen to the horizon as a chief nationalist power, and is determined for good governance, development, integrity and unity of the country.

Organisational Skills of Narendra

Narendra Modi has provided momentum to the Bharatiya Janata Party from the lowest step it stood, to the zenith where it is now. He has established the party at the core of the heart of every person in the country with his thinking, guidance, direction, hard work, political thought, authentic working style, proceedings with positive outcome and goal of development. He has taken a peek into the lowest local worker in order to make him contribute to the progress of the party to the highest point.

A quick glance at the Gujarat BJP with a brief history of the Jansangh/Bharatiya Janata Party before reverting to Narendra Modi:

In 1951, after the Bharatiya Jansangh was set up, it secured 3.17 percent votes to win three seats in the Lok Sabha. The same year, it launched four candidates in election for the Gujarat Vidhan Sabha. The four of them secured a total of 4,000 votes and their security deposit was seized. Look at the initial contest of elections and compare it with its performance in 1965 where the Bharatiya Jansangh marched to victory in Botad municipality. This was followed by victories in municipalities in Manavadar, Rajkot and Junagarh. In 1985, that is, in a period of twenty years, the Jansangh had a wealth of several municipalities, 18 legislators and 14 percent of votes in Gujarat; this was the peak of its performance until then.

In 1980, the Bharatiya Jansangh came to the fore as the Bharatiya Janata Party. In 1986, Narendra Modi was transferred from the Rashtriya Swayamsevak Sangh to the Bharatiya Janata Party. He became the general secretary of the state organisation, and he took upon the task of firmly expanding the scope of the party. He prepared a database to enroll members of the party, as well as constitute booth committees, area committees, district committees, state committees; and this effort led to a state-level data bank. This comprised extensive and detailed information of all workers in Gujarat. Hardworking and loyal people from all fields of life were brought into politics in a bid to improve upon the image of politics. It helped to bring the youth into politics, especially because of the efforts in this field. During 1985-86, the administration had decided not to take out the historical Rath Yatra in Ahmedabad due to communal riots, but Narendra Modi used his insight and strategy to befool the police and take it out.

These efforts on the part of Narendra Modi led to the party's largest victory in Ahmedabad municipal corporation election. The entire responsibility regarding election strategy, planning, operation and propaganda was borne by Narendra Modi. At that time, he gave the slogan: "Ab to Bas Bhajpa – Ek Mauka Bhajpa ko." (The BJP this time – one opportunity to Bharatiya Janata Party.) This slogan striked the minds of people quite rapidly.

As the party started to win seats in the urban areas, the opposition tried to project the party as an urban party which looks after the interests of the people belonging to middle and higher class people. However, Narendra Modi constituted groups of youths, women, other backward classes, Scheduled Castes, tribals and others in order to make the Bharatiya Janata Party a party accessible to all classes of people, right from cities to the remotest villages, and thus made it a party acceptable to all people. He gave the slogan: "Meri Bhajpa – Achchhi Bhajpa, Meri Bhajpa – Sabki Bhajpa." (My BJP – Good BJP, My BJP – Everybody's BJP.) The party now started to get the support of the towns, villages and the poor people.

In the drought that befell the state in 1985, 1986 and 1987 at a stretch, Narendra Modi studied the impact on the poor people, their problems and injustice being meted out to them, and for this, he decided to start the Nyaya Yatra in 1987. This won a massive popular support. As he came face-to-face with millions of rural people, he came to know of the problems faced by the farmers, women, youths, tribals and other classes of people, and the Bharatiya Janata Party took upon itself the task of eliminating their problems in entirety. The people supported the party in its programmes revolving mass movements and constructive programmes. The Central Government was forced to release funds for relief work. Narendra Modi linked people's welfare with nationalism, and thus gave a new identity to the party as a nationalist party. He introduced in its slogans 'Vande Mataram' and 'Bharat Mata ki Jai'.

Narendra Modi delegated work to different committees with the creation of the election manifesto committee, discipline committee, literature department, media department, propaganda department and so on, in order to divide work among workers, and thus made a large number of them active. He also introduced the concepts of wall paintings, tabs, door decorations, pens, key rings and other types of things for the purpose of propaganda, and thus he created fascination among the people.

In 1984, Narendra Modi used the concept of Footpath Sansad in Khadia area of Ahmedabad for successful launching of 'Hamara Neta, Hamare Beech' (Our leader, Amongst Us), and displayed his insight and understanding.

In 1989, general Lok Sabha elections, the Bharatiya Janata Party launched its candidates on 12 seats and won all the seats. It was due to the untiring efforts and skills of Narendra Modi that the party was now recognized all over the country.

It was now that the talent of Narendra Modi, who until now had worked behind the screen, came to the fore. In 1990, the people's mandate was honoured when Narendra Modi partnered with Janata Dal (Chimanbhai Patel) in order to form the non-Congress Government in the state. At that time, Narendra Modi undertook the role of the strategist and king-maker, and this was how he was described by the *Times of India* in February 1990. He was admired as a strategist for his role in the election mathematics so far as the list of the candidates was concerned between Chimanbhai Patel and Keshubhai Patel. In this election, the Janata Dal had secured 70 and Bharatiya Janata Party 67; the BJP's vote share increased from 14 percent to 27. The results secured by the Bharatiya Janata Party in the 1989-91 Lok Sabha elections and 1990 Vidhan Sabha elections were commendable, and behind them was Narendra Modi working as a skilled politician, strategist and kingmaker, and with this, the entire media and popular attention was diverted to him.

In 1990, the Ayodhya Ram Mandir movement was at its peak. For Bharatiya Janata Party, it was not a mere question of a temple; rather it was a source of national faith and trust. It was a national issue. For mass awakening, the Bharatiya Janata Party conducted the Ram Rath Yatra under the leadership of Lal Krishna Advani, which was started from Somnath. It was natural that the responsibility for the success of the Rath Yatra was assigned to Narendra Modi. Beginning 25 September 1990, this Yatra shook the people out of their slumber, while the talent of Narendra Modi shone on the national spectrum.

Dhirubhai Ambani – a man who could look through the man in front, the founder of the Reliance Industries, met Narendra Modi 21 years prior to it, and it was then that he had declared him to be a horse of the long race.

In 1992, Narendra Modi visited Dhirubhai Ambani in Mumbai. He was the in-charge of the Gujarat BJP. He was known in this capacity. The two talked on diverse topics. Narendra Modi impressed the other with his skills, dexterity and effect. All this while, Mukesh and Anil Ambani looked at him from a distance. They did not know him even.

Anil Ambani recalled this incident in 2009 when he addressed the concluding conference of the Vibrant Summit. He said that it was like an amazement that my father talked to a young man for so long and so deeply, normally he did not talk to anyone for more than 20-25 minutes. He says: "After Narendra Modi left, I asked my father who this gentleman was, and he said that it was Narendra Modi, a BJP worker, and I suppose he is a horse of the long race."

By 1992, Narendra Modi had started to emerge as an impressive political personality in Gujarat. The American Government too paid heed to him, and he was invited to America as a youth leader. The same time one hundred years ago in 1893, Swami Vivekananda had brought India to the fore as the world leader, America was holding the centenary celebration at that time. Narendra Modi took part in that celebration too. He was forty-two by this time. The Bharatiya Janata Party had recognized the worth of Narendra Modi by this time.

At that time, Chimanbhai Patel was in power in Gujarat. Of the total 182 members of the Vidhan Sabha, he had the support of 100 members. He had good relations with the Central Government, then led by P.V. Narsimha Rao. The Congress looked at Chimanbhai Patel as a bridge by which the Bharatiya Janata Party could be kept away from power.

When the Babri structure was brought down in Ayodhya, Chimanbhai was at the helms of affairs in Gujarat. A serious and extreme reaction occurred in Gujarat in response to this incident. The entire state witnessed Hindu-Muslim riots. A terrible massacre was witnessed in Surat. Chimabhai Patel proved ineffective in dealing with these riots. The law and order situation was so poor that a senior leader of the Congress (I), MP Rauf Waliullah was murdered in broad daylight in a busy area, Alice Bridge in Ahmedabad. Expressing his anger over this incident, the senior Congress (I) leader, C.D. Patel resigned from the council of ministers.

And then, a sudden occurrence changed the direction of the entire course of events. Chimanbhai died of a massive heart attack in February 1994. After this, the senior most leader, Chhabildas Mehta assumed the post of Chief Minister. The Congress continued with its support to the government. Chhabildas had to bow before the Congress pressure tactics in order to stay in power; else he had no other alternative. Chhabildas supposed that the condition would improve by the Vidhan Sabha elections in February-March 1995. Narendra Modi was now ready to face the elections. Keeping elections in view, he arranged for training of workers at every level. For this, a large training camp was organised in which over 1.5 lakh workers were trained. They were trained how to manage 28,000 polling booths and how to explain and motivate the voters. The training programme was quite successful by itself. Narendra Modi undertook micro-planning at the booth level. The organisation-oriented election too proved to be a success. Most part of this was managed and run by Narendra Modi himself.

Now it was Narendra Modi who was given the responsibility for the organisation and success of any public programme, mass support programme or the like that was planned to be held.

The high command of the Bharatiya Janata Party now knew it quite well about the ability and hard work that Narendra Modi could put in. Now he was made a member of the All India election committee. Being a part of the 17-member committee of the Bharatiya Janata Party was by itself a matter of pride for any worker. In the years to follow, Narendra Modi was made part of every national-level executive committee. Thus, the scope of his duties expanded and he continued to carry them out with all attention and devotion. In the nineties, terrorism was at its peak in Kashmir. The Indian Tricolour was being trampled under the feet and dishonoured. The Kashmiri Pandits were being massacred mercilessly. The entire Kashmir was under the control of the terrorists. The entire country stood against this terrorism, while the Congress-ruled Central Government was silent. The terrorists threw a challenge to hoist the Tricolour in the valley.

To create mass awareness about Kashmir in the entire country, a *yatra* was started from Kanyakumari to Kashmir on 12 December 1991. This *yatra* was named Ekta Yatra, under the leadership of Dr. Murali Manohar Joshi, the then national President of the Bharatiya Janata Party. Travelling for over one month and a half, the *yatra* was to culminate at the Lal Chowk in Srinagar with the hoisting of the Tricolour on 26 January 1992. The entire responsibility for management of the *yatra* was given to Narendra Modi. At the beginning of the *yatra*, the Tricolour was offered to Murali Manohar Joshi by Rajendra Singh, the brother of Shaheed Bhagat Singh, Devkinandan Rajguru, the brother of Shaheed Rajguru and Javed Aslam, the son of Abdul Hamid who had been awarded the Param Vir Chakra in the India-Pak War. Travelling through the country, the *yatra* proceeded ahead. Near Jullundur, the Ekta Yatra was struck by the terrorists. Four workers laid down their lives. The terrorists had offered a challenge and the Jullundur administration was of the view that no meeting should be held there. However, Narendra Modi said to them that they could talk everything else but this topic. In the meeting held under such a pressure, Narendra Modi challenged the terrorists: "Put in all your strength that lies at your disposal, no bullet has ever been fabricated that can cut through our ideas. If any one has drunk his mother's milk, let him come and obstruct the *yatra*. We are proceeding to Srinagar with the blessing and support of all Indians. No power can prevent us from hoisting the Tricolour on 26 January."

26 January was the date set for the confrontation, and the courageous had to emerge victorious; and it was displayed on this date in 1992. The nationalists, under the leadership of Dr. Murali Manohar Joshi and Narendra Modi, hoisted the Tricolour right before the eyes of the terrorists. With this, Narendra Modi got a new recognition as an efficient nationalist.

In 1995, the Bharatiya Janata Party fought the Vidhan Sabha election on its own and secured victory in 121 seats. Keshubhai Patel became the Chief Minister. With 42.51 percent votes, the Bharatiya Janata Party hoisted the saffron colour all over Gujarat. You can well imagine who could have managed all this. Does it need be told? It was without doubt Narendra Modi.

After poor display in other states, the elections for Gujarat Vidhan Sabha in 1995 brought about a major change. Now, the Congress had to ally with a number of small parties to come to the power. It had no more the services of a leader like Chimanbhai; and secondly, the inclusion of the Janata Dal (G) in the government brought out internal differences. There were four fractions within the Congress, first led by the wife of Chimanbhai, second led by Chhabildas Mehta, third led by Prabodh Rawal and the fourth led by Madhavsinh Solanki, a senior Congress leader and former Chief Minister of Gujarat. Inclusion of the BSP, led by Mayawati, too had not benefited the Congress in any way.

However, this scenario benefited the Bharatiya Janata Party a great deal. Of the state Vidhan Sabha, it secured 121 seats out of a total of 182. The Congress had to be content with only 45 seats. The Jansangh had secured the support of only 4000 voters in the first general elections in 1952; and in a period of four decades, the number of votes secured by the Bharatiya Janata Party jumped to 66,24,711. No other party had ever secured such huge popularity so rapidly. The Bharatiya Janata Party had secured victory in as many as 98 percent of the units. In some Zila Panchayat elections, the party had secured cent percent success. The media and political analysts gave the credit of Bharatiya Janata Party's victory to Narendra Modi and called him the architect of the party's victory.

As a general secretary of the Gujarat BJP, Narendra Modi extended his party's influence all round. As a skilled organizer, he strengthened and simplified the party's organisation.

Keshubhai Patel became the Chief Minister after this election. No one was surprised when he was appointed to this post, because Lal Krishna Advani had announced right before the election, on 20 February 1995, that he would be the Chief Minister should the party come to power.

Keshubhai Patel took oath of office and secretary on 4 March 1995 in a public function. He had assumed this post, but he was faced with a number of problems which had surfaced right from the beginning. He took the whole week to constitute his cabinet. Everybody wanted to be a minister, and it was a massive challenge for him. Helpless, he constituted a council of ministers comprising thirty-three ministers. He was accused that he gave a larger representation to Saurashtra and that able leaders were ignored. It was also accused that the list of ministers was finalized, not by Keshubhai, but by Narendra Modi. There is a tradition in the Bharatiya Janata Party that important decisions are taken collectively, but Shankarsinh Vaghela complained that no discussion had taken place with him. During this period, Narendra Modi was busy in training his workers in local administration; despite this, he was being blamed in different ways. In a period of two months, he trained 10,000 representatives in local administration. In the urban and rural elections held in June 1995, the Bharatiya Janata Party won all the six metropolitan elections and 18 out of 19 Zila Panchayat elections. It won 100 seats out of 101 seats in Surat Nagar Nigam.

As per the rules framed by the Bharatiya Janata Party, its general secretaries have no right to interfere in the government working. Shankarsinh Vaghela took advantage of this weakness. He wished that he should be discussed with on all important matters such as the appointment of chairmen on different councils and Nigams of the state. The faction which he was leading wanted to make Narendra Modi a sacrificial goat. Keshubhai was not in the favour of any interference in his rights. Gradually, tension grew between them. It is also learnt that before Keshubhai proceeded on the foreign tour, he met Shankarsinh and told him in no uncertain terms that he must not interfere into any matters of appointments, at which the latter had retorted, "You would not be able to remain Chief Minister on return." Keshubhai proceeded to Britain and America on 8 September 1995 with a purpose of collecting funds from non-resident Indians. He was accompanied by a large team, but he had refused to take Shankarsinh as member of the delegation. This is one of the accusations that are given against him.

Before proceeding abroad, Keshubhai had announced the names of the chairmen of different government public corporations. This further led to rise in tension. Shankarsinh rebelled. It was no ideological confrontation, nor had it to do with any principles. On 24 September 1995, Shankarsinh called a conference in Ahmedabad with a purpose to fight corruption, favouritism, autocratic tendency and increasing criminal tendency within the Bharatiya Janata Party. He could have well contacted the party high command to express his unhappiness, but he chose not to do so. His conduct could not be called fair and proper in any way.

Two days after the Ahmedabad conference, on 26 September, a meeting of Gujarat BJP was held in which over 60 legislators took part. The conference called by Shankarsinh had the presence of 47 legislators, they were unhappy with Keshubhai Government. Vaghela had attempted to incite the legislators against Keshubhai in his hunger for power. It was also aimed at enmity against Narendra Modi too. However, Narendra Modi displayed a quality of his loyalty to the party and his qualities as a devoted worker. He handed over his letter of resignation from his post of the general secretary to the state chief, Kashiram Rana. In it, he wrote as thus:

Respected Kashiram Bhai,
Regards.

Many questions today raise their heads before the expectations and aspirations of Gujarati people. The party which has been fabricated by the hard work of thousands of people is losing its prestige due to personal differences today. Now, the truth has emerged in its actual form. The events of over the last two days are a testimony to this.

I have taken to silence keeping the party interests in view. Prior to this occasion, I have submitted personal entreaties that I may be freed from my responsibilities.

Now the situation has become quite volatile. The incidents of the past two days prove my innocence; still I would continue to remain in the role of a party worker.

I can recall a story. In the court of law, two women argued over an infant; and the judge ordered to cut the child in two so that each of the mothers could be given a part. The genuine mother requested the judge not to do this. I have reached somewhat of on such a decision.

Sacrifice for the party entails my resignation from the post of the general secretary. I shall continue to work in the capacity of the party worker.

I am confident that now my name would not be taken in the controversy. I entreat you to accept my resignation.

At this occasion, I wish to express my gratitude and thankfulness to thousands of party workers through you.

I offer you my gratitude especially.

In the service of Mother India,

Yours own,

Narendra Modi

"I can cut down my head for Gujarat and the party," with these heartrending words, Narendra Modi sent his resignation to the party which shook hundreds of workers; this manifested the glimpse of a rare great politician and of a worker who considered his party as his mother. The letter was dated 28 September 1995. Injustice meted out to Narendra Modi shocked the people of Gujarat. At this, he was called to Delhi and was made the general secretary at the national level.

That day, Vaghela called a press conference to re-stress his claim in the Gujarat Vidhan Sabha. He criticized the BJP leadership severely and accused it of corruption and favouritism. To keep his supporters in his camp, he first took them to a village Vasania, about 30 kilometres from Gandhinagar. From there, he sent them to Khajuraho (Madhya Pradesh) under the constant watch of the Congress Government. These supporters were later called Khajuria.

The BJP high command decided to take strict action at this, and on the evening of 5 October, Atal Bihari Vajpayee started for Gandhinagar. There he discussed the situation in detail with the local leaders. After a specific discussion with Keshubhai, he asked him to resign from the post of the Chief Minister, who had to abide by this decision, even though he did not wish to do so. Keshubhai said even at that time that it would only encourage Shankarsinh Vaghela. The rebel members were called back to Gandhinagar and they now voted in the favour of Keshubhai. This is the occurrence of 7 October. The very next day of having achieved the confidence, Keshubhai submitted his resignation and this was how Shankarsinh joined the party again; however, he could not become the Chief Minister next time, this time Suresh Mehta ascended this post.

Vaghela had joined the party again but now he felt that he didn't have any future in the party. He had lost his trust. The BJP high command nominated Keshubhai Patel, Shankarsinh Vaghela and Narendra Modi as national vice president, member of national executive committee and national general secretary, respectively. However, the differences between the former rebels (Khajuria) and old loyals (Hajuria) could not be alleviated in a huff. In the Lok Sabha elections held in May 1996, the Hajuria leaders entered into alliance with Khajuria leaders and together they defeated Shankarsinh.

Shankarsinh first formed a farmer union called Maha Gujarat Kisan Sena. After that, he separated from the BJP and formed a new party called Mahagujarat Janata Party on 18 August 1996. The newly constituted party demanded in the Gujarat Vidhan Sabha that it should be recognized as a separate party because it enjoyed the support of one-third of the members of the BJP. On 20 August, the Rashtriya Janata Party was formally constituted in Ahmedabad. Thus, Shankarsinh severed all his relations with the BJP. All this had been done with a sense of vengeance; however, just about this time, of the 46 legislators who had defected the BJP, came back to the BJP. On 2 September 1996, about 94 BJP MLAs took oath in the Gandhi Ashram towards strengthening the unity of the party; however, Suresh Mehta's Government remained unwavering. On 19 September, when the Vidhan Sabha sat for its session, the supporters of Shankarsinh indulged in unruly behaviour, which resulted into the suspension of the session.

Looking at the gravity of the situation, the Governor recommended for the imposition of the President's rule in Gujarat, and it was implemented the next day itself. Thus, Suresh Mehta Government remained in power from 21 October 1995 to 19 September 1996. It is something amazing to note that a leader like Vaghela, who possessed great political influence, proficiency and broad public contact, could not accept party discipline. He gave up all his principles for defeating the party in conjunction with the Congress, the very party in which he had grown to prominence.

The manipulations that Vaghela exercised made it evident that he was opposing the party only in order to grab the power, and was accusing Narendra Modi continuously. He chose to blame him even when Narendra Modi was not in the government and then was busy in the training work of the party workers. However, Narendra Modi was made the scapegoat and he was sent out of the state. Now a pertinent question arises – Why did Vaghela rebel again? At this time, Narendra Modi was active neither in Gujarat nor in Gujarat politics. If we analyse both revolts, we can infer that he had revolted only with some purpose in the mind. In fact, he had turned into a snake in the grass.

Krishnapal Singh, the then Governor of Gujarat, who took office after Naresh Chandra, on 22 October 1996, invited Shankarsinh Vaghela to form the government. Vaghela had the Congress support with him, and thus, he had a total of 102 members out of a total of 182 in his favour. Of these members, 42 belonged to his party, 45 to the Congress and the remaining were independent members. Thus, Vaghela's power lay, not in his own party, but due to the Congress support. His weakness came to the fore when in the by-election for Sarkhej Vidhan Sabha seat, the BJP candidate Amit Shah defeated the Congress candidate with a massive margin of 24,000 votes. The Rashtriya Janata Party candidate lost his security even.

Now the Congress was stuck between two conflicting views. The number of its members was larger than the number of members of the RJP. Besides, the defeat of the RJP at Sarkhej had divulged the fact that it was weak from inside. Now, Congress was of the view whether it should continue to support Vaghela Government or pull it back. A long discussion took place in the Congress. The image of Vaghela was not quite clean. Soon he was being accused of corruption and many of these accusations came from the Congress. Finally, Vaghela had to submit his resignation. He got a chance to be in the power for one year. He was succeeded by Dilip Parekh on 27 October 1997.

Parikh could not hold on the post for long, he was in power for mere 70 days. After this, in the 1998 Vidhan Sabha elections, the Bharatiya Janata Party got a magnificent majority and with it, Keshubhai Patel was sworn in as the Chief Minister.

Due to the power hungry Shankarsinh Vaghela, the BJP could remain in power for only 38 days and had to bow down from the government. In the 1998 Vidhan Sabha elections, Narendra Modi came to Gujarat, he conducted public meetings and infused new life among the people with his sentimental, motivating and sharp speeches, and sowed self-confidence in the BJP workers. In these elections, the BJP secured 117 seats and thus gained clear majority. In the Lok Sabha elections, the BJP secured 17 seats.

From 1998 to 2001, Narendra Modi was made the in-charge of the states of Himachal Pradesh, Punjab and Haryana, and he showed results there.

After Narendra Modi stepped out of Gujarat, the BJP witnessed a decline in a short period until 2000 to the extent that it lost elections in municipalities, Zila Panchayats and Tehsil Panchayats; and this was very terrible. The Gujarat BJP appointed Bharat Barot Committee in order to find out the causes of the massive defeat; however, the report was so explosive that it was suppressed right there, it was not made public. Corruption had taken to the skies during the autocratic and inefficient administration of Keshubhai. Gujarat suffered further when a massive earthquake struck it in the beginning of 2001. The BJP camp was shocked into silence. The BJP had to suffer terrible defeat in Sabarmati Vidhan Sabha seat by-election which was considered to be a stronghold of the party. When a simple election could not be won, the BJP high command was shaken out of its slumber, and without any further delay, it sent Narendra Modi back to Gujarat in order to spread the saffron colour across the state. Narendra Modi was sworn in as the Chief Minister on 7 October 2001, and within first four months, the terrible Godhra massacre took place in February 2002, followed by riots. The Vidhan Sabha elections were held in December 2002. It was marked by new vigour and a new slogan: "Hamara Gujarat, Anutha Gujarat" (Our Gujarat, Unique Gujarat.) Of the challenges facing Narendra Modi, this time included the senior BJP leaders Shankarsinh Vaghela and Keshubhai Patel, and a massive challenge in the form of Godhra riots committed by people with terrorist inclination. The dreadful earthquake tested Narendra Modi toughly. However, he turned this calamity into an opportunity, he started the relief work on a war footing. He granted government funds to people to help the administration in rehabilitation work. People too stood by him in this effort, and thus they grew more eager to assist him towards taking Gujarat to the further heights of development. In the elections held in 2002, the BJP overcame all challenges and difficulties and sent a wave of saffron across the state. The BJP secured 118 seats in the Vidhan Sabha, with 50 percent of vote share; while the Congress could secure only 39 percent of vote share.

During Narendra Modi's rule, in 2005, the BJP once again came to power in Zila Panchayats, Tehsil Panchayats, municipal corporations. Its effect was seen in the cooperative fields too as market yard, cooperative banks, cricket associations and the like. With the slogan 'Jeetega Gujarat' (Gujarat will Win), the BJP won 121 seats in 2007 Vidhan Sabha elections; these 121 seats included 4 by-election seats; on a whole, the BJP secured 50 percent of the vote share. And then Narendra Modi continued to bring laurels in the elections held in 2012 in which he came back to power with 115 seats, and thus achieved a historical hat-trick. It was despite the competitive environment in the state due to the new party of Keshubhai called Gujarat Parivaran Party (GPP), CBI factor of the Congress, anti-Modi conspiracy, propaganda, negative atmosphere created by the media and the like. This time, Narendra Modi had given the slogan: "Sabka Sath, Sabka Vikas, Ekmat Gujarat". (Everybody Together, Everybody's Development and Unanimous Gujarat). Despite these spectacular successes, Narendra Modi continued to work hard, guide and inspire his workers. He himself worked very hard all the time.

By nature, Narendra Modi is inclined to think differently than what others do. He starts to think from the point where other leaders stop thinking. He has no family and no business. Day or night, morning or evening, he had only one preoccupation – My Gujarat, My Gujarat. This is the reason that this full-time politician stands alone among the crowd of hundreds of opposition leaders, offering challenges to all of them together. He is like the sun among the stars.

On 20 November, 1995, Narendra Modi was appointed as the national secretary of the BJP. Now, his field of activity centred round Delhi. In 1996, Lal Krishna Advani constituted his national team. Narendra Modi was summoned to Delhi and was given the responsibility of the party activities as the general secretary. With this, Narendra Modi had entered a new phase of politics. The Vidhan Sabha elections were due in five states – Uttar Pradesh, Madhya Pradesh, Rajasthan, Himachal Pradesh and Assam. Each of these offered a range of distinct problems and challenges, which had to be tackled with. Three-four months preceding the elections proved very significant for Modi. During this period, he got a good chance to come into contact with a number of senior and experienced co-workers.

Though this responsibility entailed difficulties and challenges, yet he bore it well. He went to different places and met people. He himself says that while working in Punjab and Jammu and Kashmir, he came to know of several facts which he did not know before. A few days later, elections were held in the states which were given in the charge of Narendra Modi. The BJP secured unprecedented success in these elections.

When Narendra Modi was called from Gujarat to work in the party headquarters in Delhi, he responded positively without any hesitation. He possesses a very clear and strict attitude towards discipline. He set out for Delhi from Ahmedabad soon after he was called. He carried with him only one suitcase. He stayed at the house of a co-worker in Delhi. He has been never seen to demand any luxury, nor does he care about them.

His thinking was truly recognized when the same people, who wanted to make Narendra Modi a scapegoat, revolted against Vaghela. When the truth came out, they were shown the outdoor. The people too decided to show the door to the power-hungry leaders. Narendra Modi himself said: "Whatever happened had no ideological basis, it was mere hunger for power."

It was due to his devotion and perseverance that he was made the general secretary of the party on 19 May 1998. This post had been occupied by such stalwarts like Pandit Deen Dayal Upadhyay, Sundar Singh Bhanari and Kushabhau Thakre. Thus, Narendra Modi was only the fourth person to reach this high post.

Narendra Modi has ever been a disciplined worker of the party. He undertakes and carries out all the tasks assigned to him devotedly and courageously. In the capacity of the national general secretary, he took over the charge of Haryana, Himachal Pradesh, Chandigarh, Jammu and Kashmir and Punjab. He worked hard in these states. He was never terrorized of the terrorists and other anti-social elements. He continued to tread his path of duty without any fright or prejudice.

He worked in Jammu and Kashmir where the BJP had not much influence. When Bill Clinton, the American President, visited India, about 36 Sikhs were massacred in Chhattisinghpura. At that time, Narendra Modi was appointed the in-charge of the area. He decided to undertake a tour of the area. Farooq Abdullah came to know of it. What happened can be well described in the words of Narendra Modi himself:

"He called me and asked how I had gone there. I said that I went by road. He said that I could put him in some trouble as the terrorists often lay mines which are hard to evade. He also requested me to go back by air. He also complained this to Advaniji that Narendra Modi was wont to visit any place anytime and he never cared for his security. Advaniji called me. I requested him that I would go back only after the final rites have been performed because I was already at Chhattisinghpura. Advaniji agreed to my entreaty, but he emphasised that I must return by air only."

In fact, this thinking of Narendra Modi is not based on any assumptions of fate, rather he has devotion towards his work. He himself has mentioned: "I used to go about Jammu and Kashmir freely. People say that my presence is known so I am under a threat. I say to them that I am doing my duty and I have no fear of living or dying."

Without doubt, he did his duty with complete devotion. When he was asked to work in Haryana and Himachal Pradesh, he did not let Punjab go out of his sight, and worked there for six months. Elections were due for 20 seats of Chandigarh Nagar Nigam. Hard work on the part of Narendra Modi bore fruit when the BJP secured 17 of these seats. When Pawan Kumar, the Chandigarh MP, met him, he remarked, "What an amazing feat it is! You are doing something wonderful. The Jansangh had no impact here, it was like a minor party here."

His loyalty towards duty is also manifested in absolutely abnormal manner at some times. When war broke out in Kargil, he was right there as it fell right in his political domain. Therefore, he continued to stay there. He has said himself: "I ought to be there as an organizer – in the capacity of a non-combatant in the battlefield." This point seems quite abnormal, or rather extraordinary, but Narendra Modi is nothing worried about. He says: "My loyalty is my chief power. Once the Prime Minister visited there, it was my duty to receive him there. Some volunteers were required to carry the military equipment, which I managed. The Prime Minister did not have adequate woollen clothing to deal with the cold environment, but he was still there in all vigour. He was saying, 'Come, and let's do something.' And these words would make people march after him. I was not leading from the front; I was just playing the role of a co-worker."

Narendra Modi has not termed this as any unselfishness. He says: "Unselfishness? No, it is perhaps devotion or dutifulness. It was my area of work. Once I invited Premkumar Dhumal, Chief Minister of Himachal Pradesh, to come and distribute gifts at Kargil, as every other soldier came from that state. Each family had a soldier; many had more than one too."

In childhood, Narendra Modi was fond of mountaineering and trekking. He had undertaken trekking in several of Gujarat's hills. Because the area of Jammu and Kashmir fell under his charge, he toured Leh, a place where you might have to face breathing problems due to high altitude. During his stay at Delhi from October 1995 to October 2001, he visited Laddakh, a place located at the last edge of India. He wished ardently to visit the places of pilgrim there. Narendra Modi loves nature. Mount Kailash is believed to be the abode of Lord Shiva, so it has fascinated him greatly. Mount Everest is 29,028 feet high while Mansarovar is located at an altitude of 24,000 feet. Narendra Modi visited Mount Kailash and Mansarovar in 1988, and offered his spiritual worship to Lord Shiva. Narendra Modi wishes that the route to Mansarovar and Kailash would be open from Leh, and the Hindu pilgrims would be able to visit there without any visa restrictions or payment in dollars to the Chinese Government. It would enable the poor Hindus to fulfil their ambition for the exalted place.

When the National Democratic Alliance or NDA Government came to power in Delhi, Narendra Modi was assigned the responsibility of inviting the state chief ministers for the swearing-in ceremony. People working in the political domain wished to meet him. He also met some officials in the foreign delegations. He explained to them what they wished to know about the new government. Narendra Modi said that they wished to know more about the BJP, its relation with the NDA, different procedures of its decision-making, mutual relations between the Rashtriya Swayamsevak Sangh and the Bharatiya Janata Party and the like. These foreign delegates were impressed by our system of organisation. They seemed to know the Congress while the BJP was much new to them.

Continuous success in elections helped the BJP to carve a niche in the other countries too. The ministers of different countries expressed their desire to meet Narendra Modi. He was at first invited by Alexandar Doner, foreign secretary of Australia. The foreign governments wished to know how the BJP is different from the Congress, what type of educational system prevails in India, and how political parties manage such a large democracy. Many of the facts were quite amazing for them. For a Commonwealth nation, like Australia to invite the general secretary of the BJP was no ordinary matter. Narendra Modi visited Australia and New Zealand in July 2001, and then visited Malaysia on the invitation of Dr. Mahathir Mohammad, Prime Minister and chairman of the United Malay National Organisation. He was the first leader to have been invited by the United Malay National Organisation.

In Australia, he first visited Brisbane where a meeting was planned for October 2001 in which the heads of the Commonwealth nations had to participate. Narendra Modi met the leaders of the two prominent parties there, namely Labour Party and Liberal Party, and discussed with them the political system in Australia. He also discussed the possibilities of joint ventures with Doner, who in turn appreciated India's achievements in biotechnology, information technology and yoga. Australia has assisted India a great deal in the fields of tourism. Narendra Modi obtained detailed information about the Frazer Island there.

The visit of Narendra Modi to Malaysia was important in itself. Prime Minister Mahathir hoisted a dinner in his honour. They discussed on different problems pertaining to South Asia and developing countries. During his visit, the then Prime Minister Atal Bihari Vajpayee had signed an agreement for the construction of a railway line. Narendra Modi reminded Mahathir about the agreement. It was a matter of pride for India to assist the neighbouring Asian countries. Mahathir immediately discussed with his officials and got the project launched worth 180 crore American dollars. Narendra Modi said: "The railways are the lifeline of India, and the Indian specialists should assist other Asian and African countries in this field. There are a number of opportunities for the Indian Railways in this field."

The Gujaratis living in Malaysia had organised an eatery camp to render assistance to the earthquake victims in Gujarat, and the funds were submitted in the Chief Minister's Relief Fund. The camp was inaugurated by Narendra Modi. This camp was attended by over 40,000 Malaysian people.

In the meanwhile, beginning his journey from a RSS *Pracharak* in Gujarat, Narendra Modi reached the high post of the general secretary working at the national level. By tradition, the *Pracharaks* and general secretaries keep themselves aloof from the media. Narendra Modi was no exception in this regard. However, the party appointed him the party spokesperson during the Kargil War. It was quite a challenge for a person who kept away from the media. He carried out this responsibility quite sensibly. As a party representative, he was now seen in different television fora and discussion panels, and he underlined his viewpoint in them. When he was asked about the overall situation in Kargil, his response took everybody by surprise. He said, *"Chiken biryani nahin, bullet ka jawab bum se diya jayega."* (Not by chicken-rice, we shall respond to the bullet by bomb.)

During the Kargil War, Narendra Modi visited the battle-field in 1999 and encouraged the troops. He, impressed by the courage and bravery of our troops, wrote a poem also, which goes thus:

Kargil
Pahle bhi ho aya tha
'Tiger Hill'
Pahle bhi dekh aya tha
Tab
Rajadhiraj ke
Shwet maun ko
Ji bharkar piya tha.
Aaj
Pratyek choti garaj rahi thi
Bamon, bandookon ki goonjon se
Barfili shilaon par
Dhadhakate angaro sadrishya
Sena ke jawanos ko dekha
Pratyek jawan ki aankhon mein umadate
Sau crore sapne dekhe...

(Kargil, I had been there earlier; 'Tiger Hill', I had visited there earlier; then I had perceived the silvery silence of the king of mountains; but today, each of the hill is echoing with gunfire; it is like burning embers on the snowy peaks; I have seen the army troops, and the crores of dreams flooding in their eyes.)

The day Indian troops conquered Tiger Hill, Narendra Modi was right in Kargil.

By 1999, Narendra Modi had won over Prime Minister Atal Behari Vajpayee's complete confidence. He was working as the party spokesperson at that time. After Atal Bihari Vajpayee met General Parvez Musharraf, Pakistan's President, the number of people visiting Narendra Modi rose further. He was given the responsibility of providing details about the meeting of the two leaders to the media. He talked to Omkar Singh, senior journalist of the Reddiff.com openheartedly and this was published on 19 July 2001.

After having ascertained if Narendra Modi had met Atal Bihari Vajpayee soon after the summit meeting, Omkar Singh asked how Prime Minister Vajpayee felt after during the summit meeting. Modi said, "Whatever occurred in the meetng is a confidential matter and I cannot reveal its details." He further informed, "As far as the nature of Vajpayeeji is concerned, there is nothing to understand much about." Omkar Singh stressed, "Was Vajpayee in an offensive posture during the meeting?" Narendra Modi said clearly, "Offence and defence are two alternative things. Atalji is not only a political leader, he is also a politician. His attitude was crystal clear when he invited General Musharraf for the talks. Musharraf had to go back without having signed any treaty; it clearly tells that Atalji had assumed an offensive posture." At this, Omkar Singh asked again, "Why does it appear to be so to you?" Modi said, "The scheme for Kargil War had been formulated by Musharraf himself. Atalji had told him in no uncertain terms that India is capable of dealing with terrorism even without his cooperation. In fact, it was a warning, rather an alternative for the Pakistan-based terrorist factions that they would be crushed should they choose to confront India." Narendra Modi explained that neither the Government of India nor the BJP described the talks as unsuccessful. He said that the process had just begun. When asked about the agreements, he said that these agreements were the same as were signed at Simla or Lahore. Omkar Singh said that the process which started at Lahore had ended at Kargil. At this, Narendra Modi remarked, "We must not forget that Pakistan has been formed on the foundation of hatred. The ideology carried by Pak leaders remains the same till date. We wish to cultivate a hope of peace and development among the Pakistani people. Pakistan should now understand that it would benefit more greatly if it maintained friendly relations with India. Ups and downs are the features of any peace process; we should proceed ahead along side them."

Though Narendra Modi had replied very clearly, yet Omkar Singh's curiosity remained still. He asked, "The opposition says that the government went for the summit meeting without any preparation." At this, Narendra Modi replied, "No, this is not the truth. This point has been raised indirectly that a minister in the cabinet did not wish for the agreements to be signed; however, no cabinet minister can do it. This rumour has been spread from Pakistan so that the Indian media is made busy to find out which minister wanted to obstruct the talks." Omkar Singh enquired next, "Sushma Swaraj was not in the main meeting, how then she arrived at Agra?" At this, Modi replied, "She is a cabinet minister. Therefore, she has every right to come before the media. If Musharraf can talk to the editors for one hour and a half, why then can Sushma Swaraj not talk about India's side before the media? The Pakistani foreign minister himself has said that in the present age of information technology, politics cannot be kept aloof from the media. The same thing applies to Sushmaji."

In the end, Omkar Singh asked, "Is the Government of India unhappy with senior editors present in Musharraf's conference?" Narendra Modi said in clear terms: "The General (Musharraf) should not have played with the media in this manner. Some editors have informed us that they were not aware that the conference was being aired live on Pakistani television. If the General felt that he could solve the Kashmir problem through a press conference, then he must do it, not once but thousands of times. He would remain where he is now."

Narendra Modi has his own tact of meeting the media. He answered to all questions, but he did not adopt any defensive posture on any point. He did not allow any media person to comment anything undesirable. When he was waiting in the studio for the interview to begin, a journalist came. He told Modi that the talks have failed due to adamant attitude of India. He wanted to know Modi's take on this comment. He retorted immediately, "You can call me adamant, you can call my party adamant, but who has given you the right to call my country adamant?" The journalist could not find anything to respond back.

In an interview given to the *BJP Today*, a newspaper of the BJP, Modi stressed that India has extended the hand of friendship by inviting General Musharraf for peace talks. He had said that they would abide by the conditions as enumerated in Lahore Declaration and Shimla Agreement, and through talk with Atal Bihari Vajpayee, they would make effort to establish peaceful relations. He further said that this talk was more important for Pakistan, and the policymakers there should take advantage of this opportunity. Pakistan has got numerous opportunities in the past fifty years to come forward as a peace-loving country, whether it is Tashkent Agreement, Simla Agreement or Lahore Declaration, but it has failed to utilize any of these opportunities optimally. Today we can see anti-terrorist inclination in countries all over the world, due to which Pakistan has fallen aloof. It would have to display its reliability before the international community.

Narendra Modi had said that there is a challenge before Pakistan to save itself from Talibisation. The decision rests with Pakistan. He had said, "Taking advantage of this situation, Pakistan should shed its basic image of the present times and should try to present itself as a peace-loving nation. The organisation of talks at the international arena is a great trick. India's firm stand in the talks is good for both countries. If it invited any negative reaction, it could harm only Pakistan."

He informed the *BJP Today* that the agenda of Vajpayee Government has always been that of peace. It was the same agenda that was adopted at the time of Pokharan atomic explosion. It was the agenda during Lahore bus journey. It was the same agenda when we decided not to cross the line of control during Kargil conflict. Narendra Modi further said, "We gave a unilateral decision to ceasefire during the Ramzan days, at that time, our only agenda was peace. Our agenda was peace when we talked with Musharraf. Our policy has always been that of peace with the Pakistani government."

Speaking about the results of the ceasefire Narendra Modi explicated, "Though a ceasefire during the Ramzan days did not have any impact on the terrorists, yet the Kashmiri Muslims were greatly influenced by it. This ceasefire isolated Pakistan even among the Islamic nations, and terrorists lost support of the Kashmiri people. There is a great difference between Indian fighters and foreign (hired) troops." Narendra Modi was of the view: "Had Lahore not happened, the outcome of Kargil War could have been quite different. The ceasefire was imposed because it was backed by the agenda of peace."

Narendra Modi speaks like a politician. He can understand and explain any political situation well. This was precisely the reason that he continued to be the focal point of the media as the BJP general secretary. The Sirf.com had invited him on the occasion of 55th anniversary of independence to talk about India of his dreams. In his interaction, Narendra Modi raised several important points:

- It is unfortunate that the problems due to which our country was divided have not been resolved as yet. It is resulting into polluting our politics.
- We have a Constitution of our own. In the past fifty years, we have made endeavour to bring justice to the weaker sections and Dalits of the society.
- It is no less unfortunate a matter that the spirit of service seen during the independence struggle has lost its existence very rapidly. Today citizens are very conscious towards their rights, but they are forgetting about their responsibilities towards the nation.
- If we have to march ahead, we will have to carry out our duties towards the country and society completely honestly. The country's history over thousands of years tells us that the country and society have not been constructed only due to the contribution of the politicians, rather all classes of people of the society have contributed on an equal footing – farmers, workers, religious leaders, scientists and intellectuals, etc.
- I entreat the media people to start a system in which no political news should be given on at least two days of the week.

- I propose that, after the death of a political leader, there should be a ban on naming any building, street or road after him for ten years.
- Today we are living in the age of information technology. For me, it does not signify information technology alone, rather it is tomorrow's India.

Referring to the Maha Kumbh fair at Allahabad, he said that India is capable so far as self-restraint is concerned. He said:

"The Maha Kumbh reveals the fact that India can do much given an opportunity, motivation and guidance. This is the fine outcome of the power of unity. The people gathering on the Ganga banks are equal, no incidents of thefts or untoward incidents take place there. This is a fine example of human man. I would say that it is an illustration of the power of Indian people. Can we not utilize this power in other fields of life? The Maha Kumbh shows that we can face any challenge capably if adequate motivation and guidance are given."

Putting his view in a dramatic manner, he concluded: "As far as I think, there is nothing impossible under the sky."

Now just imagine how many of the politicians you would ever meet who would like to be away from the media limelight for two days in a week. Who can talk something meaningful about information technology as him? Who is the one who can talk the truth in such a bold manner? It is Narendra Modi alone who can do it.

His view to inspire the community towards progress is still clearer. In a conference held at Falna (Rajsthan), he said, "I belong to this society. It is possibly the first programme of its kind in which I am taking part. Had a magazine not erred, you would have never known wherefrom I came or that I am part of the same community. I have been a member of the Rashtriya Swayamsevak Sangh right since childhood, it taught me patriotism, and ever since, it has become a part of my life.

"An individual can become great only on the basis of his community's strength. If the community does not stand by him, he cannot possibly become great, but it is not justifiable to use the community for political purposes. The community should be used to augment the community's strength.

"Politics is important in democracy. There is no crime in becoming politically important, but it cannot be done through alms, rather this strength should come out naturally. This strength comes from, not material prosperity, but from education. Politics is not everything. You cannot become a great power only on the basis of political achievement. Politics is only a tiny tool. Our first priority should be to strengthen the community. We should ask ourselves how many of us are holding the positions of doctors, engineers, advocates and scientists. How many sons of the soil have attained high positions on the basis of their talent and hard work? These are the people who strengthen the society, and not the legislators or ministers.

"If we resolve in our heart that we have to become strong economically, socially and educationally, we would be able to carry everybody along with us, and then, there would be none who could obstruct us from achieving our objective. There is a proverb in China: 'One who thinks of one year does farming, the one who thinks of ten years plants trees, that give fruit several years later; and the one who thinks of the entire generation, he constructs good man.' We will have to construct good people for the construction of a good society.

"I shall cite from the Sindhi community. When a Sindhi person inaugurates a new shop, the people of his community are present in his shop. They give the new shop-owner gifts in a closed envelope. They do not want to show their gratitude. It is no big deal for them to put five to ten thousand rupees in the envelope, but this is in the form of a gift, and not debt. It is a fine method to strengthen the community.

"Gandhiji used to say that when a man is educated, he alone is educated; but when a woman is educated, the whole family becomes educated over for generations. Therefore, we can make the entire society educated by educating our daughters. If you wish to be successful in politics, you will have to work for those sections of the society who are neglected and backward. The power resides in them."

How gorgeous these proposals are! There is no sense of communality behind them; rather he wishes to tell people how the society can be made strong.

Narendra Modi was away from Gujarat and its politics for full six years. He had given up the political arena of Gujarat for his co-workers, who kept fighting with one another. This infighting had become a type of game for them.

Other than the elections in 1999, Narendra Modi kept himself busy in Delhi in the capacity of party general secretary from 1995 to 2001. Most of this period passed travelling round the country. The occurrences of this period entailed what could happen later. On 28 June 2000, he visited Gujarat to attend a programme in which the detained and arrested leaders during the Emergency under the MISA were honoured. When he appeared on the stage, people rose to their feet and offered him a grand standing ovation. The chair for Narendra Modi was put on the stage at the end.

Thus, rising popularity of Narendra Modi drew attention of everybody towards him. In an article published in the *Indian Express* in July 2000, it was commented that the appointment of Narendra Modi at this post has increased the power of his supporters in Gujarat. It wrote that Gujarat was passing through a stage of ups and downs and there was need for a strong leader there who could establish discipline and unity there.

On 23 August 2001, a special programme called *Tap Vandana* was held in Sanskar Dham, to honour the senior *Swayamsevaks* above 75 years of age who had worked with Vakil Saheb; the occasion was the death anniversary of Vakil Saheb. The programme was also attended by Sheshadri, the *Sahsarkaryawah* of the Rashtriya Swayamsevak Sangh. At this occasion, a CD of the songs written in praise of Vakil Saheb was released which comprises songs written by Narendra Modi too.

On 10 May 1998, Narendra Modi was appointed the general secretary in-charge of organisation. This post had not been given to anybody else during the entire period when Kushabhau Thakre was at the helm. Narendra Modi became the third leader to ascend this post. In the Jansangh forty years ago and then in the BJP, this post was held by Sundar Singh Bhandari, and Kushabhau Thakre held this post for the last six years.

The conditions in Gujarat were not favourable to the Bharatiya Janata Party. The situation had become so adverse that the party could not win even a single by-election in 2000-01. When it lost the elections for Sabarmati Vidhan Sabha and Sabarkantha Lok Sabha seats, as well as elections in local agencies, tehsils and nagar palikas at the hands of the Congress, the party was totally shocked. In such a case, the party high command felt that none else but Narendra Modi could revive the party to the past glory. He was immediately summoned to go to Ahmedabad and take over the power from Keshubhai Patel.

All this had occurred quite unexpectedly. Narendra Modi himself says:

"It occurred in October 2001. An aeroplane had crashed in which were travelling Madhavrao Scindia and some journalists, one of whom was a cameraman, Gopal from AajTak whom I knew well. The final rites of Madhavrao Scindia had to be performed in Delhi. I attended it. It appeared to me that I must attend it. He used to meet me in the party office. About that time, I received a call from the Prime Minister (Atal Bihari Vajpayee). He enquired of me where I was. I informed him about my whereabouts. He asked me to meet him in the evening. When I went to meet him, he started the conversation something like this: 'You have grown fat eating the Punjabi food. Now you should shape up. Go away from here. Vacate Delhi.' I asked him where I should go. He instructed me to go to Gujarat where I was to work. Then I asked him if I was being made the in-charge of Gujarat alone or some other states too would be under my charge. I never knew that Atalji wanted to make me Gujarat Chief Minister. I was thinking that I was being given the charge of only organisation of the party there, but then Atalji intervened and said, 'No, you will have to fight the election. You have helped others in elections, now time has come when you should fight it for yourself.' I pleaded that I could not do so. I told him that I would visit Gujarat for ten days in a month to look after the organisation there. Now I was beginning to understand that he was pointing towards making me the Chief Minister. Therefore, I said to him that this was not my jurisdiction. I have been out of Gujarat for six years. I am not aware of the situation prevailing there. What shall I do there? I have no interest in it. I don't know anybody out there. At this he said that he did not know anybody when he had come to Delhi. I continued to say no. At night, Advaniji called me and asked what I had said to Atalji. I asked why. At this he said that everybody had decided something for me. I said that I was not fit for this job. This indecision took five-six days, and finally,

I had to bow before the Sangh's decision. I went there and ever since I have been there."

In fact, the Gujarat party workers were stressing for Narendra Modi to return to Gujarat and take over the chair of Chief Minister. Perhaps Narendra Modi did not know of all this. He did not want to take any interest in becoming the Chief Minister, but now he had no other option. He had to go to Gujarat, which he finally did. The then Chief Minister Keshubhai Patel said to his supporters, "My political journey would continue as a legislator and party worker."

After arriving at Gandhinagar, Narendra Modi met Keshubhai personally. After this, Keshubhai handed over his resignation to Sundar Singh Bhandari, the Governor. The day of 4 October was an important day in the life of Narendra Modi. On this day, a meeting of the BJP legislators was held in the presence of the party's national secretary, in which Narendra Modi was elected as the leader. Keshubhai Patel proposed his name, and Suresh Mehta seconded it. The meeting was attended by Madanlal Khurana and Rajendra Singh Rana, the state BJP president. The *Express News Service* national network wrote in its edition of 5 October thus:

"Narendra Modi, the general secretary of the BJP and a powerful leader of the Rashtriya Swayamsevak Sangh, who is about to take oath of office on Sunday, is likely to make major and important changes in the council of ministers in order to improve the party image in Gujarat. It is being said that Modi has been given clear indications from the party high command to ensure the prestige of the BJP and its government in the state and take it out of the troubles it is facing now. Having arrived here from Delhi, he has explained all his priorities. He said, 'I have come here to play a one-day match. This limited overs of the game requires a firebrand batsman who could score runs rapidly in a few overs.' The party sources have revealed on Wednesday that Modi will pay to three points specifically while making major changes in the cabinet, which are discipline, coordination and working efficiency. The ministers accused of corruption could be shown the door. It is clear indication that the party has only one year to prepare for the Vidhan Sabha elections to be held in March 2003."

For Modi, to be elected the Chief Minister, was a sentimental occasion. He touched the feet of his predecessor Kushabhau Thakre, and hugged Madanlal Khurana, Rajendra Singh Rana and other leaders. He said to his co-workers that they have to keep up the scoring rate. He had only 500 days and 12,000 hours for the next Vidhan Sabha elections. He further said that they would have to ensure BJP's victory in the elections. He gave a new slogan to Gujarat: "Aapnu Gujarat – Aagavu Gujarat" (Our Gujarat – Special Gujarat).

Three days later on 7 October, Governor Sundar Singh Bhandari swore Narendra Modi in as the fourteenth Chief Minister of the state. It was for the first time that a Sangh *Pracharak* had ascended the post of the Chief Minister.

The *BJP Today* remarked: "The return (of Narendra Modi) to Gujarat has infused a new life in the youth workers of the BJP, and the state BJP leaders are confident that it would benefit the party by his wonderful leadership."

Within one month of being selected as Chief Minister, Narendra Modi had an opportunity to visit Russia with Prime Minister Atal Bihari Vajpayee. In the presence of Prime Minister Vajpayee and the then Russian President Vladimir Putin, he signed a memorandum of cooperation with the Astrakhan region. This agreement led to augmentation of trade, commerce, services and culture as well as cooperation in other fields between Gujarat and Astrakhan. It was said that Gujarat and Astrakhan maintained good mutual relations in the sixteenth century. With the signing, there was hope that Gujarat's ports at Kandla, Okha and other places would be renovated.

After taking oath of office as the Chief Minister, Modi got a number of precious presents, all of which were deposited in the state treasury, and later they were auctioned to collect funds for girls' education in the state.

The legal position in this regard is that all the presents given to the person holding the post of Chief Minister are deposited in the government treasury, and if a Chief Minister wishes to keep them with him, then he has to deposit its value to the government. Despite this rule, no Chief Minister had ever done this. They used to carry the presents with them, only Narendra Modi was different from them all. Crores of rupees were collected by the sale of these presents. Narendra Modi said himself: "I can go to any extent for the sake of girls' education."

Narendra Modi had been given a time of 100 days for estimation of his work, but the so-called secular press started to criticize him even before it. However, Narendra Modi continued with his effort to make Gujarat shine at the world level with his devotion, hard work and dedication.

□

Hold Over Administration

Narendra Modi has always been a disciplined worker of the party. He carries out everything assigned to him with devotion and dedication.

People were quite disappointed and despaired before he came to the state while the workers were discouraged. On the other hand, the state was suffering at the hands of natural calamities like earthquake. The situation was so terrible that the party could not win even a single by-election. The party had suffered terrible defeat in Sabarmati Vidhan Sabha and Sabarkantha Lok Sabha by-elections as well as in local body elections at tehsil and nagar palika levels. In such a dejected state of affairs, Narendra Modi took over the post of Chief Minister, and with it he gave the new maxim: "Aapnu Gujarat – Aagvu Gujarat" (Our Gujarat – Special Gujarat).

Narendra Modi took oath of office and secrecy on 7 October, 2001. He visited his mother to seek her blessings. She said the only thing: "Son, never take a bribe even if somebody gives it." Narendra Modi had acquired the traits of hard work and propriety from his parents ever since childhood. He continued to observe these traits even after he became the Chief Minister. His only goal was social service, the spirit of service to the poor was manifest in his dealings right from the first day.

Gandhinagar, the year 2001, the day of Dhanteras.

After having become the Chief Minister, he was about to proceed to the official residence. The day was auspicious and the occasion was auspicious – the day of Dhanteras.

Everybody was busy thinking who would install the sacred pitcher (*Mangal Kalash*). Will she be some sister from the Sangh or some sister or other woman of his family? But it was not to happen. On this pious day, the sacred pitcher was installed by Ravina

Naresh Kumar Jadav, a Dalit girl, and this was how Narendra Modi started his stay in the official residence. Her father, Naresh Jadav was a class IV government servant belonging to the Dalit community.

The newly appointed Chief Minister had no experience at administration, nor had he worked on any government post. Now the only way out for him was to begin with hard work which he did. A series of meetings started in the department, it mostly lasted until eleven at night. He did only one thing that was to listen to officers and understand their work. He took training from the specialists in the company of the ministers and senior officers, and thus an understanding was created on specific subjects.

With the passage of time, he became dexterous in making the style of government working system dynamic. He had the basic understanding of work; he had large experience in the organisation. Now, he started to look at each field with a new perspective. In the year 2003, he presented a new proposal, that was to separate the agricultural feeder from the domestic and industrial feeders. The officers discussed this proposal for long, but no uniform opinion could be formed; of course, files kept moving up and down. Narendra Modi was of the opinion that it was possible, but no one was ready to do it from technological viewpoint. Finally, he found a way out – he chalked out a unique scheme called Jyotigram Yojana.

Gujarat became the first state to supply round-the-clock electricity. This scheme laid down unprecedented development in the state. The living standard in the rural area started to rise. Students were provided educational facilities, and with this, cottage industries were established on a mass scale.

It was only the beginning. When electricity was made available, computer education started in schools. When electricity supply was available in the Panchayat courts, e-governance took off. After some time, each village was connected with broadband connectivity, which resulted into e-gram Vishvagram Project. Today, the development is at such a scale that Narendra Modi, from his seat in Gandhinagar, can talk to villagers in any village across Gujarat, or any other official right from Sarpanch to Collector, and students too. The specialists are at work to give rare technological knowledge to students from the Biotech Studio in

Gandhinagar. The officers are very happy about the fact that this could not have become possible without the firm stand taken by the new Chief Minister.

Narendra Modi came to know that Gujarat was a backward state in the field of education, especially in the field of girl education. It shocked him greatly. He used his skills to remove the past shortcomings which had been in existence over years. The entire council of ministers and administrative officers now focussed their attention on the mission mode. From the month of June in 2003 was started the Shala Praveshotsav and Kanya Shiksha Mahotsav. It became an annual feature. Today, Gujarat has achieved the goal of cent percent enrolment. Due to Narendra Modi's efficiency in working with a unique viewpoint in every conceivable field, the officers of Gujarat have earned respect all over the country. It started, as if, a competition among officers and states to work better. The success formula of Modi's Government in the state is no mystery; it is simply based on the new attitude, new viewpoint and hard work.

A meeting of all district collectors was called in November 2001. It is a very ordinary event. But what happened during the course of this meeting was quite extraordinary for the officers.

All government officers were in attendance at the meeting with due preparation and mentality. The meeting was set to start from 10 o'clock. All officers, ministers and Chief Minister were present at the meeting at the scheduled time and venue.

After the lamp was lighted, the newly-appointed Chief Minister said: "We have got an opportunity to serve the people of Gujarat, and we shall all work together." Nobody knew how his voice made them all spellbound. The present officers thought that the Chief Minister would go out after lighting the lamp and everything else would devolve as it normally did before. But it was not to be so.

A collectors' meeting generally discusses revenue and government projects; one department follows another. The department secretaries and ministers attend the meeting and review their achievements. Now, Narendra Modi took his seat on the stage, and this was something of amazement for the officers thinking that the Chief Minister was to take part in the meeting. All officers started to give details of their work with due caution as the Chief Minister was present right there and he had to be impressed by their work. When the review meeting started, the Chief Minister heard them in all attention.

When the meeting was suspended for lunch, everybody was thinking that the Chief Minister was sure to go this time, but no, he took lunch with everybody; not only this, he introduced himself with all of them. After this, the officers thought that he would go now, but no, he took his place and the discussion started. He did not leave even during the tea break. He was trying to listen to and understand each department and its work. Everybody now felt that this Chief Minister was different from the others they had seen until then. He was the one who was curious and eager to know different things, and now they believed that he would certainly do something special. It encouraged and motivated the officers, collectors and ministers. They all had grown emotional when their departments were given due importance. The meeting was scheduled to end at 6 in the evening; it ran right until 9 at night. Everybody was tired but their faces glowed in delight. The Chief Minister remained present in the meeting for 11 hours, which started at 10 in the morning and lasted until late at night. He listened to everybody patiently and attentively. Now everybody could understand how the days to come were likely to be. Narendra Modi had no prior experience of the government working, and the only way that could lead to his success went through hard work that he was bent upon doing.

Amongst the topmost revolutionaries of the Indian freedom struggle, the name of Shyamji Krishna Varma is taken with due respect. He had arranged for education and boarding for armed revolutionaries in other countries, and provided them with required literature too. He had died in 1930 in Geneva. Now, in his family, there was only his wife, Bhanumati. Before his death, he had made such arrangements as to safe keep the remains of his and those of his wife for one hundred years. Shyamji wished that his remains should be brought to India after independence. The country became independent in 1947, yet the revolutionaries were forgotten about. 73 years after his death, Narendra Modi talked to the government in Geneva. He himself visited Geneva and carried the remains of Shyamji Krishna Varma and his wife back home on 4 September 2003. A glorious Asthi-Kalash Yatra was taken out from Mumbai airport. The remains were welcomed at the town of Mandavi in Kutch. Today, a magnificent revolutionary memorial stands at this place, where the remains of this great patriot were kept.

It is simply not possible to describe the emotions and sentiments of Narendra Modi while he walked out of Mumbai airport with the remains in his hands. Perhaps the remains had been awaiting abroad for a patriot person to come and emancipate them for as long as 73 years. Both Shyamji and Narendra Modi had done their duty to the motherland.

Narendra Modi has erected majestic revolution memorials at each place in Gujarat where revolutions occurred. The sole motto of Narendra Modi is to motivate the coming generations for laying down their lives for the sake of their motherland.

Working on the post, Narendra Modi completed 12 years on 7 October 2013. When he took the oath of office, he also took the oath of happiness and prosperity for the people of Gujarat. He served the state with a complete mind. Narendra Modi says: "I am busy in worshipping Gujarat." His mantra is: "Gujarat is my soul, India is my God." Narendra Modi has not taken even a day's leave from his busy schedule. Now the development of Gujarat is the popular topic to talk in the whole of world, deriving awe and respect. Gujarat is being talked not only because of its development and prosperity, because of its work in economic and agricultural field, but also its work in the fields of social, educational, health domains as well as the work undertaken to augment the self-confidence of the people. All this could be achieved only by hard work and transparent administration. Gujarat came into existence in 1960 as a state. Ever since, Narendra Modi has ruled for the longest duration. In his rule of 12 years, he has implemented such schemes and projects that were unheard of before. He gave the ideologies of Panchamrit comprising Jnan Shakti (power of knowledge), Jan Shakti (power of people), Jal Shakti (power of water), Raksha Shakti (power of security) and Urja Shakti (power of energy) for the all-round development of Gujarat.

Under the Jyotigram scheme, round-the-clock electricity is supplied to towns and villages. It has increased the scope of industry, leading to larger employment opportunities in the state. Taking concern for the health of pregnant mothers and newborns, the Chiranjivi scheme was launched and implemented. The government also announced rewards for a harmonious village, harmonious panchayat, harmonious court which go without a police case. The e-gram Vishva Gram scheme has been launched to link each village through the satellites. The computer network is used to provide quick government service in villages. Effort is also made to provide Vidyalakshmi Bonds to the poor girls and economic saving scheme for rural women.

Narendra Modi has maintained an image of a strict ruler and administrator, yet he has been extremely sensitive, pitiful and affectionate for the deprived and the suffering. Narendra Modi has a world view. He believes in *Atmavat Sarvabhuteshu* (Everybody is like myself) and *Pardravyeshu Loshthavat* (Others' wealth is something to be overlooked). He keeps thinking all the time how he can alleviate suffering of the society. He displays in his every act how a volunteer feels. Narendra Modi possesses a pure heart, he knows others' suffering, and it is his innate trait.

Sample this situation: In the public relations office, located in the basement of Gandhinagar Secretariat, Block-1, a few officers are sitting in a small cabin, 10′×10′ in size, and in front of them is sitting the Chief Minister with a laptop, and a television monitor in the front. The chairs in the front were kept for the visitors. Several people are sitting outside the cabin, some are youth and others are elderly. Some are educated and others are illiterate. Most of them appear to be poor. Of them, there is a dark-skinned tribal man sitting on the floor, he is Ranchhonbhai. He is a physically disable and cannot walk.

This suffering man has come to the Chief Minister from a village 300 kilometres away in Surat district hoping for justice. He has walked this distance on his paralysed feet. This poor, handicapped, helpless, suffering and deprived tribal has patched clothes, with an old red cloth round his neck and disorderly grey hair, holding a small bundle in a hand.

Narendra Modi is looking at this man with emotions, and the dialogue begins between the tribal and the Chief Minister:

Narendra Modi asks in an affectionate tone: "Brother, why have you come this far?"

The tribal says: "Sir, I am illiterate. People in my village say that I must go to the Chief Minister, Narendrabhai, he does justice to everybody, I too would get justice from him, and so have I come. I have stepped out of the village for the first time in my life.

"Yes, what can I do for you?"

Tribal informs: "When the order was passed from your office, the collector and tehsildar started work of house construction for Dhansukhbhai Ramanbhai Halpati of my village. In construction, however, they used this instead of cement and mortar (opens the bundle and shows), and scarce does he use any cement in it. When I raised the voice, they have broken the doors of my house and pressurized me to bring doors. Wherefrom can I bring the doors? I have no money and my house is being made of sand. If I choose to say something, the patwari threatens me to get beaten by the police."

On the television screen, Narendra Modi enquires of the collector of Surat, "What is this matter?"

An assistant officer sitting next to the Surat collector responds, who can be seen on the television screen by the complainant and the Chief Minister. He says: "Sir, he has a house in the name of his son, which had been constructed by Halpati Housing Authority in 1996-97. There is an open space along his son's house. Due to mutual conflict, the house of the complainant has been damaged, yet after the compromise, the patwari and the husband of the woman sarpanch are getting the house constructed afresh."

Narendra Modi: "The construction is not of good quality, and the complainant has presented himself in my audience to say that doors and windows are being demanded of him."

"Halpati Housing Authority has taken heed of the place and situation, and the claim of the claimant has been verified, and there is pressure on him that his son's house would be destroyed, it is a true matter."

Narendra Modi: "Start a strict action on the patwari. Is a patwari supposed to trouble the poor people? The material sample that he has brought cannot make a good house. These people are mismanaging things. It is expected of them to construct houses properly. Substandard material is being used in the construction. The sample brought by the complainant is proof enough that the work is not being done properly. Examine the matter yourself so that the construction work can be undertaken rapidly and satisfactorily."

The complainant expresses his gratitude to Narendra Modi. Many such people come to Narendra Modi to attend the Complaint Resolution Welcome Programme, which is held on the fourth Thursday of every month. This programme has been rewarded by the U.S.

Once, Narendra Modi was staying in Panchmahal district in order to hasten the benefits of the Vanabandhu Kalyan Yojana so that the last of the men could be benefited. The government procedure takes place in its normal turn, but Narendra Modi visited the district himself to meet the people, whom all he considers his family members. From the stage, he noticed an old tribal sitting away, he was looking at him attentively. Narendra Modi felt that he was looking to him with a great hope and that he wanted to tell him something.

At the end of the programme, he walked up to that tribal and enquired after his health and address. Then he asked, "Now tell, do you have a problem? Do you expect anything from us? Do you want to say something to us?"

The old tribal grew sentimental at this affectionate talk of Narendra Modi. His spoke his heart out: "Sir, our village had no electricity for years, but you have brought it to our village and illuminated it. It appears as if the dark has been eliminated from the whole life. You have given a meaning to this life."

Why do people love Narendra Modi so much? It could be possible to understand from the words of this tribal.

Jhaverbhai Savjibhai Rathod of Khatsura village in Mahua tehsil, Bhavnagar district, complained that the Khatsura Seva Sahkari Mandali Ltd. was siphoning off funds. He requested that the money should be realized from them and should be given to the people who are eligible to have it.

When Narendra Modi came to know of this, he spoke to the district collector, "My greatest objection is with the government agency that is working in the field of district cooperative area, why did it not do its duty properly? How could such unethical work continue for six years, and now only, a case has been filed against the guilty? Is this Mandali not assessed annually? Are its accounts not audited regularly? Give utmost priority to this matter and make funds available to the legitimate people. Carry out this instruction in due earnestness."

Wherever exists corruption in the government system, or work is not done timely, or properly, it is the Chief Minister himself who would call in strict words for proper implementation. The man at the end of the line too has complete hope in him for justice, and his hope is not belied; this makes the people grateful towards Narendra Modi's Government.

The government gives bonds to primary students, Vidyadeep to boys and Vidyalakshmi to girls. Its purpose is that these children would be able to make use these funds for their higher education. In case of a sudden death of the student, this amount is given to the family as assistance. The premium for this bond is paid by the State Government to the insurance company.

The daughter of Mohanbhai Chhanabhai Khetaria of Amreli district too had been given this insurance security. Unfortunately, the daughter died suddenly. The insurance company did not pay the compensation for four years. At this, the father filed a complaint with the Chief Minister.

Narendra Modi took this matter very seriously. He issued orders in which he said, "No such incident should arise in which the family members of a deceased student have to file an application. It is the responsibility of the government to ensure that the insurance amount is handed over to the families of all the students who have died. Separate arrangements should be made in each department for this, so that the insurance scheme is regularly inspected. This order should be implemented not only in the education department, but also in other departments. There should be proper coordination among farmers, anganwadi workers and police departments. This order should be issued immediately and the matter should be taken up in all earnestness. If an insurance company is not working properly, advertisements should be issued against it in the newspapers, and this should be done on behalf of the government to make out how it is harming the society. Action should also be taken against this company. Moreover, I should be given the complete report of the whole state, district-wise, detailing the number of deaths of students and the families benefiting from the scheme."

Such is the commitment of Narendra Modi towards his work. He has carried out his duty sensibly, sensitively and responsibly.

Narendra Modi has implemented a large number of welfare schemes, each of which is touched by sentiments and human affection. During the Shala Praveshotsav and Kanya Shiksha Abhiyan, the entire government, right from the Chief Minister to the Secretary level officers, visit villages in the scorching heat in the month of June, to get children admitted to school. There is an anecdote that occurred in a small village called Lihoda, located in Dahegam Taluke, Gandhinagar district. The whole village had gathered there. Narendra Modi noticed that an Asha worker stood with a child in her arms. He saw that the child was not well. He enquired into the matter. He saw that the child was suffering in the leg. Narendra Modi instructed the district collector to make arrangements for his treatment, the expenses for which would be borne by the government. The children danced to welcome the Chief Minister. He was looking at them with all attention. He noticed that a girl among the children had some problem in the eye.

After the dance, Narendra Modi called the child to himself. The teacher thought that some error might have been committed. Modi asked the girl very affectionately: "Daughter, do you have some trouble in the eye?" The girl was Neelu Makwana. She said, "I study at standard 6. I was very small when my eye got pricked by a needle, ever since my eyesight has been poor."

Narendra Modi tapped her head and instructed the collector to treat the problem at the government expense.

Like every year, a large number of sisters lined before the Chief Minister's residence on the festival of Raksha Bandhan; they all had come to tie the sacred thread of rakhi on his wrist. At this time, the black cat commandoes were standing outside the *pandal*. Narendra Modi walked into the *pandal* and with this began the programme of tying the sacred thread. He saw that the wrists of the commandoes were bare. He decided that there should be rakhis on their wrists too. He called all the commandoes inside and asked the sisters to tie rakhis to their wrists also. Now all sisters began to tie rakhis to them too. The commandoes, who were doing their duty away from their sisters and families, now had hundreds of sisters. Their rocky hearts melted, they felt some strange sensation within them; the eyes of many of them had tears.

The youth of the country wishes to know wherefrom Narendra Modi gets his inspiration. It was 2011. The Khel Mahakumbh was being organised, it is one of the most successful sports programme.

It was the inauguration ceremony, attended by different popular people including the famous artist Akshay Khanna. It was organised this year due to the motivation of the CM. Some people were also there who might be physically disabled but they were special in some specific abilities. When the players marched past, the first group that led the rest was those of such people. When Narendra Modi delivered his inaugural speech, he emphasised the vigour of these special children and how he was motivated by them. He recounted that how the success of these children at Athens had impressed him. Saying this, his eyes became moist. This liberal viewpoint of Narendra Modi gives him a unique personality, which is different from other political leaders.

A special feature of Narendra Modi's personality is that he keeps his behaviour polite and natural. In free India, the dialogues and discussions between high administrative officers and politicians are not conducted in a cordial atmosphere, they are not friendly and informal; most of these occur in a formal and artificial atmosphere. Narendra Modi found that if the ministers talked to officers in an informal manner, then it could result into wonderful outcomes. With this began the tradition of the Varshik Chintan Shivir, in which the ministers and IAS officers stay together for three days. All ministers and officers including the CM stay together. They do yoga, play games, join in cultural and recreational activities, a number of discussions and meetings take place the whole day. Senior ministers, or Narendra Modi himself, listen to the views as enunciated by junior officers. Ministers talk with other ministers on matters relating to policy and implementation. This experiment by Narendra Modi brought openness in the administration; besides, it helped to establish a wonderful dialogue and relations between the people's representatives and bureaucrats.

The Chintan Shivir of 2005 was held in the Rann of Kutch. The inmates stayed in the tent city located in the desert. The whole day, Modi took part in it as the others did. After the dinner, all inmates had gone to bed. About half past four in the wee hours next day, a junior officer felt sudden chest pain. The fellows informed the doctors. As the information went round, all officers started off for his tent. Everybody was amazed to note that Narendra Modi was right there from 5 in the morning and was nursing him as if he was looking after a member of his own family.

He discussed his condition with the doctors and got the officer admitted to the world famous heart hospital at Ahmedabad. Not only this, he kept himself informed of his progress. This incident showed how a leader should conduct himself with his co-workers and comrades; Narendra Modi had presented before them a fine example.

One anecdote had been published by the *Samyukta*, a daily Kannada newspaper being published from Hubli in Karnataka. Narendra Modi was about to visit Karnataka, it was at that time that this story of a poor tailor was published in it in order to satisfy the curiosity about Narendra Modi. The character of this story was Chandrakant Mahervade.

Somebody had told him that there was a great need of tailors in Gujarat. Chandrakant Mahervade, a resident of Gujarat, set out to Ahmedabad with one relative with him so that he might earn his livelihood there.

Chandrakant Mahervade earned his bread and butter as a tailor. He had recently married. Looking forward to lead a good and happy married life, he worked hard in Ahmedabad. He started to get work there. He rented a house at Maninagar. In the meanwhile, his wife Shobha became pregnant, she was admitted to LG Hospital at Maninagar, where she bore a beautiful girl.

Shobha stayed at the hospital for five days, but the whopping bill that the hospital handed him over was much beyond the capacity of Chandrakant. There was no chance of taking his wife with him. Unknown place, unknown people, the relatives too turned away. He was happy to have a daughter, but was worried at the enormous bill.

The security guards found him worried and sad, and enquired about it. Chandrakant narrated his tale of woe.

"Look, CM Narendra Modi is a legislator from Maninagar. He helps everybody. Go to Gandhinagar and tell him your difficulty. You will get help there," he was advised by the security guards.

Chandrakant reached Narendra Modi's bungalow in Gandhinagar. He narrated his purpose of arrival to the police officer posted there. He showed him the bill. He was asked to wait there, and the bill was sent to Narendra Modi. In a few moments, Narendra Modi walked out, he listened to Chandrakant and asked for his letterpad. He wrote something on it, signed it and put it in an envelope, and then said, "Go and give this letter to the officer there." He asked him to be patient and said that everything else will be settled amicably. Wish your wife on my behalf."

Chandrakant felt gratitude for him, and he went back to Ahmedabad. He handed over the prized letter to the hospital staff, and his total bill was waived off. He returned to his house with his wife and daughter. He recalls Narendra Modi even today. Whenever he finds Narendra Modi on the television or in newspaper, he recalls the entire course of event that took place with him and feels a sense of gratitude for him.

Service and quick decision-making are the innate qualities of Narendra Modi. Due to the Tapi river being in floods, whole city of Surat was filled with water. The CM himself took over the charge of looking after the relief work. Narendra Modi arrived at Surat and looked after health and hygiene needs there.

He was passing by a society, when a youth, along with his friends, started to shout slogans against Narendra Modi. The CM saw all this. He asked the driver to stop. The security people were shocked that the matter might take an ugly turn. Narendra Modi got off the car and walked to the youth. Tapping his shoulder, he said, "Yes, son, what is the trouble?" The young man, who was until now shouting angrily, pacified in no time. He said, "Our society has been filled with garbage. We have complained to the corporation people a number of times, but nobody has come for this. I am unhappy about this."

In no time, the CM summoned all the officers and instructed them there itself, "The society must be clean by tonight." He himself stood there for about 30 minutes. He left only after the work began.

People were happy and impressed by his immediate action. A secret of his success lies in the fact that he never postpones anything for the following day, he acts immediately.

After inaugurating a police station in Alang, Bhavnagar, he was going in his caravan to attend his next programme. It was drizzling and the pilot car was leading. Suddenly, the pilot car lost its balance and it turned over, making to the deep ditch on the roadside. Five policemen were grievously hurt.

Narendra Modi got off the car immediately and ran to help these people who were by now wet. The other security personnel saw this and rescued the wounded. The CM stood there until they all were sent to the hospital in an ambulance. He also instructed the district officer and district superintendent of police to look after all the policemen.

The favourite song of Narendra Modi is: *Vaishnav jan to tene kayie je peer parai jane re...* Narendra Modi says that a true representative of the people is the one who can understand others' pain and who helps them in their sorrows without any ego.

□

Precursor of Development

History is laden with ample evidences that farsighted and efficient leadership can help a state rise to fame, not only within the country, but in the whole world. When new records are being established the world over in the field of development; when new heights are being touched by the countries; and in such an atmosphere, if a small state like Gujarat comes out shining, its credit would naturally go to its farsighted leadership. It is fortunate for Gujarat that it has got an opportunity to be served by a guide who is not only farsighted but also hardworking, honest and devoted.

After taking command of the state in October in 2001, Chief Minister Narendra Modi has set up newer records of development, not only within the country, but also in the world. Therefore, the people of India look forward to him with optimism in his eyes. He does not present mere hope or expectation; rather he has turned into the voice of the people of India.

There is hardly a national leader in political history of the country who had ever been loved so greatly and ardently by the people. Today, the entire country is spread with a new type of atmosphere, especially for change at the helm, and a change that would establish the country's dignity and pride at the international level. The important point is that the basis of this changed atmosphere lies in Gujarat and its committed leadership.

When Narendra Modi took over the post of Chief Minister in Gujarat, he mobilized the state from the disorderly condition to continuous present-day development in the past twelve years, and it has touched new heights in its endeavour, giving a new ray of hope to the people of India.

Let us see what Gujarat has achieved during this period of twelve years.

Gujarat has traversed the development path in not one, but numerous fields. Some fields are such which have massive problems in a number of states including Gujarat. Today the country is facing challenges of poverty, unemployment, water, electricity, agriculture and many others. As a result of all these problems, the country's economy is falling back. Despite a number of schemes, poverty has not decreased; rather the number of the poor has been on an increasing high. Water, for domestic as well as irrigation, has become a massive problem. The problem is so severe that it has to be supplied by tankers in some parts of the country, like in Delhi. And agriculture, it is quite painful to talk about it. Agricultural production has increased but what of agricultural economy? What is the condition of the farmers? Agriculture and electricity are connected to each other integrally, but both are facing adverse conditions. Water is needed for farming and electricity is needed for water, but the farmer has neither enough water nor enough electricity. Therefore, the natural outcome is monsoon-based farming. It is for all of us to see.

Agriculture and industry are important focal points for poverty alleviation and achieving the desired rate of development to attain economic prosperity. When two wheels of development are kept balanced, desired development of the country can be achieved. With time, this type of development can be achieved in other fields too. This development requires a thinking to utilize the Panch-shakti, which resides in the nerve centre of all-round development.

Panch-shakti or five powers means - manpower, water power, energy power, knowledge power and security power.

If a leadership is successful to utilize the five powers in proper coordination, the path to the highest development would become natural and spontaneous.

Here resides the secret of Gujarat's continuous development, its key to development. As the Chief Minister, Narendra Modi exhorted the six crore people of Gujarat to invest the five powers, and with this, the state witnessed the nectar of development, the nectar for which the people of the country are thirsty. Today, Gujarat has become the model of development in the country.

The development and progress achieved in the first decade of the twenty-first century, especially between 2001-11, is quite amazing for all people. But it remains a milestone, it is not the destination. The development journey of Gujarat would continue in the future too.

In the past twelve years, Gujarat has witnessed the light of development in different areas as agriculture, water resources, health, education, industry, roads, buildings, electricity, tribal areas, women empowerment, rural development, upliftment of the deprived and so on. All areas in Gujarat are full to the brim with achievements.

When Narendra Modi took over the reins of Gujarat in 2001, the biggest challenge before him was to reinstate the people's confidence in the administration. However, the situation was so bad that Gujarat did not know Narendra Modi well enough as a value-based and hardworking political leader. Under such a situation, he had to establish himself as not only an efficient politician and organizer, but also a Chief Minister and able administrator. Modi's political life was connected with Gujarati atmosphere, so a class in the state knew about him; however Gujarat did not know about his work. In such a situation, it was natural for questions to rise how far he would be successful as a Chief Minister.

Beginning from the challenge of reinstating the trust of people in his personality and administration, he bore the responsibility of leading the Bharatiya Janata Party to glorious victory in the 2002 Vidhan Sabha elections.

When Narendra Modi came to power in 2001, the people's faith had started to shake in the rulers and government. Weakness of Keshubhai and inactive administration had produced adverse impact upon the people's psyche. Devastation caused due to massive earthquake in Bhuj on 26 January 2001 had further shattered the hopes of the Bharatiya Janata Party to come back to power in the elections to be held in 2002. There was every chance that the BJP would be swept clean. The greatest challenge before the ruling party and the government was to take people into confidence that it was only the Bharatiya Janata Party which could provide clean and efficient government in the state. This challenge was tougher in view of a new Chief Minister who was not known much by the people. Narendra Modi was faced with a difficult challenge to make people feel confident in his leadership that he would lead the state to unprecedented development.

It was no trivial challenge to put the state on the path of development. Its economy was in a shambles following the storm at Kandla in 1998, the drought condition ever since. This situation was further aggravated by the earthquake in the first month of January, it was like a backbreaking shock. It appeared that the state would not be able to limp back to normalcy in decades.

The work of bringing Gujarat back to the course of development seemed almost impossible as challenges of the calamities were grave, which had shaken the people of Gujarat completely. If Gujarat had to be brought back to normalcy, the anxieties residing in the people's hearts would have to be transformed into thinking, in order to convert it into energy and commission all people into development process, and this required a particular way of thinking. It was only on the basis of strong and able leadership that the state could be put back on the path of development because political and administrative capabilities were coordinated well.

Rise from the Bottom

When Narendra Modi took over the power, Gujarat was at its bottom; it was so low that it could not possibly bear with any more shocks, even a slight shock could have led to its breaking up into fragments. The priority was to bring the state out of the devastating ruins suffered from the earthquake. Accepting this responsibility, Narendra Modi took over the power. He rendered relief to the victims and made untiring efforts for their rehabilitation. People were still dissatisfied; they were feeling unhappiness, anger and regret for the State Government and administration. The earthquake had shaken not only the land and the buildings, but also the minds. Thus, Modi was faced with the responsibility not only to reconstruct Gujarat after earthquake, but also to communicate the efforts for rehabilitation and relief work through the use of media, so that the cracks in the buildings and minds could be filled up. To bring the people out of the shadow of the earthquake, Narendra Modi started to struggle; he worked very hard. He was not worried about the outcome. Modi put into operation the entire administrative machinery, during this action, the thought of *Karmayogi* rose in his mind.

It was from this moment that he made efforts to energise the entire inactive administration, and made it spring into action, and this doctrine of *Karmayogi* took roots from this.

It is true that in the initial stages he was harsh with the administration in dealing with the challenge of people's dissatisfaction. However, this process brought to him a capacity to read the people's minds and the infinite capability that lay in the government machinery; now the question was how to make use of this infinite power. From this point, he thought to train the government servants as *Karmayogis*.

Sabarmati Quenched from Narmada

Filling cracks which arose from the earthquake and those which exist between parties, Narendra Modi started to raise his talent in the new capacity. The entire Gujarat was waiting upon him with curious eyes. He started work on Sardar Sarovar to bring water to Ahmedabad. The occasion was to fill water in the Sabarmati river with the Narmada's water. After he took over the oath of office, he held the first public programme and implemented this idea, which had not been even thought about earlier. This achievement brought into reality the idea of linking rivers, not only in Gujarat, but in the entire country.

Gujarat on the March

A common Gujarati never lags behind in celebrations. It can be said that life for Gujarat is much like a celebration, a festival. Due to its fondness for festivals, the cultural heritage of Gujarat has found a distinguished feature when compared with other states. But it does not revolve round only celebrations; Modi has woven this fondness into social life in order to put the state on the path of development. Its chief characteristics have been continuous activity, perennial liveliness and Gujarati tradition of doing something new all the time. It was the honour of Gujarat perhaps, and it continues to be so now. It is the pride of Gujarat and its peculiar mark of identity. Its eternal pulsation, its peculiar vibrancy distinguishes Gujarat from all the rest.

The essence of Modi's thinking and meditation was to make the country and world feel Gujarat's vibrancy. Gujarat continues to pulsate, progress and develop; it prospers in trade and industry, all based on peace. Its social life is vibrant. Gujarat has the capability to keep even the visitors vibrant who visit here in connection with trade or employment, and the foremost priority for Narendra Modi was to make the world and country feel it.

In January 2003, that is, some time after the CM constituted a new council of ministers; he gave a new slogan for the people of Gujarat: "Vibrant Gujarat." Several former Chief Ministers had given different types of slogans, but a slogan like 'Vibrant Gujarat' was something new. It can be said that Vibrant Gujarat had become an identity in itself.

Vibrant Gujarat was a farsighted programme to make people feel vibrancy of Gujarat. Narendra Modi, in order to make feel how Gujarat's life is lively due to the concept of Vibrant Gujarat, organised the Patang Mahotsav (Kite Festival) on the day of Makar Sankranti in January 2003. And along side, during this festival, was organised a Global Investors' Summit – 2003 to celebrate Vibrant Gujarat and invite people for capital investment in the state. Both the organisations were grand.

The chief feature of the Patang Mahotsav was that the foreign kite-flyers too were invited, so that the world could know that Gujarat, considered being at strife once, is in fact very peaceful. Another reason for its organisation was that Makar Sankranti is of great significance among all festivals observed in the state. The Muslim community, especially those living in Ahmedabad, Surat and Vadodara, are closely linked with the kite industry. If this industry is developed here, the Muslim community ought to benefit from it, especially its poor class. Not only the Muslims, the other communities too would greatly benefit from the organisation of the festival, thus it becomes a tool of economic progress.

With the successful organisation of the kite festival, the world felt how the people of Gujarat love celebrations. It also threw open the doors of development of kite industry in the state.

World Conference – Impressive Organisation

Along side the Patang Mahotsav, the Global Investment Summit was also organised in Gujarat in 2003, 2005, 2007, 2009, 2011 and 2013. These programmes were increasingly successful; and from this, it appears that Modi has greatly succeeded in bringing out the state from its deformed image. Now it holds a place of pride in the world.

From the viewpoint of statistics as well as from the viewpoint of achievements, the investment summits were unprecedented. A chief feature of this summit is that all important industrialists and economists attend from the country, and they stress their willingness and express their curiosity to cooperate in the economic development of Gujarat. It has seldom happened in the history of the country that the industrialists of the first line share the same stage together. It is no trivial achievement. The prestigious industrialists present there admired the effective administration of Gujarat. Not only this, the opinions they expressed about Narendra Modi were uniform in nature. They all emphasised that Gujarat was safe in his hands. Going further, they predicted that Gujarat would reach the zenith of economic development in the days to come and would lead the remaining states in the country.

To realize the latest projects of development, there is need to transform the age-old tradition of administration. This tradition was not based on anxiety but on thinking. It also required thinking along side positive attitude and foresight. The CM knew it well that the IAS officers in the higher echelons of the administration were no less capable. He also knew that the officers at the district and tehsil levels too were very capable despite some practical limitations. The CM thought that if these officials were infused with a spirit of thinking process in a natural way, they would transform into *Karmayogis*. Modi also thought that this group generally works with a negative mentality, and if it started to adopt a positive attitude, all the pending things could be completed in a matter of a few days; not only this, wonderful results could be attained. With this thinking, Narendra Modi started the annual programme of reflection attended by high level IAS officers as well as officers of the district headquarters. Besides, a unique Karmayogi Training Camp was organised at the district and tehsil levels in 2003-04 and 2005-06. The reflection camp and Karmayogi training camp were recognized as 'we-governance'.

Thus, a variety of schemes were announced, started, completed under careful observation and supervision, and thus a structure was created by which such schemes could be materialized. With the Navratri Mahotsav, Patang Mahotsav, World Investors

Summit, Krishi Mahotsav, Kanya Shiksha Abhiyan together with a large number of other programmes organised by different departments; all these were held one after another, often the next started when the previous one was still in operation. The officers and employees were never allowed to feel at rest; continuous work and business became the natural feature of the administration. The most important thing to note is that despite all this business, the officers and employees have become habituated to this type of work. Moreover, the outcome of these schemes has led to a sense of satisfaction, which enables them to embrace the future projects with vitality and motivation.

The discussion taking place in these reflection camps, together with the follow-up for them, has showcased that these camps have played a key role in administrative reform as well as opening up the attitude of IAS officers. These reflection camps begin with meditation and yoga in the morning, and then a number of meetings are held. The district collectors present the work done in their districts, and this is followed by discussions on it, questions are asked and answers are given. The work of gram sabhas is reviewed. The Krishi Mahotsav and Kanya Shiksha movements are reviewed. All officers take part in the discussion with an open heart whether the topic pertains to the working methodology, problems and solutions, resolution of problems, limitations of the administration or others. All this results in a new environment which opens up new vistas of problem resolutions.

Necessary Change in Thinking

In the reflection camp, the CM himself reflects on various topics, at the same time, he exhorts the administration to bring out daily work out of the burdensome limitations. Let us see a part of his address: "The problem is not the mind, but the mindset. The state requires, not revolution, but transformation. The cells, which have become negative, have to be recharged. Not even a single instance has occurred during my rule when even a single officer had to be admonished. When the secretaries speak of the state's interests, they must ensure that it is in fact in the state's interest. The officers must not worry, they must think and contemplate. The goal should be such which is within sight and can be achieved. When goals are achieved, it makes us feel happy. Weaknesses ought to be there in the administration, but they can be removed by positive working. We should replace the guilt like I could not do, I did not do, with I can do, I have to do something. Show courage in taking decisions, and if anything wrong has occurred, bring it to my knowledge."

We must aim at the development of the deprived people. We must bring out the people from below the poverty line. We have succeeded in the Samras Yojana, why then do we lag behind in Tirthgram? The document sheet on the file must be compulsorily filled, and it should be considered as desirable. If the file has stopped at one place for more time than expected, it should be dealt with seriously. It should be noted in the annual private report. I am not interested in administrative reform, but in administrative efficiency. You must think to do things that results are obtained, and would do this in that way so that better results are obtained. This type of thinking has to be cultivated in employees in order to make them *Karmayogis*. We have to form the teams of masterminds. The work should not lead to fatigue, but to contentment. When you do not work, you would feel fatigue and despair. Identify the difference between success and failure, and only those officers can become true employees who invest themselves in the service of the people.

Good Governance

When the world is entering the era of globalization, how can the administration remain untouched by it? The world perspective is changing rapidly. Rapid changes can be seen in social, economic, political and educational domains. In such a situation, people and society of the country and state should feel this change and should join the mainstream, but only this joining is not going to help. Unless the administration joins in this stream, the desirable results cannot be obtained. Therefore, all people connected with the administration should realize the world perspective and march with it shoulder-to-shoulder, and for this, the concept of good governance was mooted. When the administration plays a vital role in the society, it is important that the officers and employees are equipped with specific skills. Such awareness is necessary for every employee, and for this purpose, the CM put forward a new type of idea of training the millions of employees, and this was realized too. In this training, millions of state employees took part, the chief objective of which was individual development, role of individual, positive attitude, development of individual qualities, working in team spirit, development of administrative capability and development of working methodology.

To ascertain the feedback of the two-year-long training programme, scientific evaluation was undertaken of the entire Karmayogi movement. Its inferences are very interesting. The sample survey conducted to know the overall and inclusive impact of the training camp, 89 percent of the employees felt it very useful in the area of individual development, and 86.50 percent of them felt this useful in the development of working methodology. 89.70 percent of the employees found it very useful in their individual development. For reform of administrative working, 87.90 percent of them opined that they were now equipped with a vision to evaluate their work in a broader perspective.

The more important point than the impact of training and inferences of the survey is that a large section of the employees remained connected in this scientific training. In the administrative history of Gujarat, never ever had occurred an occasion when millions of employees had been trained with some specific goals and ideas, nor such results had ever been obtained. While the ministers and higher officers were linked with the reflection camps on the one hand, millions of employees were linked in the Karmayogi training camps. As a result, a new environment of development was created in the state. They were not only ready to grab any opportunity to show their skills and efficiency in the organisation of festivals, execution of projects and schemes, but also facing any natural calamities that could befall the state any time. To persevere in such a situation required the power to struggle and indomitable spirit to maintain the cycle of development, and this credit should reasonably go to this type of movement.

The things did not stop at this juncture. Everything cannot be set right just by training or reflection. After all this, it was necessary for the Chief Minister and other ministers to understand the administration, and now efforts were made in this direction.

Now the shortcomings prevailing in the administration and their solutions were considered in order to make the state administration lively. Truly speaking, such a wholesome process requires long patience, strong willpower and foresight. Narendra Modi coordinated all these three features and thus brought into reality the new form of the administration of Gujarat.

The administration should be such that it should be able to control all domains and subjects; also it should not make others feel about its control. The true spirit of administration resides in this type of thinking. When this type of administration has to be realized, it is necessary that it is made sensitive, which requires in turn its reform. Under the leadership of Modi, the mindset and administrative structure were coordinated in order to reform the administration, and special efforts were made to infuse the spirit of duty in the administrative leadership. The reflection camps, Karmayogi camps and presentation were only different factors of this entire process.

These training camps helped to motivate millions of officers and employees of the state, and this brought dynamism in the administration; it infused energetic oxygen in it, which helped to improve the image of lifeless administration. Each citizen came to feel administrative liveliness. With it, a vitality was achieved by which the new programmes were successfully completed, leading to new vigour, encouragement and motivation.

While, on the one hand, efforts were being made to make the administration as a role model for the country and world and, on the other hand, there was a responsibility to bring out the administration out of its limitations. Therefore, it was compulsory to maintain continuity in the process of administrative reform.

In May 2003, an effort was made to understand the high features of some countries. Presentations were held to understand the administration in countries like Australia, New Zealand, Malaysia, Singapore, Canada and other countries. It was necessary to understand the way administration was carried out in different countries, so that the administration in the state could be transformed into a model. To change the mentality of routine work, a seven-point programme was presented, and then the guidance was reviewed for financial management. The organizers of the presentation put forward the broad outline including such topics as quality, productivity, initiative, discipline, commitment, amenability, public-orientation, professional efficiency, services, regulation and management, information-oriented approach and other important things. The information gathered from different countries in this presentation was reviewed with a view how to adopt suitable information in Gujarat. The organizers presented the complete details about this too.

The presentation also discussed various points such as to make the public services more efficient, autonomy of agencies, their merits and demerits, measures to root out corruption, competitiveness of salaries, selection in appointments and its procedure, computerization, units and quality of service sector, role of regions and the like. During this discussion, it was considered that the reflection undertaken in the routine circumstances too should be utilized in this process and it would bring fine results. The Chief Minister instructed the concerned secretaries to prepare working plans for implementation of the suggestions with a view to structural development of social services, guidelines to development, extensiveness of management and information system and the like.

Series of Demonstration

Discussions were now taking place day and night which all aimed at progress of Gujarat. In it, officers and policymakers presented their progress report and presentation in order to give the future picture of the state. The chief feature of this period was that the programmes commenced in the morning and lasted till late in the evening or night. The most wonderful thing was that the Chief Minister used to be present all throughout such meetings. It was like a wonderful manifestation for a Chief Minister to be in attendance in a discussion all through. He not only attended the discussion, but also examined the working of different departments in depth, and assumed the actual condition based on the data presented to him. He would also discuss the limitations as well as the achievements in order to chalk out the future course of action. He was also thinking all the time how to remove the shortcomings and improve working. All these points were raised by officers in their presentation. It was an unprecedented occurrence in the administrative history. Perhaps no other children had ever invested their mental faculties to understand the administration and assess the working of each department of the State Government.

It was natural for the concerned secretaries to think the utility of these presentations which they were carrying out. What did the Chief Minister wish to have from these? What could be the outcome of such detailed presentations? But today, we are able to see the outcome in their physical form in working, implementation of schemes and the concerned matters. We would have to agree that the series of presentations started by the administration was no pastime, it was honest and meaningful.

There is no reason to accept that a Chief Minister would know everything. In this sense, it would be quite appreciable for Narendra Modi to understand the working of each department in honest terms, and this effort has led to achieve a unique dynamism in the administration resulting into a number of spectacular achievements.

Idea of Panchamrit Yojana

The series of presentations and training camps started for administrative reform bore wonderful results. Narendra Modi gave a new idea of Panchamrit for all-round development of the state. He said that wonderful results could be obtained if the spirit of Panchamrit was implemented as the foundation stone of development revolution. What did he mean by Panchamrit? He meant by it manpower, knowledge power, water power, energy power and security power. If these powers were discovered and the process of development is started with one goal in the mind, the results were bound to be achieved. These things appeared very simple and normal, yet the way Modi linked them resulted into development in a natural way. It is inevitable to accept that development requires taking note of the domains of knowledge, energy, water, people and security. Therefore, Modi presented before the administration the idea of coordination of these five powers. Nectar revives even the dead, and if the process of development is given the nectar of these five powers, it would become lively and the administration would get spectacular results in a short period, and these results could be perceived in just the initial 111 days of his rule.

Foundation Ceremony only when Inauguration is Certain

Unless a definite time limit is given for implementation of a project in a planned, phased and time-bound manner, the results cannot be guaranteed. Sometimes it happens that the projects, liked by the Chief Minister, are started, but then they take to the backseat and hardly completed in time. To bring the administrative officers out of this mindset, Modi used to tell openly, "I have no interest in laying the foundation stone for the projects which are not likely to be completed. If you want me to lay the foundation stone, tell me the date by which this project would be completed. The date of completion should precede the date of commencement." When such an assurance is asked for, the project is bound to be completed in time. We do not mean to say that the Chief Minister or government wanted to finish the project anyhow in order to keep to the time limit, but he only meant that the time limit should be set in realistic terms. If there is a delay, it can be understood and tolerated if explained, but there has to be a time limit. Commencing a project with uncertain time limit has no meaning for the people. This is the only thing that the administration has to understand; the projects should be completed in due time keeping all the desired speed. It would make the projects dynamic and definite.

Explicit Directions

Each department was given the goal to simplify the directions and timely execution of projects. The Chief Minister had the authority to decide the priority of a project which has to be started in the days to come. The organisation of presentations and working camps for secretaries, which ran over hours, was aimed at rapid implementation of the projects as per the priority. Modi had estimated the limitations of the administration, working background of the concerned department, its working efficiency on the basis of the presentation submitted to him. On the basis of this estimation, he directed the concerned departments in clear terms to make a definite blueprint of its work in the coming five years. This was mental in form. This mental blueprint led to the construction of the majestic edifice of Gujarat. The reflection camps and Karmayogi training camps had led to activate the officers and employees. Now the need was to utilize their vitality and motivation into realization. The concerned authorities were motivated to bring results to the fore. Each department of the administration knew it well what it has to do in the coming five years. It became an important point in its agenda. As a result, each department of the administration is in a position to mention its proud achievements which it has obtained in the given time limits.

With the goals and objectives of routine administration of the state, the concept of good governance was kept in the focus in order to bring out efficient administration, effective management and the like, and with such a doctrine, the responsibilities were assigned. If we go by the information provided department-wise, we find that the form, goal and objective of the implementation of projects have yielded results in positive terms, all under the overall guidance of the Chief Minister. These results are very encouraging. His leadership is like the magic lamp to achieve name and fame. It appears that Gujarat would have been a brighter state had this mental work been invested in it in the era that had gone by before this period.

Series of Continuous Review

The goals set out for the departments to underline the development include general administration department, social justice and execution, labour and employment, Narmada and water resource and water supply, forestry and environment, revenue, legal and parliamentary affairs department, agriculture and cooperative units, sports and youth, cultural matters department, law, health and family welfare, urban development and urban-rural construction, finance, information and broadcasting, food and civil supplies, roads and buildings, energy and petro-chemicals, ports and fisheries, science and technology, women and children development, industry and mines, panchayat, rural housing and rural development, and education department. The administration department organised reliable training courses for employees keeping in view administrative reform and training.

The goal was taken to train thousands of employees in EDP under Sardar Patel Administrative Training and Study Centre. An all-purpose movement was launched to implement the required policies. The review meetings were organised with the concerned secretaries in order to look over the Five Year Plans and annual schemes relating to construction, their expenditure and material achievements.

As far as common people are concerned, the goals for work were given to the revenue and panchayat departments together with the time limit, only then good results can be accrued for the general public. Three years ago, every villager felt discomfort on looking at the working of the tehsil office under the revenue department; a person had to visit the court many times for even small things, every time he was asked to come the following day or week. It disappointed the person who made there after spending money on transportation. Therefore, the administration had a very poor image among the people. Making the working of revenue and panchayat departments efficient can help uplift the image of the entire administration. When the Chief Minister felt this, he gave special emphasis on improvement of working there.

Prosperity in Agriculture

The basis of all-round development in Gujarat is dependent on agricultural work and produce. If the state succeeded in increasing agricultural produce, it would result into the state's prosperity. Irregular rainfall, situation of drought and devastated farming had resulted into breaking up of villages. Planned efforts were needed to resolve this situation and expand agricultural prosperity. Efforts were made in 2004-05. The goal was to provide people large-scale opportunities for employment together with development of farming through agro-vision, and thus improve the living standard and income of the farmers. In the new global agricultural perspective, increase in agricultural produce and farming of the needed commodities could be aimed at in view of the industrial demand. With this goal in view, the government determined certain objectives.

The objectives included to give momentum to development through value-based agricultural production, to provide latest techniques to farmers, to teach them about the latest global economic system, to tell them about latest agricultural goods like biotech and genetic seeds, chemical and generic manures, pesticides, and to make use all of these in the state. It was also aimed to teach farmers about the proper utilisation of these resources and how coordinated efforts could lead to overall development. Further, the aim was to strengthen the market committees through development of their structural facilities, to produce healthy fruit plants in the field of horticulture, to produce high-breeding cattle in the dairy field, and to create favourable environment for the domains, and the like.

Goals were also set for the health and family welfare department of the people to look after people. It included the goals of decreasing infant mortality rate, improving mother's health, modernization of population regulation laboratories, G-swan connectivity with district offices, modernization of ayurvedic pharmacy, development of ayurvedic herbs horticulture, development of ayurvedic hospitals, opening new ayurvedic and homoeopathic medicine clinics, etc.

Potable water and irrigation water have presented massive problems for Gujarat in the past 50 years. The people of Gujarat were as good as facing the drought conditions for over 10 years now. If there is problem of potable water, you cannot think of water for irrigation in fields. The people of Gujarat have suffered due to lack of water between 1960-95. Still, the rulers paid little heed in finding a permanent solution to the problem, only temporary relief was given through makeshift techniques such as supply of water through tankers spending crores of rupees under the master plan, and give employment to the poor labourers. Sometimes, some better techniques were thought out like repair of the old and useless handpumps or installation of new ones at some places. It was all that was done prior to this period. No other ruler ever thought to solve this problem permanently.

In fact, several schemes could have been launched to eradicate this problem significantly, but neither the schemes were launched nor any effort was made to complete the few schemes that were launched earlier. The ambitious Sardar Sarovar Project was the one which could meet the needs of water for about 9000 villages and 135 small and big towns as well as providing irrigation water to 18 lakh hectares of land. It was an unprecedented scheme for any ruler. All those who came to power had known it well that the problem of water could not be solved unless Sardar Sarovar Project was completed, but none of them showed the commitment, nor did the previous governments showed any will to do so, notwithstanding the fact that this project was launched by Jawaharlal Nehru in 1961.

Narmada Water Makes to Fields

Most of the area of state was faced with a massive problem of irrigation due to lack of rainfall. Scarcity of rainfall had burnt priceless crops in central and eastern Gujarat, especially in the districts of Vadodara, Panchmahal, Bharuch, Narmada, Kheda, Anand and Ahmedabad, which could lead to massive devastation of the economy. On the other hand, the truth was that there was water in the main canal of the Narmada, but in the absence of any management effort, this water could not be utilized. Gujarat was passing through an ironical stage. On the one hand, there was water in the Narmada; and on the other, the crops were suffering due to lack of water. This problem had to be tackled anyhow. The Chief Minister considered resolving this problem, and he directed the engineers to find means to make the Narmada water available to the fields.

One main cause of the Narmada water not being made available to fields was that the canals of the Narmada Project were not yet ready, and water could not be supplied to fields without them. The condition was so terrible that there was no chance in sight to complete the canals in near future. So, there was no other way but to suggest other alternatives to supply water for irrigation, and the alternative that was decided to work upon was to use the water in the branching canals in Bavla, Dholaka, Sanand, Daskroi and Fatewadi command area in Ahmedabad, made under the Mahi Irrigation Project, which should be used to supply water in Anand and Kheda districts.

Narendra Modi directed the administration to supply water to the fields from these branching canals. Thus, for the first time in history, the Narmada water was made available for irrigation to the scorching fields. The branching canals of Sardar Sarovar Project had been completed in Vadodara to some extent, so the Narmada water was released in these canals to supply to the fields. In Kheda and Anand districts, the Narmada water was supplied through the Mahi branching canals; while in Ahmedabad, the Sabarmati river was filled with the Narmada water in order to supply it to the fields through Fatewadi canal. This supply of water for irrigation helped to save crops worth crores of rupees and it helped to increase agricultural production from 9,000 crore to 40,000 crore.

With the Narmada water being available for irrigation in several districts of Gujarat in the year 2003-04, the production of crops multiplied greatly.

Narmada Water in Kutch

The Narmada water had started to flow in villages and towns for drinking purposes, but an important need was to supply it in Kutch district. Kutch is an area where water is scarce. Narendra Modi directed the administration to supply water to Kutch, right up to the Pakistani boundary, through a pipeline. Consequently, the Narmada water descended on the scorching and dry land of Kutch on 18 May 2003. This day was historical and memorable for the Kachchi Mandus (people of Kutch). They thronged the place in thousands and had a glimpse of Narendra Modi in the avatar of Bhagirath, the mythological figure believed to have brought the Gangas onto the earth. When Modi celebrated with Narmada water in a public ceremony, the Kachchi Mandus showed unparalleled vigour, it was such a scene that could never be forgotten. Its cause was natural; none of them had ever dreamt that the Narmada would ever descend around them in Kutch. However, the Chief Minister had changed their dream into a reality. This programme was not symbolic. From this historical day, the pipe water from Narmada was to be supplied in several villages and four towns. At that time, Narendra Modi had said that this water would prove to be raw gold for the dry land of Kutch.

Hydroelectricity Generation from Narmada Water

From October 2004, the Narmada water started to fill the Sardar Sarovar up to a height of 110.64 metres. With this, electricity generation started, it being the first generation in the history of this project, which continues to this date.

Struggle with Obstacles

It is inevitable to mention the struggle that Gujarat had to undertake to raise the height of Sardar Sarovar dam to 121.92 metres, especially due to the fact that Gujarat would have gone without it without the dexterous policies played by Narendra Modi. A meeting was convened of the RCNCA in New Delhi under the

Water Resource Ministry of Government of India so that a decision could be taken to raise the height of the dam to 121.92 metres. The meeting was unnerved when it was perceived that the then Water Resource Minister, Dr. Saifuddin Soz wanted to obstruct the further construction of the dam. On the other hand, the opponents of Sardar Sarovar Project had left no stone unturned to prevent its raising to the desired height. The reason was natural. Had this dam been raised to 121 metres, it would become a turning point for Gujarat. As a result of efforts made to stall its progress, Dr. Saifuddin Soz exaggerated the matter by saying that the work of rehabilitation has not gone on satisfactorily, therefore, the dam would not be allowed to proceed further. At this time, the whole of Gujarat underwent a wave of dissatisfaction and protest. It was the time when all people of Gujarat came together to demonstrate their peaceful stand in favour of the dam, and such a demonstration had become inevitable too. It was a testing time for the Chief Minister too. The Supreme Court had ordered that necessary rehabilitation work was in progress in the concerned states; how could the approval for construction be overlooked and the construction stalled, and how could it be tolerated?

Narendra Modi played a strategic move to struggle against the Central Government. He decided to undertake a 52-hour fasting at GMDC Maidan, Ahmedabad unless the approval for raising the height was approved. In the presence of thousands of people, saints and seers, as well as people representing several voluntary organisations connected with Sardar Sarovar Project, Narendra Modi sat on fast. On the other hand, the flag-bearers of different parties in Gandhi Ashram, Ahmedabad, leaders of voluntary organisations, trade unions and other small and big organisations started their symbolic fasting to raise their voice against the anti-Narmada elements, and all this was done in a very peaceful manner. As a result of these collective efforts, the then Union Minister for Water Resources had to bow down. The vital role played in the whole event brought to the fore his fine personality as a great political leader.

Narendra Modi also encouraged, along side increasing the capacity of Sardar Sarovar Project, rainwater storage movement in Gujarat. The rainwater storage movement had taken root right from the year 2000, but it gained momentum during the period of

Narendra Modi. Now, a series of check-dams were started on small and big rivers in the state.

Narendra Modi also put forward an idea to construct barrages in each village for water harvesting project in Saurashtra to provide water to the dry rivers. In the initial phase, this responsibility was given to the irrigation department in 2003-04 and 2004-05, in a bid to revive the dry rivers.

The fact remains that his specific style of awakening the mass power is unique to Narendra Modi. This attitude can be seen in few political leaders. We scarcely find the mentality in leaders to invoke common people in a bid to get fine results in a project. But here the matter was quite distinct.

The water revolution that started in the state in 2000-01, continued to burn more brightly in the coming six years. Now, the outcome of this effort is that millions of cubic water is stored underground through thousands of barrages, while a number of dry rivers in the state have been revived.

The height, that Modi gave to the water harvesting project and revived the dry rivers, occurred due to his unique way of thinking along very clear lines. When it rains well, all ponds are filled up and the overflowing water makes to the sea, and a method was to be thought out to conserve this water, so that the ponds are full and rivers flow with water round the year, only then the scarcity of water could be tackled. All this planning had been done with this in view, as a result of which, dry rivers could be revived. This project materialized into reality the idea that not even a single drop was to be allowed to flow to the sea after all the ponds were filled up. It helped to fill the dams and rivers to the brim.

Benefits of Water Harvesting

The water level rose in the state due to people's cooperation in Sardar Patel cooperative water harvesting scheme in which over one lakh barrages were constructed in Saurashtra, north and east Gujarat in tribal areas. The water could be found in wells from minimum 15 metres to maximum 30-35 metres. It was an amazing occurrence for Gujarat. This increase in water table may not be a thing of wonderment for average farmers in Saurashtra and north Gujarat, but it certainly pleases them. Earlier the wells dried up in summer, but now they still had water even after having used it in two crops, which farmer would not feel happy about it?

Water harvesting led to a new direction of rural economic development. The first outcome was that the people who had migrated to cities in search of employment started to move back to their villages.

Diagnosis of Electricity Scarcity

The construction of barrages helped in irrigation and potable water supply. It also helped in generation of hydroelectricity, especially in the areas of north Gujarat, a new light was seen because scarcity of electricity was tackled here. The water table was continuously rising in hilly areas of Sabarkantha and Banaskantha districts, which filled the wells with water. Now, an average farmer does not have to spend money on electricity for drawing water from wells.

Water harvesting has also brought wonderful results in tribal belts. A tribal who lived in a hut some time before now has started to live in a *pucca* house. *Pucca* houses, fields filled with rich crops of cotton, wheat or arandi, rising incomes are the features that please the farmers; now water is available right in the backyard, which has made even the poor people feel like a prince. Now people don't have to beg because of natural calamities.

For the long-lasting solution of water problems in Gujarat, the Sujalam-Sufalam Project was launched under which water harvesting, raw spreading, water harvesting by canals, pond deepening, underground pipeline supply of water, establishment of irrigation projects in different tribal areas, construction of obstacles to prevent salinisation resulted into availability of water for irrigation. Such projects have played a vital role in agricultural development of Gujarat.

The Chief Minister, on the one hand, started the barrage construction movement, and on the other, where it was not possible, the rainwater harvesting project was launched in order to restrain the flowing water; for it boribunds were constructed; this idea was given by none other than Narendra Modi himself. The more the water is collected, the more advantage it would beget. At some places, a very ordinary technique was adopted, that was to obstruct the flowing water by placing sacks full of sand or manure to make a small dam, so that the water takes five times longer to travel the same distance, and it would be the ripe time when maximum seepage of water would occur, resulting into higher water table underground; which is going to benefit the place like never before.

Besides providing facilities for irrigation, Narendra Modi also emphasised the need for education, research and extension of agriculture with a view to development. Agriculture is the culture of India, so is science. Therefore, Narendra Modi made efforts to bring the two together. If agriculture is science, it should be made to the fields through agricultural scientists. He said that unless scientific researches were made to reach the fields, they would remain as good as dead. When Narendra Modi, in 2002, found that the agriculture universities in the state possessed over 700 agricultural scientists, he opined that their reaching out to farmers would help to serve agriculture in true sense of the term. Therefore, in the convocation ceremony held at Anand in 2003, he said that unless the work of scientists did not reach the farmers, the process of research would remain meaningless. He also said to the scientists: "You conduct newer experiments with farming, conduct newer researches, discover newer varieties of seeds, I suppose you do all this for the sake of farmers."

Laboratories in Fields

It was natural for the Chief Minister to think that scientists conduct research for the benefit of farming, but the researches conducted in laboratories scarce made to the fields. If these useful researches did not reach the fields, what for use were they? The conditions in laboratories and fields are quite distinct. It does not mean that the scientific researches taking place in the laboratory have no concern with the practical life in the fields. Most of the researches are conducted keeping in view the actual and practical situations, but this too was true that hardly any research reached the fields. Therefore, the Chief Minister gave a new slogan to the agricultural scientists: "Lab to Land." The idea behind this slogan was to deliver the scientific researches being undertaken in laboratories to the fields. Not only this, the scientists should step out of the laboratories to go to fields and feel the actual conditions prevailing there, and then conduct researches accordingly. If a scientist's intellect and farmer's insight are brought together, it would turn gold even brighter. Therefore, Narendra Modi put forward a new thinking, and with time, this took a concrete shape too.

The work undertaken under the Krishi Mahotsav includes such matters as distribution of agricultural kits, guidance of farming, inspection of crops by scientific methods, change in crop pattern, animal husbandry enrichment, water harvesting, housing projects, gobar bank and self-help camps, provision of women employment, agricultural camps at tehsil headquarters, panchvati scheme and village-wise crop pattern, and the like.

The organisation of Krishi Mahotsav has resulted into great benefit to the farmers in tribal belts in districts like Valsad, Dang, etc. Who would explain to tribal farmers the correct method of farming? Who would tell them that water harvesting leads to increased water table? Who would tell them that animal husbandry would lead to increased milk production? The tribal farmers who found it hard to keep the body and soul together, how could he have the capability to buy farming or horticulture or animal husbandry kits? And what could be better if such numerous farmers were benefited by the Krishi Mahotsav?

Thus, Gujarat moved from rainwater-oriented farming to irrigation by other means. With it, it also introduced the system of research, education and expansion of farming; all these efforts have culminated into amazing results. If Gujarat has become a leading state in agricultural field, its credit truly goes to this formula.

Emphasis on Girl Education

The major problem being faced in the state was about low girl education and literacy rate. Narendra Modi stressed on the need for girl education and made arrangements for it, which bore positive results. In the last five years, priority was given to educational field, especially girl education, for which the Kanya Shiksha Rath Yatra and Shala Praveshotsav were started from the year 2003-04. These movements have led to increased rate of enrolment and girl education.

The Kanya Shiksha Rathyatra proved to be a unique movement. Like the Krishi Mahotsav, this programme too requires the presence of the Chief Minister, education minister, state ministers, district in-charge, secretary, district collector, district development officer, IPS, IFS, secretarial officers, and officers of other departments including education. All of them visit different villages in the hot month of June and organize programmes to get all girls admitted with a spirit of social service. This programme has proved to be very successful. This movement has also resulted into increased awareness among parents and guardians for education, especially for the girls. Under it, all admissible girls are got admitted to primary school. Besides, effort is also made to re-admit the dropouts. Under this programme, people are also explained about different government schemes and such problems like unfavourable sex ratio between boys and girls as well as unequal rate of birth, female infanticide and female forticide, and awareness programme for 'Save girl' campaign. The villagers are also acquainted with the social problems arising from these things. The parliamentarians, legislators and district, tehsil and panchayat officers are present in the Kanya Shiksha Rathyatra. In the current year too, the Kanya Shiksha Rathyatra was organised on 15-16 June for admitting girls in schools.

The Chief Minister himself visits a number of villages in this movement, not in the capacity of a Chief Minister, but as an alms-seeker. It is no trivial matter. Whichever village he visits, he lights the lamp of education there. He begs before the people for education. He begs in his unique style, which is so impressive that all those guardians who have not yet admitted their children in school accept his advice immediately and happily.

E-governance

Common people feel for the administrative improvement especially from the working of the revenue department. The image of the administration depends on the offices under the revenue department working at rural, tehsil and district levels. Rural and urban citizens have to often visit these offices in connection with their land records. The working in these two offices touches the common people. The more rapidly it is done, the more simplified it is, the better administrative image is presented before the people touching their hearts. Narendra Modi, during his rule of 12 years, has kept this point in the focus, and has taken effective steps to make the working of this department result-oriented and impressive through the use of technology. For this purpose, several types of schemes have been started. It was during this period that the people of Gujarat came to know about a new term called e-governance.

The revenue department is one of the oldest administrative structures of the government. It plays a vital and result-oriented role in different types of national programmes and different government schemes. This department is spread through at the rural level, right up to the remotest area. Each tract of land in the state has been measured, and land records are recorded in the revenue records. Basic information regarding land, crop pattern, irrigation research, cropping area, irrigation area, irrigation rights, ownership rights, land revenue and land use change, etc. are the details that are entered here, and they are updated from time to time.

The chief functions of the revenue department include land records, land measurement, land revenue, land management, survey settlement, rights letters, land grants, land acquisition, land use change, evaluation, document registration, stamp duty, agricultural land maintenance, disaster management and the like. The revenue department looks after the sensitivities and aspirations of the people.

Modernisation of Revenue Department

E-dhara means computerized land record management. Its chief factors include a fine model of e-governance, clean and correctly planned land records, evolving technology, effort to deliver benefits to the remote areas, momentum in public service and use of technology to strengthen the administration. The revenue department started the e-dhara programme in order to bring about revolution in the field of land management. Under this programme, there are e-dhara centres working at 225 tehsil headquarters. The land offices are clean, useful and computerized for rapid and simple service. The revenue department, on 15 August 2004, has done away with the hand-written records system and has approved only computerized records system. This has helped to provide the people safe and transparent computerized land records numbering 1.54 crore which includes 98 lakh 7/12 records and 56 lakh 8-A records.

E-gram – Computerisation of Gram Panchayats

The important schemes that the panchayat department has started in Gujarat includes E-gram Vishva Gram scheme. The exchange process of information through computer has been started in order to bring the rural people of the state to the world perspective. Computers have enlivened the urban centres, and villages should not lag behind, this is the purpose behind this scheme. The gram panchayats, tehsil panchayats and zila panchayats have been linked with the secretariat at Gandhinagar through the computer network. The State Government has made an effort to provide e-service in villages like it has done in towns and cities. It is only in Gujarat that 12,151 gram panchayats have been connected with computer network for giving e-service. In this sense, Gujarat is the only state in the country which provides e-service in villages. Of the total 13,693 gram panchayats, computer facility has been made available in 12,151 panchayats that comes to nearly 88.74 percent, which is a unique achievement. In its first phase, it has made possible for the issue of death and birth certificates, income certificates, caste certificates, character certificates, residence certificates, etc. as well as availability of forms and applications for different government schemes.

For this work, all zila panchayats and 222 tehsil panchayats of the total 224 have been linked with the Gujarat state wide area network. For training of panchayat members and government servants, a facility has been provided for satellite-based direct digital reception system, it also works for dispensation of information. In each tehsil panchayat office, the touch screen kiosks have been provided in the tehsil information centres by which necessary information as well as records is made available to the people. It is through e-prima software that the panchayat records are available online. At the rural level, arrangement has been made to provide 7/12 and 8-A information to the farmers by the gram panchayat by using the tehsil/district-level server for information. Under the cyber service, facility is also available for dialogue with farmers through the use of Internet, as well as for providing other information regarding agriculture, education, information, health, employment and the like. E-gram also has provision for depositing electricity and telephone bills, insurance and postal services, etc.

Panchvati Scheme

Chief Minister Narendra Modi has, on the one hand, started the e-dhara programme to resolve the rural problems by providing the infrastructure to the gram panchayats; and on the other, to increase rural prosperity and eradicate social inequality; he has also put into operation other schemes like Tirthgram and Panchvati. Generally, there are available parks and gardens in towns and cities for children to play; but now, a scheme has been launched in villages to provide infrastructure, like parks for children to play and for the elderly to sit together. The panchayat department has implemented this scheme in a number of villages. Inaugurating this scheme in the state's villages, Narendra Modi said: "Right from the origin of our ancient culture, trees have been inseparable parts of our life. Our religious scriptures, texts and Vedas too have delineated the importance and utility of trees. Our Vedas have accepted the peepal tree as the universe incarnate; therefore, women and girls go round it for worship. The birds inhabiting the peepal are considered the form of soul and God." With such imagination, the Panchvati scheme was launched in the state which kept in view the significance of trees and conservation of environment.

The rural people of the state have maintained their diverse culture. The forests adjoining the villages were rich and green; village children played and swung on the trees, and thus enjoyed the environment to the extreme. However, this treasure has vanished with time, resulting into adverse impact upon rural life. However, to resolve this problem, the green cover has been reinstalled in different areas, especially in villages, and it has been provided in the form of parks and gardens. This scheme has been implemented by the panchayat department. Under this scheme, selected trees are planted. The different varieties of trees include peepal, banyan, harad, bel, ashok and other fruit trees. Generally, these parks are created on an open and even land measuring one thousand square metres or more. To awaken the spirit that this park belongs to me and my village, an amount of ₹ 50,000 has been prescribed as donation from the villagers. This place is also equipped with the facilities of latrines and bathrooms, so electricity too has been provided. For electricity, the solar systems have been provided. Such facilities are available in several parks. If there is a village or pond in the adjacent area, then this scheme also includes different devices for entertainment such as boating and seeks to provide necessary infrastructure for that purpose.

To mobilize public support and participation, an idea of contribution was mooted under which people of a village have to contribute ₹ 50,000, while the State Government renders an aid of ₹ 1 lakh. People can contribute in the form of cash or kind. The gram panchayats offering cash are given priority.

Tirthgram Scheme

You have seen that the Panchvati scheme is unique in itself, so is the Tirthgram scheme. We can find tendencies of evil such as tricks, crimes, police complaints, drug addiction, thievery, atrocity and the like, in social life in towns and cities. However, there are numerous villages in the state where no police complaint has been launched, nor has any FIR been launched, nor has any serious crime taken place for several years. To make feel the people of such villages something special about it, Narendra Modi has spread the concept of Tirthgram with a purpose of brotherhood, social harmony, peace and all-round development. The panchayat department started this scheme in 2004-05. Under it, norms were set for the eligible villages. In the gram panchayat elections, a panchayat elected unanimously was declared as Samras Gram, and such a village was given priority in the scheme. The villages where no crime has taken place in the past five years are given priority for Tirthgram and other development schemes. Such villages have no production, sale or consumption of drugs.

The other norms of selecting villages under the Tirthgram scheme include cleanliness, higher rate of girl education, low rate of dropouts, cultivation of social harmony and goodwill, lack of social disputes, settlement of cases through negotiation and discussion, lack of dispute between religious places and villagers, and availability of all facilities to all poor and tribal people. These norms also include participation of villagers in mid-day meal scheme, construction of school classrooms, Vidyalakshmi bonds, purchase of educational resources, untouchability eradication and its strict adherence, participation in construction of agricultural ponds and boribunds under the water harvesting scheme and the like. The panchayat department has constituted a committee at the district level under the chairmanship of the district collector. The panchayat department has implemented a guiding system for selecting the villages under the norms. Thus, preparation has been made to strengthen and modernize villages with people's participation. The village is the unit of development of the country. The country can witness development only when the village is developed. The efforts made for realizing this mantra cannot be negated because of their definite commitment.

Concern for Salt Workers and Families

Narendra Modi paid special attention to the economic progress of fishermen and tribals. Speaking on the problems concerning fishermen, Narendra Modi says: "If you are deprived of salt for one week, you will have the better of it. Our salt workers work on the seashore with their families so that we can get useful salt; they don't care for their health. If they care for us, doesn't their welfare pertain to us? Therefore, I have decided to link the concern for salt workers and families under the Sagarkhedu Project. These people will be provided mobile hospitals, which will access these people in order to look after their health. In order their children can be admitted to school, it is under our consideration to provide them all types of facilities including housing, education and other facilities."

When Narendra Modi announces the all-round development schemes of Sagarkhedu, how can he forget about the problems of the salt workers? In his address, he expressed his desire for their all-round development. He said:

"The State Government has taken upon itself the task of different welfare schemes for salt worker families."

10-Point Programme

The employment-oriented programme is in operation for five lakh families for the forested people. The purpose of this programme is to increase agricultural production in order to create opportunities for employment, to increase activities in animal husbandry, dairy industry and agriculture, to provide qualitative training to tribals, to improve their skills in science and technology in order to link them with suitable employment, to give priority to the tribal families in which the women are the heads of family, and so on.

If the girls have to go to the nearby villages to study, then the bus pass would be given free of charge. This scheme has been put into operation.

Effort has been made to provide milk at eight to ten rupees per litre to tribal children of Amirgarh and Danta, whose number is exceeding 52,000. It helps to supply all the essential ingredients to their bodies. This experiment was started seven months ago. It has resulted into increased school attendance. Not only this, it has improved health of the tribal children, making each child all the more active. Care of tribal health has led to better health of Gujarat.

Tribals are given their *pucca* houses with a package of ₹ 15,000 crore. There should be no tribal who has to live under the trees at night. Each tribal's hut should have electricity. An IIT has been established in a tribal tehsil. This has helped to give momentum to the tribal youth. They are now looking out of labour work in order to live a life of pride and self-respect.

The Vanbandhu scheme has established newer dimensions of development for the tribals. There is no tribal area where development has not been felt like water, education, agriculture, animal husbandry, gardening, horticulture, health, forest wood, child health, land grants, road and infrastructure, electricity and the like.

Highway to Rural Development

When Narendra Modi took over as the Chief Minister in the year 2002, he conceptualized a modern rural Gujarat based on all-round development according to the Panchshakti. It seemed to him that when an urban citizen gets three-phase electricity round the clock for domestic consumption, why can this not be given to the villages? If small and big industries can be developed in cities by giving round-the-clock electricity in cities, why then can small and big industries not be set up in villages if electricity is provided there? Lack of electricity has resulted into devastation of farming, lack of basic infrastructure like roads and water, lack of employment opportunities, which has resulted into disintegration of village life. This problem could be resolved only if this facility is given to villages, and this task will have to be undertaken at war footing. All other facilities were being provided in Gujarat villages, but electricity was not being provided for 24 hours for domestic consumption. In fact, the Jyotigram scheme is not only an ambitious scheme, but also a highway to rural development of the state. It is the lifeline of rural Gujarat.

Gujarat is the only state in the country to provide 24-hour three-phase electricity to its 18,000 villages and 8,000 towns, without any cut. This seemingly difficult and impossible work has been taken over by the government, because it understands the problems and pain that people have to undergo without electricity.

It is only Gujarat where electricity is made available to towns and cities, as well as the villages now, round the clock. The villages are supplied electricity under the Jyotigram scheme. It has resulted into five times increase in employment opportunities in villages, and small and big industries are being set up there. The Jyotigram scheme is not mere supply of energy for domestic or recreational purposes, it has become a part of economic revolution of the villages, leading to revolutionary impact on the economic power of the entire state. The distance between villages and cities is being bridged up. Modern education and e-gram schemes have changed the entire scenario of development. Now, doctors are also heading to rural areas in order to give their services there.

The Jyotigram scheme has taken birth from the pain and pity of darkness of the small man. Feeling sensitivity for the poor rural community, this has helped the government to abolish distinction between town and village. This has helped the farmers to save their crops from getting scorched. Three-phase electricity has also led to increased farmers' income because the process of value-based transformation of agricultural products has started.

Perceptible Advantages of the Jyotigram

- Round-the-clock power for domestic consumption and cottage industry and continuous eight hour supply to farming.
- Continuous increase in agricultural output.
- Improvement of rural economy and cessation of irregularities.
- Villages became self-dependent, and they have not to be dependent on cities for daily articles.

- Decrease in transmission and distribution loss, as well as transformer failure in the state.
- A step worth emulating by other states.
- Increase in income due to prevention of electricity theft.
- Development of industries due to good quality and continuous energy in rural areas.
- Economic prosperity in rural areas due to increase in opportunities in local employment.
- Better health and education services.
- Control over migration of rural people towards cities.
- Improvement in living standard of rural people and availability of electricity as per the daily routine.
- Controlled electricity supply at predetermined times for farming, but continuous supply of good quality led to increased underground water table.
- Due to better consumption of electricity, knowledge of rural people improved about the country and world.
- Re-establishment of electricity supply at the time of natural calamities as well as provision for Jyotigram light.

The first Jyotigram scheme was launched in eight districts. Inspired by its success, it was launched in whole of the state on 17 November 2004. Today, the entire Gujarat is shining due to the Jyotigram scheme.

The style of administration of Narendra Modi has been quite distinct. His style of working is to overcome the problems completely, exhaustively, and it is due to his leadership that Gujarat has been able to eliminate a number of problems in the last 13 years which had been eating into the state. Not only this, he has invited people's participation in the resolution of complicated problems and thus has displayed a great insight.

The social-cultural impact of the Jyotigram project has been the increased consumption of electronic goods, better health, nutrition, family planning, better execution of government schemes and increase in income, also people's awareness has increased towards opportunities of growth in income.

Increased facilities and comforts have helped in improved education among rural women, better recreation, social status, income and the time spent on these factors of life, while the time on daily domestic work has decreased by about 26 percent.

The industrial tendencies such as diamond polishing, make-up goods, agro-processing, etc. have gained momentum. Due to the scheme, 53 percent of the families have got opportunities to work at night. This momentum to rural economy has led Gujarat from dark to light.

Development and New Forms of Garbage Disposal

In the past one hundred years, the world's population has increased from 200 crore to 600 crore, and in Gujarat, 40 percent of the population resides in urban areas, which is likely to touch the 50 percent mark in some time. Urbanisation should become not a problem, but an opportunity, and it should be the path of development. New initiative for development will motivate other states too. Gujarat had earned fame in cotton industry even before independence, now it has led the rest in white revolution and green revolution. Gujarat has initiated steps to manage solid waste management in order to turn 'waste into wealth' and recycle the dirty water, so that these become useful for the social structure. Gujarat has also initiated steps by providing 24-hour electricity to the rural areas leading to creation of employment there and thus restrain migration to cities. In urban development, Gujarat has mobilized public participation at a large scale in order to take a grand leap towards development.

Challenges in Urban Development

In the past few years, Gujarat has identified the significance of the issues like roads, solid waste management and water supply, and has made the cities quite livable in terms of water supply lines, gutters and roads, etc. Healthy rural development is necessary to stop migration of rural people to cities; at the same time, there is need to provide civic facilities in urban centres for health and education.

The present State Government is following Narendra Modi's foresight and insight in order to achieve development, which has resulted into positive outcomes. The working of nagar palikas has been made more effective through conceptual administrative reform, drinking water schemes, organisation of programmes like Vikas Path, solid waste management and plantation for environmental conservation, all these steps have led to better urban development.

Renovation of Towns

In the earlier times, there was quite a lax system under which hardly 25 urban planning schemes were launched. Now, after urban development has been achieved, around one hundred urban planning schemes have become possible. As a result of administrative reforms, real estate development has become excellent in Gujarat. The available infrastructure has led Gujarat to unprecedented development. The traders dealing in concrete, earth, sand, stone, labour, masons and the like have immensely benefited by unprecedented increase in employment.

In 124 nagar palikas, the Samadha scheme has been approved. 24 of them have freed themselves from the debt of the electricity board. Effective renovation of the Gujarat Housing Board and Slum Clearance Board has been done. Priorities of development include disaster management.

Gaurav Path

To develop at least one main city road, the government has chosen as the Gaurav Path; all encroachment is removed from it, it is greened, evened and equipped with such facilities as footpaths and street lights. The houses on either side of a Gaurav Path have to follow a given colour code, and thus the participation of common people has been sought in it.

Chiranjivi Scheme

To decrease the death rate among newborns, the Modi Government has launched the Chiranjivi Scheme, which has won accolades and success. This scheme has also been awarded with the Asian Innovative Award by the *Washington Post* in Singapore.

The Beti Badhao Andolan (movement for saving daughters) has led to improvement in sex ratio, which has jumped from 802 to 870. The medical checkup of students is being taken over and is being done free of charge, including free treatment and surgery facilities.

Vitamins A and D are being given as nutrients to 10 lakh children under the age of three years at present with 4,400 *anganwadis*. With the aid of the World Bank, 30,000 tonne waste is being treated; this step has been appreciated by the Supreme Court too.

The concept of medical tourism has proved to be successful. Several foreigners and NRIs land in Ahmedabad by every international flight with a purpose of medical treatment and surgery here. 85 mobile vans have been provided for medical services to salt workers, fishermen, tribals and those living in remote areas. Town health centres have been started in urban areas. The then Union Minister for Health, Ramdoss declared that the Chiranjivi scheme of Gujarat model will be launched in the entire country from the next financial year. According to media news, the Government of Uttar Pradesh is considering to launch the Chiranjivi scheme for safe delivery in private hospitals for the women belonging to BPL families.

Narendra Modi has written about this scheme that it was started in the state for the first time in Gujarat in order to transform women's lives and to provide free medical care and treatment to them in hospitals. As a result of this scheme, the number of mothers and children has improved. The Nari Gaurav Niti or women improvement policy has been initiated to make women power a partner in the development process.

The Government of Narendra Modi has issued the following instructions in this regard:

1. An infant should be taken care of right from the time of conception.
2. It should be ensured that the women in the initial conception stage should register themselves in the nearest health centres, and they should go for medical examination for at least three times.
3. It should be ensured that the delivery is undertaken at the health centres. If it is not possible there, it should be ensured that it is completed by a trained maid/nurse.

Matra-Vandana Yojana

The Matra-Vandana scheme has been launched for protection of health of mother and child. This scheme has been extremely successful. It provides for a budget of ₹ 23.80 crore. For it this, the Gujarat Government has also been awarded.

Some of the important points of this scheme are:

- Awareness should be created among people towards health of the newborns. Safety of newborns is very important, so proper and immediate steps should be taken in this regard.
- People should be made aware of the things that they should keep in view before and after birth of a child, so that both mother and child remain healthy and safe.

Beti Bachao Abhiyan

The Modi Government launched this scheme in order to control foeticide and declining sex ratio. The sex ratio is the most unfavourable in prosperous states of India like Punjab, Haryana, Delhi and Gujarat. According to the 2001 Census, the number of girls on every 1000 boys is 798 in Punjab, 819 in Haryana and 883 in Gujarat. After Modi's initiative in Gujarat, the results in the 2011 Census showed up, and the sex ratio increased to 918.

Some states have taken this tendency very seriously and have taken various steps to control this. Like the Beti Bachao Andolan (Save Daughters Movement) in Gujarat, other states have put into force other schemes. The sex ratio among children below seven years of age is continuously falling in the country. In 1981, this ratio at the national level was 962 which has nose-dived to 927 in 2001.

This indicates that our economic prosperity and better education have no positive impact on this problem. To eradicate this problem at present, there is need to create social awareness as well as implementation of anti-natal and post-natal checks.

The Modi Government in Gujarat has made every effort to stop the misuse of modern technology which can discriminate the sex of the foetus. Strict laws have been enacted against female foeticide, and its pilot project was launched in five districts of Gujarat, where 22,163 infants took birth, out of whom only 87 infants died, else this number could have been as large as 812.

The success of this scheme has led to its implementation in the whole of state, which was appreciated by the Union Minister for Health himself and instructed to implement it in the whole country.

The Indian scriptures have revered woman as goddess. Gujarat is a state where women are actually revered, respected and it is where maximum efforts have been made for their empowerment. It has greatly succeeded in resolving the gravest problem of female foeticide.

Recently, Narendra Modi said that people should take pride in the birth of a daughter rather than going for female foeticide. He started all types of programmes along side Beti Bachao scheme. Today, Gujarat has become the safest place for women and girls for working. The number of BPOs has continuously increased in this state.

In this state, the security of women is carried out like a duty. If we compare it with other states, we find that other states far outnumber it in crimes against women as well as female foeticide.

Narendra Modi had started the Beti Bachao scheme about a decade ago, and entreated section of the society to realize the value of a daughter's life. Besides, the health ministry of Gujarat has launched a website called betibachao.com. This website is a place where people can lodge their complaints.

A two-day workshop was organised to make aware of the Pre-natal Diagnostic Technical (Regulation and Prevention of Misuse) Act, 1994, which discussed the relevant points.

Karmayogi Scheme

To cultivate loyalty towards work among government servants in Gujarat, this scheme has been launched. It has proved quite effective. All employees are given special training and model code of conduct within the limits of the Constitution. The government servants are called social servants in Gujarat. There are certain clear instructions for them what they should do and what they should not. Some instructions revolve around the following:

1. Always remember that you are a government servant and public servant. You are given salary, allowances and other perks from the public funds in return for your services. Thus, you fall under the term 'government servant'. You are liable to be treated under the provisions of the IPC 1860, together with Anti-corruption Act of 1988.

2. Each government servant in the state has to do his best by being honest, fearless and neutral by conforming to truthfulness, devotion, commitment, capability and justice, so as to contribute in the state's development.
3. Maintain the image of an honest, just, logical, clean and unprejudiced, friendly image of the government servant.
4. Demonstrate honest and unprejudiced spirit in settling matters. Your attitude should always be reasonable.
5. Behave with people, subordinate workers and co workers with proper etiquette.
6. Good behaviour is an important key to success. Behave with others as you expect others to do with you.
7. Never forget to carry out your duty efficiently. Each duty is sacred and dutifulness is the greatest form of worship to God.
8. Never neglect your duty and never bring down your devotion to work. If a worker shows a shortcoming or carelessness in matters other than those pertaining to decision-related errors or others, action can be taken against him under the provisions of conduct rules and regulations as well as standing orders.
9. Take your decisions without prejudice or unreasonableness. Your decisions should be reasonable from all viewpoints.
10. While settling matters or files, you should not be influenced by individual likes or dislikes, prejudice or preconceived notions, etc.

Kanya Kelvani Yojana

To bring awareness towards women literacy and education, the Kanya Kelvani Yojana or girl education project proved very significant. This is the reason that the rate of women literacy is rising more quickly than that of men. The women literacy rate is rising at 12 percent per annum. As a matter of fact, the literacy rate in the country at present stands at 74 percent. This rate in Gujarat, as per the 2011 Census, stands at 79.31 percent, and it is 70.73 for women.

It cannot be negated that with increasing women literacy, India has treaded on the path of progress. It has expanded opportunities for human resource, but also a change has come about in working and environment. Women literacy has encouraged to better girl education, as well as better child health and all-round development.

Women literacy has also aided in decreasing infant mortality rate, and it has helped in encouraging population control. Of course, there is much scope for improvement in these fields. Awareness is necessary for equality between men and women.

Narendra Modi has chalked out several policies for women education, so unprecedented rise in literacy can be seen in Gujarat.

Balbhog Yojana

This scheme was launched with a view to provide mid-day meals to poor children in the school. Under it, children are given tasty and nutrient food at lunch. It helps to improve their health as well as to engage them in study. It has also improved the condition of dropouts.

The Central Government instructed that cooked food should be served to children at mid-day. At present, the Narendra Modi Government has modified these norms to prescribe that the meals should constitute at least 450 calorie energy and 12 gram protein.

Under the chief objectives of the Balbhog scheme, the State Government is investing a large capital for educational schemes. Its optimum benefit can accrue only when children are freed from malnutrition and become able to receive education to their full capacity. This scheme is an important link in realizing this objective. Through this scheme, the following objectives of universalisation of education will be realized:

1. Increase in enrolment in primary classes, so that no person remains illiterate.
2. To make children stay at school for the whole time and check their tendency to dropout.
3. To develop the capacity in poor income group to have education.
4. The chief objective of this scheme is to provide nutritious food to children.
5. When children of different castes and religions partake food together, they cultivate the spirits of social harmony, integration and mutual brotherhood.

Integrated Child Development Scheme

Under this scheme, called Integrated Child Development Scheme (ICDS), Gujarat, for the first time in 2001, brought all child development schemes under one roof. At present, there are 336 schemes under the ICDS under implementation.

Let us have a glimpse of the programmes under this scheme:

1. There are a total of 50,123 *anganwadi* centres in the state.
2. 2,767 of these *anganwadi* centres are running from government buildings.
3. 93,290 women and girls are working in *anganwadis*.
4. It provides guidance and nutrition to 16,21,929 pregnant women and girls.
5. The number of benefited children stands at 28,57,296.
6. To deliver the benefits of this scheme to distant and remote areas, the government has started the *anganwadi* van system.
7. For the first time in the country, the Gujarat Government has provided each *anganwadi* centre with two gas cylinders, a gas connection, a gas stove and a cooker for making idli.
8. Each year, 36 lakh children are examined medically.
9. 5,200 poor children are given free medical treatment and surgery to treat them for kidney, cancer and heart related diseases.

Efforts to Make the Poor Self-dependent

The most important decision of Narendra Modi was to organize the poor welfare fair in each district. This organisation was like a *mahayajna* in the service of the poor. Organised in each district, the employment resources were increased for millions of economically backward people. Some of them were given money cheques, and others lorries or sewing machines, tractors or land plots. A total of 342 poor welfare fairs were organised in the whole of Gujarat in which an amount of ₹ 26,000 crore was disbursed for employment purposes. These people comprised tribals, scheduled castes and other backward classes.

Perhaps it must have been the first attempt of this kind to distribute the benefits of government schemes in the presence of thousands of people. In it, the poor were given resources to fight with their poverty. The people attending these fairs felt that they would now be able to live a life of dignity and would be able to undertake some business of their own. Prior to this, the middlemen used to make fool of the poor to grab all the benefits themselves. However, in these fairs, the Chief Minister or ministers were present themselves to disburse the benefits, which led to elimination of middlemen. Officers, right from collectors to peons toured different villages to find out where these benefits were essential. These fairs have materialized into benefits for 30 to 60 people in each village, comprising barbers, cobblers, tailors, drivers and the likes. Narendra Modi states: "My government functions for the poor. These poor welfare fairs have been organised in order to help each of my brother and sister to live a dignified life." A good aspect of these fairs came to the fore. Narendra Modi recalls his experience and states: "A poor barber was given his apparatus, so he was enthused to open a stall in Himmatnagar. When his income rose, he came to meet me at Modasa, and gave donation of ₹ 251, and expressed his gratitude to the poor welfare fair, because his good income was outcome of the fair."

Narendra Modi agrees that not only he, but everybody, including each of his opponents, knows that these fairs are the power of the poor; these are dedicated to them; they are a meaningful effort to infuse consciousness and self-respect in the poor. These fairs are helping to make the poor self-dependent.

Yajna for Panchamrit Sankalpana

You can find poles apart distinction between Gujarat of 2001 from that of 2014. They are as distinct as chalk from cheese. In the past one decade, Narendra Modi has transformed the complete image of the state. Nobody had ever imagined in 2001 that the state would earn the epithet of the leading developing state of the country with its unique touch. This thought was unnatural and unrealistic then. It was the time when the state was faced with a number of problems. Even after several dimensions of development had been added, a prosperous Gujarat could not be imagined, because the state lacked an ideal, farsighted and determined leadership to give momentum to the process of development. In its concrete sense, development of a state is one thing, and to present it with pride in the country and world is another thing. Of course, Gujarat has achieved a distinguished place in the entire country in the past 12 years.

Challenges to BJP

Just recall the days of October 2001, how difficult they were so far as carrying further the process of development was concerned. The Bharatiya Janata Party had considerably lost its reliability as a ruling party, and it was faced with a massive challenge to bring the state out of this uncertainty and instability and the entailing negative impacts. It was the time when the state had not yet risen above the droughts in the preceding years of 1999, 2000 and 2001. The drought or semi-drought condition for three consecutive years had shaken the foundation of economy in the state. The foundation of all-round development could be laid only on prosperous economy alone, and when it was in a shaky condition, how could one think of all-round development? Despite all this, Narendra Modi led the state out of this conundrum to achieve the pinnacle of development in all fields.

Narendra Modi started his journey towards development with the organisation of public welfare fairs in the initial years. It cultivated a sense of self-confidence among the people. Addressing one such fair, Modi stated: "The government is not doing any favour. It will play the role of a servant to help the poor and suffering and depressed people to make them self-dependent. It would lead the poor man towards self-dependence, only then the might of the society would be awakened. For this, we have to coordinate and blend the powers of knowledge, people, energy, water and security, and it would lead to the production of nectar. The society that partakes of this nectar would taste eternal development."

In the past twelve years of his rule, Gujarat has achieved spectacular achievements. We can summarise it in its spirit in which the officers and employees have been transformed into *Karmayogis*, and this remains the greatest achievement of the administration. The truth remains, that in the absence of the efforts undertaken by Narendra Modi, Gujarat would not have changed for any better.

Stream of Development

If we compare the situation in 2001-02 with the achievements six years later, in all fields including agriculture, irrigation, water supply, education, road and transportation, health, revenue, panchayat and rural development, fishery, forestry, social welfare and other departments, we find that what has been achieved in these six years could not be achieved in a forty years' period. The distinguished achievements have been realized by Narendra Modi in the course of mere 12 years. Under the agricultural department, agricultural economy is at its zenith. Work in educational research and distribution has led to agricultural development at 10 percent, which is higher than that of any other state in India. At one time, the average annual agricultural value produce stood at ₹ 9000 crore rupees, which has multiplied to ₹ 1,00,000 crore in this period. The Narmada water has been supplied to over 9000 villages through efforts in irrigation, water supply and water harvesting measures. If we talk about the energy department, no other state in India provides 24-hour three-phase electricity in the villages, which Gujarat has achieved through its Jyotigram scheme. In the same way, the revenue department started different schemes in order to take the state to the pinnacle of development through the e dhara, e-gram, Vishvagram, Vanbandhu, Sagardhedu, Female foeticide prevention, girl education, road development and the like.

How has all this development materialized? Narendra Modi examined the process of development in the past 40 years, and then contemplated over it. He undertook study of the obstacles faced in the path of physical development, challenges to development, programmes undertaken for development and the outcomes of their implementation. He also studied the development process under the government machinery, and then he set down to consider the uniqueness of state development, continuous development despite objections, his strategy, continuity in policies despite a change in government, development-oriented administration with perspectives of change and the related matters, and the present form of Gujarat came to the fore from the outline that was imagined thus.

Government Becomes Lively with Panchamrit

The foundation of development of a state is laid on the basic infrastructure and resources, its ideological flow, water resources, energy and its conservation. Whatever thought that Narendra Modi put into state's development, came to the conclusion that the heritage of the state should blend five equal and harmonious powers which could irrigate the process of development. These five powers were the power of knowledge, the power of water, the power of people, the power of energy and the power of conservation. The blend and coordination of these five powers resulted into the nectar called *Panchamrit*, which can make the society eternal and lively.

Power of Knowledge

In the past few years, Narendra Modi has made people taste the nectar, a blend of five powers or forces, due to which, the entire state is experiencing an amazing wave of development in each field of life. This blend has proved to be the foundation stone of development in the state. Therefore, it is necessary to understand the concept of *Panchamrit* in some detail. The State Government proceeded towards the power of knowledge. It attached significance to intellectual property and organised reflection camps aimed at state's development. Under it, the points included are educational infrastructure, global education and employment board, Jnanrath project, distance education, girl education, education in information technology and biotechnology, human resource utilization in research and creation of employment opportunities, and the like.

As far as the field of education is concerned, the fact would have to be accepted that the level of girl education was poorer and weaker in the state when compared with other states. With an objective of bringing about qualitative improvement in it, the movement was launched with Shala Praveshotsav, which resulted into better girl literacy rate, and the number of girl dropouts too came down. Under this campaign, the people of Gujarat witnessed a large-scale mobilization of resources for admission of girls in school in the districts and tehsils where the girl literacy rate was low. This witnesses positive results. Even average children have the constitutional right to receive primary education, but it is a folly to think this right would automatically get education too. Therefore, the Praveshotsav campaign became the tool to draw children to school in towns and villages. This campaign witnessed massive people participation.

For the initiation of power of knowledge, each girl getting admitted in school gets a bond of ₹ 1000, and each girl completing education up to seventh standard is given this amount together with interest. Besides, the girl students belonging to BPL families are also given 60 kilogram of free grain, and temporary shelter for the wandering families in order to enable them to admit their children to school. These measures have transformed this campaign into a lively manifestation.

Among the other fine aspects of the power of knowledge, such points have been linked such as purification campaign, training of teachers through Karmayogi campaign, and the like. Strict action was taken against those who have taken education as the medium of earning and market for trade. The purification drive helped to make education more effective. The diagnostic tests were constructed for children in primary and secondary schools. The children found weak in mathematics and science subjects were given special training. Thus, successful effort was made for improvement of educational quality. In order to enable the youth of Gujarat compete with the students of other states, the subjects like mathematics and science were included in English medium.

The children who rose from primary education to higher education were covered under an accident insurance scheme in order to provide them a security cover.

For extension of education in tribal and remote areas, four new B.Ed colleges were started together with 71 PTC colleges and 603 secondary schools, and thus realized the dream of class to every teacher and teacher to every class.

Besides the establishment of Kutch University, Nirma Institute and Dhirubhai Ambani Institute were given the status of universities for education in technological, professional and computer and information technology. This power of knowledge has led Gujarat to stand in the first row of the developing states.

Power of Water

Along side the power of knowledge, the State Government launched various schemes of Sardar Sarovar Project for storage of water in order to make the earth green and prosperous, and this has led to positive results in Gujarat. There was a time when women and girls had to walk for miles to fetch a pitcher of water on their heads. Year after year, the small and medium size ponds, wells and borewells dried up. The water table fell from 15-200 feet to 1500-2000 feet, compelling the farmers to feel the scarcity of water for farming. This resulted into exploitation of groundwater. Narendra Modi realized the importance of power of water, and made the concept of water storage more acceptable, and as a result of which, there are more than 85,000 barrages, 1,75,000 ponds, thousands of boribunds in addition to revive the village ponds, border ponds, baoris were revived to supply water to the fields and homes in order to make the earth green and moist. As a result of this, millions of cubic metre water could be stored, resulting into wonderful achievements. The areas of Saurashtra, north Gujarat and east Gujarat, where the works of water storage have been undertaken, the borewells and wells are no more dry, water is filled in them to the brim. Once long ropes were needed to draw water from them, but now one can drink water with the cupped hands. The dried borewells are all full of water; and this is a common sight. The people of the state had never imagined such a scenario to occur in their life.

Along side water storage, water management was taken afoot through drip sprinkler irrigation programme. This scheme was launched with a provision of ₹ 1500 crore, which helped to provide drip irrigation to 4.50 lakh hectare area. This has proved to be a vital basis for water management. In the last four years, good rainfall occurred with which a large amount of water was collected and stored, strengthening the state's economy to a higher level. The credit for this development should go to the power of water.

Power of Energy

Energy is the basis on which industries can flourish. It gives momentum to industrial development. Narendra Modi took the initiative of providing cheap and timely electricity to industries with an urge to generate it. We can find qualitative improvement in electricity generation and distribution in Gujarat.

The gas produced in the state was used for electricity generation, with which the state achieved a commendable outcome in the field of energy. The entrepreneurs now had to face fewer difficulties to get electricity. If we talk of Sardar Sarovar dam, with the increase in its height to 121 metres, electricity generation caught speed. Besides, steps were taken for electricity generation by windmills. At present, work is afoot to generate 5,000 megawatt electricity from oceanic tides.

Encouraging policies were formulated for wind energy and tidal energy. The ₹ 1500 crore gas grid project too was launched, in which domestic gas and industrial gas was planned to be distributed through pipeline. It should be worth mentioning that the state has also started projects in LNG, CNG fuel resulting into qualitative improvement in the energy scenario in the state.

Along side, the energy department has taken strict action against theft of electricity, resulting into almost non-existent thefts at present. For this, the Vidhan Sabha passed the anti-theft law which was got sanctioned by the President too, which provides for a strict punishment of three years' rigorous imprisonment as well as a fine of ₹ 2 lakh. This effort has borne optimum results. As a result of such efforts, the occurrences of electricity thefts have decreased and the importance of power of energy has been established.

Power of Security

It is the most important of the five powers. How can the process of development be sustained in a society where the sense of security does not prevail. Development can take place only when the state is infused with an atmosphere of peace and trust. Gujarat has the image of a peaceful state, though a number of efforts have been made to disturb peace here in the past few years. The fear of terrorism was felt by Gujarat, especially from the neighbouring countries, in the year 2001-02. Had terrorism not been suppressed by a determined political willpower, Gujarat too would have become a centre of terrorist activities. The state not only suppressed terrorism with the participation of security apparatus, but also has risen to the status where the world's industrialists look forward to this state, and it has become possible only due to peace prevailing here. In the last three years, investments running into crores of rupees have been made in the state under Vibrant Gujarat scheme. The leading industrialists of the country too have their eyes on Gujarat for setting up their new units, and all this has become possible only due to security prevailing here.

The works undertaken under the power of security include the Gujcoc law which was passed and sent to the governor for approval. Drugs worth of crores of rupees have been seized. Heavy fines were imposed on people guilty for Godhra massacre under the POTA, as well as steps have been taken for effective curtailment of economic crimes and irregularities, and fines and sentences have been imposed without any discrimination. The units of Chetak commandoes have been constituted to contain terrorist activities. Also, women police stations have been established. For security on the border towns and villages, steps have been taken to develop them together with formulation of adequate laws to prevent drugs and narcotics trafficking. The Gujcoc or Gujarat Control of Organised Crime Act has been passed to take steps for control, containment of organised crimes. Also, the Gujarat Protection of Interest of Depositors Act has been passed to provide consumer security in banking organisations and other acts to improve qualitative reforms in the management of cooperative banks, national security and legal systems, encouragement to security personnel in the border areas, effective exchanges with army, navy and air force personnel, discussion between security officers and civilian officers, joint patrolling with the Coast Guard, establishment of Coast Guard station at Jakho, positive attitude on the acquisition of speed boats, support to the POTA to contain terrorist activities and the like.

Power of People

The optimum utilization of human resource can make the present more progressive and efficient. Narendra Modi attached significance to this aspect in order to achieve a number of positive outcomes. The number of barrages has reached up to 85,000. Its success was the result of people's participation and proper utilization of human resource. The state could overcome the drastic impact of the earthquake, due to the important factor of the power of people. First time after the establishment of Gujarat, democracy has marked a historic milestone. All elections for panchayats, nagar panchayats, municipalities, municipal corporations and Vidhan Sabha as well as Lok Sabha have been conducted fully peacefully. The people who consider Gujarat not peaceful are in fact shocked by this fact.

The power of people has spread all over Gujarat. There is infinite power in the gram sabha, where people themselves can think over and decide the matters. The government administration is of the view now that it has given up its slumber in order to make the administration active and dynamic. The Chief Minister sits in his office and conducts dialogue with people through video conferencing, and it is at this time that he can see people's awareness and aspiration for development.

The people of villages are all too eager to get rid of quarrels and enmities; they wish to support the Samras Gaon scheme. More than 5000 gram panchayats have become Samras or harmonious. Is it not a good sign for the gram panchayats for unanimous elections? The entire village should come together to take decisions regarding development, giving up their personal scores, and this is proof enough of the villages marching towards Swaraj or self-government.

This government is committed for all-round development of the villages. It has made the villages peaceful, self-dependent, as well as has linked them with the world by creating essential infrastructure. Gram sabhas have been held in more than 18,000 villages. On the line of 'waste to wealth', gobar (cowdung) is being used to generate energy, and this new viewpoint has produced results. It now produces gobar gas, natural manure and energy. Gujarat became the first state of the country to achieve the goal of all rural roads. It is also the first state to support farmers in purchase of agricultural produce at the maximum support price. The government bought bajra, peanut and makka.

Thus, the five powers have been irrigated well for the development of the state in the past 12 years, as a result of which development has blossomed here. It is now hoped that it would become a banyan, a massive tree of development in the days to come. Therefore, we can say that Gujarat in 2014 has touched its glory. Gujarat has tasted the nectar of progress. It is the *Panchamrit* of sensitive leadership and progress, and it gives a unique place to Gujarat, as well as leaves a distinct mark on the pages of political history. The day is not far when Gujarat would be known for its dignity and progress.

□

Techno-savvy Modi

In the general elections, there was an interesting programme linking him with common people in a dialogue. It was called *Chai Pe Charcha*, or discussion at tea. It was also called *Chai Chaupal* or tea meeting. Modi used the technology in order to conduct meetings with millions of boys and girls across the country while sitting in Ahmedabad or Mumbai over a cup of tea. The Lok Sabha elections in 2014 have been completely high-tech, under the influence of social media. The credit for this should go to Narendra Modi.

Now, technology has taken large strides. It enables a person, sitting in Ahmedabad, to talk to a person sitting in America, and this exchange of messages takes place within seconds. Today messages are exchanged from trivial topics like what is to be cooked in the kitchen, to the interesting videos and documents. However, it is something to be learnt from Narendra Modi how this technology should be used for professional purposes.

Today people of all age groups have interest in the Internet. The Google and Youtube find out interesting videos in a matter of seconds. Narendra Modi knows this fact well, and he knows the art how to get connected with the youth and women voters. When the elections had not yet been declared, even then Narendra Modi discussed with youth and other techno-savvy people through the *Google Hangout* on 21 August 2012. About forty lakh people joined in this discussion. When we talk of Modi and technology, we can say that he is not merely linked with it, rather he has been using it for his purposes right since its inception in India.

When the digital diary, pager and computer arrived in India, Narendra Modi started to use them all skillfully. Rajiv Shukla, former journalist and presently a big Congress leader, informed people about not only what Modi talked in the interview, but also what his lifestyle is. This programme showed two faces of Narendra Modi. On the one hand, he is using the computer; while on the other, he was drying clothes in sun in a very simple manner. Narendra Modi was a Sangh *Pracharak*, ever since he has remained in touch of latest technology. He utilizes it in his work related to organisation, propaganda and linking with people.

Ever since online news and newspapers are available on the computer, Narendra Modi's daily routine includes reading the news early morning in the wee hours over a cup of tea. Generally, the information department of Gujarat has experienced that the Chief Ministers used to be sent the headlines from newspapers in the office. But when these headlines were sent to Modi, he would say that he had read them all, and asked to send to him if there was something new. What I mean to say is that his homework is always up to date.

The web media is used most by the Gujarat Government. People-oriented information is passed to people through WhatsApp and SMS.

When Narendra Modi became the Chief Minister for the first time, the most important decision that he took was to connect the monthly meeting of district collectors and chief officers of the government that used to be held in Gandhinagar, through video conferencing. Its greatest advantage is that now the collectors do not have to travel a long distance up to Gandhinagar. It also saves on the time, energy and petrol being spent on these meetings.

Narendra Modi has adopted technology as his weapon. These days, Arvind Kejriwal is much in news. He keeps dramatizing things in order to be in news. After he was sworn in as the Chief Minister in Delhi, he announced great promises to the people, and when people came in large numbers, he fled on seeing the crowd. At this time, a point was raised in the country why Narendra Modi does not hold Janata Darbar; why he does not meet the people directly. However, the youth is not wont to accept anything on the platter. When the Internet was searched, it was revealed that Modi was in constant touch with the people right since 2004, through the use of technology. This programme is called Swagat Online. This programme has also won national and international awards.

The full name of Swagat is State Wide Attention on Grievances by Application of Technology. It is with the use of video conferencing that Narendra Modi can hold dialogue from his office with the people at village, tehsil and district levels. He listens to their complaints and finds solutions to them.

The social media is quite popular among the youth these days, especially the Facebook and Twitter. It is like a blessing for leaders like Narendra Modi, due to two factors:

1. Social media does not fall under any control for the most part, it controls only inciting statements or vulgarity. Whatever control exists lies in other countries like America.

The newspapers can be seen to oppose certain people in accordance with their policies. This thing applies to television channels too. However, there is no such barrier on social media like Facebook or Twitter.

2. It can be used to give any message, also pictures and videos can be uploaded. Narendra Modi is quite popular among the youth, and its greatest factor lies in his continuous touch with the social media.

Besides, the Youtube is also used to counter any propaganda against him by uploading videos. When a speech of Narendra Modi is not published in the newspapers, it is put on the social media, if you are looking for his speech, you are sure to find it there.

At present, Narendra Modi has his own website – www.narendramodi.in at which he takes out time from his busy schedule to write on it. This website is available in all languages of the country, including Sanskrit.

Narendra Modi also keeps uploading videos of his programmes. All those rallies he has addressed, all those programmes that he has addressed, all those things can be seen on the website, because all his news cannot be seen on the television channels or newspapers due to some opposition to him. Sometimes, the opponent newspapers and television channels present his news in a very negative light. Modi is gaining ground in the social media, and this cannot be due to a few people, there is a team of dedicated supporters behind it. Skilled people sitting in Ahmedabad, Gandhinagar, Delhi and other places of the country are giving it the practical shape. All these people wish to see Narendra Modi as the Prime Minister, so they are benefiting the Bharatiya Janata Party with their technique and knowledge.

This is the reason that Narendra Modi addresses large rallies in Odisha, Kerala, Maharashtra, Uttar Pradesh, Bihar, Punjab and other states. While he is still on the go in a rally, parts of his speech start to be uploaded on the media in the form of small clips. His live speeches are broadcast on a number of sites and other means of communication.

Narendra Modi has linked all gram panchayats with e-connectivity. Today, each gram panchayat has the Internet, and this programme is called 'E-gram – Vishvagram'.

The last Vidhan Sabha elections in Gujarat have been a talking point not only in the country but in the entire world, and its sole reason was the 3-D technique. The 3-D technique used by Narendra Modi attracted people at more than one place. Its factor is that he is very popular among the people, and everybody wishes to see him nearby. When a leader talks to people, it benefits him in elections. Therefore, Modi adopted the 3-D formula, which helped him connect with millions of people at the same time.

The 3-D holographic presentation technology is quite distinct from video conference. This technique was for the first time used by Prince Charles of Britain in 2008 when he addressed the World Energy Council, he had used it only for six minutes. This technology is favourable to environment, so it leaves little carbon footprint, so Charles liked it much. This address was also recorded in the palace. Normally, this technology is used in the world to launch a product in the market or for recreation purposes. However, the Bharatiya Janata Party made use of this technology for election propaganda. The specialists reveal that for it, a three-dimensional stage has to be constructed, on which the three-dimensional image is carved for presentation to the viewers.

It makes feel the audience as if the person is present right before them, body and soul. This technology involves a great expenditure, because one camera lens and projector are used for live broadcast. But this to be viewed without the specs are needed a video projector, a small cabinet installation, high quality TFT plasma or LCD screen, HD player, video server, DVD player, lighting and audio system. The speaker has to address by the HD camera and it is broadcast using the HD TV projection system.

3-D makes people believe that Narendra Modi is right before them. This technology has proved its worth, and in the successful campaign of Modi, this technology has played a vital role.

In the beginning of the chapter, we talked of *Chai Pe Charcha* programme, for which the organizers are using distributed video conferencing and hybrid technology, which coordinates DTH broadcast high speed Internet and satellite uplink.

The CAG (Citizens for Accountable Governance) is a voluntary organisation. It fits two large flat television screens on each tea stall connected with Videocon DTH Integrated television screen, by which the company gets marketing slot in place of the television set. The webcam and high speed internet provide mutual dialogue at most places. The predetermined audience wishing to ask questions is provided with a television crew together with outdoor broadcasting van linked with live satellite uplinking facility.

15 to 20 questions are asked in a session. This programme broadcasts Modi's authorised website live. When Narendra Modi is linked to the people through the hi-fi technique and speaks to people over a cup of tea, they feel connected to him directly. Gaining popularity can be learnt from none else but Narendra Modi.

□

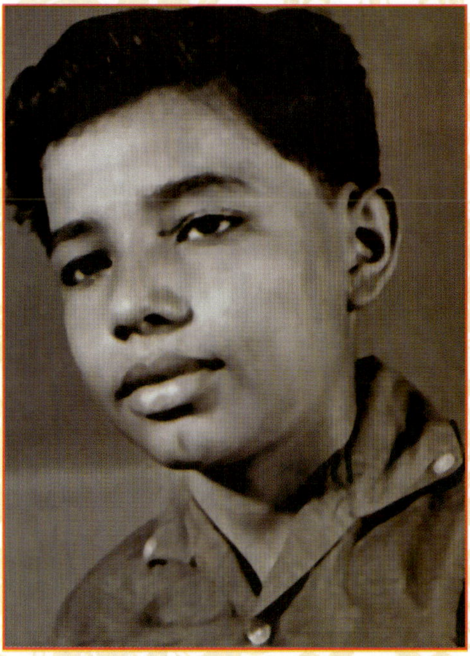

Child Narendra Modi.

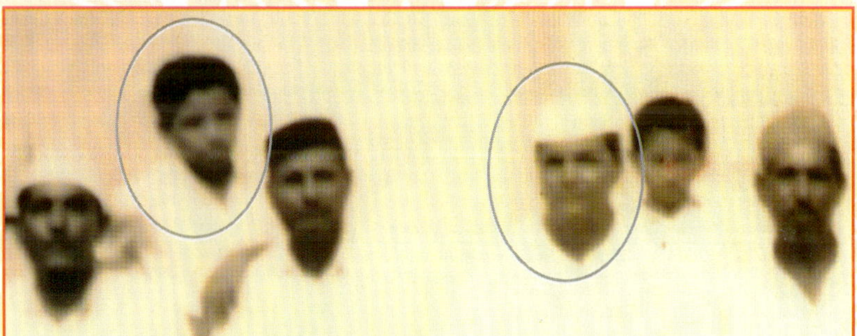

Narendra Modi with his father Shri Damodardas and other family members.

Father Shri Damodardas Modi.

With affectionate Maa Smt. Heeraben.

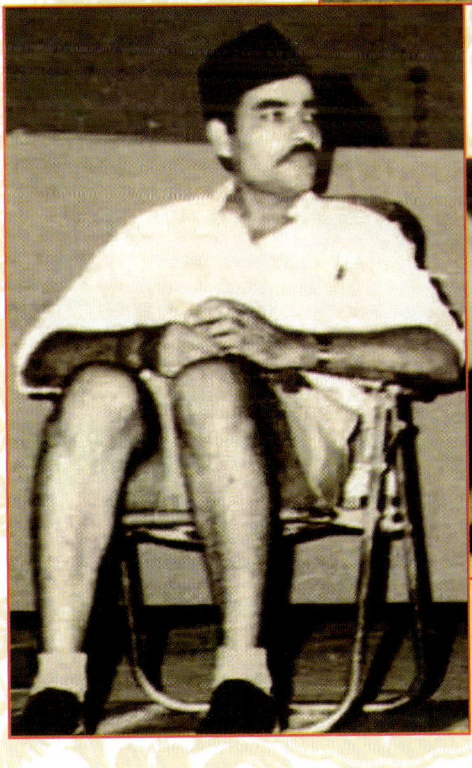

Adolescent Narendra Modi.

On the bank of Kailash Mansarovar.

In a cheerful mood.

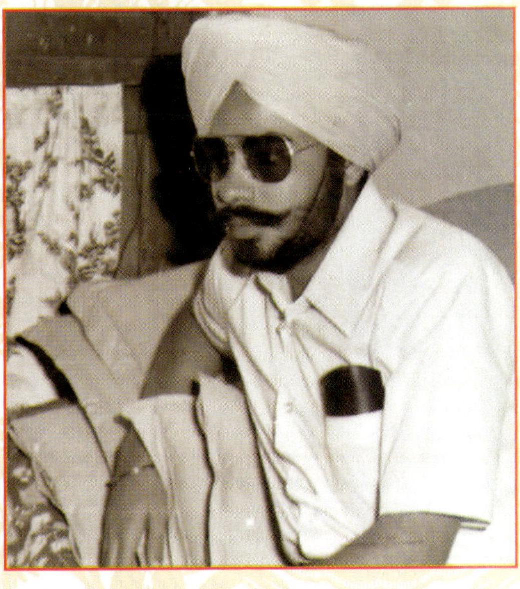

During emergency disguised as a Sikh youth.

The launch of Narendra Modi's book 'Patraroop Sriguruji', by Shri Balasaheb Deoras, the third Sarsanghchalak.

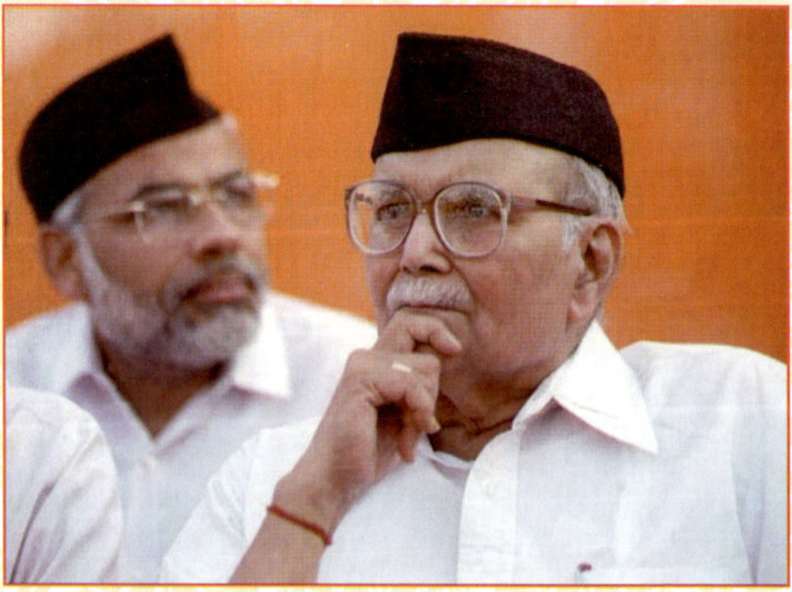

With Prof. Rajju Bhaiya, the fourth Sarsanghchalak.

In dialogue with Shri K.S. Sudarshan, the fifth Sarsanghchalak.

Honouring Shri Mohanrao Bhagwat, the present Sarsanghchalak.

With Shri Lakshmanrao Inamdar (Vakil Saheb) who played a vital role in moulding Narendra Modi's personality.

Common man Narendra Modi listening to a speech in a rally.

Hoisting flag at Lal Chowk at the conclusion of the Ekta Yatra.

With Sangh officials of Gujarat state when Narendra Modi was a Pracharak.

With Shri Atal Bihari Vajpayee, former Prime Minister.

With Shri Lal Krishna Advani, former Deputy Prime Minister.

With Dr. A.P.J. Abdul Kalam, former President of India.

With Smt. Sushma Swaraj, Union Minister of External affairs.

With Shri Arun Jaitley, Union Finance & Defence Minister.

With Shri Shivraj Singh Chauhan, Chief Minister of Madhya Pradesh.

With Shri Manohar Parrikar, Union Defence Minister.

With Dr. Raman Singh, Chief Minister of Chhattisgarh.

With Shri Rajnath Singh, Union Home Minister.

With Shri Amit Shah, National President of the BJP.

Discovering the world over a cup of tea.

Not only a good writer, but also an earnest reader.

Occasion of launching of Shri Narendra Modi's Hindi book 'Setubandh'.

Doing Pranayam and exercise to stay fit.

In dialogue with the future of India – the tiny tots.

Serving food to students.

Presenting a sewing machine to empower the economically weaker women.

Honouring an elderly woman.

With troops on India-Pakistan border in Gujarat.

Paying respect to the women.

With super star Shri Amitabh Bachchan.

With melody queen
Smt. Lata Mangeshkar.

With world renowned yoga exponent Swami Ramdev.

With world renowned spiritual leader HH Dalai Lama.

With Jagadguru Shankaracharya Jayendra Saraswati.

With HH Sri Sri Ravishankar.

Shri Narendra Modi taking oath as the Prime Minister at Rashtrapati Bhavan on 26.5.2014.

Shri Narendra Modi taking charge of the Prime Minister of India, at South Block in New Delhi.

PM Narendra Modi is greeted by Bhutan's PM Tshering Tobgay.

PM Narendra Modi with USA President Barack Obama at White House.

PM Narendra Modi with PM of Japan Shinzo Abe.

PM Narendra Modi with President of China Xi Jinping and his wife Peng Liyuan.

PM Narendra Modi with Hillary and Bill Clinton.

Prime Minister Narendra Modi with Russian President Vladimir Putin, Brazilian President Dilma Rousseff, Chinese President Xi Jinping, and South African President Jacob Zuma at sixth BRICS summit.

PM Narendra Modi with PM of Nepal Sushil Koirala.

Prime Minister Narendra Modi with Australian Prime Minister Tony Abott.

PM Narendra Modi beating a melodious tune on drum and playing a Japanese flute during his visit to Japan.

PM Narendra Modi addressing the 69th United Nations General Assembly at the U.N. HQs in New York on 27.9.2014.

PM Narendra Modi addressing the Officers and Jawans of the Indian Armed Forces at Siachen Base Camp during his surprise visit to Siachen on Deepawali 2014.

PM Narendra Modi launching the 'Saansad Adarsh Gram Yojana'.

Prime Minister Narendra Modi launching the 'Pradhan Mantri Jan-Dhan Yojana'.

PM Narendra Modi releasing the 'Virat Purush Nanaji', collection of the writings of Rashtrarishi Nanaji Deshmukh.

Prime Minister Narendra Modi launching 'Clean India Campaign'.

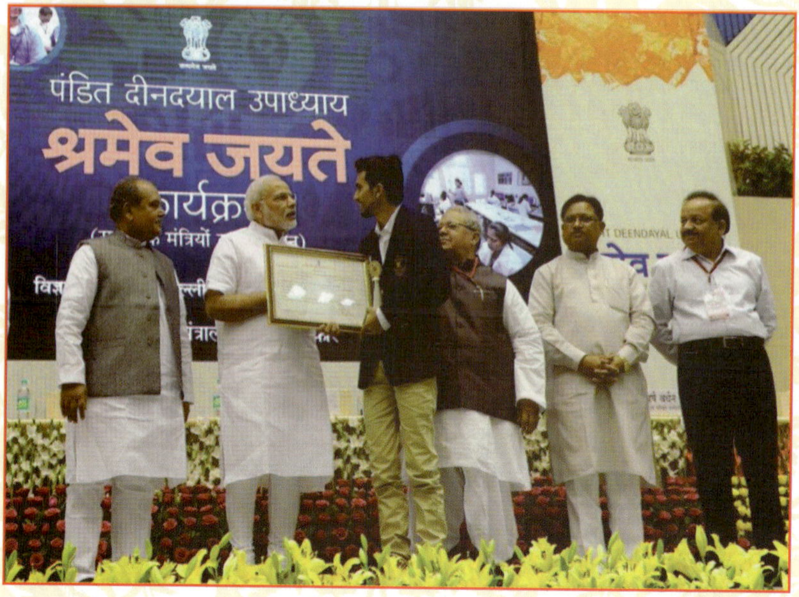

PM Narendra Modi inaugurated the 'Pandit Deendayal Upadhyay Shramev Jayate Karyakram' organised by the Labour Ministry.

PM Narendra Modi congratulates scientists at the Indian Space Research Organisation (ISRO) mission control centre in Bengaluru after the successful orbital insertion of Mangal – the country's Mars Orbiter Mission spacecraft.

One Hundred Steps of Development

Leads in Poverty Elimination

1. Gujarat stands at first place in poverty elimination programme for the last ten years continuously under the Prime Minister's 20-point programme.

Per Capita Income at ₹ 75,115

2. The per capita income in the state has jumped four times from 19,283 in 2001 to 75,115 in 2011.

Leads in Employment

3. Gujarat leads the other states in providing employment to the youth. According to a Government of India report, Gujarat has the least rate of unemployment, which stands at 1 percent.

₹ 13,000 Crore Aid to 85 Lakh Poor People

4. A direct aid of ₹ 13,000 crore has been disbursed in the state to 85 lakh beneficiaries through the poor welfare fairs.

₹ 21,000 Crore Aid to Fishermen

5. The ₹ 11,000 crore scheme has been completed for fishermen, and another new package of ₹ 21,000 crore has been put into operation.

₹ 40,000 Crore to Tribals

6. The tribal welfare scheme has been completed with ₹ 17,000 crore and a new package of ₹ 40,000 crore has been put into operation.

₹ 25,000 Crore to Urban Poor

7. ₹ 13,000 crore scheme for the urban poor has been completed and a new package of ₹ 25,000 crore has been put into operation.

Self-employment to Thirty Lakh Women

8. Under the Mission Mangalam, 30 lakh women have been given self-employment through 2.25 lakh Sakhi Mandals, in which an amount of ₹ 1,700 crore has been invested.

Free Stamp Duty for Women

9. Women are not charged stamp duty if they buy property. Until now, 12 lakh women have taken its benefit, amounting to a total of ₹ 440 crore.

Samras Award to 250 Women Sarpanchs

10. 250 women sarpanchs have been given the Mahila Samras Gram Award (the women elected unanimously for the panchayat) together with a grant for development to the gram panchayat.

22 Lakh Houses in 11 Years

11. In the past 11 years, 22 lakh houses (averaging 2 lakh houses per annum) have been constructed, while in the preceding 40 years, a total of 12 lakh houses were made (averaging only 30,000 units per annum).

Piped Water to 74 Percent Houses

12. 74 percent of the houses in the state are supplied piped water for drinking.

Piped Gas to Seven Lakh Houses

13. Seven lakh houses in the state are supplied gas by pipeline.

Maximum Literacy Rate

14. In the past decade, the rate of literacy has jumped a high rate of 10.6 percent. Women literacy rate has jumped by 13 percent from 58 percent in 2001 to 71 percent in 2011.

Cent Percent Enrolment in School

15. Cent percent enrolment was achieved in admission, and the rate of dropout fell from 22 percent to mere 2 percent.

Qualitative Improvement in Education

16. Focus was turned to qualitative improvement in education.

Five Times Rise in Engineering and Management Seats

17. The number of seats in engineering and management has risen five times. There were 22,535 seats in 2001 which have gone up to 1,23,592 in 2011.

Increased Number of Colleges and Universities

18. The number of colleges rose from 442 in 2001 to 1,762 in 2011. 31 new universities were constituted in which are included 11 special universities.

Security Power University

19. The first security power university has been set up in the state, the first time in the country.

Forensic University

20. The only forensic science university has been set up in Gujarat, the only one in the world.

First Petroleum University

21. The first petroleum university of the country has been set up in Gujarat.

Engineering Fee at ₹ 1500

22. There are 19 government engineering colleges in which the fee is just ₹ 1,500.
23. An increase in medical seats by 4000 has enabled the Gujarati children to study at home.
24. Distance education programme has been launched through satellite spectrum.

25. First in the country, the Government of India has delivered 36 megahertz satellite transponder.
26. Under the SCOPE, three lakh students have been trained in the English language.
27. Under the Empower programme, 1000 students have been given training in computer in each tehsil.
28. Under CM fellowship, the youths are empowered for commendable contribution.

18 Lakh Children in Sports Mahakumbh

29. For sports development, a sports university has been set up. In 2011, more than 18 lakh students took part in the games. The Chess competition too was launched.

Benefit to 33 Lakh Patients

30. 33 lakh patients were treated under 108 emergency health service. Of these, 11 lakh were connected with emergencies in pregnancy and delivery.

Gujarat Medical Services Corporation

31. The Gujarat Medical Services Corporation has been set up recently to provide almost free generic medicines and diagnostic services.

Medical Expenses for BPL Beneficiaries at two Lakh

32. Under the Chief Minister Amritam Yojana, the BPL families are given a grant of ₹ 2 lakh towards medical expenses.

Mother and Child Care

33. Welfare of mother and child is looked after through the schemes like E-Mamta, Chiranjivi, Balsakha, Fortified Food, Khilkhilahat Van, etc.
34. 69 lakh deliveries are undertaken in hospital in the PPP-based Chiranjivi scheme.
35. The infant mortality rate has dropped from 62 per thousand in 2001 to 44 in 2011.
36. The mother mortality rate has fallen from 202 per thousand in 2001 to 148 in 2011.

37. Under school health examination scheme, the health of 1.5 crore children was examined.
38. Effort is being made to make Gujarat free from leprosy and polio.
39. Gutka has been completely banned in order to prevent cancer and other perilous illnesses in the youth.
40. The Nirmal Gram award has been given to 4,281 Gujarat villages.
41. The rate of agricultural development was 10.8 percent in the previous decade, compare it with only 2.3 percent national average.

One Lakh Crore from Agricultural Produce

42. The agricultural income increased seven times from ₹ 14,000 crore in 2001 to 98,000 crore in 2011.
43. Milk production increased by 66 percent.
44. It is leading in cotton production. Cotton production jumped from 23 lakh bales to 123 lakh bales in the last six years, which is as much as 465 percent.
45. The Krishi Mahotsav were held from 2005, the purpose of these month-long programmes is to acquaint the farmers with modern and scientific methods of farming.
46. Four lakh new agricultural connections have been installed in the last ten years, as compared with a total of 6.3 lakh connections in the preceding forty years.
47. Farmers were given 42 lakh farm soil health cards.

Construction of Animal Hostels

48. 1.2 crore cattle were treated in 30,000 animal health camps. The country's first animal hostel was constructed. 112 animal diseases were treated.
49. The area under irrigation increased from 108 lakh hectare to 145 lakh hectare, showing an increase of 37 lakh hectare.
50. Seven lakh hectare area was provided with dripping irrigation and sprinkler irrigation.
51. 65 lakh water harvesting structures were created which included boribunds, agricultural ponds and barrages.

Water Table Improved, Narmada Water Supplied to Dry Lands

52. The dark zone was removed to supply electricity in 57 tehsils.
53. There is no equivalent in the country where the underground water table has increased from 3 metres to 13 metres.
54. The Narmada water was supplied to the dry Kutch land and thirsty land of Saurashtra and north Gujarat.
55. The Narmada flood water was filled in the Saurashtra dams under the SAUNI scheme.
56. Continuous increase of 10 percent or more was maintained in three sectors of agriculture, industry and service sectors.

Vibrant Includes 100 Countries, Investment of 21 Lakh Crore

57. In the fifth Vibrant Mahotsav in 2011, agreements ranging to ₹ 21 lakh crore were undertaken, in which more than 100 countries participated.
58. Gujarat became the auto hub with the arrival of Tata Motors, Maruti and Ford.
59. The annual average development rate of tourism stands at 10 percent, while it is 16 percent in Gujarat.
60. The state contributes 60 percent in ship building.
61. To benefit 18 districts out of 26, a 565-km-long dedicated freight corridor has been undertaken on the either side of which is being taken the work of massive industrial corridor ranging up to 150 km.
62. 13 special investment regions will be set up with the world's best facilities.
63. The process of Dholera Sir has been started, which is two times as big as that of Shanghai.
64. In the coming times, the Gift City would become the financial hub.
65. All districts connected with G Swan will create Asia's largest fibre network.
66. In the interlinking of rivers, ten districts of the state have been included.
67. The water grid has been spread over 1900 km.
68. It is the only state with statewide gas grid over 2200 km.

69. Roads are being constructed right up to the remote rural areas, which include Kisan path, Pragati path, Vikas path, Pravasi path and Gaurav path.
70. Under the Jyotigram scheme, all villages are supplied round the clock electricity, seven days a week.
71. The capacity for electricity generation has increased from 9600 MW in 2007 to 15,750 MW in 2012, which is as good as two times in only five years.
72. Electricity generation is two times of the national average.
73. The height of the Narmada dam was raised up to 121.92 metres. The Narmada river and canal have been used to produce 1,450 MW hydroelectricity.

Sardar the Highest

74. The world's highest statue of Sardar Patel will be installed near Sardar Sarovar dam, called Statue of Unity.
75. The first riverfront project of the country is the Sabarmati Riverfront Project in Ahmedabad.
76. The Ghogha-Dahej ferry service is under execution.
77. The BRTS project has been successfully executed winning a number of international awards.
78. The Panchamrit framework has led to development in energy, water, knowledge, human resource and service.
79. While maintaining the revenue overload, the 11th Five-Year Plan was raised to 1,11,111 crore rupees.
80. The 12th Five-Year Plan was made for 3,00,000 crore rupees, which is three times of the previous one.

Seven New Districts, 20 New Tehsils

81. Announcement was made for seven new districts and 20 new tehsils in a bid of decentralization.
82. The tehsil government was activated in order to give more powers to the local administration.
83. The panchayati raj institutions were strengthened, each gram panchayat was given the right to spend up to five lakh rupees under its discretion.
84. The villages without any social dispute or crime were declared Tirthgram with a grant of 2 lakh rupees. At present, there are 1,075 Tirthgrams.

85. The gram panchayats elected unanimously were given the Samras gram panchayat award with an award of ₹ 3-5 lakh development aid. Recently, 8,428 villages have been declared as such.
86. To hasten the justice process, the evening courts have been established, which is a unique step.
87. The Swagat Online in the Chief Minister office has helped to settle disputes of consumers very quickly. Until now 2.25 lakh cases have been settled. The UN has given the public service award for it.
88. The land documents are computerized under e-dhara.
89. The NA planning and application is a transparent process.
90. The golden jubilee of Gujarat was celebrated on a grand scale, under which were held Gujarat Mahotsav, Gujarat Khel Mahakumbh, Shatranj Mahotsav, etc.
91. The one-year-long Swami Vivekananda 150 Jayanti Mahotsav was launched, and this year was declared as the Youth Power Year.
92. The presents and gifts given to the Chief Minister were publicly auctioned and the proceeds were deposited in the girl education fund.
93. The Supreme Court appreciated the state for public distribution scheme and TP scheme.
94. Each fortnight – one award, aggregating to over 250 national and international awards.
95. The UN award was given for VASMO, Swagat and disaster management, and the Commonwealth award was given for VASMO and disaster management.
96. The country's first climate change department was constituted.
97. It is a state to receive 3,500 crore worth of carbon credit, having a share of 17.28 percent in the country.
98. The rooftop solar power production policy has been launched in cities.
99. The canal top solar power production has been launched on the Narmada river.
100. Near Patan, Asia's largest solar park has been constructed with a capacity of 500 MW.

□

How Gujarat Succeeded

Today 'Gujarat model of development' is a favourite topic of discussion. It comprises economic, social and government model of the state. This topic has to be understood in the right perspective.

Gujarat is a progressive state and is on the march so far as development and administrative matters are concerned. In the past few years, progress has been achieved in all areas, especially rapid development has taken place in Kutch and Bhuj. Recently, these areas witnessed devastation due to the earthquake, but now everybody is amazed at the level of development reached here.

You can ask anybody and he would confirm that Narendra Modi possesses quite different qualities when compared with other leaders and chief ministers. When you meet him, your consciousness will say that he is different from others. When you rise above that consciousness, and glance at the administration, government machinery and history of independent Gujarat, you will find a number of factors which stand out and make Narendra Modi a unique leader. The former leaders possessed power and patience, but he is the Chief Minister who has ability, desire to work, ambition and sentiments. We have had several leaders in the past who possessed ambitions and aspirations and capabilities, but the people of Gujarat can see today that he alone possesses all these aspirations, desires and capability. He is imaginative and insightful, and all these qualities present him a definite personality. We shall try to glance at his positive qualities, which distinguish him from others.

Narendra Modi is a leader who goes out to people. There are few leaders in India with this capability. It has been seen that pregnant women wish to have a child like Narendra Modi, so they visit him to touch his feet and seek his blessings. A large number of people wish from the core of their hearts that Narendra Modi should be the CM again. This is not a political pressure on people, but Narendra Modi has succeeded to establish sentimental and emotional relations with the common man. His fans comprise of the people of cities and villages, and include youths, adolescents, elderly and women. The people of India living in other countries appreciate his style of working.

His entire time is devoted in thinking how better development can be achieved in the state. There is an instance. Just one month prior to the declaration of Gujarat Vidhan Sabha elections, he wished to go to Switzerland. His chief objective was to invite that country for investment in the state. In fact, most of the political leaders have an aim, that is to come back to power any how, and they set down to prepare for it one year in advance. But, for him, having foreign investment in the state was a more important work even in the election year.

The main factor of success in Gujarat is his unique way of thinking about problems. He looks at a problem in a different perspective, and tries to identify it. He invests his time to look at the problems closely, because he understands that if a problem is understood well, half of the solution would be automatically arrived at. He listens to any matter put across him very seriously and then sets down to find its solution. He does not take any superficial step, nor does he go for any shortcut method. He imagines for the complete change from bottom to top and imagines for the future, and thinks out solution with a long-term perspective. After that he works on the roadmap which comprises his objectives, goals and procedure, and in the end, he works on the process of implementation. He does not only like a real process and representative, but also a real, reasonable man. He has the capability to adopt others' good qualities and monitor others. He may not be a management graduate, but his tact, intelligence and novel style of working are topics of teaching in management schools.

Narendra Modi is a talented individual. He can think over any project and can implement it in the whole state in a minimum time. He is quite curious to know the outcomes too. The interlinking of rivers is being actively thought over in the rest of the country, but he has already linked rivers in the state successfully; that means, the rivers that had run dry for years are full of water today. In the same way, the 300-kilometre-long canal 'Sujalam-Sufalam Yojana' was formulated, leading to availability of water in the water-thirsty areas. This scheme has led to supply of water over 56,599 square kilometre area. Also, 12,621 transformers have been supplied in over 18,000 villages, and under the Jyotigram scheme, 9,681 small villages have been linked with electricity in a period of 30 months, connecting the entire area with water and gas grid. All villages have been linked with broadband under the E-gram Vikas Gram scheme. All these instances show the quick implementation of projects.

Despite his capability to launch multi-million projects and imagine the outcomes, he does not overlook the small outcomes and local technology. He says that science should be worldwide, but technology should be local. In the area of water, he propagated the boribunds, which is a local technique. A boribund means a sack filled with stone and pebble in order to prevent the flow of water. In the seminar for Vibrant Gujarat, he glanced over global specialisation and encouraged and respected the experiences and experiments of the local farmers. He also approves the recommendations and suggestions by the government servants. He respects the views and suggestions forwarded by common man, who can send these to him through e-mails and letters.

He is a decision maker who carries a process right until its outcome. He does not link administrative foresight with political needs. Under his way of politics, he reminds of the administrative decisions and keeps his focus on deeds, and these things help him to raise Gujarat as an efficient and developed state. Several institutions working under the Gujarat Government have obtained ISO certification, which in fact is not a state requirement.

Narendra Modi belongs to a backward caste, so he started work in the backward areas. In his youth, in the capacity of a common man, he confronted different types of problems, the most serious of which pertained to water and electricity. Now he has got an opportunity to solve them, and is making efforts to solve them through proper planning and systematic way.

Narendra Modi vociferously opposes the view where more attention is paid to the development of infrastructure and industrial units, but the backward areas and departments are neglected. What can be a bigger problem than this? When he launches the Jyotigram scheme in the state, he never thinks that this belongs to a particular area or department, rather he links it with all areas and departments. He launches projects for the people facing problems, such schemes include Van Bandhu scheme, Sagarkhedu scheme, poor prosperity scheme, and others. These schemes do not limit themselves to only certain areas. Narendra Modi works for all the people living in the state.

While maintaining good relations with the people, he is of the view that they should be included in the development projects. The facts of state's success includes 3,00,000 water harvesting structures, Krishi fairs and Kanya Kelvani Yatra and so on. He has transformed the government schemes into large movements in order to encourage people's participation in them.

He states that least administration is the best administration, so he has made use of information technology in order to simplify and enable the administrative process. This state was nowhere in IT and e-governance areas in 2001, but today, it leads the rest in e-governance. This benefit has accrued, not to IT, but to people. When it is used for the common man, his life becomes comfortable and easy. In all important offices of the state, one-day governance centres have been created where people can get their certificates and documents quickly. Now he is busy in connecting all gram panchayats with computer and broadband connectivity. E-governance results into transparency in administration.

Narendra Modi states that his government does not run of its free will. Our progress is due to social reform, and whatever reform occurs is due to the policy, because policies are formulated keeping the needs of people and society. Under these goals, the officers are clearly instructed that the system should continue to be transparent and uniform, and right decisions should lead to everybody's development.

He looks at the applications of common man the way they should be. He attaches importance to resolution of problems under the Swagat programme. This quality of his sends a message to all officers and people. It is not dependent on the officers to settle a problem, rather it is the system which has to decide how to solve a problem, and this is done using the latest techniques. The essence of all this says that only the Chief Minister is not responsible to the people, rather the entire cabinet, officers and others linked with the problem are responsible, and they should be held amenable.

The organisation of fairs and festivals on the occasion of Navratri, Makar Sankranti, Sharad Purnima, Taranetar and the like are not meant for only tourism purposes; it is to mark the interest of the youths towards these fairs and festivals, especially those who live abroad. The stepwells that had fallen in non-use long back have been revived as Jalmandirs in order to make them places of attraction.

Narendra Modi is an individual who links himself with all subjects concerning the state and people. He wishes to motivate all people and give them insight. He starts with a new technique by insight. In the last seven years, he has thought out solutions to the problems which were considered to be unthinkable not only in the state but in the whole country.

He had started the rehabilitation work by including different committees and officers to work on the earthquake-affected houses. His effort revolves round sentimental utilization of manpower rather than the officers bound in rules and regulations. Other instances display that he has taken the lead in making the justice administration quick, video conferencing with prisoners and courts, organisation of evening courts, women courts, different committees for irrigation and potable water, Chiranjivi scheme for pregnant women belonging to BPL families, roaming ration card, health card and the like.

It has been mostly observed that most of the ministers often indulge in blame-game and prejudice, but Narendra Modi is quite distant from these negative traits. He enjoys an honest and truthful image. He keeps his relatives away from individual benefits. His personality can be a prohibitive trait in the personality of a common man, but it is only a slight part for a politician and society.

As per the rules, all gifts given to the Chief Minister have to be deposited in the state treasury, or have to be auctioned. However, the former Chief Ministers thought it better to keep this rule only on paper. In the history of the state over the preceding 41 years, 13 Chief Ministers had deposited a mere 4.55 lakh rupees in the treasury under this rule. Compare it with Narendra Modi who deposited all these gifts in the treasury regularly. Not only this, he found a unique way of utilizing this treasure. He devoted this amount for encouraging the Kanya Kelvani scheme. As a result, people donated him money worth millions in this account. From the year 2003-04, an amount of 17 crore rupees has been received as gift to him.

The Modi Government was assigned with an important task to transform the working methodology. The reflection camps held in the beginning discussed that the errors committed with bona fide intentions can be forgiven. This helped the officers skilled in quick decision-making, they now felt confident. The bureaucracy too started to approve projects. The officers who are involved in their projects and also assist in the projects of other departments, derive pleasure from it. The officers are motivated that all these projects are meant for the welfare of the people, and many tasks are undertaken without the officers' leadership and government investment, people participate and contribute in them.

Narendra Modi is of the view that grateful and contented employees express pleasure and satisfaction for customers, clients and others. The government has started the Karmayogi campaign in the state to enhance professional efficiency of officers and employees, with a purpose that these traits become evident in their own personal lives too. The Karmayogi campaign provides training in working efficiency, pranayam and yoga.

How decisions are taken in development projects and their work plan, can be seen best in the cabinet meeting held every Wednesday. This meeting is held from 10 to 12 in the morning or 12 to 2 in the afternoon. You might think what use is this two-hour meeting for the development of the entire Gujarat and its various problems. Narendra Modi has chalked out a magnificent system for it. On the Monday preceding the cabinet meeting, the Chief Minister, cabinet ministers and officers meet the people, and on Tuesday, members of Parliament, Legislative Assembly and other representatives are approached for information about the whole state. After this, in the cabinet meeting on Wednesday, different ministers have to bring details of the problems and development projects under their respective departments.

The Chief Minister himself attends these meetings and asks for details. If some work is found pending, explanations are asked and relevant details are summoned. If a minister tells about certain problem in his department and its solution, then the Chief Minister intimates the concerned secretary to make effort for its solution. Not only this, if the assistance of the Chief Minister himself is needed, it is rendered too.

Gujarat's development gained momentum due to these efforts; also, this system became an example of transparency in administrative work. The cabinet ministers and other leaders who have been in more than one government accept that there is a great difference in the working methodology of the former governments and that of Modi. Ever since its coming to power, the Modi Government has undertaken large-scale reforms in the government and working methodology of the administration, the positive outcome of which can be seen today.

To minimize political differences in the villages, the Samras Gram scheme was considered. The gram panchayats falling under this scheme have been encouraged and rewarded too.

The administration model constructed by Narendra Modi is not on the basis of appeasement but on the basis of work. When it comes to stabilizing the rates of electricity, he turns to the electric regulatory commission for professional advice. He did not bow before the farmer movement. In return, he made them believe that he understands their needs well. Farmers need only water, and not electricity. In the years to come, he started the surface water scheme called Sujalam Sufalam. Now, farmers can get water for irrigation at a small price, because the water level has gone up. Encroachment has been removed to a large extent in the urbanisation drive. The electricity thieves have been caught. Now more people have applied for electricity connections, but no movement or blood-shedding has taken place anywhere. People are aware that he has come for a long time. A common man thinks that he is different from others in terms of his professional approach, individual truthfulness and determination. His resolve and capability have won him fans not only in the state but in the whole country. His being elected for the fourth time clearly shows that good administration is good politics. Not only this, his stable politics is the symbol of development-oriented politics.

□

Satyamev Jayate

Time : Quarter to eight, Date 27 February 2002, Place : one kilometre from Godhra railway station. Under a well-planned conspiracy, Gujarat was pushed into a terrible and barbaric situation. 58 innocent Hindus, including women and children, were cruelly burnt in the S 6 coach of Sabarmati Express. These passengers had been killed so brutally that humanity shivered; the description of this beastly act is just beyond words.

In reaction to this demonic act, riots broke out, in which a number of innocent Muslims and Hindus were killed. Narendra Modi tried his best to contain these riots. Despite his earnest efforts, the so-called proud secular powers, the foreign-funded NGOs and media pointed fingers at Narendra Modi ceaselessly and blamed him in every possible manner in order to bring to the fore a flood of false and deformed reports of news. This occurrence was attempted to be looked from the deformed mentality of false secularism. These secular forces did not try to establish peace in the state, rather they conspired to further inflame the sentiments and spread the riots, while Narendra Modi was struggling to establish peace and goodwill in the state. He delivered a heartrending statement in the Vidhan Sabha for the sake of peace. He said:

"I don't understand how degraded we have become. We wish to see the caste even in an incident like death. Death has no caste, the colour of blood does not change. But now, all norms are being given up to specify the colour of blood. What will five crore people of Gujarat expect from us? There is the election contest to settle political scores. You will get a lot of opportunities to explain to the masses and do politics with their changed minds. However, at present, Gujarat is undergoing a time of calamity where forbearance is being measured by the deaths of the innocents. Is this time necessary for such politics? There is a need to spare a thought for this.

"Whether the incident pertains to Godhra or after it, it is not at all reasonable for any civilized society. It is a blot for the entire humanity. It is no incident by which anyone can go out with a raised head. There is no difference of opinion in it. However, the sinful atrocities committed in Godhra or thereafter should not be allowed to come to the situation in which some people commit the error and we all spring to our feet to use a foul language for our Gujarat. Is all this justified?

"What do all these incidents show? Rise above the petty politics and think over. This trouble pertains to all of us, and we all have to resolve the matter together. The thing to think over is the problem that no such effort is being undertaken here. There is some effort in which determined efforts are being made to impede the development and advancement of Gujarat towards progress. This government is resolved to maintain peace at any cost.

"What is this mentality? Is the truth only our vote-bank politics? Where has our vote-bank politics taken us in the fifty years? We have not set at rest despite the dismemberment of the country, we must not forget about this history. Therefore, now the time has come when we have to decide how we can move forward defending the Constitution and values in the atmosphere of determined peace.

"I wish to say that this contemplation should rise above politics. The thought of Gujarat's future should be undertaken rising above political tricks. We should worry about tomorrow's Gujarat. Its good cannot be achieved when we keep an eye on the chair. I have no hunger for power. I have never dreamt of power. I have no interest in treading the corridors of power. The people have assigned me the responsibility of ruling Gujarat, therefore, I am resolved for the state's all-round development and welfare. I have never thought of wrapping politics in selfish desire for power, nor has it ever shown in my conduct."

Gujarat squeezed itself out of the riotous situation. The false propaganda of the so-called secular powers was turned down by the people. Even the Muslim community was not influenced by these false secularists and foreign-oriented NGOs, and all people expressed their trust in Narendra Modi.

The editor of *Manushi*, Madhu Purnima Kishwar conducted an interview with Zafar Sareshwala, a well-known trader of Gujarat. A part of the interview is being reproduced here, which explains the authenticity of Narendra Modi and his non-communal views.

Zafar Sareshwala belongs to Sunni Vora community. His family arrived from Saudi Arabia about 250 years ago and settled down here. The Sunni Voras are sometimes taken for Daudi Voras. They form only a small part of the Muslim community. In fact, the members of the Sunni Vora are spread over the whole of Gujarat in significant numbers. This is an orthodox Muslim community and is linked with small and medium size industries, and they have achieved much success in these. Most of the *Madrasas* in Gujarat are run by this community. Maulana Vastanavi, an Islamic scholar, is a Sunni Vora. People talk only of Deoband, but quite an old *madrasa* of Sunni Vora community is located at Dabhel, which was set up about 100 years ago.

Zafar says: "The people who talk of 2002 riots forget that these were the result of several riots that took place earlier. Very terrible riots had taken place after partition in 1969 in Ahmedabad, in which over 5,000 Muslims were killed. However, there were no 24-hour television channels then, and no detailed and correct information was available then. A small incident focussing on a cow occurred, and it took the form of a terrible occurrence. At that time, the Congress was in power under the leadership of Hitendrabhai Desai and Indira Gandhi was in power at the centre.

"Our office and factory, etc. had been burnt down during the 1969 riots. The area police station was located at the Relief Road. Right in front of the police station are located a mosque and shops belonging to Muslims. This mosque and shops were burnt down. When Indira Gandhi toured these riot-affected areas, she visited this place too. I can remember that clearly. I was five years old then. My grandfather was there too. Indira Gandhi got down the car and asked him how the mosque and shops could have been burnt when the police station was only 40 metres away. In the 1969 riots, the Muslims had been massacred in a preplanned manner.

"Leave alone sentence, no one charge sheet was given. Anyone can see the report submitted by Jagmohan. The entire community had been annihilated, no one had survived. Why are those riots not talked about? 5000 Muslims had been killed in 1969 in Ahmedabad alone. What happened to those 5000 families, no one talks about that.

"After that in 1985, even more terrible riots took place. This followed by several small and big riots over months. My factory had been burnt down then, and my house was in no better condition. At that time, Madhavrao Solanki was in power in Gujarat and Rajiv Gandhi at the centre. From 1985 to 2002, people had come to conclude that riots were inevitable to recur every couple of months. The curfew remained in force for two days. When the riots occurred in 1987, Congress's Amarsinh Chaudhary was the Chief Minister. After that, Chimanbhai Patel of the Congress was in power in 1990 when the riots took place. This time again, my factory had been burnt down. My factory was burnt down again in 1992 when Chimanbhai Patel was still in power.

"All Dalit riots had taken the form of anti-Muslim riots. In almost all riots, our office and factory were burnt down, we had to face disrespect, because the police refused to record the FIR. No FIR was ever written those days which came from the Muslim community. Moreover, we had to face the wrath of the insurance companies. I can recall that when in 1992, I was doing well in business, my factory was burnt down. Our insurance amount was 1.50 crore, but the insurance company gave us only 9 lakh rupees as the damages claim. No one has ever written about these burnt down offices and factories belonging to the Muslims. Were all those insurance companies run by Narendra Modi?

"After each spate of riots, these were the same Hindus who helped us back to rehabilitation. I always say that had the Gujarati Hindu been communal, no Muslim would have ever survived here. But the Hindus are not communal.

"After the 2002 riots, we were fully devastated economically. Its cause was that we were linked to the share market. It is no trivial thing or a matter of joke for a Muslim to suffer losses who provides employment to 250 people. At least, 200 families got their livelihood from us. We could not come back to our former situation. Our bank guarantee was withdrawn. The banks refused to give loan to the Muslims. These national or private banks are not run by Narendra Modi.

"To improve our condition post-riots, I contacted the ICICI bank and offered my house as security for the loan. In the end, the relationship manager said to me, 'Zafar Bhai, this 'M' word has become a barrier in your work. There is an unwritten rule not to give loans to the M people.' He said that he possesses a list of all negative people with him. Had that list been framed by Narendra Modi? A number of Muslim-majority areas like Kalupur, Jamalpur and the like fall under this negative area list. If your house is located in this area, you are in the negative list. In Paldi, only Faiz Mohammad Society was kept in the negative list, because it is a Muslim society. When we are not eligible under all bank norms, we are not given loans.

"Our family business is centred at Ahmedabad. During the 2002 riots I was in England. We were once again confronted with a situation where we had to bear with a tremendous loss. It beset us with a feeling of despair and disappointment. There was no one to talk to us. I lived in Derby. During the riots, three Gujarati Muslims and two other people of Derby had been murdered near Himmatnagar. They were on a visit to their ancestral village. They did not know anything of the riots. They were confronted by the rioters on the night of 27 February. They were taken aside and killed mercilessly. One of them was Aswal who was my neighbour in England. They were shaken terribly. It appeared to me that something ought to be done. We decided to take the Gujarat Government to the International Court of Justice. At that time, Lal Krishna Advani, the then Home Minister, was about to visit England. I filed a case in England's high court against Advani pleading that this man ought not be given entry into the UK. I based my argument on the fact that Louis Farakhan, a fundamentalist of Nations of Islam was about to come to the UK but the government had not accorded him this permission.

"I pleaded if you can stop Farakhan from visiting England, then you must stop Advani too. My case was accepted by the high court at London. Advani went back from Spain itself because he had not to bear with this insult. This case was later rejected, but I had pleaded my side in this. My opposition was pointed not against Modi, but against the entire administration.

"I assigned my case to a reputed British company working in the legal field spending a large amount, and got a case prepared against Modi. As the things moved, it appeared to me as if I had become a hero. I grew restless. I asked myself what could happen if this case was taken to the International Court of Justice. At the most, this matter would make to the television, and I would become the poster boy of anti-Modi campaign. However, what would be its outcome? At that time, the peace talks between Egypt and Israel had begun by the US. Egypt was about to meet Sharon, this was facilitated by George Bush. The problem in Egypt had existed for the last 60 years, but what had they achieved? We were looking at the condition of Muslims all over the world. We had fought, we did what all was possible, but what did we get from all this? I was very disappointed to look at the future of the Egyptians. About three million people were shelterless and living in Lebanon, and their condition was pitiable. If we looked at the camps in Egypt, even the slums in Mumbai would look somewhat like the paradise.

"It appeared to me that these three million refugees would not have been living such a life had they adopted the method of dialogue. Now who would decide what the Egyptians and Gujarati Muslims should do? The critics, who sit in magnificent buildings in air-conditioned offices and cushioned chairs, do their job of criticising, and get a fat salary spread over seven digits. They do little work than sending e-mails during their course of work spanning 9 in the morning to 7 in the evening. We have to live in Gujarat, we have to live and die here, and we are being controlled by such people who are not at all needed to visit India even, they have not to walk the streets in Ahmedabad. They are hardly worried to take even a single positive step here. All Islamic people in the world are equal. My spell was shattered. I thought that the Muslims of Saudi Arabia are the Muslims of Saudi Arabia, and those of Pakistan are Pakistani Muslims. Let the matter of Gujarat go. Within India, the Muslims of Lucknow are Lakhnavi, they are hardly moved when a Muslim dies in Gujarat. The worst thing that I felt is that if you are a Muslim of Ahmedabad, those of Surat would not come to protect you.

"I went round every mosque in England to plead for financial aid to the riot-affected people. I used to tell them that they did not have to give me any money, they should send the money direct to the people working for the riot-affected people as they were in dire need of money. They had to reconstruct the houses. During this time, it appeared to me if we had degraded to the status of beggars – the entire Muslim community had degraded to that status. I heard about the refugee camps. I told my brothers that these refugee camps should be closed down, let not the Muslims turn into beggars.

"There was no reason I could not afford to live a life of luxury in England. I ran a financial company there. I worked in a team with a Sharia scholar, and formulated economic products as controlled by the UK Financial Services Authority. I started the first Islamic Equity Fund, it was the first of its kind in the world. I delivered lectures in London and Harvard on Islamic Institute of Finance. The entire concept of Islamic finance and Islamic fund was mine. I was proficient in this field. However, I saw that no one had any sympathy for giving anything to the dead or his family. They had nothing to do with them. The people were happy with their present lot. Their indifference hurt me greatly. People sat in their drawing rooms and partook of mutton and chicken and discussed Gujarat. This scenario was terrible. I said to myself that we didn't need such people. We did not need their pity. I had launched a battle against Modi. Now it could not be possible for me to return to Gujarat. At this time, it appeared to me that we could not solve the matters if we did not sit together and talk on any issue including those of the Muslims in Gujarat. I asked myself if I had to begin talking, why not start it with Modi.

"I talked about this to two-three chief Islamic scholars. At that time, we came to know that Modi was about to visit England on 17 August 2003 in connection with his first Vibrant Gujarat summit. I decided to go and ask him when he himself lived at Vadnagar and lived with Muslims, then what the difficulty was for him with them. I put forward this view before the Islamic scholars too. They said that if I had to resolve this matter, I would have to talk to Narendra Modi. If I did not need the solution, I could continue with my differences and conflicts. They warned me about several difficulties that I could have to bear. I asked them what they felt from the viewpoint of Islam. Guide me about the Quran and Hadis.

"They read out ten *ayats* (verses) from the Hadis and the Quran, explained them to me and said that I must talk for the sake of peace. One scholar explained Suleh Hudabiyah and asked my purpose behind all this. I said that I wanted the solution and nothing else. After the riots, the Muslims had lost all connections with the administration. If this severance continued over a long period, it would make you fully isolated. We have to run schools, *madrasas* and hospitals. We need to talk to the administration at every level. Whom will you talk to?

"This understanding scholar encouraged me, then I asked myself how the cat has to be belled. How could one man meet Modi? I had already started a campaign against him and had taken the matter to the International Court of Justice. Therefore, I contacted Mahesh Bhatt, my friend and a well-known director-producer-scriptwriter of Indian film industry. Mahesh Bhatt has been quite active about democratic rights, especially the rights of the Muslims in India. When riots occurred in Gujarat, he was the only person to reach there on the third day itself, and he stood firmly behind the Muslim community. He said that he wanted to see us all economically capable, and that he was ready to accord any assistance that might be needed.

"All these years, I found that Mahesh Bhatt is a very authentic person. I talked to him about my new viewpoint. I informed him that Modi was coming to England and that I wanted to talk to him. Bhatt said that I must meet Narendra Modi. All problems should be resolved through talks. Two World Wars have been fought, but the solution could be found only through dialogues.

"Later I asked him how I could meet Modi. He said that he could consider to help me if I wanted to meet him with a desire to find an adequate solution. A few days later, Bhatt rang me up and said that his friend, Rajat Sharma has close relations with Modi. I have talked to him. He has advised me to e-mail him about all this and send the message for a meeting.

"After this, I e-mailed to Rajat Sharma with several questions. I expressed regret on the entire unfolding of events. I wrote to him that I had got down to fight with Modi, but after having applied all the options, I find that no solution could be found this way. Of course, I had become a hero in the entire occurrence, but I did not want to be one. I wanted to meet Modi in this connection, and I asked what problem he had with the Muslims. Rajat Sharma forwarded this e-mail to Modi. I have come to know that Modi at first lost his cool, and then he said that it was Zafar who had launched a campaign against him and had led people against him. I also accept that he must have seen my family background and would come to conclude that I belong to a good family. He clearly said that he had no agenda and wanted to meet with me to talk about the 2002 riots.

"It is worth mentioning that when we met Modi, he was not a hero. People scowled at him, they called him Hitler. You must understand his background at that time. There was no question of prejudice expected from him. If we take note of today's condition, you can find a long queue of people who desire to meet him.

"The meeting was thus organised with him through Rajat Sharma. He informed us that Modi would reach London on 17 August. After that, I requested Rajat Sharma to accompany him. He asked me why he wanted to embroil me in this matter. I pleaded that it would be better for us. It was the reason that Rajat Sharma accompanied us to London.

"Modi invited us to meet in a hall of Bembley. I said to him I wanted to have a personal talk. He agreed to it. We met at five in the evening at Saint James Court, where he stayed. As soon as I met him, the newspapers carried the headlines that Zafar had taken a U-turn in the Modi matter. The people close to me commented on me adversely, earlier they considered me a hero.

"I said to my critics that they should find a way out to defeat him in the election if they opposed Modi so much. The truth remains that Modi had secured victory with a majority. People had voted him to power. If you are clever and insightful, then you should find ways to defeat him. If you cannot defeat him in election, and continue to oppose him sitting over there, and you don't want anyone to talk to him too, how you think the matter can be resolved.

"I published an entreaty and said that I welcomed Narendra Modi, because he had been elected as Chief Minister democratically. After this, a large number of people opposed me. All the newspapers criticized me sharply, and I turned from a hero into a villain. After my meeting with Modi, all people of the Muslim society in England turned their eyes from me, but I did not listen to them. I responded to my critics that it appeared to me the better path. I have no personal agenda. If Egypt can talk to Sharon, why then could I not talk to Narendra Modi? Why can't you see Modi as Sharon?

"Some Maulanas told me that we conduct dialogue even with our opponents and enemies, then Modi is our own man, he is one of us. We can catch his collar. These couple of Maulanas had the courage. Then we received guidance from the Quran and the Hadis, and I got the courage to speak my mind. Even if one hundred crore Muslims went against me, I would not be ready to leave this path of mine. I got 100 e-mails from all over the world criticising me scathingly. I had decided that it was my *jehad*.

"After I received a call from Mahesh Bhatt, we met Modi at five in the evening. Mahesh Bhatt said to me in his peculiar style, if I was going to meet Narendra Modi. He advised me that I need not meet him if I had not the courage to say that peace cannot prevail without justice. In response, I said that he is the Chief Minister, I did not know how long he would talk to me, or would not meet me at all, he might take my petition and ask me to come again. Mahesh Bhatt hoped that everything would settle amicably. He asked me to go and meet him. I went with my brother and a well-known Islamic scholar to meet Modi. Being a businessman, I can bear with scathing criticisms, however, the Maulanas were termed as *qafir*, and they were much disrespected later."

It is worth mentioning that Mahesh Bhatt has been seen in the media criticising Modi quite severely. At this, Madhu Kishvar said that she could not believe that it was he who had encouraged Zafar to talk to Modi. Due to this, to confirm Zafar's claim, I went and met him in Mumbai and tried to know if he had played a role to take forward the dialogue that was started with their historical meeting in August 2003. Mahesh Bhatt confirmed every single word that Zafar said. Thus, the first meeting of Zafar with Modi was presented.

"Let me show how I met Modi," Zafar continued with his talk. "When we entered the building, there was a storm in the heart, I was anxious about the outcome. I was much nervous. He shook hand with me and said in Hindi, 'Aao yaar.' (Come friend.) Thus, he lightened the atmosphere. There was a swing there, and Modi asked me sit on it with him. At that time, Modi was talking of Gujarat's dignity. I asked him if he had isolated me from the other Gujaratis. He asked how. I said that I hail to Ahmedabad and thus I am a confirmed Gujarati while he is from Vadnagar. Truly speaking, you are not that Gujarati. In response he said that I had force in my claim.

"Rajat Sharma and about eight-ten people were present in the meeting. I started my talk by saying that he had come for campaigning under Vibrant Gujarat aimed at economic development of Gujarat, but this development would remain incomplete without justice. The Western countries have sway over the world because they mete out justice to their citizens. The people of our country keep fighting with one another. I have not come here to talk only of Muslims. All people in our country are facing injustice. Peace cannot be established without justice.

"After this, Maulana Mansuri talked for long about the need for justice. A leading industrialist of Gujarat was also present in the meeting. He was looking at his wristwatch again and again. Modi had a number of appointments in the evening, but he did not ask him not to look at the time. Modi expressed a desire to be with us for as long as possible. He said that I could take as much time as I wanted, but I had to speak my mind out.

"After this we discussed the riots. We asked him what he was doing in the morning of 27 February 2002, and why he had not called the police and army and why he had not gone to Juhapura and refugee camp. What all questions the SIT asked him, we had asked all those questions there. Even then we were severely criticized, was it justified?

"Maulana Mansuri conducted himself quite harshly before Modi, but Modi behaved with him quite respectfully and talked to him. The Maulana was a scholar. Modi kept listening to him, which was unexpected from a Hindu hero. Maulana said that they would forget everything if justice was meted out. He asked for assistance, only which could settle everything else. We were demanding justice not only for the Muslims who constituted 15 percent of Gujarat's population, but for the Hindus too who were facing injustice. It was necessary that justice is given to everybody. It was maturity of Modi that he listened to the Maulana despite the force of victory in elections behind him. My younger brother, Talha too was present in the meeting. He had especially come from India for this purpose. Talha had witnessed all the events unfolding there, and had worked actively in the refugee camps. Maulana Mansuri stated, 'Look, nobody could reject this reality that more than 1000 Muslims have been murdered. I want to ask only this much that whatever good or bad happened from Palanpur to Vapi and Bharuch, whatever the problem was, whatever the discord between Hindus and Muslims was, all that is your responsibility. Therefore, we have the right to question you. How could such a terrible incident take place under your rule?'

"Modi responded to these questions peacefully. He said that it occurred in his rule and he had to mitigate it.

"We did not want anything from Modi. We did not want him to do this or that. At first, I asked him if he included the 60 lakh Muslims among the five crore Gujaratis when he talks about them. If yes, we could talk further. If he chose to say that he represented only the four and a half crore Hindus, then there was no sense in talking.

"Narendra Modi said to me that all of us were his, and there were no two opinions about it. We all were part of the five crore Gujaratis. He said, 'When I brought the Narmada water into the Sabarmati, did I stop it near Juhapura. When it reached Nehru Bridge, who was benefited the most?'

"After thoroughly listening to us, he said that many of my contentions were true, but some were exaggerations too. He said that he was quite new in administration in 2002. In fact, he had been made the Chief Minister just three and a half month before the riots. Then he told us which all steps he had taken in that challenging atmosphere prevailing after 27 February.

"We felt what he talked was solid. It was due to the reason that earlier, the riots under the Congress rule went on for months, and many of them scored higher number of deaths, while these riots had occurred only on three days.

"Modi had come to power in such unruly times. When it came to select his constituency for contesting election, he could not convince Haren Pandya to vacate a secure seat for him, and in the end, he fought election from Rajkot, and he was declared the winner on 26 February 2002. Perhaps the time was not right. He was to present the budget in the Vidhan Sabha the very next day. It was at this juncture that he had to face the terrible event of Godhra.

"He listened to my talk very attentively and patiently. We were impressed by him by the fact that all data was on his fingertips. It was our experience that no one ever heard of the problems facing the Muslims. We had witnessed the riots in 1969, 1985, 1987 and 1992, no Chief Minister had ever listened to us, and all these years, the Congress Chief Ministers were there. I can recall that after the riots in 1992, a delegation of the Muslim community went to meet Narsimha Rao. This delegation was made to wait for four days. He did not even consider this fact that the delegation had come to meet him during the month of Ramzan. I had refused to go and meet him. I said that I could not bear with this disrespect. Why should I bow before anybody for availing my Fundamental Rights? However, my uncle went to meet him. Rao did not meet us the day that was fixed for the appointment. Therefore, my uncle came back. He said that there was no sense in meeting a man who would not meet despite the appointment.

"Another delegation had to wait upon for four days, and it was given only two minutes' time on the fourth day. It was the condition of Muslims under the Congress rule. The people who went to meet him were all prosperous and well-to-do, they were leading Muslims, you can categorise them as Tata or Birla. I said to myself that I would not go to anybody with a begging bowl.

"Even for a moment we did not feel that we were talking to a Chief Minister. I am not the kinds who could be bought and sold. Modi asked us to talk of that day. He asked me if any mosque was under the control of a Hindu. Is there any Muslim who has not got the aid? I told him that I was not ready with those data. I said that we had gone to him to ask only this if he had any trouble with us. Modi took out a piece of paper and gave it to us. He said that it was his telephone number and he was available for us round the clock, at midnight or early in the morning. He promised us justice.

"We never imagined that this meeting would last two and a half hours. I had hoped to be with him for mere five minutes. Most Prime Ministers or Chief Ministers don't meet a common man longer than that, nor do they talk at such length. Generally, they tell to give the application or petition. We talked to him for such long and touched every big and small matter."

There was an incident concerning Syed Shahnawaz Hussain, a Muslim leader of the Bharatiya Janata Party too. According to him:

"Near Chota Udaipur, there is a *madrasa* run by an educational trust of Vastanvi. In the 2002 riots, a group seized this *madrasa*. There were about 400 students in it. I was in the cabinet of Vajpayee. Numerous Muslims of that area telephoned me. I talked to

Narendra Modi about the danger to the lives of those children, and requested him to take immediate action. Modi cooperated fully, but all the news that came out was negative. Everybody talked of the number of dead, but nobody talked of the people who were rescued and saved."

The accused in the massacres in Moradabad, Bhagalpur and other places have not been punished as yet. The largest number of riots took place during Nehru rule. Terrible riots took place during the rule of Indira Gandhi and Rajiv Gandhi. Gujarat has been the place where riots have broken out even before independence. But all these things are presented as if communal riots have taken place only during Narendra Modi's rule. Were the riots during the Congress regime not communal by nature?

In 2003, Nazma Heptulla narrated to me an incident about contacting Narendra Modi during the Gujarat riots. At that time, she was the vice chairman of the Rajya Sabha as a Congress member. She is the granddaughter of Maulana Abul Kalam Azad, a leading freedom fighter and first Education Minister of free India. Heptulla joined the Bharatiya Janata Party in 2004. I telephoned her to confirm the following incident. She said:

"The riots had flared up. Just then, I received a phone call from the office of Agha Khan that there was threat of a Muslim colony being attacked, it was located in a Hindu area. He rang up Advani, who was the Home Minister then. He immediately rang up Narendra Modi, who in turn telephoned and said, 'Nazma sister, you don't have to worry. I shall take care of this matter myself and give security to them.'

"He did what he said. He sent a regiment of the army to save the colony and all the people were saved. Local Muslims informed me that their colony was surrounded by the Hindu colony, and in case of an attack, they would not have found a way out, because nearby Naroda-Patia was such type of area. It is my experience that Narendra Modi responded very rapidly on whatever complaints were brought to him."

SIT Report

The special investigation team or SIT was constituted by the Supreme Court in order to enquire into the accusations against Narendra Modi. The court watched over its working. It is quite clear in the SIT report how the police and army saved the Muslims from the rioters. This report mentions the action of quick reaction teams (QRTs) which did not allow any harm to be done to the Muslims.

Despite prejudice and discrimination at various places, generally the police and the army had saved numerous lives. The news reports of that time reveal that many officers had risked their lives to help people. Such stories came to light later, some of which are as follows:

- Ahmedabad police saved 5000 people from Noor mosque.
- In Mahesana Sardarpura, 240 people were taken to safe places.
- In Por and Nardipur villages, 450 people were taken to safety.
- In Sanjoli village, 200 people were rescued.
- In Fatehpura village of Vadodara, 1500 people were rescued from the clutches of the rioters.
- In Kavant village, 3000 people were taken to safety.

Zafar recalls his talk again. He says that two months later, he contacted his office in October and intimated about my name and phone number. Within three hours, Narendra Modi telephoned me. I had never heard of any Chief Minister to respond to a common man so quickly. He said that he had been called after such a long time. Zafar says:

"I wanted to know if he would talk to me or not. Modi asked me when I was coming back to India. I said that there was a difficulty. I had revolted against him and now his police would be all too ready to arrest me. I would be imprisoned and nobody would ever come to my rescue. He stressed to know when I was coming, and when I told him of my return, he made all the arrangements for me to return safely.

"When I came back, he enquired of his secretary when I wanted to meet him. When I went to meet him, he asked me to talk on some problem. He said that it was not necessary for the Muslims to vote for him, but it was necessary for the government to do its duty.

"All such accusations that the Modi disrespected Muslims and planned riots in elections fell flat in the Supreme Court. Due to politically motivated riots, Gujarat's police and administration has become communal. Most of the riots took place during the Congress rule, which continued to rule the roost right until 1995. While Modi controlled riots within three days and restored the state to normalcy."

To empower the Muslim community, it is necessary to make it self-dependent. One may find it strange, but after riots, the Muslims are being encouraged for education. Until 2001-02, there were only three Muslim schools in Ahmedabad, this number has gone up to 17 now. There is a Muslim college too. In FD College, more than 1000 girls study. Zafar said that his sister and sister-in-law run a school in a poor area in Shahpur, where more than 650 girls are studying. It is desired that such type of work is done. Using foul words against Modi on the television cannot make one non-communal. We don't want this type of non-communalism. If something has to be done, it has to be done at ground level.

The licence raj is a terrible problem in any part of India. However, schools and colleges can be set up in Muslim areas quite easily. It has been an unwritten rule in decades that there is no need of approval for opening a Muslim school, but no Muslim had ever thought about it. But the condition has changed altogether today. If you wish to do anything in any field, right from teaching to irrigation, the government encourages you and aids you.

Zafar recalls to have told Modi that he wished two things from him. One was logistic support and the other was administrative machinery, they should not impede the progress. Modi gave his word and he kept it too. Today, the administration is quite active so far as Muslim educational needs are concerned.

Zafar recalls: "I can cite several instances. For example, there is a school in Bapunagar, a Muslim area. It was a Nutan school run by a Hindu trust, however, when the number of Muslims rose, the school management sold out this school to the Muslim management. Today, 1400 Muslim girls study in the morning and 1400 boys study here in the afternoon. One Sunday night at half past ten, I received a telephone call telling that there was a problem. It was that the school building was about to be demolished and the police had already reached there, and there was a plan to demolish the building in the morning. I asked what I could do in it. He said that none else but Modi could save the school. It is half past ten, how can I ring him at this odd hour? But he stressed. This incident occurred in 2007. I telephoned Modi at quarter to eleven. His secretary received the call. He informed that Modi was not in town. I requested him to tell Modi that he should ring me up before seven in the morning. The next day, Modi rang me up at 6.59 and asked what work I had with him so early in the morning. I informed him about the Muslim school at Bapunagar. I told him that I did not know whether it was authorized or not, but it was going to be demolished by the AMC, and that had to be saved anyhow. He said that it was an illegal building and the high court had already ordered to demolish that building. I pleaded that after all it was a school. Modi responded by saying that it was the matter of a school and if it was demolished, the responsibility of the future of those 2800 children would be on his head. Modi stayed the demolition that day, and then his officers advised us how to regularize the building."

The Modi Government is often accused that the Muslim community has lagged behind economically in Gujarat. It is assumed that the political environment and government policies are anti-Muslim to the extent that they have been suppressed economically. Zafar is a leading industrialist, and he has a flourishing industry. Due to this, he maintains a different viewpoint. According to him:

"If you look at the fresh statistics, you would find that the condition of Muslims is far better than ever before. Their condition is much better today. Open your eyes and look at the facts. Many of these are as follows:

'To judge the financial condition of a Muslim, the simplest way is *zakat*, because he pays it on his property. It is an aid given to the needy. It is used for meeting basic needs of the poor and for satisfaction. Suppose, I pay ₹ 2500 as *zakat* this year, it simply means that my property stands at ₹ 1 lakh. If the next year I paid a *zakat* of ₹ 5000, it would mean my property has jumped to ₹ 2 lakh. The amount of *zakat* is rising in Gujarat with every passing year. In fact, you would find that fifty percent of the *zakat* received in the country's *madrasas* comes from Gujarat, and the rest comes from the rest of the country. Had the Muslims grew paupers under Modi, the amount of *zakat* would have come down in Gujarat. However, the wealth of Muslims has increased in the past ten years.'

"I shall cite another example, it pertains to the sale of BMW cars. We sell BMW cars, the cheapest of which costs ₹ 30 lakh and its costliest version comes at ₹ 1.50 crore. When we started its dealership, we never thought that we would be able to sell more than 2-3 cars to the Muslims. However, in the past year, we have sold 11 percent of the cars to the Muslims. The population of the Muslims is just 9 percent of the whole population.

"The rates of land too have extraordinarily risen in the Muslim majority areas. You will not find land less than ₹ 50,000 per yard in a good society. This cost far exceeds that of the Hindu colonies. Where we live, in Paldi extension, there is no bungalow which costs less than five crore, and the Muslims are buying them. Where is the money coming to them from?

"It remains the truth that most of the Muslim businessmen are centred in cottage, medium and small scale industries. Their share stands at 7 percent in the entire population, while their share in the field of SME stands at about 22 percent. Today, if a Muslim wishes to undertake an industrial enterprise, there is no obstacle or discrimination in getting the government approval, else the Muslims would not have progressed so greatly. The mantra of Modi is very simple, the law is equal for everybody. Have your rights as the citizens, irrespective of the fact whether you are a Hindu or a Muslim, but don't ask for any special favours on the basis of your caste or community.

"The increase of small and medium industries in Gujarat is more than 75 percent. I shall cite its cause too. Small and medium enterprises develop where large industries are located. For example, when Tata brought the Nano plant to Gujarat, several ancillary industries were needed to meet the needs of different parts.

"Muslims are happy that Modi has not adopted the policy of discrimination against any community, whether Hindus or Muslims. He looks at all six crore people as Gujaratis. There is no need to talk of the Muslims separately. Tell me, when the President of the US speaks, does he talk in terms of whites or blacks, Hispanics, Indians-Pakistanis, Chinese or Koreans? If they set down to do so, hours would be passed counting them all. He talks of all Americans in the same breath. Modi too talks of all Gujaratis and he works for them all. It is a good thing. The Muslims are so capable that they can have their share in the projects and opportunities created for them. We expect only two things – first, the logistics facility that only the government can provide, and second, please don't put any barriers. The Modi Government has kept these two promises.

"Today Gujarat's Muslim trusts Narendra Modi, he is happy with his projects, schemes and works. The happiest and most prosperous Muslim lives in Gujarat. The Muslim community has taken the step ahead forgetting all about 2002. On the other hand, Narendra Modi has been proved fully innocent from all charges regarding the riots.

"False secularism and Tiesta Setalwad's NGO has tried their best to embroil Narendra Modi in the legal cases. Despite being proved as innocent right from 2002 to 2014, effort has been made to put him in trouble in every way. However, the SIT and the court of justice have held him fully innocent, and they have declared this verdict openly. They say that there was no role of Narendra Modi in the riots. The court has turned down all allegations of these secularists and NGOs. The truth has prevailed."

At that time, Narendra Modi wrote in his blog: "It is the law of nature that only the truth triumphs – Satyamev Jayate. Our judicial system has expressed this fact, and it appears appropriate to me that I should place my views and sentiments before the people of the country.

"When this event comes to a close, I can remember the things that occurred in the beginning. The terrible earthquake in 2001 had filled Gujarat with a feeling of helplessness together with death and destruction. Hundreds of people died and millions became homeless. The entire public life was affected; the means of livelihood were destroyed. At such unimaginable time of terrible calamity, I was given the responsibility of bringing solace to the people and undertaking reconstruction. We committed ourselves fully to face this challenge.

"Though within just five months, we were shocked by another event that was in the form of inhuman violence in 2002. The innocent lost their lives, the families became helpless. The property which was made through labour over years was destroyed. It was a terrible shock for Gujarat which was limping back to normalcy after the devastation that took place due to the natural calamity.

"My inner-self was filled with profound pity. It is simply indescribable. Suffering, pain, pity, trouble – possibly no word can adequately express those sentiments. It was a heartrending event, one is sure to shiver on thinking that inhuman and unfortunate event.

"There was suffering of the disaster victims on the one hand, and that of the riot victims on the other. It was essential for me to confront such a situation with all my might, keeping aside my private pity and trouble; I wanted to invest all my capability in working for peace, justice and rehabilitation.

"In that challenging situation, I often remembered the views expressed in the ancient scriptures that the people at the helm of power have no right to share their suffering or trouble with anyone. They have to face all this all alone. It was so with me too. I kept feeling my trouble, my pity, which was quite sharp. In fact, when I remember those days, I pray to God that any other individual, society, state or country may not see those cruel and unfortunate days."

Narendra Modi writes further: "It is the first time that I am sharing my terrible pain with you, which I have felt all these days right since then.

"It was with these sentiments that I appealed to the people of Gujarat for peace and patience following the incident of Godhra violence. It was to ensure that no danger should be posed to the life of the innocent people. I had said the same thing in my meeting with the media in February-March 2002. I had stressed that it is the political will of the government as well as its moral responsibility that it must maintain peace, beget people justice and get the guilty punished. I talked of the same thing during the goodwill fasts. I said that such hateful acts do not look good, and I felt immense pain from them.

"In fact, as a Chief Minister, I laid stress on ensuring how the spirit of unity and integration could be strengthened. To do this, I started a new address – My five crore Gujarati brothers and sisters.

"While on the one hand I was suffering from pain, I was being accused, on the other, of the death of my Gujarati brothers and sisters and harming their interests. Can you just guess my emotions and sentiments that pain me greatly? I was blamed for committing these very incidents.

"For many years in succession, I was being accused and blamed, and no opportunity was spared to attack me. I felt all the more pain that people who attacked me were out to meet their private and political interests, and they had in fact blotted the image of the state and country. The wounds that we were trying our best to heal, effort was being made to scratch these very wounds again and again. It is unfortunate that the very elements who tried to present themselves as the votaries of the victims did the most disservice; they presented all types of obstacles in getting the victims justice. They never try to understand that they have only augmented the suffering that those people were already undergoing.

"Despite this, Gujarat chose its own way. It chose the way of peace and neglected violence. It chose the way of integration in place of disintegration. It chose the path of goodwill over hatred. It was no easy task, but we were ready to tread the long path. I moved ahead of this indefiniteness and fear, and established Gujarat as a fine example of peace, goodwill, integration. I feel satisfaction today for all this effort and achievement, and I give its credit to each Gujarati."

The Gujarat Government has tried to tackle the riots in every way. Discussing this, Narendra Modi writes in his blog:

"The Gujarat Government tackled violence so rapidly and decisively that there is no parallel example in the country elsewhere. Yesterday's judgement is the completion of the review process, coming full circle, which was undertaken under the supervision of the highest court in the land, the Supreme Court. I have gone through the tests – the *Agni Pariksha* – which has now been accomplished. Today I feel relief and peace.

"I am grateful to all those people who have stood by me in these trying times, who could look through all the falsehood and trickery. Now the clouds of propaganda have been dispersed. I hope that the people, who wish to understand the true Narendra Modi and get linked with him, would feel stronger and committed.

"The people who feel satisfaction only on giving pain to others, they would not stop attacking me. I don't expect of them to do it either. However, I appeal to them in all politeness that they should not continue to give a bad name to the people of Gujarat in an irresponsible manner.

"Going by my pain and anger, I pray to God that my heart should not be filled with any bitterness. I don't see this judgement as a mark of personal victory, nor do I look at it as defeat of others. I have appealed to all my friends, especially the opponents, not to do so either. I have continued to think so right from the Supreme Court's judgement in 2011. I undertook goodwill fast for 37 days, and through it, I transformed this positive judgement into constructive work. I have worked for strengthening integration and goodwill in the society."

In the end, Narendra Modi writes: "I feel this thing in all earnestness that the progress of any society, state or country lies in goodwill and brotherhood. These are the foundations which can lead us to development and prosperity. Therefore, I appeal to everybody to achieve this goal, and work to ensure happiness on everybody's face.

"Let us once again say – Satyamev Jayate."

□

Modi in World Media

Narendra Modi remains in news all the time, call it Modi market or helplessness of the news market. Whether it pertains to the stories revolving round Gujarat's development, or cancellation of his address at Warten, or his appreciation in the national executive council of the BJP, or opposition by Nitish Kumar, or his innocence being proved in the Gujarat riots – the situation is such that the English proverb comes adequate for him – "Either you hate him or love him, but you cannot ignore him."

This is a great success for Narendra Modi. He has eclipsed the Indian media with his persona. His impact is quite perceptible on the international level too.

The *Time* is a weekly published from 1923 and has the largest circulation in the world. Its readership is 25 million, of which 20 million are Americans. On its issue of 26 March 2002, Narendra Modi has made to its front page. With this, he is included among the list of Indian stalwarts who have occupied the front page, these people include Mahatma Gandhi, Vallabhbhai Patel, Jawaharlal Nehru and Indira Gandhi.

Narendra Modi has completely transformed Gujarat. His story of success is being sung the world over. The *Time* has confirmed Gujarat's development by describing the state as the one having the highest rate of development which encourages trade and commerce.

According to this magazine, it is due to the efficient working and leadership which takes the task to the finish. These traits are missing in India, but can be amply seen in Gujarat.

The magazine states that progress has been halted in other parts of the country due to corruption and land acquisition struggles. In such a situation, Gujarat has found out solutions to both problems. The article admires the state on this account. Modi has exploited the natural resources of the state to the maximum, and thus has transformed the very structure of state's economy. Discussing the strong points of Gujarat, it says that it is the only state where large industrialists as well as small farmers can rely on 24-hour continuous flow of electricity. It also mentions that large business houses pay premium in Gujarat, due to which subsidized electricity is provided in Gujarat. Under other strong aspects of the state is included efficient and systematic bureaucracy. In the past ten years, Gujarat has risen as the auto hub.

Jyoti Thottum, a graduate of Yale University, is the bureau chief of the *Time* magazine's south Asia division. In 2000, in the capacity of a journalist, she has worked on events like the 2008 Mumbai terrorist attack and civil war in Sri Lanka. Having interviewed Narendra Modi and putting him in the magazine, Jyoti says in another article that her meeting with Narendra Modi was very adventurous and many of his qualities just amazed her.

She says that Modi might be considered a man devoted to the Hinduist way of thinking, yet his personality is somewhat different. In support of this, she says that he went ahead to demolish 120 small temples in order to get a four-lane highway constructed up to Gandhinagar, despite all the opposition from the Hindu nationalists. Jyoti states that it is a thing of much amazement for her. She says that you cannot find the aura as present in the educated politicians who have studied at famous educational institutions. Despite, his English can be called quite good. The article also records the experience of Virendra Mahiskar, the CEO of a construction company. According to him, the process of submitting bid for Ahmedabad BRTS was conducted online and it got completed very rapidly. He was not at all compelled to bribe the officers or get photographed with the local leaders.

Jyoti claims that there is a section of the Muslims who want to put the event of 2002 behind them and want to move ahead. In support of this thing, she mentions Mohsin Sheikh, a Muslim artist, and says that the benefit of development of Gujarat is reaching all people, without any discrimination on the basis of religion or faith. Jyoti is also of the view that the Congress-led government is being severely criticized due to corruption and lethargy. Further she says that fine opportunities are in the offing for Modi. The article concludes on an optimistic note and says that if India became a little of China, how it would look, Modi presents a glimpse of it.

The Brookings Institution is America's oldest and prestigious think-tank working from 1916. An organisation called Foreign Policy has accorded it the first place in the annual think-tank index. This institution is known for the quality of its work, independent working system and its influence on America's policy institutions. It is counted amongst the world's most reliable think-tanks, and its estimates are often directed. William Antholis, the managing director and senior fellow of governance studies, has been touring India for the last two months, meeting and discussing with the country's leaders, industrialist houses, administrative officers, intelligentsia, educationists and others, in order to understand India and states.

Having talked to Narendra Modi for 90 minutes, he was much impressed by him and has, in his blog, called him as the most popular and powerful leader in India. He wrote in it all that he found out about Gujarat and its influential leader. The Brookings considers Gujarat as the growth engine of India and considers it one of the seven most powerful states in India. The article says that it is difficult to find Gujarat's economic development elsewhere. It also notes that Gujarat's 10 percent annual growth is higher than any area in the world including China. Gujarat took the lead in Vibrant Gujarat summit, climate change, recyclable energy, roads, high speed phone connectivity and continuous electricity in villages. These aspects are the points of success for this state. Narendra Modi has achieved what other states could not do in agriculture. Attributing personal traits to Narendra Modi, this article describes him as an efficient administrator, a nationalist who takes pride in his country, neutral in work, an efficient policymaker and an individual taking interest in technical matters. There is no difference between what he says and what he does. He is an efficient and skilled politician. He does not follow New Delhi, rather inspires it to take after him. The model of Gujarat development has been the mantra of Modi for development of the whole of India.

Antholis also talks about how Modi is the most influential leader in Indian politics. He says that you can hear people talk of him all over India. He has often heard that he remains the most efficient leader of India, and given a chance, he would completely transform India's economy. Antholis opines that Modi will have considerable influence on Indian politics in the years to come. He is a leader with whom India should acquaint itself. The *Economist*, a weekly with 1.5 million readerships over 200 countries, claims that its readers comprise influential officers and policymakers. It is one of the most competitive and clever periodicals.

The *Economist* has described Gujarat as China's Guanddong, and says that Gujarat has implemented several things which are seldom put into practice in India. Besides, it is also estimated that the rate of production is very fine, and rural workers are getting employment. This Gujarat can be a role model for future India. In China, Guanddong did the same in 1990. Admiring the rapid rate of development of economy, the article says that Gujarat's economy can well register two-digit growth. It has occurred despite the fact that India's growth rate has come down. Gujarat's model of development has been appreciated widely. The renowned consultancy company, Mackenzie too has appreciated Gujarat comparing it with other states of India. It tells how the trader class in the state has got all appreciation.

In several matters, the magazine has described the achievements in continuous flow of electricity, gas and water. It says that the State Government is an institution in which the influence of bureaucracy has been reduced to the minimum, bribes are not asked for and officers do not interfere in things. Appreciating all-encompassing developments, the magazine says that apart from the criticism of some sections, we can say that adequate growth has been registered in India on several fronts.

□

Way Forward, Move Forward

Narendra Modi was declared as the prime ministerial candidate of the Bharatiya Janata Party for 2014 Lok Sabha elections. It has possibly not occurred before that despite being the Chief Minister of a state, Narendra Modi was being looked at by every common man in each nook and corner of the country. It is the man to listen to whom all people are curious. When he comes at television, the channel's TRP skyrockets. People listen to him from the stage or screen much like people watched the popular serial *Ramayana*. They are curious and eager to know what he says, which policy he emphasises, or what controversy he might utter which they could use for their selfish interests. Not only the supporters, but also the opponents are of the view that Narendra Modi remains the most popular leader in the country. It is confirmed by different surveys that have been conducted in the country. There is no leader who can come anywhere near him, including Manmohan Singh, Sonia Gandhi, Rahul Gandhi, or any other leader of the Bharatiya Janata Party itself. Today, the youth is after Narendra Modi, the magic of Namo is doing rounds; he remains the first choice for the post of the Prime Minister.

Most of the surveys have brought to the fore the fact. In a news channel survey conducted with Neilsen, 48 percent of the people wished Narendra Modi to become the Prime Minister, and only 7 percent people preferred Manmohan Singh. No other leader was anywhere near him. In an open survey conducted on a news site, 90 percent of the people mentioned Narendra Modi as the first choice for the post of Prime Minister.

The results in different elections further strengthen his claim to this high post. He has won Gujarat elections three times in a row with a heavy majority. Despite entire force of the opposition, media's negative attitude and propaganda by different foreign-funded organisations, his stature has further risen. This remains the strength of Narendra Modi.

Narendra Modi has succeeded to link the youth with him. This thing has come to the fore in several surveys. There is a large section of the youth in the country facing problems pertaining to unemployment, development, rising costs and corruption. Modi presents these issues with a vision. He displayed a glimpse of his idea in a speech that he delivered in Sri Ram College, where the youth favoured him greatly. In his speech at the FICCI, he spellbound the women entrepreneurs, not only this; he popularized Jasuben's pizza too.

An important role is played by his harsh decision-making image to make him popular. He can take decisions without any pressure. He possesses a unique courage. Today, Narendra Modi is felt like one's own by everybody, right from the common man to the highest industrialist. He has influenced millions of the industrialists and youths, and they share his concerns and views in the construction of India, and they have joined in his campaign.

Narendra Modi is a strong, aggressive, sharp and clever leader. He has marched ahead under the training of the Sangh. He can understand different matters minutely. It is not that his way ahead is easy. You can see the record crowd in his rallies that he conducted at Delhi, Rewari, Bhopal, Kanpur, Patna and other places, and it has only confirmed that he leads the other leaders by miles.

In the meanwhile, Modi has emerged on the social media as one of the most popular personalities. Even his critics consider him as the *Brahmastra* of the Bharatiya Janata Party, and no one seems to have any clue how to confront him. The sole objective of Narendra Modi is to reconstruct India to make it the superpower in the 21st century, and to establish it as the *Jagadguru*. The 21st century belongs to Asia, and it is the most appropriate opportunity to bring India to the fore as the leader of the world, and launch it in the age of peace and prosperity.

Narendra Modi states that we require not only good governance, but also pro-people, pro-active good governance. To realize this dream, we must have a government which has the ability and capability to control the power that it could take the country towards a new direction, working with the aim of India

First. Unfortunately, India is facing massive problems like corruption, inefficiency, lack of decision-making and political instability. As a result, people have felt motivated. Scams, rather big scams, are the things of every day. No steps are being taken to get the guilty punished, which is quite unfortunate. People are losing confidence on the government. Common people and investors are in search of some secure alternative. It is a hard work to re-establish confidence in the government.

How is Narendra Modi different from other politicians? He is committed to people's welfare and governance keeping them in the centre. He is of the firm view that there should be only one religion, one faith of governance that is India First. The only holy text of the government should be the Constitution. The power of the government should be only the people's power, and the work of the government should be only welfare of the 124 crore people.

Today much is being talked about saving India. India is a young and enthusiastic country, and now it requires a leader who can guide it, direct it and lead it. There was a time when India had several leaders of the global stature. Now we have to fill this void with a personality who can infuse optimism in the Indians. When he talks of the Statue of Unity, a new hope of national principles is awakened in us, when he talks of India First, we recall to minds our patriots. There is no other alterative but to accept the reality. Narendra Modi has himself applied the mantra – 'skill + will + zeal = win'. We can bring about a change, as he repeats the words of Swami Vivekananda: Rise, awake and persevere until the goal is achieved.

□

Challenge to Challenges*

Several elections have been held since independence. Right from the beginning, from the times of the Jansangh, from the times of the Bharatiya Janata Party, we all have much experience of working in elections. However if we look at the elections of the past, these elections in 2014 are quite different from them the earlier ones.

The country had never seen this type of a terrible situation before when such a large democratic country had been rendered leaderless, policyless, with doubtful credentials, and their honesty too was under suspicion. The country had never witnessed such days in its history as in the past few years. The country had never seen the demonic form of corruption as we have seen in this decade. We have never seen the farmers committing suicide, youths wandering for employment, mothers and sisters worried for their dignity and respect, hungry children suffering from the rising costs. Therefore, the election in 2014 was not only the election of change in power. It was an election of hope and ambition of the millions of Indians. It was the election of the heights that Atalji and Advaniji touched in the beginning of the 21st century. It was the election of the aspirations and dreams of taking India to the newer heights. Therefore, national councils of two chief parties were held in the land of Delhi. If one analyses, it becomes evident that the Congress session, held two days before, appears to be the *jehad* to save the party, how to save the Congress, how to keep the party united, it was the topic of their *jehad*. They were trying to keep themselves

---

*The complete statement of Narendra Modi, delivered in the national council of the Bharatiya Janata Party, organised at New Delhi on 18-19 January 2014.

united, while here we were concerned with how to save the country. This turned out to be the basic difference in 2014 elections. The Congress workers all over the country came to Delhi with great hopes. They were told that on the 17th of the month, their candidate for the Prime Minister would be declared, they were curious and eager to carry with them the gift of the prime ministerial candidate with them. As BJP's Arun Jaitley has said that the Congress workers came to take the Prime Minister, but they had to be content with three gas cylinders.

The points that were raised there, it seems pertinent to me to mention them here. The democratic traditions were cited for not declaring the prime ministerial candidate. Is it the truth? I hope that the people would discuss these points like they discuss other points, but no discussion is taking place for the last four days. There must be some fine reasons behind it. The country wishes to know what happened to the democratic traditions when the first Prime Minister was preferred after independence. Despite the wish of everybody, Sardar Vallabhbhai Patel was not allowed to become the PM. What do you talk of traditions?

I wish to know that on 31 October 1984, when Smt. Indira Gandhi was assassinated, Rajiv Gandhi was in Kolkata, he came running all the way, went to hospital and in a little time, the ceremony to swear him in as the next PM was held. The Congress party talks of traditions. I wish to ask them if any parliamentary meeting was held at that time. Did the Congressmen choose their PM in a parliamentary party meeting? Do you have any notes or minutes of that meeting? Is there any system? No, there is none, nothing. A couple of heads come together and decide upon the fate of the country, and the swearing in is held immediately. And today, they are out to teach us traditions. Going further, the UPA came to power in 2004. The UPA was to form the government. I can say with emphasis and surety that no one in the parliamentary meeting selected Dr. Manmohan Singh as the PM, or as their leader. But later Madam Sonia Gandhi nominated Dr. Manmohan Singh, and he was sworn in to the highest post. We cannot save ourselves by talking of parliamentary traditions. Sister Sushma has commented, Rajnath has commented, Vankaiya has commented, Arun has commented; there can be several reasons for their not contesting elections. Everybody put forward this in their own ways, but I can see one human reason; sure there is a political reason too. The human reason is that they can see their defeat clearly written on the wall, they can see their devastation before them. Will any mother get ready to sacrifice her son? Which mother will sacrifice her son on the altar of politics? And therefore, a mother's heart took this decision. No, save my son.

These days, the tea vendors are being much talked about. Every tea vendor in the country is puffing up his chest. There are two more factors of their running away from elections. The first is that the tradition in which they have been born and brought up, the way they have proved their family as superior, when such people live such kind of life, their heart too is formed in such manner, autocratic mentality overcomes them, and then they set down to think that the Lok Sabha elections are important and the Congress should win them. Therefore, when it comes to fighting with a tea vendor, it becomes a matter of prestige. They are feeling shame that there is no equality. They are famous, I am a labourer; and such well-to-do people find it very degrading to contest with a lowly worker. They think it disrespect, insult to themselves. How can they fight? Not only this, it is a matter of anxiety to have the traditional thinking of high and low, poison of casteism, superiority complex in the mind, birth in an aristocratic family. They have been born in such a high family which has maintained honour over ages, while the man confronting them was born in a backward caste; he is an individual whose mother filled water in the neighbouring houses, cleaned utensils, how could I fight with such a person? All these are the causes which are out of the political circle. Therefore, we look at the elections in 2014 in this perspective. Just imagine when we go round the streets and meet people. We ask them what they thought of the people who continued to remain out on 27 October when the bombs were being exploded and they continued to worship their deities. It reminds me of the scene when people thronged in their fight for independence, the spirit for which Bhagat Singh, Sukhdev and Rajguru kissed the gallows; the freedom for which the youths passed their youth in jails. After so many years after freedom, the election of 2014 has brought that very spirit. At that time, people got an opportunity to die for freedom. At that time, *Swaraj* infused a new life into freedom. Now, the new generation is striving for *Suraj* or good governance.

The young men of the country feel that they did not get a lucky chance to die for freedom, but now they have got a chance to live for good governance of free India. This is the spirit of this election. I can see that victory in this election, and it is due to this fact that the people who are least concerned with the Bharatiya Janata Party, who have never got an opportunity to work as BJP worker, who are as yet untouched by politics, millions of such people arrive at BJP offices, write me letters, comment on Facebook, give messages on Twitter; they all ask for work, they all want to work for us. It is their ambition, their aspiration to fight for the 2014 elections. The spirit that prevailed in the freedom struggle, in the struggle for *Swaraj*, can be seen to have manifested itself in these elections.

The country has been independent for over six decades. Much is talked about the poor people's concern. Much is being talked about development. But just have a glance at the map of India. What was the shortcoming in our policy-making? When we look at the Western sector, we find that development has taken place there, though it might be slow, yet it can be seen. But if you look at India from the central part to the East, you will find that it is crying for development. Why is such a situation being created? How has this imbalance come to happen? I would like to give the Indians the faith that when you give the Bharatiya Janata Party an opportunity to serve you from May of 2014, we shall give you the guarantee that the area lagging behind in development would move ahead. We shall bring it to match with the Western part. My Mother India has two arms, one weak and the other strong, no this cannot be my Mother India. Therefore, we are of the opinion that whether it is Bihar, Bengal, Jharkhand, Assam, Northeast, Odisha or the entire eastern area, the whole of Uttar Pradesh; brothers and sisters, we would like to proceed ahead with the dream of balanced development. If we have to make our country strong, then the regional expression should not be taken as a calamity. In the past decades, the politicians have taken the regional expression in terms as if there is a volatile change over Delhi, as if it is a burden. Regional expression can also become a great opportunity for development.

It is not a challenge, it is an opportunity. The ambition to proceed ahead in each state should be linked with Delhi, and it would lead to rapid development. I am completely confident about it.

Our country has a federal structure. It cannot be limited to the articles of the Constitution. We shall have to respect the Constitution in letter and spirit, we will have to take pride in it. It is a matter of great bliss for me that I have been on the post of the Chief Minister. Now, the party has chosen me for a new responsibility. As a Chief Minister, I know well the importance of the federal structure. I have felt the difference between the favourable government during the regime of Atalji and unfavourable government at Delhi. Due to my own experience, I can understand the pain of each state. I can understand the pain that every Chief Minister faces. I can understand the value and significance of federalism. Therefore, brothers and sisters, the Bharatiya Janata Party takes interest in strengthening the federal structure and empower it. We want to proceed further. Today there is an attitude that we belong to Delhi, we give it to the states, this is not a dignified manner to talk of things. We promise to change this scenario. There is no elder or younger brother. Both brothers have to carry Mother India on their shoulders together, this should be the spirit to prevail.

Today it is considered that the Prime Minister and his cabinet would take the country ahead. I think somewhat differently. I wish that there should be a team of the Prime Minister and all Chief Ministers, who should carry the country together. Not only this, the central council of ministers and states' councils of ministers should together form a greater team. The centre's bureaucracy and states' bureaucracies should work together as a large team. If we form this atmosphere, no problem can confront us for long. We can overcome our problems and then we can take the country ahead as per our dreams. Good governance is essential for the country. Bad governance is at the root of the problems facing the country. We have to root out maladministration. We have to emphasise good governance, and his good governance is not meant only for the rich, it is meant for the common deprived people, it is meant for the Dalits, it is meant for the exploited people. If there is good governance, the government will run well. A poor man's child will get education. If there is no good governance, a poor man's child will not be good.

We want to proceed ahead with good governance. These days, there is much talk. We have to decide whether we have to rely on the oft-repeated talks, or have to rely on the track records. We have much heard of the talks. Now is time for the country to decide on the basis of track record whom to rely and whom not to. This decision requires the heart. Act, act, act, we have heard much of acts, but now we don't need act, we need action. Defection and wavering should be made the things of the past, we must proceed ahead for development, delivery. Therefore, we have to walk ahead of good governance in order to accept the basic rule of development and delivery. In the last decade, hardly has a day passed when the Prime Minister did not form a committee, a committee for every problem. My countrymen, the country is burdened with the committees. We don't want committees, we want commitment, the country needs commitment.

So large is our country. When I glance at Mother India, when I look at life, then I come to hear that there is something which keeps us alive and thriving. My Mother India is like the seven colours of the rainbow, which illuminate Mother India. The first colour is that of India's cultural heritage, our family, our family system. This family system has existed over thousands of years and this has made us, saved us, taken us forward, grown us. We have to further strengthen this family system. Our policies, our schemes should strengthen this system, we have to think about it.

The second colour of the rainbow is the colour of agriculture, our cattle, our village. Mahatma Gandhi called our country a country of villages. It is a very important and bright colour of our rainbow. We have to make it brighter by working for farming, animal husbandry. We have to make policies for uplift of villages and rural poor. We can take pride in this.

The third colour of the rainbow is that of India's women. Our women power, that was once the image of renunciation and penance, has been downgraded. If we have to make our rainbow glorious, we will have to empower our mothers and sisters. We must pay attention to their education and training. They possess our economic and social heritage.

The fourth colour of our rainbow comprises water, land, forest and environment. It is our heritage. It is our wealth. If we have to keep India leading in the path of development, then we have to take care of this fourth colour, we will have to preserve it, we will have to safeguard it with latest technology. And the most important is our youth power. We are fortunate that India is the youngest country in the world. Our 65 percent of population is below 35 years. If a country possesses such a large demographic dividend, possesses such a large youth power, nothing could be beyond its power. In the days to come, the world is likely to be faced with a serious calamity. If we prepare for it today, our youth will have the power to construct the entire world. We have to think about it.

Our youth power is subject to certain matters of anxiety. We cannot allow this colour to fade in the name of modernity and Western influence. When we get the news that drugs, narcotics and the like are devastating our youth in some areas, then we have to set aside politics in order to save them from this vice. We have to adopt zero tolerance in this respect. We have to protect the youth. If there is smuggling from abroad, we have to carry out our responsibility and stop it completely. We have to protect the youth power in order to make it the basis of our rising to the helm in international affairs.

The sixth colour of the rainbow is our democracy. A country equipped with demographic dividend can rapidly move ahead in the world, so our democracy is our greatest wealth and capital. We can face the world with this power with us. We have to think out how to make this colour of democracy more potent. We have to take forward our democracy from the representative system to participative democracy. We are proud that we follow the tradition of democracy. But the need of the hour is that all common men experience the qualitative trait in human democracy. People should be filled with the feeling to respect democratic traditions, through our conduct, through our behaviour, through our dealings.

And the seventh colour of the rainbow is extremely important, that is knowledge. Whenever mankind has lived in the era of knowledge, of learning, India has led the world. We are the worshippers of knowledge. Every mother blesses her child saying, "Child, grow into a learned man." Every mother utters these words.

We have to proceed further towards making this colour stronger, brighter.

How can the glory of these seven colours be exalted further? How can new strength be added to them? How can new ideas be infused into them? We have to proceed with them all. Brothers and sisters, the recent Congress session stated that the Congress party is an idea.

We too are of the opinion that there can be no party without an idea, nor can there be a movement but the difficulty is whether it has any idea or not. What idea it has, which idea it has. There is one thing for sure. The country is sure about one thing that the Congress is now thinking hard. There is need to understand this thinking. What is the thinking of the Congress? What is the thinking of the Bharatiya Janata Party? I plead with the people of my country to pay attention to my words. Their thinking is that India is a beehive, it is a honeybee. Our thinking is that India is our mother. Their thinking says that poverty is a mental state, our thinking is that the poor is God for us. Their thinking goes that they don't get fun unless they talk of the poor. Our thinking is that when we listen to the poor, when we remember them, we cannot sleep the whole night in pain. They don't get fun, we don't get sleep. There is a difference, there is a distinction between the two ways of thinking. They think that money doesn't grow on trees, our thinking is that money grows in farms and granaries which prosper with the labourers' hard work. Their thinking is to divide the society and rule, and our thinking is to unite the society and develop it. What a great distinction this all is. Their thinking is family lineage, our thinking is nationalism. Their thinking is that politics is everything, our thinking is that national policy is our everything. Their thinking is how to save the power, our thinking revolves round how to save the country. They have just now said that the ticket will be given to those who have the Congress in their hearts, their thinking is that they will run the country who have the Congress in their hearts. Our thinking is that the ticket will be given to those who have India in their hearts. This is the distinction between their thinking and our thinking.

Therefore, when the 2014 elections is before us, I wish to say to my countrymen that for the last sixty years, you have chosen the rulers. You have liked rulers for yourselves. You have given the power to the rulers. Today from the altar of the Bharatiya Janata Party, I entreat my countrymen to hand over sixty months to your servant, and not to a ruler. Give sixty months to this servant and give a chance. The country needs, not a ruler, but a servant. This is the demand of democracy that everybody might get an opportunity to serve the country.

Today, we are drawing an outline of the coming future. Rising costs are a massive problem before the country. The hearth of the poor is seldom put on. Mother and child cry over starvation, they have to sleep on hungry stomachs. Can rising costs not be contained? Is there no remedy? What is the situation of the country? We have no real time data. When it comes to the farming season, we don't know which crop is being sowed and where, nor do we know how much produce we got from a crop, and what is our need? We must have real time data of everything. On its basis, we can decide how much crop has been produced and how much we have to import or export. But what happens today is that we export the things we need and the country has to go hungry, and in such a situation, the same crop is imported. None knows what kind of this commerce is. Therefore, we urge that we have to act so that a common man is not marred by rising costs while the farmers are not exploited. There should be a price stabilization fund in the country. This fund should interfere the market costs in order to protect and preserve the poor man's bread and butter. It is the need of the hour that the national agricultural market is erected. The black-marketers should be punished and such tendencies should be effectively checked. If such steps are taken one after the another, it would be in the interest of both farmers and country.

If Atalji's Government can check prices, if Morarji Desai's Government can check prices, then I must convince you that the Bharatiya Janata Party Government can very well check the rising prices.

A country with such a massive youth power striving for employment has to emphasise on the centre for excellence. We have to lay stress on skill development. How can feedback be taken for skill development? If a chemical factory is working at a place, then how the workers in it should be developed in skills? If an automobile factory is being set up at a place, how then the youth can be trained in the relevant skill development, we need to think about it. If we think and plan well, then we can fight against unemployment very well. Brothers and sisters, we have no planning for human resource. If you ask the planners how many science teachers will be needed in 2020, you will not have the answer. They cannot tell the number of nurses needed in 2020. Friends, let us now plan human resource, accordingly we should develop human power. The individual prepared thus would be certainly employable and will be employed too. The wealth of India is its youth. They should be skilled. They should be given the opportunity to work. There cannot be a greater wealth than them to take our country towards progress and growth. We wish to take that forward.

Respectable Advaniji has started a massive war against black money. A worker of the Bharatiya Janata Party has committed himself with Advaniji's dream that we must do it. We shall make the legal arrangements that might be needed. If there is a need to form a task force of the specialists, it would be made too. However, each paisa that has been looted and stashed away will be brought back in the country, and it would be invested for removing poverty and for people's welfare.

This is the time of globalization. We cannot do this alone as a country. We will have to establish ourselves in the global competition. If we have to move ahead in the world, we will have to grow ourselves. If we have to move ahead in the international level, good governance will come handy to us. The same importance should be given to human resource and infrastructure. Now India cannot afford to delay and postpone it. We must lay stress on next generation infrastructure. Whether it is roads, railways, water grids, linking of rivers, agro-infrastructure, gas grids, we have to pay attention to all these. If there is a gas grid, the quarrels for cylinders would be ended. Why should optical fibre network not be made? Should the whole country not be connected with the optical fibre network? India is blessed with a very long seacoast. Why should we not create facilities there for infrastructure and thus create a place for ourselves in the world trade. We have such a large railway, but not much attention has been paid to it. You can see the transformation in Japan, why did it come? Japan had the concept of bullet train, and with it stood the whole country. China too followed it. We have such a long railway, but we have not thought along modern lines. Why should the railways not have their own universities where the manpower needed by the railways is created? Why should our country not undertake research and innovation in our country and set up a university? This is a moot point. This has to be thought out. It needs time. You just cannot imagine how massive power the railway can become in the country. The existing railway network should be modernized, and by it we would be able to give momentum to the development path of India. Vajpayeeji had created the golden quadrilateral which brought India to the fore in the international arena.

It is the need of the hour. India will complete its 75 years of independence in 7-8 years. This will be the diamond jubilee occasion. Is it not the need of the time that we formulate Vajpayee's thinking in order to construct a diamond model of the bullet train? When the country celebrates its diamond jubilee, we should have completed the work by which the bullet train could move in four different directions. You can see, the world would start to look at India in a new perspective.

We cannot think of isolated India in the world. I am not discussing who is guilty and who is not. But we are not in a position to show our face to the world in the capacity of a society, a civilized society, a cultured society, an educated society. What is happening to our mothers and sisters is simply hateful. It is the responsibility of us all that we respect our women. Our social responsibilities must include women security and dignity. We shall have to create that environment. We shall have to make effort to create that system in order to make this social life. We will have to proceed further on the mission model 'Save the girl child, Educate the girl child'. There cannot be a greater blot in the 21st century if a daughter is killed in the mother's womb. Millions of daughters are being killed in the womb. It is the responsibility of us all that we proceed ahead with a mission to save the girl child and educate the girl child. We will have to change our attitude towards women. We have looked at the woman as the homemaker, now is the time when we should look at her as the nation builder. If we look at her as a nation builder, then our thinking would undergo a change, and we can rise before the world as a new power.

It is unfortunate for our country that we took urbanisation as a challenge or threat, when we should have taken it as an opportunity. The cause of our problems is our wrong thinking. Urbanisation should be considered as an opportunity. We should accept its role in development. The policies should be formulated in that form. Why should there not be one hundred new cities, modern cities, word-to-word concept, knowledge cities, health cities, sports cities, specialized cities? Why not? We can dream of hundreds of new cities keeping in view the needs of the country. On the same lines, we need the concept of twin cities where two cities are located nearby. This will beget us a new development model. In the same way, a big city should be surrounded by a network of satellites towns. All this should be taken as an opportunity. This will take the form of project. It will need cement, iron, for which we will need factories producing cement and iron, as well as other factories. All this will require manpower. A large number of youths will get employment. You can just imagine. If you are worried about the GDP, you just can find an answer in it.

Should every common man, poor man not have a house of his own even sixty years after independence? Why should he be made helpless that he has to pass his nights under the sky? Why should we not dream of millions and millions of houses, and connect states in this dream, and then get down to work on the mission mode. The Centre and the States should work together. Even the poorest of man should have a house of his own. Let us proceed in this direction. Brothers and sisters, our country cannot run without water, land, forest, agriculture, cattle. Our agriculture should become modern, our productivity should increase, we should have the concept of 'per drop more crop'. We must think how more crops can be produced with each drop of water. There should be deep irrigation, spring irrigation. How we should embrace modern science, how should we encourage such policies? We will all have to work on the mission mode for necessary development of India as well as best development of farming. We need to pay special attention to agro-infrastructure.

Atalji gave us the resolve of linking rivers with agro-infrastructure. We have to take forward this concept. The Amul dairy is successfully functioning in Gujarat for so many years. Can large states not witness the white revolution? Can the farmers there be so strengthened as to meet the needs of milk of that state? We shall have to move in this direction, and then our farmers will not have to face such troubles. Therefore, I say that for agricultural development, we will have to accord attention to one-third agriculture, one-third animal husbandry and one-third tree plantation. How unfortunate it is for our country that the land has not been measured here. Today, satellite technology should be used for exact size of the land, and how much of it is under farming; all this data should be made available. Today the farmer has to waste part of his land in erecting boundaries, then he would not need do it, then he would plant trees instead. Today we have to import timber, then we would be saved from importing it. If we have to strengthen our farmer, then we will have to work in this direction. And I am confident that if we carry out these suggestions, we can reverse the circumstances.

Electricity too falls in the same category. What type of country we are! Electricity generation factories worth 20,000 MW are non-operative. There is no fuel for them. The coalmines are closed. Can we not dream of power on demand? If the states take the initiative, and the centre aids, then round-the-clock electricity can be supplied in each home. With this, the life of common man can be transformed.

If we have to keep our head high in the 21st century, there should not be any compromise in education. We need to lay more stress on educational sector. Why should each state in India not have an IIM? And an IIT? An AIIMS? It is our aspiration, our dream that there should be IIMs, IITs and AIIMSs. We should guide our effort towards taking education to a higher plane. We wish to make it better. Today, if a common man is inflicted with some disease, then his entire financial condition becomes shaky, he is fully devastated. Therefore, we need to change the approach. As in education sector, there is need to shift our approach from teaching approach to learning approach; in the same way, we can address sickness in the health sector. There is need to address our wellness.

We are worried for disease, illness, and little think of health; therefore how preventive healthcare, paramedical forces should be linked together, we have to think about it. We have much talked of health insurance. In the 21st century, we will have to guarantee it. We don't have to get stuck up at health insurance. We will have to promise health insurance.

Can there be a war against poverty? Is poverty only a matter of slogans? I can speak with all the confidence that we can fight against poverty through financial planning, people's participation, small scale and cottage industry; we have to link all these tendencies in a bid to fight against poverty. To fight against poverty, the poor should be empowered, that is, we have to empower the poor. We have to take them out of poverty. We must give them a chance. And wherever we have given the chance, good results have been achieved. We shall have to take this forward.

After this, there is yet one more point. I have said that when we have to stand before the world to face it, we must undertake India's branding. We know that years ago, when we bought some thing, we could find words on it – Made in Japan, and we immediately bought it. Is this not the need of the hour that we stress on Brand India. When I speak of Brand India, I speak of five Ts – talent, tradition, tourism, trade and technology. These are the five Ts on the basis of which we can erect the strength in taking Brand India in the world market. India should produce and the world should buy it, for it we will have to upgrade technology. We will have to make the most of our talent. We will have to acquaint the world with our traditions. There is much force in tourism. 'Terrorism divides, Tourism unites.' We should carry forward the traditions like technology and trade. These days, we are faced with a new terminology. Some people say 'Idea of India'. This cannot be the preserve of any one. It can be yours, of his and of his. It can be of all people. It can be mine too. Therefore, the idea of India cannot be bound in any limits. I wish to present before of you 'my idea of India'. My idea of India – Satyamev Jayate; my idea of India – Vasudhaiv Kutumbkam; my idea of India – Sarva Panth Sambhav; my idea of India – Ekam Sad Vipra: Bahudha Vadanti; my idea of India – Na Tam Hame Rajam, Na Moksham Na Punarbhavam; my idea of India – Janani Janmabhumishcha

Swargadapi Gariyasi; my idea of India – there is God even in the plant; my idea of India – Vaishnav Jan To Tene Kahie, Je Peer Parai Jane Re; my idea of India – Vachchha Kachchha Man Nischal Rakhen, Par Dhan Nav Jhale Hath Re; my idea of India – Yatra Naryastu Pujyante Ramante Tatra Devta; my idea of India – Nari Tu Narayani, my idea of India – service to the poor; my idea of India – Nar Karni Kare To Narayan Ho Jaye.

Now when I am speaking of my idea of India, and when we are going in 2014 elections, we shall together raise the slogan. Just clench your fists and speak with all your might. I will speak and you will speak after me. I will speak – Vote for India, and you will speak with raised hands – Vanshvad se Mukti ke liye (for freedom from dynasty) – vote for India – for freedom from favouritism and prejudice, vote for India for freedom from corruption, vote for India for freedom from rising costs, vote for India for freedom from maladministration, vote for India for country's security, vote for India for people's security, vote for India for houses to live in, vote for India for food to eat, vote for India for medicine to the poor, vote for India for welfare of the poor, vote for India for educational reforms, vote for India for employment for the youth, vote for India for women's dignity, vote for India for a progressive India, vote for India for India's integration, vote for India for one country, vote for India for great India, vote for India for politics for good governance, vote for India for politics of good administration, vote for India for politics of development, and vote for India.

Today we are proceeding in our areas, we must proceed with the resolve of victory. We should embrace victory, each of our companion should become victorious, and we must remember that victory in election is conceived at the polling booth, polling booth is the breeding ground of victory, and we have to take all care of the mother, of the breeding ground, it is our duty to safeguard it. Therefore, the polling booths must be safeguarded, we must think of them, we must have a resolve to win the polling booths. Let us proceed ahead with this resolve, let India become divine. To realize this dream, we together should transform the country's might into votes.

With this expectation, I am grateful to the national leadership that they have given this responsibility to an ordinary person like me. Therefore, when a tea vendor fights an election, you will go and tell the country that Modi is an individual who has nothing of his own, and if you say so, you are sure to get wealth from ten crore families. Even the poorest of person will come forward to donate to the Bharatiya Janata Party. We should decide that we shall fight the election with the money that the common man donates to our party. Recently, our workers in Kerala achieved this feat. In 2012 Gujarat elections, the volunteers visited each house and collected five rupees, ten rupees, hundred rupees to fight the election. The government in Gujarat has been formed thrice, in a way it is the government for the seventh time. But I have got the opportunity for the last four times. I fought the election with money contributed from common people. We have to carry forward this tradition. We have to follow it and abide by it. And when a poor mother's son, a tea vendor is in the field, the country will fill our coffers, it is my confidence, it is my faith, it is my trust.

□

Interview with Narendra Modi

(Please note that this interview was taken when he was CM of Gujarat)

Will you tell us about your place of birth?

I come from Vadnagar in Mahesana district. This area of Vadnagar is interior area and was known as Hatkesh area. Vadnagar was once the capital of Gujarat. Its old name was Anartpur. There lived two famous musician sisters – Tana and Riri here and they were contemporary of Akbar. It is believed that when Tansen sang the 'Deepak raga', his entire body started to burn, and an individual was required who could sing the Malhar raga. The emperor sent his troops to Vadnagar, but the two sisters communicated back that they did not sing in anybody's court. This is the attitude that my village possess. I have inherited this attitude. Tana and Riri refused to go there to sing, and it is said that Tansen himself had to come to Vadnagar.

How was your education in high school?

When I was in high school, the teachers looked not at the homework, but at my good and short points. They always cared for me. They used to guide me for overcoming my shortcomings, and I can remember all that today. I tried to attend school, not by body, but by mind. Due to this, I can recall the day. When I was in school, I was there with both my body and soul. We often are present at a place by the body, but not by the mind. It is essential for one to be present at school by the mind too. It is not true that education can be learnt within the limits of the textbook. Education can be obtained from nature and anything around too. Education is a continuous process.

I used to score good marks. It appeared to my father that I was a bright student, so he wished that I must study science in the university. There was Veljibhai Chaudhary, my father's friend. He was my schoolteacher. He was of the opinion that I have a good understanding of literature. He advised my father to take me forward towards literature stream. He said that my power of understanding and assimilation was good. Few people spoke English in our village, English was not the medium, but he could learn English well. My inclination towards the Sangh continued during school time. I used to be quite busy at school. I can recall that there was no wall in the compound. We all came together to hold a charity show, gathered money and got the wall constructed. It is my nature. It is my proclivity. It was all teamwork.

Will you tell about your practice?

My life was somewhat of a different kind. I did not study. I did not go to any college. I left home at the age of seventeen. Lakshmanrao Inamdar urged that God had given me the ability so I must do something. With his inspiration, I appeared in external exams and became a postgraduate. You can say that I just passed the examination. In one sense, I did not study. No teacher has ever taught me. When I started work as a *Pracharak*, I was kept to maintain the Hedgewar Bhavan. I had much faith in Vakil Saheb. I had once said to him that it would be good if I got a chance to stay with him in the beginning. It would train me. Anyway, he handed me over the maintenance of the Hedgewar Bhavan.

You conducted plays in student life. What was their background?

I did many plays at school. Vadnagar was a small village. Our village was much influenced by the plays. When I studied, my school completed 25 years. The school did not have a compound wall. To make it, all students decided that a charity show should be organised. For it, a play was organized. We undertook several plays like *Peela Fool, Jogidas Khuman* and the like. I also wrote the plays. Bhogilal Bhojak was at Vadnagar at that time. He was a popular artist of the film *Narsingh Mehta*. He was linked with theatre. He came to us as the director and trained us.

At what age did you become a Sangh Swayamsevak?

During my childhood, the Rashtriya Swayamsevak Sangh was active in Vadnagar much before independence. I came into contact with the Sangh in my childhood. I can remember that Vakil Saheb conducted the first meeting in the village, he was the *Prant Pracharak*. I have also written a book on his life.

You were fond of reading and going to library right from childhood. Is it true?

I became fond of reading from the age of about eleven years. The talks that were given at the Sangh often mentioned the name of Chhatrapati Shivaji. I thought much about him. My image in the village was that if I was to be found out, I must be looked for in the library, you were sure to find me there. Our village was small, but our library was good and large. If somebody ever wanted to see me, he would come to the library. I had read Rajgopalachariji's *Mahabharata* and *Ramayana* in English. My teacher had instructed me that if my faith and languages were blended together, I was sure to like such books. There is a book on Chhatrapati Shivaji in Gujarati written by Vaman Mukadam. This book extends over 600-700 pages. I can remember that it was not comfortable for me to carry this book. I carried the book home at that age. I read this book mindfully. Then I liked Vivekananda too. Whenever I got an opportunity, I read him. In the beginning, whenever I was required to deliver a speech, I would try to quote him. I used to discover his quotes on all topics. I don't know why, right since childhood when I came of my own, I felt myself near Vivekananda. I came to know about him in the Rashtriya Swayamsevak Sangh for the first time; perhaps I was born with those traits from the previous birth.

Did you take interest in games in childhood?

My background was such that I did not get this fortune. My father had a tea stall near Vadnagar railway station. The financial condition of the house was not good. I studied and went to the railway compartments to sell tea. Whatever money I got from it, I gave it to my family. I sold tea for a long time in the railway compartments; therefore, I had little interest in games. But I got time in the morning at five, then I took interest in yoga. I found swimming easy. I used to swim in the pond for hours together. There was a small temple in the middle of the pond. I took much interest in hoisting the flag there. I used to swim and hoist the flag there. Besides, I did not have luck to take part in games. Now there is no interest too. Now it has become quite impossible.

Did you have leadership qualities from the childhood?

Of course, you can say so. I can remember that in 1962, during the Indo-China War, the military troops passed from Mahesana. The bus or train fare from Vadnagar to Mahesana was about eight to twelve annas. I used to go to Mahesana railway station and get busy in distributing tea and biscuits among the jawans. I can remember that war due to this reason.

In the same way, when I was in the eighth standard, many areas of the country faced floods. There was a terrible flood in the Tapi river. At that time, I accompanied with one of my friends to go to the Janmashtami fair in the village in order to render assistance to the flood victims. Our fathers used to give us a rupee to spend at the fair. With that money, we put up a tea stall in the fair. Whatever money we earned there, we sent for the assistance of flood victims. I loved to do such things right since childhood.

Was this assistance an inherited trait or did you possess leadership qualities by nature?

A streak of social service was in my family for sure. My mother's nature is certainly service-oriented; she had some knowledge about medicines. She gave some medicines to children which had to be taken before sunrise. Children used to line up before our house right from five in the morning. Mother knew about fifty types of such medicines. The environment at our house was such. My mother was illiterate, but she possessed a divine power. We used to get up early to help her. We used to sit the children systematically and render all help that was needed. This sentiment exists in all my family members. Perhaps I am not a leader in prevalent term of analysis, but it can be said that I was a person who took initiative. I am a person to start things.

How old were you when you left home?

I was about 16 or 17 years. I renounced home soon after school education. After my high school education, I said to my parents, "I am going and I don't know when I will come back."

Why did you leave home?

The first thing that I had to understand was to find out what the world is. I passed two years in the Himalayas. A transformation was taking place in me then. I used to visit different places, I wandered about. I went to Kolkata, I stayed for some time in the Belur Math. I can remember a childhood incident. It appears to me that whatever incident takes place with me, it occurs in some context, though these contexts may appear isolated, yet they are somewhat related to one another. I was in the fifth standard, at that time. I myself had corresponded for admission to Balachadi in Gujarat. I thought it necessary to go for service to the country. But my father refused me permission. He said, "It is not your work. You will not go." Ever since, this thing was on my mind that I have to do something. It appeared to me that if that was not my way, then some other way would have to be searched out. This was the right path for me. I set out from home, I was in search of something, I didn't know what. I did not meet any specified people. I was searching something within, but I did not get any satisfaction. I met spiritual people, I discussed with them. At my age then, nobody took me seriously. I was such too, it appeared to me. Some of them thought that I was an absconder. Many people asked me to go back home and asked me who would feed me and who would keep me. I got different types of experiences. Then I wished to go round the Narmada. This *Parikrama* goes for 14 months, it is done on foot. But I could not complete it. This wish remained unfulfilled.

After that, I roamed about in whole of Gujarat. I came into the contact of Vakil Saheb and the Sangh. If somewhere I found the Sangh *Shakha*, I would go and attend it. I met Sangh officials. I met respected Guruji too. On tour, I visited the Sangh office at Ahmedabad. Vakil Saheb said to me, "Brother, you have energy, you must utilize it. Stay here." He had a great influence on me. It was thus how I started to live at the Sangh's state office Dr. Hedgewar Bhavan in Ahmedabad.

I lived in Hedgewar Bhavan and did Sangh work. I had no experience to run the daily *Shakha*, yet I became a *Pracharak*. A Sangh *Pracharak* is an individual who dedicates his whole life to social service and national service. In a sense, he lives a life similar to that of a *Sanyasi*. It is as good as an exception to become a *Pracharak* without having completed its training or experience to run a *Shakha*. At that time, I was about twenty years. I met a large number of people at that time. I became close to two people amongst them, one of them was Eknatji Ranade. He got constructed a memorial at the rock where Swami Vivekananda sat and meditated for three days to look at the glory of Mother India. Another personality was Dattopant Thengdi. I maintained spiritual relation, rather intellectual relation with both of them. They too had much affection for me. I could speak my mind to them easily.

Once, Eknatji wished that I should stay with him and take charge of Vivekananda Centre. On the other hand, Dattopantji wished that I should stay with him and assist. However, I continued my work as a *Pracharak*. At that time, I had the advantage of education, exercise, discussion and understanding the officers. One day, Vakil Saheb said to me, "Narendra, God has bestowed so much on you, so you must study further." I asked what I should. He advised me to study history and Sanskrit. I asked him how I could study then. He stressed that I must study whatever the case may be. After some enquiries, he collected some information and said to me, "You can become a graduate of Delhi University without attending a class, as an external student. It was how I became a graduate of Delhi University.

How did your experiences go when you lived at Hedgewar Bhavan?

When I started to work as a *Pracharak*, the entire responsibility of managing Hedgewar Bhavan was assigned to me. I had infinite respect for Inamdar there. I said to him that it would be very fine if I got a chance to work with him, it would be as good as training for me. Any way, I was given the responsibility of the office at Hedgewar Bhavan. I am habituated of getting up at five in the morning; it has been formed due to that. I got up at five in the morning, went to fetch milk and made tea. Then I rang the bell to wake up everybody at quarter past five because about 20-25 people lived there together. Morning prayers were held, the great people were remembered; this programme lasted about 8-10 minutes. In the meantime, my tea would be ready, which I offered served to everybody one. After tea, everyone would wash each other's plates as there was no servant there. I would clean my surroundings and then make for the *Shakha*. In the shakha are held physical training and prayer. On return, I would prepare breakfast for everybody. We had a fine term there: 'P for P in boy P on P' this meant 'Poa, Pracharak in Prantik Karyalaya by Premchand on Path'. Here there was a boy called Premcand, I was very small then, about thirty years ago. He too was with me. He had come from the village just then. He used to assist me in the office. He would mop and clean Hedgewar Bhavan in the morning. I would wash Vakil Saheb's clothes. It was my inclination. I would read newspaper. If Vakil Saheb went to meet somebody, I would accompany him. After that, I was given the responsibility of *Vibhag Pracharak*. I was given the charge of *Sahvyavastha Pramukh*. Vakil Saheb has played a great role in moulding me. He loved me like his son.

Did you receive the degree in political science without any study?

No, I worked for it. I used to bring books to the *Karyalaya* and study there. Later the Emergency was imposed. I was underground then, still I went to Delhi for examination and passed it too. Later I left studies and wrote a book on emergency – *Sangharsh Mein Gujarat* (*Gujarat in Struggle*). At that time, there were two professors of political science in Gujarat University – K.D. Desai and Pravin Seth. They both urged me to go further and do MA and PhD. At their request, I started MA in political science from Gujarat University and stood first.

What did you do during the Emergency?

At that time, the rulers had tried to choke democracy. The leaders of political parties and social institutions had all been put behind bars. The entire country was as good as a prison. This was a struggle for the protection of democracy. I too worked in it as a soldier. I stayed at different places during the 19 months of my underground life. I had a warrant in my name. I would travel round Ahmedabad, Gujarat and the country. I would meet people, hold meetings, distribute pamphlets and so on. At that time, there was a volunteer in Bhavnagar Jail. We got the information that he was not well, so I went to jail to enquire after his health and about others, and came back in about two and a half hours. I worked for about two and a half years just like this.

Did you disguise during the Emergency?

If you think ordinarily, it is not much difficult to live underground. You don't have to do anything but to skip the police anyhow. However, for a fighter, especially an underground one, it is quite difficult for him to fight continuously and keep himself safe from the police too. The number of underground workers was quite large in Gujarat. It was about one hundred in the beginning, which comprised members chiefly of Sangh, Jansangh and Vidyarthi Parishad. Many of them had been arrested. Many workers had to surrender themselves. About 35 workers had been arrested, and now the number of free workers was about 35. This number was of those who had the MISA warrant on them. Besides them, there were scores of others who worked underground; they had to stay underground so that the government or society would not doubt them. The underground workers had to be careful so that their identity did not disclose. The Sangh *Pracharaks* who normally wore dhoti-kurta, now took to modern dresses and kept strange names. The members within the family were addressed like Dada, Mama, Bhai, Bade Bhai, Chhote Chacha or Bade Chacha, and an effort was made to keep away all others. Among workers, we worked with such names as Dixit, Umesh, Ajit, Chaudhary, Anand, Amit, Navin, Lalji, Prakash, Ranjit, Batuk, Timir and so on.

As the number of underground workers was large, the person in-charge of the state had to remember the names of all workers at state and central levels. Their dresses were quite camouflaged. They all had to adorn the dresses and work like Parsi, Voraji, Mullaji, Sardarji, LIC officer, swamiji, Pradhyapak, doctor, agarbatti agent, journalist, astrologer and others. It was also important that this disguise looked quite normal. This disguise became so natural for us that we had to introduce ourselves in the families well known to them. A panditji, dressed as an astrologer, had to predict the future, rightly or wrongly. As a swamiji, I stayed at volunteers' houses, and wore saffron dresses. Once while I was sitting at one such worker's house, a professor of Swaminarayan sect came. The family members introduced me as a swami from Udaipur. Now a debate was held between a sanyasi and a chance-swamiji. The swamiji anyhow managed to save his prestige, but did not allow the opponent to have a feeling that he was not the genuine saint.

When I became a sardarji, I would tell jokes on sardarji, and I would do it knowingly. Children in several families would request for such jokes too. It was quite difficult a task to change ourselves into the disguise, but the time and situation taught us everything.

You had an arrest warrant but yet you were not ever caught?

There were a number of fronts to fight during my underground stay. We were always on the lookout for any opportunity where we could oppose the government. In order to keep the people in jail motivated, we would keep them acquainted with different news, programmes and schemes. The chief cause behind it was that the prisoners had a psychological barrier to know if any fight was continuing outside or not. We had to take risk for that too. Once, it was necessary to have contact with some important leaders, who were kept in Bhavnagar Jail. It was not possible to communicate through some message. I had to visit the jail and discuss some points with them, and a plan was chalked out for it. To visit the jail for an underground worker was like committing suicide. With due preparations, I arrived at Bhavnagar in the middle of September 1976. I went to jail with a woman. The meeting was held. I stayed there for one hour, held discussions and returned safely. Keshavrao Deshmukh, a Sangh *Pracharak*, was caught. He must have the message from Mumbai, and how we should have it, we planned for it. This paper was quite important. At Maninagar, we sent a woman at the railway station to offer tea and breakfast in the afternoon. She was given a bag, newspaper and books. The woman was also instructed what she had to do on return. She tricked the policemen and exchanged the papers, newspaper, books from Deshmukh's bag, and thus those papers reached us safely.

How will you feel if you are called egoist?

Ego – I think you have to have two hands to clap. It is somewhat the same situation with ego. If the person in front has no ego, I wouldn't feel it a bit. For example, a saint is visited by a large number of people, but he would never say that the person in black shirt has a high ego and the person in red is a proud man. A saint would not utter anything like that, because he doesn't pay attention to all this. A saint has no ego. My ego will touch the other person only when he has the ego. Therefore, I don't agree that I have any ego. One more thing, I am respectful by nature. I became the Chief Minister only because of this, and years have passed since.

Do you do yoga or *dhyan*?

Yes, I do it daily and whenever I get time.

You devoted your life to Mother India, why?

It has always appeared to me that I have to give something to the society. I will not be able to give to the society however big I may earn. There are some barriers in life, they would stop me. If I have a scooter today, I will wish to have a car tomorrow, so that I can do social service. Then it will appear to me that I should have a larger, costlier car. The same thing goes with house, better house, costlier house. It will go on just like this. I will continue to accumulate all these for social service, and will be involved in a vicious cycle. I said to myself that I must free myself from all these barriers; I should do for the society what I must. You can begin with what you have.

You worked in the Sangh. How did you come over to the Bharatiya Janata Party?

In fact, I was a Sangh *Pracharak*. I worked for *Shakha*. We had an elderly *Pracharak* – Nathabhai Jhagda. Years back, he was the organisation in-charge in the Jansangh. He did not keep well, he was suffering from diabetes, so everybody was of the view that a young man was needed. Everybody wanted that the person should be the one who could work hard, and run around. This is the reason why I had to come into this field. One day, I received a call from Balasaheb Devras, the *Sarsanghchalak*. Abaji Thatte was on the other side. He said that Devras wanted to see me. I went to Mumbai on the scheduled day. There, Balasaheb welcomed me and took me to a room, and then he closed behind him. He seated me. I wondered what the matter was. I was called by the *Sarsanghchalak*, it was something extraordinary for a *Swayamsevak*.

He talked to me about the origin and structure of the Jansangh, and how it evolved. Then he said to me that he wished that I must work in this field. He expressed his confidence in me. It was a very fortunate day in my life that the *Sarsanghchalak* had called me. The whole day, he talked to me; we were together for six hours. He talked to me on intrinsic and extrinsic matters. He also explained to me in black and white what political events took place at what time, how development took place, he told me about individuals, what turns came in their lives, and what I was supposed to do. In the end, he said that he wished to assign me some work. I said that it could have well been done by the local people; it was nothing to call me for this. At this he said that the topic was such which he himself wished to discuss with me. I was the exception after 1952 that the *Sarsanghchalak* had decided to call and talk to a *Pracharak*.

When the Jansangh was formed, the *Sarsanghchalak* had himself decided on Deen Dayalji and Bhandariji. After that, whenever I met Balasaheb, he would say that he had decided this. He expressed happiness to see me as a father does on seeing his son. It was extremely an important decision of my life. That day, it was decided that I have to work for the BJP. I used to attend the BJP meetings and sit in a corner to look and listen to everything that went on. I did this for close to two years. I did not mix up with people much. I became acquainted with everyone. Then in 1989, was made the general secretary, and after that, my first direct experience came from Somnath-Ayodhya Yatra. The national media witnessed my skill in organization for the first time. It was after this event that I came into the open.

You wished to do everything that the organisation assigned you, didn't you?

Yes, the same way. You would not get to see my photo anywhere. It is my nature that I do well whatever I am assigned. But everybody looked at me that this is the youth who works.

After that, my scope of responsibilities expanded. Whenever a committee was formed at Delhi, I used to be nominated in it. If there was a committee of five people, I was one of them. What Balasaheb said to me, everything occurred just like that. In a way, I was being readied. All people of the organisation were making effort for my development.

How many languages can you speak?

Marathi, Gujarati, Hindi and some Punjabi, English. Besides, I like to listen to Bangla music and songs, I can understand them too. I have also translated Marathi books into Gujarati.

As the organisation in-charge in Gujarat, you won the BJP in elections right from the panchayat to Vidhan Sabha, why did you then all of a sudden leave Gujarat for Delhi?

It was the decision of the organisation. I do silently what responsibility the organisation gives me or ask me to do.

You were in Delhi, and then you had to come back as the Chief Minister. How did it happen?

It happened in October 2001. Madhavrao Scindia had just died; his cremation had to take place in Gwalior. In the accident, a number of journalists too had died, that included Gopal, a cameraman with AajTak. I knew him well. He used to visit my office often. It appeared to me that I must attend his cremation. I went to Delhi to attend his cremation. I was there when I received a call from Atalji's office; I was told that the PM wanted to talk to me. He asked me where I was. I told him that I was in the Shamshan Ghat. He laughed. I asked him what the matter was. He said what he could talk while I was in the Shamshan, and invited me to visit him in the evening. I told him that I would see him at half past six in the evening. When I went to him, he said, "You have grown fat eating the Punjabi food. You need to slim down. Go, go from here, vacate Delhi." Joking is part of his nature. I asked what the matter was. He said that I had to proceed to Gujarat and work there. I asked him if I was required to work in Gujarat or other states too. I did not know if he wanted to make me the Chief Minister. I thought this work might pertain to the organisation. I said that I looked after four-five states, and wondered if I had to look after the work of only one state. He said, "No, no, you have to contest the election. You have cooperated with several people fight election, now you must experience it yourself. We all have decided it." Five-six days elapsed since this discussion took place. After all, I do whatever the organisation asks me to, so I came here, and ever since, I am busy in this work.

When you came into politics, did you ever think that one day you would become the Chief Minister?

I worked for the organisation in the capacities of state general secretary, national general secretary and other responsibilities. The day I was decided for the post of Chief Minister, it was somewhat different. I had never imagined that I would ever descend into this field. I had not fought the election for a classroom monitor even, so election was not my choice, but I knew well of election strategy. I worked from the core of my heart when it came to fight election and got the party win. Even today, it does not appear to me that I am Gujarat's Chief Minister. I always think how I can serve the common man the most. I think myself as isolated from this post. Now I think that this is my work and I have to do it mindfully, devotedly.

How do you evaluate your journey from an organizer to a Chief Minister?

It is true that I have had a long experience in direct politics in the Bharatiya Janata Party and organisation. Basically, I am inclined towards the organisation. It is natural for me because I have passed my life in the organisation. However, an important point is this that I work for organisation in essence. Many people work and they all are related to public life. They fight elections and lead people. And now when I am in the government, I have several responsibilities with me, but I don't think any of us is different from the rest, or isolated, or higher, or lower than the rest. Some of them have experience in administration and the others in organisation. Some have capability in leadership. It appears to me that everybody possesses a unique quality; I too have my own qualities. I am carrying out the responsibility of Chief Minister with these qualities. I have worked for the organisation all my life. Now, my share of work includes organisational work as well as administration. I saw the secretariat first time after I became the Chief Minister, but I accepted the challenge. I got an opportunity to serve the people. My whole heart is in the service of the people. I am working with this spirit.

Will you tell something about your daily routine?

I get up at 5 in the morning; I am habituated of taking a cup of morning tea. Then I have the habit to visit the Internet soon after. I read papers, especially of Delhi. I check e-mails if any. If possible, I reply to them in a sentence. After that, I have a regular habit of doing yoga, asan, pranayam and the like. I have faith in God, so I pass some time in meditation. Of course, my infinite faith lies in Supreme God. This appears essential to me not for material happiness, but for mental happiness. After all this, I take bath and get ready. If the newspapers have come, I go through them. I start work after 7-8 a.m., I meet the visitors, if possible, I reach office at ten. I don't return unless I have finished the day's appointments.

It is perhaps for the first time in India's history that the office of the chief executive remains open late at night. My office is the centre of my tendencies. I try to stay back in Gandhinagar on Monday, Tuesday and Wednesday and work there. If possible, I visit different centres of the state on Thursday, Friday, Saturday and Sunday. I myself seek the feedback about the work under progress in the state. I inspect how government schemes are being implemented. I meet people. I take feedback from them. A phone call may come however late at night, I am sure to call back. It may not be possible to do so for one or two percent people. The people who ring up regularly have seldom anything worthwhile to say. This is my way of working.

Don't you have breakfast in the morning?

No, I am not habituated of taking breakfast. By nature I wish to see the newspapers, but they come late, so I open the Internet. When I was in Delhi, I got to see other papers of Gujarat, so I opened the Ahmedabad edition. Yoga, asan, pranayam all these are my regular features.

Do you worship?

Yes, I do it for a maximum of two hours. I do pranayam and yoga daily. I meditate, but there is no specific methodology. I chant a little during the Navratras. I fast, partaking only, water during the Navratras. No milk, no tea, no juice, no salt, no sugar, no fruit – only water. I worship Ambaji, Shakti. I have been doing it for years. During Advani's Somnath-Ayodhya Yatra, I was tested hard. The entire arrangement of the journey was on my shoulders and those were the days of Navratras. I took only water, and ate nothing. The third day, Kamla Bhabi, the wife of Advaniji, came to know of this. She had tears in her eyes. She said to me, "Narendra, this is not the way to work so hard. You must give rest to the body." I said, "This is my real life, I take pleasure in it."

Which is your favourite religious song?

Vaishnav Jan To Tene Kahie. When I was in the organisation, I used to deliver lecture on this song for close to one hour. Suddenly, I had a thought in my mind which I developed further. I used to tell them that the *bhajan* is about 400 years old yet it still applies to each leader or worker in politics. Just replace 'Vaishnav Jan' (people of God) with Jan Pratinidhi (people's representatives).

Jan Pratinidhi To Tene Kahie Je Peer Parai Jane Re
Par Dukh Upkar Kare Toy Man Abhiman Na Ane Re.
Parastri Jene Mat Re, Pardhan Nav Jhale Hath Re.

(A people's representative is the one who can understand others' suffering, he serves others but has no ego in the mind, he never touches others' women, nor does he put his hand to others' money.)

I used to give this *bhajan* to my workers as a document, only I changed one word in that. I love this song. I would like to tell you why Gandhiji liked it. The more you hear it, the more meanings you find in it. I can say only this that Narsingh Mehta was not only a poet, but also a thinker. He knew how people lived 400 years ago. There is no word in it which would not guide the politicians.

What types of books do you like to read?

Those books which are useful for humanity; I like to read the material related to human values – in books or on Internet. Today I am somewhat habituated of Internet. I can find anything new on it in brief. I read it. There is no one particular book which has influenced me, still I would say that Vivekananda's many books have impressed me. I was also impressed by the books on Sharada Maa and Ramkrishna too. In sum, I like such books.

You have written many books. What are you writing now?

No, there are several topics on my mind, I wish to write too, but it is not possible for lack of time. But I want to begin one.

Do you take to autobiography, memoirs and correspondence too?

I have an old file of my correspondence. I wrote my first book *Sangharsh Mein Gujarat*. At that time, I had nothing but pen and paper. I had no reference books to help. I completed this book in 23 days. I have a different type of memory. I have written seven books. Of these, *Aankh Aa Dhanya Chhe* is a compilation of poetry, *Premtirth* is a collection of stories. I don't keep any notes, I write by memory.

Whom will you consider your role model?

The definition of a role model can be set in different ways. If it comes to justice to the deprived and the suffering in the society, I remember Martin Luther King or Babasaheb Ambedkar. If it comes to not surrendering before anyone, I remember Abraham Lincoln. If I talk of a statesman and society's cultural heritage, I remember Mahatma Gandhi. If we have to talk about organisation, I remember Pandit Deen Dayal Upadhyay. And if we have to talk of firm determination and clear-cut speech, I remember of Sardar Patel, who stood before the Nizam all alone in order to undertake integration of India. There can be nobody like him in body language and resolve.

Who is your role model, whom you can call your influencer or motivator?

Vivekananda. In fact, I passed a couple of years in the Himalayas. I passed much time in Ramkrishna Mission too, that too when I was small in age. First my mind was inclined in that direction, and then it turned towards the Sangh work, and doing this work I reached here. Else with my family background, I was talking of it to somebody, had I become the school principal, my family would have distributed sweets to the whole village, because it was a big thing for its member to become a school principal. I belonged to an ordinary family, a very ordinary one.

How did you cultivate interest in literature and recreation?

I was fond of writing poetry. I will tell you an anecdote. It occurred way back. The images were being installed in a Hanuman

Mandir in south Gujarat. I was invited there. If you go to that area, your vehicle will continue to drive and drive, the village will be faraway, not to be seen soon. On the way, I saw the tribals of Dharampur, living with scarce means, having bodies like coal. I saw that scene for first time in life. On my return journey, I thought of a poem, I wrote it in Hindi – *Maruti Ki Pran Prathishtha*.

I sent this poem to my friend, Mahesh Mehta who lived in America. He and Dinkar Mehta are my relatives, so I sent it to them. I also wrote a letter with it, which I found just yesterday. As a poet, I wrote the name – Brahmachari Hasavanandji. In the paper, I also wrote the horoscope of the poem.

I wrote that looking at the constellations of birth; it appears that the poem has the yoga of Mangal. That is, there is no chance of the poem going with the poet. I wrote this type of astrological language in it. I also wrote that this poem would continue to roam around the world with its poet and he will have to go far. I wrote its second part. In it, I wrote the method of reciting poetry that the depressed people should be invited to poetry recitation, and not those who laugh naturally. This poem is not meant for such people. A few such things were written on the paper. As the *Prasad* of Lord Hanuman's poetry, they taught different physical exercises.

I first worked as a columnist in *Sadhna*, a weekly, and then during the 18 months of Emergency, I published a weekly named *Satyavani*. I also wrote a play which protested against untouchability. This hobby did not stand in the way of politics. Aspiration, ambition, glamour or power would have become a barrier in politics for me, but fortunately, I have been a conscious being in this religious society of Gujarat. I don't see any antagonism between literature and politics. Though I have not stepped into literature, I am not yet ready for this enterprise mentally.

You have a fantastic sense of humour?

Humour or satire comes to me quite naturally. For example, one day Atalji was unhappy, he said, "What is this security, you cannot meet anybody, you cannot go anywhere, you cannot do this, you cannot do that." At all times, he expressed his sentiments. He was tired of security limits.

Once I said to him, "Atalji, if you want to evade security, I can tell you a fine method."

He asked, "What is it?"

I said, "When you set out of home, keep some poetry books with you. Looking at them security people will keep away from you."

He laughed loudly.

Atalji has a fine sense of humour.

Once we had to attend the dinner at a person's house during our stay in Jammu and Kashmir. He was very enthusiastic and was welcoming everybody at home. A fine, juicy vegetable was on the plate.

Atalji asked, "What is this?"

The host said, "It is Srinagar variety, it is dam-alu (mashed potato)."

The potatoes were hard, they could not be broken, so Atalji said, "Are these dam-alu or dam-nikalu (what takes out life)?"

Such a fine sense of humour he had.

Did you acquire this sense of humour?

I have sense of humour right since childhood. I was in school when I was a favourite of a teacher. He was my father's friend. Once he went to meet father and said that God has bestowed much on this boy, but he does not make use of it. He said that he always applies one trick or another the whole day. For example, my teacher taught the Newton's law quite seriously. We all friends were in the class, so I remarked if it was the fact. He said earnestly that it really happens. Then he wrote something on the blackboard. Before he spoke anything, I remarked again, "Is it so?" First he thought that I was asking quite seriously, and then after ten-fifteen minutes, he felt that I was playing a joke. He complained to the principal who was my father's friend. He said, "He has talent." He illustrated my strange things which were replete with talent, even in jokes. He said, "There is something in Narendra, cultivate him."

Then he advised that I have command over language, something should be done to promote him.

Mr. Chaudhary was our teacher of English. My father instructed me so I was with him for some time. He worked hard with me. It was the chief reason, I had all this from childhood whatever name you may give it – trickery, naughtiness or whatever.

In rallies you enchant millions of people, you just fascinate people with your speech. Did you have this art of speaking right from beginning?

It appears to me that I must have cultivated this skill. Actually, one can say, I am not an orator, I am a communicator. It started ever since I started to attend big rallies. It is the common practice that you address some people in the beginning, so and so, so and so. I didn't do this then. I stand by the mike and have a glance over the audience in the ground. I don't know how this has developed. If I do this, people would get bored up, and my half a minute would be over. If I did this, how I would look like. I want that somebody in the audience should speak first, and then a dialogue should take place. For example, when I stand up and look ahead, I should ask which language I should speak – Hindi or Gujarati. Suppose I get in Gujarati. I love to have this fun.

Let me show an example. In Delhi I went to attend a function organised by the *India Today* which was also attended by speakers like Toffler, Clinton and President Abdul Kalam. When I stood up to speak, I had my written lecture with me, but I said that somehow I would not be able to read the written one. The topic was the development of states. I said how long we would continue to walk about with a dustbin, let us go about with flowerpots. Are we destined to follow the dustbin system in this country? I am telling you that after me, President Abdul Kalam and others quoted this in their speeches.

I had a programme from Kashmir to Kanyakumari. During the journey, we had to hoist the Tricolour at Lal Chowk in Srinagar. At that time, the terrorists had put a poster on a wall that only a son of his mother should come to hoist the Tricolour, he would not go back alive. At that time, I had made all the way from Kanyakumari to Kashmir, delivering speeches enroute. In my lectures, I would surely tell: "The terrorists must listen with open ears, I shall arrive at Srinagar's Lal Chowk on the morning at 11 o'clock on 26 January, I will not come in a bulletproof car, I will not wear a bulletproof jacket; I will not carry any arms with me; I will come with a Tricolour in my hands, and on the morning of 26 January, it will be decided who has sucked his mother's milk. Shatrughan Sinha was with me during this dialogue delivery. Later in a meeting in Jammu, he said, "I have seen actors shift from film industry to leadership (politics), but there is complete possibility that Narendrabhai will shift from politics to film industry."

All this occurs quite naturally. Now I can find that this has become a source of power for me.

You are fond of photography, are you?

There was a time when I used the latest digital camera. Scarce there is a camera which I haven't tried my hands on. But I never shot anything other than natural scenery. My photo exhibitions have been held before, which comprised slide shows of my photos. Today too I keep a camera and if I got a chance, I would shoot too. I went to Kutch on the previous Sharad Purnima, I went on an outing on a camel-cart, I shot Purnima with the camera.

What is the arrangement of your meals after you became the Chief Minister?

There are peons here. I don't eat the lunch, I keep khakhara. I have khakhara and coffee, and if I return home in the evening, I like to have khichri.

And to maintain yourself, Food and all that...

I am not fond of eating. I eat almost five hundred times a year in others' homes; if I count morning and evening, it would come to about 500 new homes, and for about 30 years, I sought alms for food. I went to people to have food, so I didn't develop any particular taste in eating. I ate whatever I got. Secondly, my nature is not to tell in advance about my arrival. I eat whatever is given. If I don't get anything, I don't eat, thinking it God's will. I return home without food then. People know it. Nobody asks me if I would like to eat.

If I visit a person at the mealtime, if he says, "Come and sit, food is ready." And I will eat whatever is available.

Do you observe fasts?

I have a small temple at home. I chant much during Navratras. I rise at about three in the morning to do extra chanting. I don't take anything in Navratras. I take only fruits in Chaitra Navratras, but I am only on water during the month of Ashwin.

People look at you in different ways, some say you would have excelled had you entered the literary field, some say that as a Chief Minister, you take to finish whatever you take in your hands. How do you feel about it?

People have different ideas about me. I am known to fully complete the tasks that I am given right since beginning. When I worked in Punjab, my co-workers opined that I was in the wrong place; I should have been an industrialist instead, because I used to create the entire corporate system by my managerial skill.

We can see emotions in your eyes, which keep changing rapidly. They show cleverness at one time and naughtiness at another...

In a programme in Mumbai, Suresh Dalal had described my eyes. He said: "The cartoonists take your beard at the centre of their sketch, but I ask my audience to keep his eyes in the centre." Secondly, the playfulness of my eyes hasn't come alive after I became the Chief Minister; it has been there for years. An individual analysed that there is no problem. Your eyes display what is there inside you, just manage your eyes, conceal their feelings, and you have no problem. I said it was impossible. I have never hidden anything.

Do you get your speeches written?

When I had just come, there was a problem because I had come here after a gap of about six years. There was a gap between me and Gujarat. I did not know about the questions, decisions and disputes prevailing here. I was fully isolated from here for the six years. The Gujarati newspapers had been stopped. I was fully isolated. Then this responsibility came from the blue. I had never met anybody, right from the peon to the chief secretary. I saw the chamber of the CM after I had been sworn in, and visited the Vidhan Sabha only after I became a member. Earlier I hadn't visited its gallery even. I did not know of the system here. Therefore, I asked my secretary to tell me what I had to speak. I used to ask him to draw out points for the speech. I did not know them. I looked at the points once or twice. If you have to go to a vegetable shop, you must go with the bag, I came to know of this fact. Wherever I went, the speech written by the secretary proved to be useless, I spoke other things, of course, on the given topic. Therefore, I bade farewell to the speechwriter. They too said that it was a better option. Ultimately, I did not like what others wrote. It appeared to me that my older practice was quite useful.

You have a wonderful memory, haven't you?

Of course, it is a good wealth. You can stay in politics only when you have a good memory. I called the secretaries for a meeting on the first day, and from second day onwards, I called them by name. They wondered about this. Generally, their names were not known even by those Chief Ministers who had been in the post for five years. Our Ashok Bhatt Khadis used to call them all by name.

It is very advantageous. Many people were in jail during the Emergency. But I was out. I was underground. Babubhai Jashbhai Patel, former CM, too was in jail. There, he dramatized *Shakuntalam* in Sanskrit. People were impressed. The letters coming from the jail described all these things. Babubhai was a good actor.

What was the special factor of your success as a CM?

The special factor for success as a CM is teamwork. The opportunity that I got to incline the entire system as the Karmayogi movement will bring a positive result for a long time to come.

You have wonderful self-confidence. What is its cause?

It is chiefly due to the tendency to go into a matter, and having no personal ambition, aspiration or hope. They who have truthful thoughts are approved. Ultimately, the truth attains victory, and not individual.

What is the greatest success and greatest failure in your life?

I am too small to evaluate this as of now. It has no relation with success or failure of private life.

You work for 18 hours, yet you are always fresh and active. What is the secret?

I get relaxed from the diversity of work. Even there is diversity in government files. I also get relaxed on changing the place. I attend the water scheme programme at one time and then in educational programme the next. Fatigue is related to our philosophy. If you have no philosophy to take something by heart, you will not get tired. If I think giving interview a burden, it would make me feel fatigued, but if I take interest in talking to you, then I would not get fatigued. Basically, it is my attitude towards work. I think that you get tired by taking rest, and not by working. When you have finished a work, you get satisfaction and bliss. The people of Gujarat have handed me over a responsibility, and development is my agenda. Sky is the limit, I must work to it. The more I work, the less it is. I have to carry development right up to the poor man's hut. I have to bring Gujarat forward among the most prosperous states of the world. I have much to do to realize this dream. I have many dreams, I have to work hard. Once, my speech was scheduled in Mumbai. There is a popular astrologer sister, Vasudha Bagh. One of her books was published by Suresh Dalal. She had invited me for the launch of her book *Mera Bhagyavidhata*. I was required to speak on this topic, but I had not thought much about it. I stood up, and thought and said that my fortune is my responsibility. My responsibility determines my fate. Each responsibility of mine opens up a new vista. I carry out my responsibility with commitment; it opens up the next door.

Don't you get bored up being in security all day?

You have spoken my mind. Life is so bore, just beyond words. Entire freedom is gone. The security surrounds me as soon as I step out. I feel pity for those who give me security. I am a workaholic, and they have to stand morning to evening, they have to work harder due to me. As a human, I sometimes feel the condition of the country. It is quite painful. The cause of security in temples too is terrorism. Terrorism has produced the environment of insecurity in the country.

Do you love to listen to music?

I love the Himalayas; therefore, I listen to the *Call of the Valley* (Shivkumar Sharma and Hariprasad Chaurasia). The flowing stream, its sound, but I don't get the time now. After I became the

CM, the things like favourite have receded into oblivion, due to lack of time. Of course, I listen to *Chidanand Rupo Shivoaham Shivoaham* to get relaxed in the car. By the time the car stands still, I am fully refreshed.

Which is your favourite film song?

Kishor Kumar's *Kuch to log kahenge, logon ka kam hai kahna.* That's all. I have nothing to do with the later part. Truly speaking, I love sad songs.

Do you listen to songs in other languages?

I have the divine gift of understanding a few languages. I listen to Bengali songs from the heart. When I am in the car, I listen to Bengali songs. I am habituated to rise early. The Bangla Akashvani begins its programmes from five, and my Akashvani begins from seven. Due to this reason, I have the habit to listen to Bangla Akashvani. I enjoy both Bangla and Gujarati songs equally well.

You are techno-savvy. Do you use the computer?

There was a time when I worked and searched on the computer for hours. I found new things. I would know what is going on in the world, what new research is going on in technology, I know how to surf, but it has decreased now.

If somebody seeks your advice on personal or family matters, what do you say?

I like to talk to such people. You may not agree that many hopeless people ring me up. They tell their family problems. I share their anxiety; this is my contribution. The things we talk are useful for myself too. I shall give you an example. This happened before I became the CM. A sister rang me up in the morning. I did not know her. She talked about her family. She said many things. I asked her to write down all that she wanted to say about different people, nothing should be left out, keep writing until the last. When you think that you have nothing to write more, just tear off the paper without reading it again. No person would be able to do so more than a couple of times. I say that if you cannot tell something to a person, just become his co-guide.

What is the saddest thing in your life?

Pleasure and sorrow are parts of life. I adopt sorrow to enjoy life. I have no complaint with anybody. I have no aspiration from anybody, I have no personal agenda.

Who is the person who has made the greatest contribution in your life?

I worked as a Sangh *Pracharak*, many people cooperated with me. Of these, I got cooperation from Lakshmanrao Inamdar or Vakil Saheb. Besides, I discussed things with Balasaheb Devras, Bhaurao, Dattopant and Eknath. I got guidance from them too.

What is your faith about prayer?

Of course, definitely; I take prayer as a mode of remembering God. I pray Omkar in the morning daily. This sound emanating from the navel has energy. I chant in the evening sometimes. Water cleanses the body, and prayer purifies the inner-self. Of course, prayer works, there is no means to measure it. Of course, but this is my argument that if you are wont to think about the presence of somebody at a particular hour, then that person is God Himself, you can just take this.

Who is the person with him you can speak your mind?

There are three such people. Two have died, I shall tell their names. One was Vakil Saheb on whose life I wrote a book. Now he is no more. My life after teenage passed in his company. He knew all my things, pleasures and sorrows too. After him, I was in the company of Dattopant Thengadi. We met once or twice in a year. He lived in Delhi. He lived there continuously. I too had my responsibilities. I invariably talked to him personal matters, but he too is no more. Whenever I felt weak, I expressed myself before them. I agree that these people knew me well – inside and outside. There should be someone such in one's life. There should be a shoulder you can place you head to cry. Sometime back I got a call from a relative brother. He was so sad that he broke down. I sent an SMS to him. You cannot feel relieved if you flow bucketful of tears, just a drop or two at a shoulder of a favourite person can do the job. He sent the SMS a little later saying Satisfied.

Do you love watching movies?

I love art or slow films which possess a thought-process. I like offbeat or art films, like *Manthan*, the one which storm your thinking and through which action and process may begin and not reaction. Now it is not possible. Now I am fasting, I have to give the result. I must work as a devotee, only then will I be able to give the result.

Being happy means?

No complaint and no aspiration. They are like two tracks of the railway. You don't find respite in them. The cause of suffering is aspiration.

Can you get success without honesty?

Honesty can lead to different results. The question is that of measuring tape, what norms you use for it, what is its basis. If I speak on my experiences, I would say that you can succeed by authenticity. Different people have different scales.

You are known as an honest leader. What do you wish to say about corruption?

I never had to claim that I am honest. People think that I am honest. As far as corruption is concerned, there are two types of corruption in the society.

The first grave problem is government corruption and the second is corruption in personal life. Government corruption is a very grave and worrying thing, it should be stopped, but it should begin from the top. The people at the top must not encourage it, then those below them will keep away from it. I mean to say that when it happens, the people to think on these lines will increase. All political leaders have to think about this corruption. Second, corruption has entered personal daily life. For example, we pay money to take reservation in the railway or get admission. This blot can be removed by awareness.

Is politics possible in today's atmosphere without corruption or enmity?

On the basis of my experience as the Chief Minister of Gujarat, I can confidently say that nothing is impossible.

Where do you find yourself twenty years later?

I have never decided anything in life. I don't know anything about tomorrow. I have no plan for myself. I have no roadmap. It is God or organisation that plans for me. But I can assure you that wherever I may be, I shall work as devotedly, as joyfully as I do now. And yes, I shall do what I am given.

Do you think India will become a superpower?

Are we not a superpower today? We are a superpower in the world in terms of human values and life-related attitude.

Our basic thinking has never been in race for money. However, after economic aggression, we have to come forward to protect our super elements.

In fact, in the history of ten years, it appears that India has a global duty. God has determined India's duty to do good of the world. India has to play this role. I am confident that India has done it and will continue to do so. Its divine and internal power shall inspire it to work for the world's well-being.

How could you link people of all classes in your projects of people's welfare?

The poor welfare fairs were organised in Gujarat. It is my experience that if a state level programme has to be done or lakhs of people have to be gathered, then it comes to appreciation. We undertook only district-level programmes under this scheme which were attended by three-four lakh people. It was the kind of participation. People showed will to link in the journey to development. I shall give you an example. We are running a movement for conserving water. We undertake construction of check dams. We also hold Van Mahotsavs for conservation of trees, Shala Praveshotsav for admission of children to school, Beti Bachao movement for protection of our girls. There are numerous such schemes that are run by people's participation.

You are much criticized in newspapers and news channels. How much are you upset by it?

Not a bit (he stresses). There is no negative word in dictionary which has not been used for me. I remain totally detached.

Secondly, if I haven't done anything wrong, why should I be upset? I am not a man to move along my image. I try to do good of six crore Gujaratis with witness to God. I am a human, so I might have erred in doing the truth or right, but one thing is sure, I haven't thought ill.

Modi Government assists the industrialists. Foreign car projects will only bring industrial development, this is said so by the opposition. How will you react?

Industrial development in Gujarat takes place quite naturally. My government works most in improving the human development index. Why do these Congress fans of mine never talk of the tribal welfare scheme costing ₹ 15,000 crore, Sagar Khedu scheme costing ₹ 11,000 crore, urban poor scheme ranging ₹ 13,000 crore. My government started the Beti Bachao or save daughter movement in 2002; at that time, the gender ratio was 802:1000, which has improved to 870:1000. In the world, India's position in human development index stands at lowly 126th, this is shameful, we are busy in reducing mother and child mortality rate. Right from common man to the President talk of the need to run a movement in this direction for the last thirty years, but we have attained success in this field under Chiranjivi scheme. Now, a poor pregnant woman heads to the hospital and feels safe there. We supply fortified *atta*, fortified chocolate, fortified oil to fight malnutrition. We have fought not only against terrorism; we have also fought against malnutrition. In villages, we have schemes like Sukhadi for pregnant women, voluntary schemes for giving milk to the poor in rural dairies and the like, and these schemes are run by people's cooperation. The government is constructing five lakh houses for the poor in rural and urban areas. The Scope programme has been taken up for improving education and English for the youth in order to improve their employment prospects. In short, the Gujarat Government has paid attention to all aspects of life, from food to nutrition, education to health.

You talk of injustice to Gujarat. How far is it true?

I will speak of injustice meted out by the Central Government. I request the people of Gujarat to pay attention to this, especially with a view to the benefits of schemes that are given to other states. For example, Tamil Nadu was given ₹ 13,000 crore for construction of national highways, while no fund has been released for Dandi March; gas is found in Gujarat, but there is no gas for Pipavav. Electricity allotted to Gujarat is shifted to Maharashtra, it comes to as much as 200 MW at night. Why, because it would be considered bad if there is dark in Mumbai, this is the excuse that is given to do injustice to Gujarat. The MCOCA is in operation in Maharashtra for organised crimes, but the GUJCOC is not approved for Gujarat. Gujarat is a neighbouring state to Pakistan. Just think, how Delhi could enjoy if people in Gujarat die?

What are the achievements of your government's rule?

These achievements are not limited like the limited colours of the rainbow; there are hundreds of them. This government began work with the Panchamrit scheme at the basis – which are : power of knowledge, power of water, power of energy, power of people and power of security. You will find hundreds of achievements in each of these aspects. For example, when I was new to the government, people said that they should be given electricity for as long as they could eat food in the evening. Now we can give it. There is water crisis in Gujarat. We started the water management scheme. We worked most on check-dams, boribunds, farms and ponds. Everybody spoke about linking of rivers, right from the common man to the President, but this is the government that interlinked rivers. Now, there is water in the Sabarmati round the year. What is the reason? It is Narmada's river that flows in Sabarmati. We have revived twenty rivers in the state. We have started girl education scheme in the state. When I came to power, only 60 percent people went to school. Today, all hundred of them go to school. Earlier, 50-52 percent dropped out, which has reduced to mere 2-3 percent. In 2010, we celebrated the golden jubilee, and took a resolve to bring it down to zero.

In the same way, Gujarat is better off than other states so far as it relates to malnutrition. There is arrangement for fortified *atta*, fortified oil, clean water to fight malnutrition. On the other hand, we used technology and e-governance to create the infrastructure for the 21st century. We started the movement to connect all Gujarat's villages by broadband connectivity. Our villages possess the facilities which may not be available in the world's cities; it would help them connect to the world. Gujarat was not at all number one in investment. Now it has come to occupy the number one position for the last few years. According to the data released by the Reserve Bank of India, of the entire investment, 26 percent has gone to Gujarat and the remaining 74 to the rest of the country. We took on our hands the task of drip irrigation. For it we had Sujalam Sufalam scheme, Jal Sanchay scheme and Jal Sinchan scheme. We adopted a holistic approach in them. Secondly, we took three important decisions, which would have impact on the whole country, they are the integrated development package of Vanbandhu Welfare scheme costing ₹ 15,000 crore, Sagarkhedu scheme costing ₹ 13,000 crore and ₹ 11,000 crore package for the urban poor.

You have always fought with terrorism. What do you say?

There should not be even a single blast in Gujarat. I used to raise my voice against terrorism then. I am not alone. I can see the atmosphere in the whole country. Even an ordinary citizen of the country is of the opinion that strict action must be taken against terrorism. All the surveys undertaken in India have concluded the same thing. There is soft pedaling against terrorism in the country. It is due to this factor that innocent people die and terrorists enjoy. Terrorism is a proxy war. What do we do at a time of war? The government announces blackout, and we keep dark. Every citizen participates in the war. In the same way, it is a proxy war. We have to follow the rules about it. We will have to accept the rules of security, only then can these people be controlled. At a time of war, all people, whether the PM or ordinary citizen, speak the same language, the country discusses only one thing, that is to defeat the enemy and embrace victory. The entire country celebrates victory. Terrorism is a proxy war. We all must raise our voice together and say, eradicate terrorism.

What is the remedy to end terrorism?

Terrorism in India is thirty years old. The survey tells us that after Iraq, India has suffered most by terrorism. More troops and officers have been killed at the hands of terrorists than in war. It is sponsored terrorism. They get boys from here, their sentiments are played to recruit them. These youths come from well-to-do and educated family. The terror of terrorism is increasing, but there is no one to check them. They come fearlessly and go away. The country may or may not do anything, but Gujarat is not going to sit idle unless zero tolerance attitude is formed, until new terrorists are recruited. If we do not check terrorism, we will have to see innocent people die. The Central Government will have to introduce zero tolerance in all states. Gujarat functions at zero tolerance mode, and we are of the opinion that if terrorism has been eradicated from Punjab, the same way it can be done from the whole of India too.

Gujarat holds schemes like Shala Praveshotsav, girl education and the like. How did you think about them?

Truly speaking, the Kanya Kelvani Shala Praveshotsav came into being out of suffering. When I became the Chief Minister for the first time in 2001, in the meeting with secretaries, I got detailed information about working of different departments and the actual condition of different areas in the state. During this process, I also came to know of educational condition in Gujarat. I found that Gujarat stood at 20th place in the country, it was behind Bihar even. It moved me. I was shocked by it. I felt helplessness; it was quite troublesome for me. Such a poor condition of education in Gujarat! This must change, and it was the time when I thought of girl education or Shala Praveshotsav. We started to implement it immediately, and today Kanya Kelvani or Shala Praveshotsav has become a mass movement. Today, due to this programme, the dropout rate, which stood at 29 percent five years ago, has come down to two percent, and it is our endeavour to bring it further down to zero. To meet this objective, the State Government has provided all those facilities which might be needed.

What is the goal of the Bharatiya Janata Party?

Our dream is to make Mother India prosperous, wealthy to the highest extent. It is aspiration, our dream to accord Mother India the place of the *Jagadguru* or world's guru. It is our dream to make Mother India fertile and prosperous. Our goal is *Sarve*

Bhavantu Sukhinah, Sarve Santu Niramaya, Sarve Bhadrani Pashyantu, ma Kashchid Dukhbhagbhavet. Our goal is *Vasudhaiv Kutumbakam*. Our goal is *Sahnavavatu Sahnau Bhunaktu*. Our goal is *Rashtriya Swaha Idam Namah*. Our goal is *Tyen Tyakten Bhunjitha*. Our goal is *Hindu Sarve Sarvo Sahodara*. Our goal is *Na Hindu Patito Bhav*. *Karmanyevadhikaraste Ma Faleshu Kadachan*. From my direct concrete knowledge, I am of the opinion that we must feel contented in public life, even in a field which is degrading like politics, such an organised team and workers are possessed by the Bharatiya Janata Party alone.

You have made several achievements under your leadership. Which of these is the most satisfying?

There are numerous achievements, there are innumerous things which beget us satisfaction and joy, but the most blissful of these was the Chiranjivi scheme. You may know that India stands at 126th place in the world so far as world human development index is concerned, that means, we have a very lowly position. The death rate among the people living below the poverty line and mortality rate among mothers are quite high. At birth, a large number of mothers or children died. So, God blessed me with an idea by which the Chiranjivi scheme got into shape.

The government does not have sufficient number of delivery houses. We announced that the government would pay for any delivery if the mother went to a delivery house. Not only this, the government would pay for the fare from home to hospital. Besides, the government would also pay ₹ 200 per day to the caretaker of the pregnant mother.

And if the mother or child could not be saved, the government would pay a compensation of ₹ 10,000. We started the pilot project in five districts in the beginning. 2,400 poor mothers registered their names under this scheme. We could save 99 out of 100. One mother died and we are very sorry about it. Out of a total of 1400, 1355 got a new life. We shall continue to regret the loss of 45 mothers. The good thing is that a new hope has been lit in the lives of very poor families. Now, this scheme has been implemented in the whole of Gujarat. The *Finance Times* of London has awarded the Silver Medal under Asian Innovative Scheme. The Central Government too has approved of this scheme.

How did you conceive about the Gujarat global investors' summit?

The summit in 2003 was a special effort. It was an innovative experiment. The enterprise in 2003 was taken in a very negative environment. The elements bringing a bad name to Gujarat continued with their negative activities. Still 2003 proved to be successful. People came to understand this. In 2005, the negative environment had diminished. It was like a wait. What will happen? Will it happen or not? How? And so on. Later, a massive environment was created in the summit. Investors, managers and people displayed self-confidence. The goal of Vibrant Gujarat Global Investors Summit was to bring recognition to Gujarat. We invited the world to come and see Gujarat, and invest here; we succeeded in our effort.

If there is investment, employment will rise, but the special achievement is that this two-day summit led to a global attachment in the Gujarati entrepreneurs, which would bring rich dividends to the state. This benefit cannot be weighed in a scale. Have confidence in Gujarat, and we succeeded to give this message. Confidence and trust are the greatest wealths of Gujarat, and I feel very contented on this achievement. This investment ranging over billions will bring qualitative development in Gujarat, lakhs of people will get employment. A fine quality of Gujarat is that it rose to face the healthy trends and provided a market to the goods produced by other states and foreign companies, with this started industrial development of Gujarat.

Narendrabhai, after you came into the government, much change has been witnessed in government's national festivals and cultural celebrations, their quality and form. Will you explain all this?

The first thing is that the celebrations on 15 August or 26 January were held quite simply; only a small amount was granted, and a few government officers and other officials joined together to hold programmes, there was no participation of the people. This celebration is significant from the view that the new generation and people could feel pride in their heritage. When people are made aware of the sacrifices of the ancestors, it helps to join them in the process of progress and development. We started a process of improvement in them. The state-level programme was held in one district, with an aim that the incomplete development work should be completed there, and a system was made for this. Due to this, the district's administrative machinery woke up. People came to feel that these programmes were just theirs. These celebrations were not for the sake of celebrations, the goals for these were mass awareness and development, and we infused these goals in the national festivals and Gujarat's establishment day in order to establish them at a higher plane. Due to this, our *Karmayogis* were introduced with their inner strength, and people felt pride in themselves.

The second good aspect of this programme is that we present magnificent cultural programmes on these three occasions. We make an effort to raise the quality and presentation of these programmes to the national and international levels. It helps in understanding history. The important historical dates are dramatized. Thus, amendment, improvement, artistic aesthetics, development of local artists, modern technology and global fluency of presentation through continuous practice, recreation due to compiled practice, comprehension of history, and the achievement of social traits like national pride, patriotism and self-pride – all these are the qualitative achievements that these programmes give us.

With the holding of Khel Mahakumbh, a massive environment for sports was created in Gujarat. What is your vision about it?

We must accept one thing that the Gujaratis are not much inclined towards games and sports. With the development of television and the like, our youths were turning away from physical labour. Sports are not meant for winning awards. For it, we have created an environment. At the time of golden jubilee celebrations, we thought out Khel Mahakumbh. At that time, the three main goals were: (1) to create sports environment in the state, (2) to refine sports skills, and (3) to create awareness towards sports in the society.

It is true that an environment has been created today, we have achieved quantity. In the first year, 13.15 lakh players participated, which rose to 15 lakh and last year it was 17.62 lakh. It is a positive sign. Now, we have to carry the programme to the next level. Therefore, we have established the Golden Gujarat Sports University. I have now to create coaches with scientific thinking. We have to construct sports school in each district. A sports school will be a hub while the university will produce good players and physical training teachers and coaches. I have to create centres of excellence of the international standard in order to prepare world level players. This year, we have formed a group of players below 12 years of age. The 1000 good players of this Khel Mahakumbh have to be minutely monitored and mentored in order to bring them to the national scheme. I have cultivated sportsman spirit in the Gujarat youths right since childhood in order to construct a divine and magnificent Gujarat. This task would also solve a number of social and economic problems. It is a great movement. In the next five years, this will become as important a sector as industrial and agricultural development. Besides, multipurpose centres will be created in small towns to compile the tendencies of youth development, in order to have positive impact on quality of life, senior citizens and public health. I want to create such an environment. This environment will help in doubling our rate of development.

You have implemented the gram sabha concept for rural development. Is this true?

The development of gram sabha is a step in the right direction. In a gram sabha, a villager can question a government officer about the result of a certain procedure or task. Fifty or hundred people should gather in the gram sabha; they should check the accounts and conduct an open discussion, whether the patwari comes or not, whether he works or not, what happened to the road, if there is some trouble and the like. There is a school in the village but teachers are not regular. There are several barriers in such public works, and the gram sabha is an effective tool in their eradication. Awareness has come about in villages due to the gram sabha. Besides, on account of this, an atmosphere of mass participation has been created for village development. It is through gram panchayats that the gramsevak, patwari, sarpanch and teacher come together in order to bring about a change in the village.

This innovative enterprise of the gram sabha has achieved success in undertaking public works by collective effort. Now, many of the problems are resolved locally. Even a backward person can speak out his mind. His confidence has augmented in telling what he wants to.'

Round-the-clock electricity in villages, it appears something like a dream to the outsiders. How did the Jyotigram come about which is something impossible?

In Gujarat, every common man wishes for state's development. Everybody is resolved that Gujarat should develop. I don't want partial or one-sided development of the state. I don't accept a situation in which Gujarat shows development in two or three aspects. Each village of the state has to be developed. Development has to reach the last man. This stream of development should reach every village, this is my resolve. As Gujarat pulsates, Vibrant Gujarat became famous the world over. It is my effort that every village should pulsate. I am confident that by the leadership of the sarpanchs and everybody's efforts and hard work, each village will come up in Gujarat. I feel pain on seeing our villages. I can remember when I started the Jyotigram scheme, the leader of opposition in the Vidhan Sabha was Amarsinhbhai Chaudhary. When I announced the Samras village, he came to me and said, "Narendrabhai, you have become the Chief Minister just now, you don't have much administrative experience. Somebody has handed you a fireball. It is simply impossible to supply round-the-clock electricity in villages. You will be trapped. I plead with you personally and in confidence. I did not say so in the Vidhan Sabha, but I say it privately. Narendrabhai, you will be embroiled. This is not the work which can be accomplished. You will be fixed if you promise it." I joked to him saying that I would not have been assigned this responsibility had this job been so easy. It is difficult so I have been appointed. Of course, the task was very tough; it was a hard nut to crack, but there was a pain in the heart. If there is electricity in cities, why is it not in villages too? Today take any major city in the country including Delhi, Mumbai, Kolkata, Chennai, Bangaluru, Hyderabad or any village of India, but Gujarat is one state in which we supply electricity 24 hours a day, seven days a week, and it is three-phase electricity.

You are much interested to make women sarpanchs. Is it not a problem for a sister to become a sarpanch?

When a sister becomes a sarpanch, it is sometimes painful. When I worked in Haryana, an incident happened. There was a meeting, everybody was introduced there. A brother stood up and said that he was an SP. I said he might be an SP, but the meeting was that of the Bharatiya Janata Party, it was not a government meeting, and he had nothing to do with it, you must not attend it. At this he said, "I am an SP and I attend all the meetings." I said, "Brother, this meeting is not meant for an SP, it is a meeting of BJP volunteers. You must know it, you must not come to it." I was then told that SP meant Sarpanch Pati (husband of a village head [wo]man), and not a superintendent of police. I plead with the sarpanch sisters to have control in their own hands, and not hand it over to their husbands.

I can recall that five years ago, some sisters of a village in Umreth tehsil came to see me. They were about 70 in number. I wondered why they had come. They said that their village had decided that not a man will be made the panchayat member; the entire village has been handed over to the women. It was a matter of pleasure for me. I asked them, "What do you intend to do of the village?" The dialogue that took place then continues to inspire me today. Those seventy sisters said to me, "Sir, we have to do something so that there is no poor in the village." The panchayat does normal things like constructing a pathway, writing letters for grants, and the like. But these sisters wanted to abolish poverty from the village. They requested me to instruct the district officer to give them aid. In the five years, these sisters worked to provide employment in the village. This concept was thought out by the elected women, not all people in the country have ever thought about it. Men may appear strong, but they are not so in fact. If there are ten women, ask a man to go and talk to them, and he would not go. If there are ten men and ask a woman to go and talk to them, she would go boldly and speak her mind. So courageous are the women. The first sentiment that they should have is to improve the village somewhat. I must not allow anything wrong to happen here.

How did you think about Shala Praveshotsav?

The former Chief Ministers said that they did not know. I don't know if the previous regimes felt pain or not. This is not my point of discussion whether the earlier government machinery was anxious about it or not. But I feel anxiety for this. I need people's cooperation to eliminate this anxiety. Therefore, I go from village to village. There can be no greater sorrow in the modern times if the offspring is not educated. Many people would say to their children that they did not get education despite such a long life, and what benefit it will give. They will say that they have earned their livelihood well. I wish to say to such people that you have lived a life of misery, you must not allow it to happen to your children. You did not have the chance to look at good or bad, but do you want these youths to live life the way you did, do you want them to live life in the same conditions that you did? The time you lived in was a completely different world. Now the times have changed, the same situation cannot go on now. Therefore, I visited the villages to go to people to eradicate this suffering.

Life is changing, age is changing. What is the means to fight poverty? What are the means to fight drought, scarcity of water, milkless animals, dry farms, unbearable poverty? Which means can work in such a difficult situation? If there is a means, it is education. It is a tool which will save you from difficulties; education is the tool to fight in any situation. Without it, life will be useless.

People are of the view that government employees don't work, you call them *Karmayogi*. What does it mean?

Just imagine about a typist and a guitarist. A typist types in his government job, which skill does he use? Fingers. He earns his livelihood by the skill of his fingers. He does his work, he is an employee. A guitarist too earns his livelihood by the skill of his fingers. But look at a typist and a guitarist after twenty years. A typist seems to live a life of burden, he drops his shoulders, seems to have squeezed down, it appears to be so. And look at the guitarist, he might not get food to eat, but he becomes a *Karmayogi*. The creation of his fingers fills bliss in his life. There is a difference between the two. A guitarist too uses his fingers, but his life blossoms in the later half, while a typist stales in the later life. If you are in this bus, you would like to change the seat. What is the reason? Because he has lived the life as an employee, so I say that there is need for one to become a *Karmayogi*, not for school, not for teaching, not for student, but for oneself.

How far have you succeeded in inclining the bureaucrats towards people?

Not only the media, but the entire country is talking about it that we wanted to make our employees *Karmayogis*. A difference has come about in our rule. Ever since our government has been formed, our workshop is held from five in the evening to eleven at night, which is attended by all officers, secretaries and ministers. A department gives presentation on one day, and then a discussion takes place on it.

The IAS officers informed me that they had worked in the government for twenty years, but now only they could realize what a government is. When the industrial development department gave its presentation, the education department said that it would require transformation of the teaching system. If this did not happen, you would not get the human resource you need.

Every year, we hold a three-day camp for the field staff, in which all officers and ministers together undertake yoga, discussion and training, it helps to enhance team spirit and unity. In this programme called Swantah Sukhay, there is no government label, there is no GR. I told the government officers to do all that they like. An officer got check-dams constructed at Ambaji for providing potable water. It brought employment to the people and water to the fields. We distributed a questionnaire to about three and a half lakh employees, out of a total of five lakhs. From it, we found where the government is going wrong, and what we should do to improve it. Now we are set to implement their suggestions. The employees have much energy and experience.

We have trained all government employees in pro-people governance. Earlier, when somebody was transferred to the personal management department, it was considered to be a punishment posting, but it is no more so. The workers, who have been trained in this, say that this camp should be extended from three to four days. Such good experiences are coming to the fore. I hold a meeting with the trainers every quarter. The training of about 1,55,000 employees has been completed. The entire system is witnessing a positive change. Besides, we also have a one-day governance. If an employee is not present from 10 am to 5 pm, he has to answer for it. There are 225 centres in the state where work is done with the help of IT.

When it comes to pro-people governance, the method of resolving people's difficulties should be sturdy. I hold gram sabha three-four times in a year, and I take class one officers with me. All people of the village attend it. They have the right to say what they wish to. In this way, we have resolved about six lakh problems.

My Swagat programme has become a talking point in the whole country. Every month on the fourth Thursday, an online programme is conducted through video conferencing. Earlier, the ministers held the Lok Darbars, it is its modern form. Under this programme, all the district officers are linked to me. Now the situation is such if a government officer doesn't work, a villager may tell him if the work is not done, he will complain it to the Chief Minister online.

Narendrabhai, the farmers in Gujarat are becoming financially prosperous when compared to the other farmers in the country. How far is this true?

We have taken the steps of agricultural development and irrigation in order to prosper the farmers in the right direction, it has resulted into positive outcomes. Every year from Akshay Tritiya, begins an agricultural festival which has become a historical movement for agricultural revolution in the state. This government has directed the farmers towards scientific farming and energized cattle-based economic system. The nature too has bestowed its blessings, and the state has not witnessed any drought in these years. The parched land of Gujarat is now green, so the prosperity of Gujarati farmers is a talking point everywhere. The farming produce in Gujarat ten years ago was ₹ 14,000 crore, which has now jumped to ₹ 80,000 crore. The agricultural growth rate in the entire country stands at mere 3 percent, which is in two digits in the state at 11 percent. To enable the farmers to have more produce at a lower cost, we have created greenhouses, net houses, sprinklers and other scientific methods of irrigation, these projects have been implemented. Besides, the soil health is examined and cards are distributed in order to estimate the farmers' productivity, and thus we take suitable steps for improvement of farming.

This is common perception that industrial development leads to less land for farming. What is the condition in Gujarat?

When normal development takes place, the land for farming is compressed, but Gujarat is an exception in the country. Here, together with industrial development, the land for farming too has increased. It is no mean achievement. Its main cause is that the barren land, which was lying useless for years, has been made useful for farming with means of irrigation. The entire country discusses it, even the world discusses it, and I must say proudly that the Supreme Court of India too has appreciated the land policies in the state.

There are accusations that the State Government is encroaching upon farmlands in its movement for industrialization. Is this true?

Gujarat is the only state in the country which has created the special economic zone. We are the first state to create the SEZ in 2003. The land given for all SEZs in the country has a share of fifty percent in our Gujarat. Still, no agricultural dispute has ever taken place here. It is due to our way of working. We don't want to take a farmer's land. Those who wish to take a farmer's land, they should go and convince him, and give him the price he wants, and meet his demands. It is up to the farmer to give his land or not. The government does not get involved in this matter. It is the way of working in Gujarat, and this is the reason that there is no controversy or dispute in Gujarat, while it normally happens in the rest of the country during the course of industrialisation.

Many people term Gujarat's development as Modi's mantra. Will you explain it?

There is nothing like Modi mantra. I am far from these things. The natural tendency of our country and people vests in power and ability; if we link them, there will not be any failure. We have done just this in Gujarat. We take pride in people's qualities and achievements. People's participation and mass movements are very essential for development. We shall utilize these for development. When the government comes along people, development takes place in its true sense.

Secondly, there is no definite model for development. It is prepared as per a state's capability and features. If we follow any model blindly, it would not solve the problem. Rather, a new system should be used at the local level, and then the basis should be encouraged in policy. For it, we have thought much in order to mark the chief path of Gujarat's development. We have made the strategy of Gujarat's development as a model of 360 degree growth, at the centre of which are six crore Gujaratis. We have created an environment by which development reaches these six crore people. We have worked hard and contemplated. As a result of this contemplation, we have created and established a new system of development in the state called *Panchshakti*. It coordinates power of people, power of knowledge, power of energy, power of water and power of security in order to undertake a movement for all-round development.

We should get habituated to work to become the best of all. We have to see where we stand in comparison to the people who are best in the world. The state should be guided in this direction. Our direction should not be that we are better than yesterday. We might be better than yesterday, but where do we stand as compared to the best? And how can we reach there? This is a moot point.

Who will you give credit?

I have to explain one thing. In the run up to development in the past eleven years, we have initiated development process in various areas and attained success. We would not have touched such heights of development had we not with us the blessings of six crore Gujaratis. This is the direct result of insight and understanding of six crore people, my team of six lakh co-workers and their commitment towards people. I pay gratitude to the people and all employees of the State Government.

You are very optimistic towards the present-day youths?

When you shout 'dark, dark', it does not eliminate dark. Dark can be eliminated if a lamp is lighted. We are living under a negative burden, so we see dark even in the lamp. If we find dark even in the lamp, we have got to change our mentality.

When we were small, we had read a small story in the syllabus – *Alice in Wonderland*. That story makes us think whether we have taken the right course or not. A girl called Alice has lost her way in a fair, and she asks Auntie Cat about the right path, who says, "Never say you have deviated from the path, rather say that you don't know where you have to go. Your path is where you are going now." Let us learn from this Alice of Wonderland that we must decide whether we have deviated from our path or not. If the goal is definite and the path is definite, we would know whether we are on the right course. Only then will we get an opportunity to come to the right path. This is my view that we should set a goal which is achievable, which should be possible and not yet in hand. It should appear that I would run a step or two and catch it easily. If I move forward, I am going to get it. This work has to be done. Everybody will get the momentum only when this is done. It may appear a trivial thing, but I can visualize the outcome we will get.

There is competition everywhere and the youths are undecided. Which formula will you give them for success?

In an issue of the *Reader's Digest*, there was a question in which the people were asked to reply from their experience: "What is the distance between success and failure?" Write from your own experience. Don't write an imaginative tale, write no article, just write from your experience. An American engineer wrote, which I think, is useful for all of us.

While digging a goldmine in Africa, a company reached far down and discovered gold in it up to a certain depth, and then no more of it was found. The company felt that the source has been completed and all gold has been extracted, and there is no more scope there. The company departed from there with all its goods. After this, an advertisement was given for the sale of the mine. A young American engineer read this advertisement. This is a true account of his life. He decided to buy the mine and submitted the tender. He bought the mine at a very low rate. He started to dig. They had to begin where the previous company had left. He dug for another three feet, and you will wonder, he got the richest goldmine right there. He wrote in the *Reader's Digest* the distance between success and failure is just three feet. The company which had left, had it dug another three feet, it would have become the richest company in the world. But the poor engineer got that wealth. The *Reader's Digest* reader wrote further, "Friends, don't stop at three feet, because success might still be looking for you."

Tomorrow is yours. I cannot dare say that today is yours. The youth must worry for today. Those who have power today, tomorrow comes to touch their feet; so give up the worry for tomorrow. Try to make today great. The brighter it is today, the stronger you will be to enlighten tomorrow. And we must achieve this capability. The youth must not look back to yesterday; he has to link himself with tomorrow. The youth must be linked with today. Today and youth should be inseparably connected. Every today of his should give him vigour and energy, he should possess energy within, his inner-self should be bright, he should have confidence in himself. The ocean that overflows with confidence, even a boat of aspiration can cross over.

What is the real power for success?

We will have to form the team and get success. I am of the opinion that Hillary and Tenzing are two fine examples. After they scaled Everest, journalists asked them both who reached the peak first. They said they were both together. When asked who stepped on the peak first. This question was asked again and again, separately and together, that one of them must have stepped first. Both of them replied that they together stepped on it. This is called team. It is a great thing. Else, did Hillary need Tenzing or the other way round after they came down? One of them could have well said that they were together, but just that he was a slight ahead, or the like. Somebody may be greedy. It is fifty years since. Hillary stayed at Nepal for fifteen days, but he did not have any change of heart. I suppose that this was the greatest power that got him success in life.

What is your view about age?

In the future, information will be the power.

IT = Information Technology.
My heart:
IT: India Today.
And
BT = Biotechnology.
My heart
BT: Bharat Tomorrow.
desire + power = resolve.
resolve + perseverance = achievement.

When a desire changes, it becomes playful, it is called the wave. When it is static, then resolve is formed. When resolve is blended with perseverance, it becomes achievement.

The people have expressed faith in you again. You have become the Chief Minister for the fourth time. The record of ruling Gujarat for eleven years continuously goes to you. What is the secret about it?

There is no secret about it. Of course, the credit goes to six crore Gujaratis and their insight and understanding. This is the victory of the people of Gujarat, this is the victory of the women of Gujarat, who have raised their voice. It is the victory of the youth who took over the responsibility of the election. It is the victory of the farmers, of the poor people, of the senior citizens, who continued to stand with us throughout. This victory is that of all-touching, all-inclusive and all-round development model and good governance. In democracy, power and wish are above the rest.

Ten years ago, I suddenly happened to take over this responsibility. Prior to it, I had no experience of fighting elections or administration. I have been brought up in an ordinary family. Right from the age of seventeen years, I have lived life in society, with common people; I lived like a saint, an alms-seeker. I have felt people's sorrow and pleasure. I had no experience of the government, system, administration, resources. But I had the feeling of the questions, problems, pain and suffering of common people. Therefore, I thought first how to solve their problems, and then thought over the system that could get people rid of their problems. I put my resources at work. The outcome took the people into confidence. This government has been cut from a different kind of fabric. People came to think that this government would do somewhat better. Several welfare measures were undertaken with development in view; my true intentions and clean policy did not mean any appeasement towards anybody, this development was guided only towards development and people's welfare, and nothing else. This government completed eleven years of development. We continued to implement the policies, and without any anxiety over advantage, we adopted the transparent policy. In this decade of development, Gujarat has created the dignified form of democracy first time after independence. The government has aimed at service, and the society has become development-oriented.

- Balanced development is the first priority for the government, whether it is village or city.
- There are Swagat programmes for complaints and their eradication.
- Energy is the mover of development.
- Optimum utilization of solar energy.
- Gujarat solar power capital.
- Coordination of power of people with power of water in irrigation and water management and water distribution areas.
- Roads are the carriers of development.

The role of government was to bring people in the ambit of development. People's capable movement of development was created on the land of Gujarat with the participation of six crore people.

The rural area has been neglected all over the country. Why did it change for the better in Gujarat?

The agricultural festivals were held in 18,000 villages for basic problems relating to rural economic system and agricultural development. 6,50,000 check-dams, farm ponds and boribunds were created in order to store and harvest water. The Jyotigram scheme provided 24-hour three-phase electricity to the villages. In the field of animal husbandry, 2700 cattle health fairs were held in order to protect health of millions of cattle and they were administered immunization injections to end 112 types of animal diseases. In a decade, the state registered a growth of 66 percent in milk production. The Gunotsav scheme helped in bringing about qualitative changes in education. 108 rural ambulance services were made available. Due to several such schemes of rural development facilities, farming and farmers became partners in prosperity. Now economic enterprises were started in villages. Direction for new employment was created through skill-development centres numbering 300, that taught traditional skills. Not only electricity, Narmada water, *pucca* roads, but also broadband connectivity to all gram panchayats, communication technology services help people to get land records. The grievances redressal programme called Swagat Online has made inroads into villages. The gram sabha, Samras village, Tirthgram, Pavan gram and the like helped to create an environment for development without any dispute or controversy. 11,000 villages became clean, and now villages competed to become clean. The Kanya Shikshan Yatra has improved primary education. 45,000 *Anganwadis* look after children. 44 lakh children and mothers get nutritious food for eradication of malnutrition. The Chiranjivi scheme has created a new vista in mother and child care. Millions of sisters in villages undertake a business worth ₹ 1000 crore annually by joining the Sakhi Mandal numbering two lakh. And Khelkood Mahotsavas have made villages fine places. Development breathes life into villages. Urbanisation is looked at not as a problem, but as an opportunity, and rural development has been linked with people in order to bring qualitative change in social, economic and educational life. The poor welfare fairs have given the poor a new energy to fight poverty. The villages too pulsate with vibrant development in an atmosphere of harmony. Whether it is village or city, the mantra of development for this government has been all-inclusive and all-touching.

How did leap in development augment opportunities for employment?

It is foremost to know that Gujarat considers education as a tool to create a cultured society, and as far as employment is concerned, Gujarat has stood first in the country in the last decade. Gujarat alone has created 70 percent of total employment in the country. Even for the employment-oriented institutions, Gujarat has provided a long-term perspective. In order to get skilled manpower, 300 skill-enhancement centres were started in the state. A Gujarat's student should be able to understand the world, he should be able to communicate with the world, so the SCOPE programme has been started in order to teach him English. Under skill development, more than 3000 courses have been started. Gujarat has started the technology university. Each technical university runs ITI and polytechnics. The seats in technical education, engineering and medical education have multiplied to three times.

You undertook several development tasks in Gujarat. Which of these is your favourite?

This is a too tough question to answer. A widow mother rings up in the morning to bless saying that her son met an accident but was saved by 108. I felt that a great job was done. In the afternoon, I got calls that the Jyotigram is a fine scheme. There was a time when there was no electricity in the evening at dinner time, now people don't eat in dark. Others came and said that there was none to listen to their complaints when Swagat Online was not there. But today we have people to listen to us. While wandering about villages for girl education, an old granny comes up on the pathway and says that no one has ever seen the school building for four generations and today children are going to school. Rajiv Gandhi said that he sent one rupee of which only 15 paise reached the beneficiary, the rest vanished on the way. I undertook the poor welfare schemes in order to deliver the whole rupee to the poor. When the Government of India obstructed Sardar Sarovar dam, I sat on *Anshan* in protest. When I became the Chief Minister, two-three topics came into my mind. I had not met any member of my family for 30-35 years, because I had been out of home, I did not know even my own family members. I held a programme to meet family relatives and children face-to-face.

I met my childhood friends after 35-40 years. It appeared appropriate to me that I should see them. I also held a magnificent programme in a Gujarat college in the honour of teachers who had taught me in childhood. At that time, the governor Nawal Kishor Sharma had delivered a sentimental speech saying that he had never seen such a programme before.

How did you think of Statue of Unity?

All countries of the world try to create their mark of identity. Our country is linked with the Taj Mahal and India Gate which are historical monuments over ages. The Eiffel Tower in Paris and Egyptian pyramids are globally known. America is going to make use of modern technology in order to construct a new type of pyramid. You must have heard about 102-storey twin towers which America had built. Malaysia built a 104-storey tower to present its technology. After independence, whatever we have, is quite old and ancient, for example, the Taj Mahal, Gateway of India and Parliament have become the marks of India which were constructed prior to independence.

After the country's independence, we must come out proudly. Sardar Patel is the foremost personality to unite the country right from Kashmir to Kanyakumari. Whenever we talk of unity and integrity of the country, we find the name of Sardar Patel leading the rest. He took little time in merging the native estates into India, which is like a gift of unity. It was a wonderful occurrence for the world. The more we sing in his praise, the less it is. We have now decided to construct the Statue of Unity as homage to that great personality. Today, the Statue of Liberty is the tallest in the world. We have to make the Statue of Unity double the size of the Statue of Liberty. Secondly, Sardar Vallabhbhai Patel was the Iron Man, he was the son of a farmer, he worked for unity. All farmers in the country need iron tools to work on their farms. Because Sardar is a farmer's son, we have decided to collect iron from the farmers, get it melted and create a massive and glorious statue, so that the farmers and the world might feel that such a great man ever took birth in India. I have to communicate this thing to the world, it was how the idea of Statue of Unity came to my mind.

Before and after independence, development is seen in the society as pertaining to majority and minority classes. How do you compare development in such an environment?

In the past ten years, it is Gujarat that has realized the real definition of development politics, and I wish to say it proudly. First five crore Gujaratis, and then five and a half crore Gujaratis have done wonders in people's participation in development. The foreigners who divided India into two parts departed, but after independence too, the rulers relied on vote-bank politics, and divided the country and society into minority and majority. Some of their hunger of power must have been satisfied. However, had the capability of such massive power of 120 crore people not been divided, India today would have become a superpower.

The Gujaratis have resolved right from the beginning of the 21st century that vote-bank politics will no more be effective. Gujarat too has borne with the discrimination based on majority and minority. It has experienced pain and suffering. There is no need to recall to memory the violence and tremor in the first four decades of its birth. But one thing is certain that the leap of development that Gujarat has taken would continue to impact the world. This is the definition of the attitude of development of six crore Gujaratis.

The people who are misguiding people in the terminology of majority and minority, they have simply cheated people even today. Sachchar Committee, appointed by the Government of India, surveyed the condition of minorities in Gujarat and concluded that the minority community has taken part in prosperity and development of the state. Now Gujarat does not wish to look back. We have not to go with such people. The term 'six crore people' is not a group of words, it is the collective display of the power of society. There is environment of peace, goodwill, harmony, unity and brotherhood, it is the global goodwill of six crore Gujaratis.

You are in continuous touch of modern technology. On the basis of your experience, what do you feel how important these means are in today's politics?

Technology has empowered people, and in politics, the political leaders have been required to prove their efficiency. Technology is like a doctrine for politicians, if they are able to use it in the right direction, it would become a powerful means to change the situation. Today, it has connected the common man with the worldwide web or information technology connectivity in order to empower them. However, people have to participate in presenting a common man's voice in democracy in all matters including resolution of problems and policy making.

In the past, politicians used technology for contact with people and propaganda, but now, due to wide impact of web, technology, Internet and social media, technology has emerged as a challenge for politics, and a complete change has occurred for the citizens in democratic politics.

The information technology has enabled a common man in different sources, and now he can deliver his voice in politics, development policy and formulation of programmes. Earlier, there was no contact of politicians with the common people for five years after the election. But now, people can become lively participants in each process and activity of politics. It has resulted into the situation in which politicians have to prove their worth. No politician can ignore people's voice today; it is no more possible due to the use of technology. Politicians should not look at technology as a problem, but accept it in its true sense for the significant objective. Its inspiring illustration is the election campaign in Gujarat in which I addressed the people simultaneously at 53 places through 3-D holographic technology. Social media were used by millions of people to have a dialogue with me, mutual discussion took place, due to which I have got an opportunity to understand a common man's anxiety, questions, dreams and aspirations. The internet has turned the citizen into netizen, for whom there is no limitations of geographical boundaries.

Technology can be used to bring about qualitative change in not only politics, but also in administration. Technology can change responsibility, transparency and working style of the administrator. Good governance has become a political agenda now. We should accept the effect of technological communication, Internet media and digital conversations in order to make them feel good governance. The Internet technology is becoming a game-changer in decision-making and policy formulation. Now, politics is no more governed merely by the elected representatives.

In a democracy, there is importance of people's voice, and in Gujarat, Swagat Online has presented a satisfactory remedy for a common man's problems with the use of technology. Not only this, it can help us bring about qualitative improvement in politics and administration. In Gujarat, Bhaskaracharya Institute of Space Application and Geoinformative has used satellite technology in order to undertake satellite mapping in a strategic manner and has brought about many reforms. The pilot project of development, SIRS has been used to map the land, right from modern landscaping like Smart City to forest land of the tribals, and thus give everybody their due.

The Gujarat Government today has used technology to plan and implement watershed management, disaster management and other programmes. Gujarat is the first state in which technology has been used to resurvey the entire land. All panchayats have been linked with broadband connectivity under e-gram Vishvagram scheme, due to which e-sevam, e-dhara and other welfare activities have become transparent. In Gujarat, after the use of Electronic Voting machine, e-voting has been successfully used in local self-government elections.

Advanced technology of social media can start a new chapter between the government and people, and Gujarat has taken lead in this direction. Technology is a medium for citizens' empowerment in order to bring about a qualitative change in politics, but it should be used in the proper direction.

What should be done to awaken the society's capability?

The society is capable, it should be awakened. Before we step out of poverty, it appears to me that we should step out of ideological poverty. Poverty kills any society, any individual, and if an individual is ideologically poor, then he remains a poor man all his life, he can never come out of it. Many people state that they are helpless as they were born in such a society, they are helpless to earn their livelihood by labour. What else have they? Nobody can advance with such mental poverty.

However, if there is resolve in the mind, then you can come out of any situation. If the attitude is right, its outcome is bound to be positive.

I can remember a true anecdote. Years ago in childhood, I was standing at Mahesana railway station. Somebody gave a loaf of bread to a beggar, who kept it on his palm and ate it joyfully. The train was yet to come, so I observed his activity minutely. I went to him and said, "Brother, you have nothing in your palm, then why should you touch it on your palm before biting it?" In fact, I wanted to know his mental state. The beggar said, "Sir, somebody gave me this. I don't like it plain, so I imagined as if I had salt in the palm, I am in fact imagining it salty." I said to him, "You will never come out of this poverty. When you have to imagine, why should you imagine salt, why not srikhand?"

Mentality is a strong bound. It appears that our society is bound by this mentality. Now the time has come when we should break away from it. We will have to do it ourselves with our capability, self-confidence. We will have to forsake this mentality that somebody would come and set everything right. When you stand erect, capably and confidently, you are sure to get glory.

What type of nation do you imagine?

Our scriptures have written:

Sarve bhavantu sukhinah, sarve santu niramaya,
Sarve bhadrani pashyantu ma kashchitadukh bhagbhavet.

This means that modern science should cover public life. It is not necessary to have schools like the *gurukuls* today. In the changed times, there should be institutions matching today's needs. The ultimate goal is that there should be provision for everybody's total happiness. We do not look at an individual only in economic terms. We look at him holistically, with *dharma*, *artha*, *kaam* and *moksha*. We should develop a system in which all these four aspects of life are fulfilled, are realized, and such a system should be developed in the modern times. This work has to be done by those who know it. The people like us are assigned with the duty of bringing people together. Just think, contemplate and give something to the country. The people in government should implement it in practice, in conduct. I am confident we will be able to give the world something worthwhile.

You have been declared the prime ministerial candidate of the Bharatiya Janata Party in the coming Lok Sabha elections. How do you feel about it?

I carried out different types of duties in the Bharatiya Janata Party as a worker for many years. I used all my understanding, vision and power for the extension, expansion and development of the Bharatiya Janata Party. The party has always given me an opportunity to serve the country. The national leadership of the party has given a very important responsibility to a person like me who belongs to a very ordinary family of a very small town. This party, which is now like a massive banyan tree due to the effort and guidance of Atalji and Advaniji, will certainly kiss victory due to the effort put in by lakhs of party workers. I express my gratitude to all workers, big and small, senior leaders respectfully and politely.

I would like to promise my party, lakhs of workers, supporters and country that I would leave no stone unturned to make the Bharatiya Janata Party victorious in the 2014 elections. I would make every effort to fulfil the hopes, aspirations and expectations of common people and workers in every way. I wish blessings of my crores of countrymen that in these calamitous times, they should bless the Bharatiya Janata Party in order to enable the country come out of the present crisis. I am confident that from Kashmir to Kanyakumari and from Atak to Cuttack, the whole country will support the Bharatiya Janata Party's lotus with a new direction, new hope, new ambition and new thinking.

□

Growth Chart of India with Narendra Modi as PM

Modi visits Bhutan to assert regional sway

With an aim to develop friendly ties with the neighbouring countries, Modi took his first foreign visit to Bhutan on June 15 after taking over the position as country's Prime Minister. An avid reader and socialiser on web, he tweeted on his return to India that he was touched by welcome song sung by primary school students during the luncheon hosted by His Majesty the King of Bhutan. Hundreds of school children dressed in traditional red and green tunics had lined the route from the airport waving the Indian flag as his motorcade arrived in the kingdom which had remained closed to outsiders for centuries. He was given a ceremonial welcome in Bhutan's capital Thimphu nestled in mist-covered mountains. His talks with the Bhutan's King Jigme Kesar Wangchuk and Prime Minister Tshering Tobgay strengthened the bond between the two nations. The Himalayan kingdom of Bhutan is home to over 1.5 billion people but is held back by bristling rivalries. This country, which made the transition from absolute monarchy to parliamentary democracy in 2008, is struggling with high unemployment and a growing national debt.

Strategically placed between India and Tibet, Bhutan had remained aloof since 1951 after China took its control of Tibet, which borders with Bhutan. Relations between the capitals of the two countries Beijing and Thimpu remained traditionally strained following a border dispute. However in a surprise move in 2012, the then Chinese Premier Wen Jiabao and his Bhutanese counterpart, Jigmi Y Thinley met on the sidelines of the UN Conference on Sustainable Development at Rio De Janeiro. During the meeting, the two leaders expressed their willingness to establish diplomatic relations and discussed measures to speed up efforts to resolve the border dispute and to step up bilateral ties. But Bhutan did not pursue the move apparently to avoid creating any misunderstanding in its ties with India. On the other side, China had been building ports in Sri Lanka, Bangladesh and its 'all-weather ally', Pakistan. It overtook India as the biggest foreign investor in Nepal in the first six months of 2014.

During his first trip abroad, Modi assured Bhutan of India's support. It was his attempt to assert India's influence in South Asia where China is steadily making inroads. He opened a Supreme Court building constructed with Indian assistance. He also laid the foundation for a 600 megawatt hydroelectric power station, part of an energy cooperation plan to feed demand in Bhutan and India. By and large he aims to make India the dominant foreign investor across South Asia as well as the main provider of infrastructure loans, just the same way China has done in much of the rest of Asia and in Africa.

On the promise of making his country an economic and military power, his decision to make petite Bhutan his first destination was the latest in a series of unconventional policy choices. He had previously invited South Asian leaders to his oath taking ceremony as a prime minister and exchanged friendly letters with Pakistan's Prime Minister Nawaz Sharif in a bid to re-establish India as the dominant power in the region.

"Modi's Bhutan visit shows an astute sense of the region's critical importance to India's economic dynamism and strategic strength", said Alyssa Ayres, a South Asia expert at the New York-based Council on Foreign Relations.

Historic visit to Nepal

Narendra Modi became the first Indian prime minister to visit Nepal in 17 years. During his visit he stressed the importance of the constitution writing to the Nepalese leadership including President Ram Baran Yadav and Prime Minister Sushil Koirala. To enhance the bilateral ties between the two countries, he gave the 4 C's formula – cooperation, connectivity, culture and constitution. At the same time, he assured Nepal that India did not want to interfere in its internal affairs. Not dictating anything, he asked the Himalayan country to choose its own course in its endeavour to build a stable and prosperous democratic republic.

"Nepal is a truly sovereign nation. We have always believed that it is not our job to interfere in what you do but to support you in the path you decide to take," he said while addressing the Constituent Assembly of Nepal.

He announced 1 billion dollar line of credit (LoC) to Nepal. It was decided during his visit that the Pancheswar Development Authority will be set up and a detailed project report will be finalized within a year. The two sides also agreed to conclude a Power Trade Agreement (PTA)—a framework pact for the commerce and power sector within 45 days.

The two prime ministers directed the concerned authorities to conclude negotiations within 45 days on the Project Development Agreement (PDA) between the investment Board of Nepal and GMR Group of India for the development of Upper Karnali hydropower project.

Manufacturing tycoon China invites Modi

A proposal from Chinese president Mr. Xi Jinping was sent to Modi on July 15 saying he was looking forward to his September visit to India and also welcomed Mr. Modi to visit China in 2014. He proposed for a 'negotiated resolution' to the boundary dispute at an early date, as the two leaders had held their first ever meeting in Brazil.

Being a staunch follower of Swami Vivekananda and believer of the tenet of 'Vasudev Kutumbakem', Modi is always willing to peacefully settle the boundary issues through friendly negotiations. India and China have had common civilisational heritage, and links through Buddhism, and both countries can do more together to tackle their common challenge of fighting terrorism.

Both the countries recently signed a first ever Memorandum of Understanding on setting up China-dedicated industrial parks, as Commerce Minister Nirmala Sitharaman held talks with her counterpart Gao Hucheng in Beijing, during the Vice President's visit in China in June. Modi said that maintaining peace and tranquility on the border was essential for resolving the issue.

Targetting the three super powers

Next in pipeline after Nepal and Bhutan was Modi's plan to invite Japan, China and the US for investment through his 'Make in India' strategy and with this let the Powerful-trio compete with each other. His 'Make in India' campaign made a big splash in China as large number of investors flocked to the special investment promotion events organised by Indian missions highlighting the country's fast-changing investment liberalisation process. Modi clearly showed that his government was more committed to economic development and that India hoped to learn from China's economic success.

When Chinese president, Xi Jinping visited India along with his wife and other ministers, he was given a red carpet welcome at Ahmedabad airport in Gujarat. This had happened for the first time since every delegate was received in Delhi earlier. Modi wanted to present modern India to the Chinese president. What else could be the priorities of a person like Modi who had made his own life as a pilgrimage and had undertaken the challenging Mansarovar yatra– He suggested the setting up of an additional route for the Kailash Mansarovar yatra in Tibet to which president Xi gave assurance. The president and his wife Peng Liyuan were also given a ceremonial reception at Rashtrapati Bhawan in Delhi.

The Chinese President, got a hybrid of a Nehru-Modi (khadi) jacket, a walk on the Sabarmati river front, a cultural extravaganza by the local dancers, a lesson or two on the spinning wheel of Mahatma Gandhi and sampled 125 Gujarati dishes.

The Chinese President said he wanted both the countries to launch a batch of exemplary projects in infrastructure, such as railway construction, to enable more balanced and sustainable trade. The issue of rising trade deficit in China's favour, reaching $ 29 billion last year, was raised by Modi. Mr. Xi welcomed India to join its initiative to set up a new Asian Infrastructure investment Bank as a founding member, the official from Xinhua news agency had reported.

A fair, reasonable and mutually acceptable solution at the earliest was sought by Xi to resolve the dispute between India and China.

The Modi effect

Modi's speech was telecast in Beijing with elaborate presentations in which over 250 investors, officials as well as media people were present. A special business event and round-table discussion on investing in India's Manufacturing Sector was held to seek China's investments in the backdrop of $20 billion commitment made during the visit of the Chinese president. Besides railway modernization, bringing bullet train to India, China is to invest in two big industrial parks.

Notably a manufacturing company TBEA has already invested in Gujarat. Chinese investors will play more important role in India in the coming ten years in India and there is no doubt Chinese investments in India will grow feel the industrialists. Modi's speech had brought about sense of clarification about India's commitment to promote foreign investment.

The Chinese have felt that India has many advantages in terms of labour, youth power and open culture. Former Indian ambassador Surendra Kumar says : "Narendra Modi doesn't have to ditch any one of his suitors for the other; he can afford to play beach ball with all the three Japan, China and the US and let them compete with each other. No other Prime Minister of India was so fortunate, not even the sophisticated and urbane Jawaharlal Nehru whose charm captivated Lady Mountbatten."

Modi strongly drew attention to the long pending border dispute during his meeting with the Chinese president, stressed on the need to demarcate the Line of Actual Control and flagged the visa issue and trade balance. Mr. Xi traced ancient Indio-China links, referred to Buddhism and the Silk Route, remembered the service of Dr. Dwarkanath Kotnis and liberally quoted from Indian icons Rabindranath Tagore and Jawaharlal Nehru. It has been a tradition with the visiting Chinese leaders to meet the family of Dr. Kotnis and Xi met the sister of the famed physician, Manorama. Kotnis had given his precious life in China serving in the World War.

He reiterated the relevance of the Panchsheel and praised India's economic progress and stressed China's desire to create a peaceful periphery to focus on its pursuit of economic progress for her people. Quoting from the Bengali poet Thakur Rabindra Nath Tagore's verses on friendship, "...If you think friendship can be won through war, spring will fade away before your eyes", he stressed on the virtues of amicable relations between neighbours, peace and cooperation in the region as had been envisaged six decades ago in the Panchsheel treaty among India, China and Myanmar. At the 60th commemoration of the Panchsheel, he asserted that China would follow the five principles of Panchsheel even as it is ready to work with the West to uphold world peace and development. He also underlined how India and China together, with 2.5 billion people, could transform not only Asia but the whole world. He further exhorted India to join the SCO and Maritime Silk Route but wanted India to facilitate China's membership of SAARC and cooperate in international forums on issues of common interest. As had been expected, the joint statement committed the two sides to a reasonable and mutually acceptable solution of the border dispute and to pursue it as a strategic objective. Clearly Modi's reference to how even a toothache paralyses the whole body pressed the right chord on Xi's heart hinting on the dire need to resolve the border dispute.

It is naive to expect that the border dispute, discussed by Special Representatives seventeen times in the past, could be resolved in one visit. In his speech at the Indian Council of World Affairs event, Xi referred to China as the largest country in the world and India as the largest country in South Asia. It reflects China's overall perception of India. "A clarification on the LAC (Line of Actual Control) is very important. It has been pending for years, it is time to start it again," said Modi. If there is peace and stability, friendship and cooperation on the border, we can utilise the possibilities and contribute in each other's growth, and give a new direction to the world economy."

India, China ink a dozen agreements under Modi Government

India and China exchanged 12 documents of understanding, the first agreement was on a new route to Kailash Mansarovar, while two pacts were on trade development. There were also agreements on audio video co-production, on cooperation in railways and on exchanges between cultural institutions.

As per the agreement, China will be opening an additional route to Kailash Mansarovar via Nathu La. Modi thanked the Chinese president Xi Jinping on behalf of all Indians for a new route to Kailash Mansarovar. This new route, which will be opened through Nathu La, will be in addition to the existing route via Uttarakhand. Modi said, "My decision will help more and more Indians reach Kailash Mansarovar, in particular the old, as transportation on motorcycles would be available on the new route. The pilgrims will be benefitted in a big way. Besides that, this road will remain safe during the rainy season, too."

On improving the trade deficit, he said, "I raised the issue of trade imbalance between the two countries. I urged President Xi to give our companies better market access and investment opportunities in China to which the president agreed. We have much scope to increase economic cooperation, as it was way below the potential." India-China bilateral merchandise trade stood at $65.88 billion in 2013. While India's exports to China was valued at $14.50 billion, its imports were much larger at $51.37 billion, resulting in a large trade deficit. He was pleased with the inking of agreements for two Chinese industrial parks in India and Beijing's commitment to invest around $20 billion in India over the next five years. "I invited Chinese investments in infrastructure and manufacturing sectors. I am glad that two Chinese industrial parks will be built in India."

Visit to the land of the rising sun Japan

Japanese PM Shinzo Abe went out of his way to receive Modi in Kyoto when he went there on August 30 in the first leg of his 5-day tour. A pact was signed under which Modi's Lok Sabha constituency Varanasi would be developed on the pattern of Kyoto 'smart city' with the help of Japan. As an example of Indo-Japan Cooperation, Tokyo will help India in providing financial, technical and operational support to introduce Bullet trains, a project that Modi has been actively pursuing.

"This is not just raising the relationship from one category to another... Our relationship is not only regional in its framework, but will have a global impact," Modi said.

Following the visit of Modi to Japan, the country announced doubling of its private and public investments in India to about $34 billion over the next five years for developmental projects. The two countries decided to elevate their ties to a special strategic global partnership but failed to conclude a civil nuclear deal.

During his summit talks on the third day of his visit with Japanese counterpart Shinzo Abe, the two leaders reaffirmed the importance of bilateral defence relations in their strategic partnership and agreed on greater defence equipment and technology cooperation. The two countries decided to expedite talks on sale of US-2 amphibian aircraft to India for enhancing maritime security. Five pacts covering defence exchanges, cooperation in clean energy, roads and highways, healthcare and women were also signed while vowing to take their relationship to newer level. He also decided to speed up negotiations on civil nuclear deal that could not be concluded.

Japan also lifted ban on six Indian entities including Hindustan Aeronautics Limited (HAL) which had been imposed in the aftermath of 1998 nuclear tests.

During his visit, Modi invited Japanese investments while hard-selling India as a conducive destination for business particularly for the manufacturing sector. He told the Japanese businessmen that India was awaiting the investments with a 'red carpet' and not 'red tape' as rules and procedures have been eased by his government. He expressed gratitude to Japan for reposing 'trust' in India and demonstrating its friendship with a quip "yeh fevicol se be zyada mazboot jod hai (this bond is stronger than that of fevicol)".

"There has been talk about billions and millions. But there has never been talk of trillions," he said, referring to 3.5 trillion Yen (USD 35 billion or 2,10,000 crore) promised by Japan to India through public and private funding over the five years for various works, including building of smart cities and cleanup of the Ganga river.

Modi may have failed to get the nuclear deal in Japan but signing an agreement to make Varanasi, his constituency, a smart, green, modern city and got a pledge for $35 billion in investment is no mean achievement.

The broad smiles on the faces of the two Prime Ministers and their body language said it all, reported a news daily. In the coming years, a lot more will flow from Japan. The India-Japan strategic partnership looks real; it's not a one-night stand.

Fortunate enough, the three countries US, China and Japan came courting to Modi's country, India. While we might have enjoyed time-long links with China and Japan and Modi himself attaches importance and priority to relations with China, independent India has many more things in common with the US than with either China or Japan. This is the only melting pot where three million people of Indian origin have made their dreams come true occupying some of the highest governmental positions. So, while both China and Japan can play major roles in India's economic transformation with their investments, to fulfill India's regional and global aspirations a strategic partnership with the US is indispensable, feel the economic experts.

Modi markets Brand India to top CEOs in US

Next, Modi heads to the US to meet President Barack Obama. A devotee of 'Shakti', Modi refrains from food during Navratras (nine auspicious days) and he continued his regime during his visit to US as well. There were no gala dinner parties, no toast raisings, even non vegetarian food was out of question for the guests since Modi had sent a prior request to the US authorities. Obama respected his diet restraints and the Indian ethos.

The US that boycotted him for a decade had taken a U-turn after his election and gone out of the way to build a productive relationship. The visits of eminent people from US to India viz., Assistant-secretary Biswal, secretary of state John Kerry, defence secretary Chuck Hegel, and further the appointment of Richard Rahul Verma as the next US ambassador to India, underline American keenness to put the recent past behind and expand and deepen relations with India under a strong, nationalist Modi whose line 'Sabka saath, sabka vikas' was tried by Mr. Kerry during his visit.

At the backdrop, the US is still recovering from the economic downturn and with an unemployment rate of around seven per cent, is still the superpower of the world can significantly increase greater access to its market, easier working environment for Indian IT and pharmaceutical companies, higher technologies, alternative energy resources, joint research programmes in select fields, and a whole range of defence deals it had never before offered to India. In return, it is India's regional profile that the US wants to fit in its Asian and global strategy. Japan too wants to keep India on its side to counter Chinese assertiveness. And China's strategy seems to dissuade India from getting too close to the US and Japan.

Modi embarked on five-day visit to the US at the end of September. The Madison Square where the Indian community had arranged his welcome and address became 'Modison Square'. At the breakfast table on Sept. 29 with the CEOs of top US companies, he spoke with the knowledge and authority of a business honcho who could market India as an investment destination better than anyone else, say the witnesses. He had not taken along any minister or official with a technical commerce background as part of his entourage. The reason being, he is the best negotiator, and he knows exactly what he wants for the country from the top CEO of any global multinational. He spent around 15-20 minutes with each CEO during face to face talk with six individual CEOs of top US companies and institutions. He interacted with leading individual CEOs, including Google's Eric Schmidt, David M. Rubenstein of The Carlyle Group, Citi group CEO Michael Corbat, Doug Oberhelman of Caterpillar Inc., Indra Nooyi of Pepsico and Michael Ball of US-based global pharmaceutical company Hospira Inc. and Kenneth C. Frazier of Merck and Co. The top business honchos of US on the list of one-on-one meetings were: W. James (Jim) McNerney Jr., chairman of Boeing; Laurence D. Fink, CEO of American multinational investment management firm Black Rock; Ginni Rometty, president and CEO of IBM; Jeffrey R. Immelt. Chairman and CEO of General Electric; Lloyd Blankfein, chairman and CEO of Goldman Sachs; and Henry Kravis, CEO of American private equity fund Kohlberg Kravis Roberts and Co. (KKR).

The initiator of Vibrant Gujarat, Modi was very conversant during the business talks. With great confidence and elan with the officials he placed the needs of investment before the CEOs clearly, promising all help, and getting firm answers, say the people who saw him in action.

He promised a red carpet treatment for investors minus the frustrating red tape. Notably The Vibrant Gujarat biennial event was launched in 2003. It has grown in the last 12 years to emerge as 'a global business hub' and has established Gujarat as a major investment destination. The next year's summit, to be held in January, is being tagged as the 'Devos of the East'.

In an appreciative move, Modi did not took a train of people from his cabinet on his visit abroad, rather the business tycoons like Ambani accompanying him paid their own travel fares. Minister for external affairs Sushma Swaraj who was already in New York joined him when he arrived in New York. Among the other top officials accompanying the prime minister on his major trip were National Security Advisor Ajit Doval and Foreign Secretary Sujatha Singh.

Back home, he initiated a number of projects which created a wave in the nation towards betterment.

Swachta Abhiyan turns a big success

The country witnessed a majestic launch of 'Swachh Bharat Mission' on the occasion of 145th birth anniversary of Mahatma Gandhi on October 2. Modi asked his countrymen to help build a nation that fulfils the dream of the father of the nation.

"Gandhiji's thoughts and beliefs remain a great inspiration for us. Let us dedicate ourselves to building the India of Gandhiji's dreams," he said. He visited Rajghat shortly before launching his Swachh Bharat Abhiyan that aims to clean up India in five years. He made a surprise visit to Mandir Marg Police Station and took stock of cleanliness. A keen votary of 'Clean India', Modi had given several exhortations in this regard. In his Independence Day speech, Prime Minister Modi had talked of the Swachh Bharat campaign and called for India to be clean by October 2019, Mahatma Gandhi's 150th birth anniversary.

In his Madison Square address in US to about 18,000-odd Indian Americans, his reference to this issue received a major shot in the arm, with India and the United States both agreeing to work together on this front.

PM invites nine public figures to contribute to Swachchha Bharat Abhiyan (Clean India) and share their experience on social media

He recalled how the nation's farmers had responded to first Indian prime minister Lal Bahadur Shastri's call of 'Jai Jawan, Jai Kisan', and made India self-sufficient in food security. He said that out of Gandhiji's two dreams – Quit India, and Clean India, the people had helped to ensure that the first became a reality. However, the second dream the 'Clean India' still remained a far-fetched reality.

Modi said it was our social responsibility as citizens of India to help fulfil Gandhiji's vision of Clean India, by his 150th birth anniversary in 2019. He exhorted people to fulfil Mahatma Gandhi's vision of Swachh Bharat.

He said that according to the WHO, an average of ₹ 6500 per person was lost in India due to lack of cleanliness and hygiene. Swachh Bharat would therefore make a significant impact on public health, and in safeguarding income of the poor. It will ultimately contribute to the national economy. He extolled the people to devote 100 hours every year towards the cause of cleanliness. He emphasized the importance of building toilets as much and even more than building temples stressing sanitation not be seen as a political gimmick, rather connected to patriotism and commitment to public health.

He invited nine public figures from the country: Mridula Sinha, Sachin Tendulkar, Baba Ramdev, Shashi Tharoor, Anil Ambani, Kamal Hasan, Salman Khan, Priyanka Chopra and Team Tarak Mehta ka Oolta Chashma – to make a contribution towards Swachh Bharat, share the same on social media, and invite nine other people to do the same, hence forming a chain. He urged people to share their contributions on social media using the hash-tag #MyCleanIndia.

The whole India participated in the campaign from a small office babu to a bureaucrat, from a street child to a school student, from a housewife to a businessman – almost the whole country supported the cause and realized the importance of cleanliness.

A common man of India pledged with Modi on October 2 -

I take this pledge that I will remain committed towards cleanliness and devote time for this. I will devote 100 hours per year that is two hours per week to voluntary work for cleanliness. I will neither litter nor let others litter. I will initiate the quest for cleanliness with myself, my family, my locality, my village and my work place.

The three country visit for world Summits

Narendra Modi visited Myanmar in November, the sixth country after he took over his office on 26 May in 2014. He visited

Bhutan (6-7 June), Brazil for BRICS summit (13-16 July), Nepal (3-4 August), Japan (30 August-3 September) and the United States (26-30 September). In a span of six months in office, he completed visiting nine countries in six foreign trips. His ideology is to fast-track ongoing projects and launch new avenues of cooperation with the countries with which India has deep historical and cultural ties over centuries.

He led India at the India-ASEAN Summit and bilateral meetings with the leadership of Myanmar. He joined regional and global leaders to ensure stability and maintain balance in the region. The ninth edition of the East Asia summit reportedly emphasised on freedom of navigation and Sea Lanes of Communication in East and South East Asia amid China's growing ambitions in the region. The East Asia as well as India-ASEAN Summits made Modi catch up with several leaders. The participants at East Asia Summit were USA, Russia, China, India, Japan, South Korea, Australia, and New Zealand besides all ten members of ASEAN.

At Group of 20 nations (G-20) Summit

Adding another feather to his cap of firsts, Modi became the first Indian prime minister to visit Australia in 28 years after Rajiv Gandhi. He was accorded a red carpet welcome during his first bilateral visit to Australia during G-20 summit where he highlighted that India and Australia shared a special bond. Like America, the Indian diaspora in Australia too went crazy meeting him and taking selfies. He unveiled a 2.5 m bronze statue of Mahatma Gandhi which is installed at Roma Street Parkland in Australia's Queensland. At a civic reception hosted in his honour by Queensland premier Campbell Newman at the city hall, he exhorted the global community to take a cue from Gandhi's teachings of non-violence and love in meeting challenges like terrorism and global warming.

Along with the leaders of the Group of 20 nations, he vowed to implement an anti-corruption action plan as part of a drive against the use of shell firms and trusts to engage in tax evasion and money laundering. "We endorse the 2015-16 G20 anti-corruption plan that will support growth and resilience," the leaders said in a Communique released at the end of the two-day summit.

The G20 countries recognized that bribery imposes a heavy price on the public and private sectors with the annual cost of bribery estimated by the World Bank to be 1 trillion dollars.

Propositions by Narendra Modi

Narendra Modi proposed a global virtual centre for clean energy research and development, with adequate public funding, and invited G20 countries to invest in India's expanding energy sector. He made the proposal while observing that increased access to affordable, assured and clean energy supply for all should be a primary goal of the global community. "It is a major economic opportunity for all countries. Energy efficiency is the best source of clean energy. In India, for example, building energy efficiency in areas such as buildings, household appliances and industrial goods is receiving strong attention. I invite you to come and invest in this sector in India," he said.

Modi also said he believed that change in lifestyle, connecting with nature will be the most enduring response to energy challenges. He called for an ambitious and innovative effort to make renewable energy, especially solar energy, competitive with conventional energy. "In Gujarat, the canal-top project worked well and saved water, too," he said. On the second day of the summit he pitched for global cooperation on repatriation of black money stashed abroad showing that bringing back Indian black money stashed in foreign banks was his priority.

He encouraged the proposal of discussion on innovative funding models to ensure rapid expansion of renewable energy in a decentralised manner in rural areas. In countries like India, there are vast opportunities for those wishing to invest in clean coal technology.

Second PM to visit Fiji after Indira Gandhi

Modi became the second Indian prime minister to visit Fiji after Indira Gandhi at the time when the islands are shifting to the new democratic system. India has had close links with Fiji Islands, as it is home for a substantial minority of people of Indian origin. The majority of the Indians in Fiji are descendants of those indentured workers and early Gujarati migrants. History says that when the colonisers required labour to work on the sugarcane plantations, about 60,000 Indians were brought as indentured labourers to Fiji in three decades. In the early decades of the 20th century, Gujarati traders began arriving in Fiji to set up small businesses. A Gujarati community dominates the retail sector in Fiji now.

Modi announced a $75 million line of credit for the country's sugar industry. "It is a new day and a new beginning in our relations with Fiji. Fiji could serve as a hub for stronger Indian engagement with Pacific islands." During his meeting with Bainimarama, The Fijian counterpart, Modi sought greater security and defence cooperation with Fiji. He also announced a visa on arrival for Fijians and assistance projects that included a parliament library and doubling the scholarships and training slots in India for Fijians.

And thus the list of his accomplishments goes on.....

□

A letter by Narendra Modi before the legendary win in 2014 polls...

Dear friends,

It was the final day of electioneering campaign for the Lok Sabha elections in 2014. I conducted my final rally at Balia in eastern Uttar Pradesh, which is the land of Mangal Pandey, the leader of 1857 revolution.

After I was assigned the responsibility of being the Prime Ministerial candidate of the Bharatiya Janata Party on 13 September 2013, I toured the whole of India. The friends in my party informed me that I conducted about 5800 programmes in all including rallies, 3-D meetings and *Chai Pe Charcha* and the like, I travelled 73 lakh kilometres, and addressed a total of 440 programmes and rallies. This number includes the Bharat Vijay rallies too, which were started from 26 March 2014 with the blessings of Maan Vaishno Devi.

It was once again that I got a pleasant opportunity to look at the diversity of India, vigour of the people and glory of our culture. I have toured the country earlier too while working for the organisation, but the experience this time was unique and different.

I got an opportunity to get people's blessings like never before. Generally, a campaign lasting such long is considered very tiring, but I can feel satisfaction and bliss, it is an experience which a meditator attains after a long penance. This campaign gave me an opportunity to get people's blessings in the whole of my country.

When I glance over the entire campaign, the three terms that rise in my mind are – extensive, innovative, satisfactory.

During our election campaign, we have tried to deliver the agenda of good governance and development in every nook and corner of India. People are tired of listening to false promises, corruption and the oft-repeated dynastic statements in order to conceal their failures. They wish for a better future, and the NDA remains the only alliance which can bring about this transformation.

I was the happiest on seeing motivation and untiring work of the workers. It is one thing to watch a rally on television or social media, it is quite another experience to work on the grass root level. We do not look at this election campaign with a limited viewpoint of victory or loss. An election campaign is a memorable experience of a worker's life. It is an opportunity for strengthening and expanding an organisation, it is an opportunity to infuse confidence and strength into the relation between people and organisation. The workers visited from house to house, and conveyed the party message from people to people; we feel proud about them. Our campaign remains the tale of the hard work that every worker has put in, who has contributed selflessly for the creation of a better India.

During the entire campaign, we received continuous cooperation and guidance from the senior party leadership; it continued to give us infinite strength and inspiration, and workers were adequately motivated.

This campaign will ever be remembered for the innovative experiments. In politics, generally there are one-way messages; but we deviated from the convention in our *Chai Pe Charcha* programmes, which were innovative in spirit. The *Chai Pe Charcha* programme was held at more than 4000 places in the country. I sat in this programme for hours together, listened to the people's views and responded to them on different matters. I can remember that one such *Charcha* took place at Vardha (Maharashtra) where I met those families of the farmers who had ended their life by suicide. It was an occasion of extreme sorrow. Our farmers are helpless and compelled to lose their lives so many years after independence; while the government remains a mute spectator. How long can we allow this to continue?

Yet another innovative experiment was Bharat Vijay 3-D rallies. In one month, I addressed 3-D rallies at 1350 places in 12 rounds. I could see people's enthusiasm towards these 3-D rallies. Many youths thanked me for visiting their villages through social media and e-mail. People told our workers that they wished to meet Modiji on the stage.

For the first time in election history in India, a special Volunteer Portal India 272+ (http://www.india272.com) was launched. Millions of workers connected to it and greatly contributed online and at grass-root level. I was greatly benefited by their views and contribution. There remains infinite opportunity to revolutionise campaigning and create a paradigm shift in consultation of well-wishers and directing volunteers' contribution.

The social media was utilized in the campaign like never before. Many people showed me a number of creative messages, slogans and infographics on WhatsApp, which were quite popular. I took my own selfie after I cast my vote and requested you to send your selfies too. I talked to my friends in the print and electronic media. I was interviewed by Hindi, regional and English media.

The affection that I have obtained during the past eight months is simply unforgettable. The incident that occurred in the Patna rally on 26 October 2013 will remain etched in my memory. A number of bombs exploded there, but people's determination proved stronger over them. No man left the ground; I gave a clear message that day which I have kept repeating during the campaign – We can take a decision whether we should keep fighting with one another, or we should fight with poverty together. The first option will take us nowhere, while the second will raise our country to the zenith of finest achievements.

I should like to thank my countrymen, who have taken part in our rallies, 3-D programmes and discussions. People of all age-groups, castes and religions participated with us. I often said that it is not Narendra Modi or any one person who is contesting the election. The people of India have shouldered the responsibility of these elections, and each citizen of India has become a transmitter of change.

I conducted rallies at a number of places where the climate was very hot, yet people were present in them in large numbers. A few days ago, I was at Vishakhapatnam, when it started to rain all of a sudden, but the people remained where they were. I have no words to thank them. I wish to assure the people of India that I shall repay their gratitude in the form of unprecedented development, which will become the foundation stone of a strong India.

The campaign has ended today, but one final phase of voting remains. I appeal to all people, especially the youth, to go and vote to create a record. Those who have to vote in the final phase, they all must go; please motivate all your family members and friends to vote; every vote counts for the country.

During my tour of India, I have directly experienced that our country is unique, it has a specific responsibility. There are numerous instances in history how our country has guided the world from time to time; and today, it is once again needed that India play the role of *Jagadguru*, the world's spiritual leader. Come, let us all create and construct a strong and developed country together that will guide the world.

10.5.2014

Yours,

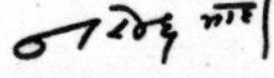

Narendra Modi

□

Major International initiatives undertaken after becoming PM

In the course of his 5-day visit to Japan in August end, the PM Narendra Modi signed a number of bilateral agreements, resulting in doubling of Japanese investments into India. With this Indo-Japan ties are being elevated to 'Global Strategic Partnership' status. Japan is the fourth largest investor in India, and the two countries conduct bilateral trade of about $16 billion, of which Japan enjoys a trade surplus. Japan is also India's largest bilateral donor. A quick glance shows :

- Japan has committed to **doubling its current investment** in India to $35 billion over the next five years. This will be primarily towards developing India's infrastructure and will involve Japanese firms. The agreement also envisages a doubling of Japanese firms doing business in India.
- Japan has also pledged $500 million towards the **Public-Private Partnership Infrastructure Financing Project** to the India Infrastructure Finance Company Limited (IIFCL). Additionally, Japan will also provide about $156 million for the Guwahati Sewerage Project in Assam.
- Both countries will work towards industrial infrastructure development with the creation of Smart **Community projects in six Indian states** as part of the Delhi Mumbai Industrial Corridor (DMIC) Project. The DMIC project will involve cooperation in developing power plants, assured water supply, high-volume urban transport, logistics facilities and skill development programmes for youth in regions along the corridor.
- **Ponneri in Tamil Nadu, Krishnapatnam in Andhra Pradesh and Tumkur in Karnataka** have been marked as

potential industrial nodes, and officials from both countries have been instructed to finalise the Master Plan and the **Development Plan** of these cities by March 2015.

- Modi also inked a Memorandum of Understanding (MoU) between the Ministry of New and Renewable Energy of India and the Japan Bank for International Cooperation (JBIC) in the field of new and renewable energy. Both sides have also asked their officials to move forward on the civil nuclear energy program, which has been held up from the Japanese side since India's nuclear weapons tests in 1998. Additionally, both countries will cooperate on **building highly efficient and environment-friendly coal-fired power plants**, and on cooperation in Clean Coal Technologies (CCT).
- India and Japan signed an agreement on the development of the Shinkansen system **Bullet trains** for India, starting with the Mumbai-Ahmedabad corridor. As part of this deal, Japan will provide technical, financial and operational support for such trains. Japan also said it would help India improve connectivity with its neighbouring countries, besides improving transport routes to the North Eastern states.
- Japan has agreed to **ease foreign end-user entities** list for India. As a starter, it has removed 6 Indian space defence-related entities from its restricted list. Both countries will also conduct talks to identify future areas of cooperation.
- The Joint Working Group will work on **speeding up cooperation on the US-2 amphibian aircraft**, which will include transfer of the aircraft and its technology to India. Both countries will also work on the roadmap for development of the Indian aircraft industry.
- Japan will work with India on **creating smart cities, starting with the Kyoto-Varanasi project.** As part of this, Japan will help India Varanasi – Modi's Parliamentary constituency – develop urban infrastructure to make it a 'smart' city. Japan will also help India improve basic amenities across selected cities.
- Modi will set up a Special Management Team within the Prime Minister's Office to deal exclusively with

Japanese investment. This special cell will **facilitate Japanese investments** so that they do not get bogged down in red tape.

(Source : Business Standard)

And thus the list of achieving milestones goes on....

□

What People Say about Narendra Modi

"India is faced with many challenges. In such a situation, there is need to adopt and preserve the Buddha's teachings and principles. The Gujarat Government is doing this well."

—**Dalai Lama** (*Spiritual Guru, Nobel Laureate*)

"Narendra Modi has several qualities. May God make him the next Prime Minister. My blessings are always with him."

—**Jayendra Saraswati** (*Jagadguru Shankaracharya*)

"Development is not making to the villages due to contradictory decisions and lack of transparency. In such a situation, the Gujarat model is proving effective. It is being used to deliver the benefit of modern technology even in rural areas."

—**A.P.J. Abdul Kalam** (*Former President of India*)

"We all wish to see Narendra Modi as Prime Minister. I pray to God that he should control the reigns of the country."

—**Lata Mangeshkar** (*Bharat Ratna Awardee*)

"At present, the commitment and devotion that Narendra Modi has shown for development of Gujarat is welcome. I wish to pray that he should serve the country and he may be blessed with that ability."

—**Pramukh Swami Maharaj** (*Shastri Narayan Swarupdas*)
[*Bochasanvasi Sri Akshar Purushottam Swminarayan Sansthan (BAPS)*]

"Treading on the ideals of Mahatma Gandhi, Gujarat has become the only state where corruption is being effectively controlled."

—**Justice V.R. Krishna Ayyar** (*Former Justice, Supreme Court*)

"The people of Gujarat are according Narendra Modi with majority for long. He has the capability to determine the country's vision."

—**N.R. Narayana Murthy** (*Founder, Infosys*)

"The leadership of Narendra Modi is worth emulating. He has the capability to lead the entire country."

—**Ratan Tata** (*Former Chairman, Tata Group*)

"We have a farsighted leader in the form of Narendra Modi. He is a source of inspiration for everybody."

—**Mukesh Ambani** (*Chairman, Reliance Industries*)

"Narendra Modi has come stronger in economic development. He is the proper man to take India out of financial crisis. Narendra Modi is the better option to improve upon the directionless government administration and falling rupee."

—**Christopher Wood** (*Well-known economic strategist*)

"I visited Gujarat and saw the roads from Ahmedabad to Surat and Vadodara. I saw that the roads are quite good even in villages. There is electricity even in huts."

—**Mahashweta Devi** (*Well-known writer*)

□

Untiring Journey

- 17 September 1950: Narendra Modi is born at Vadnagar, a small village in Mahesana district (Gujarat).
- Begins to attend the Rashtriya Swayamsevak Sangh Shakha at the age of about eight years. Shared work with father after school, his father had a tea stall near Vadnagar railway station.
- 1956: Worked as a volunteer in Mahagujarat movement at a small age.
- 1962: During India-China War, he voluntarily served the troops at railway station despite his small age.
- During the flood in the Tapi river, 12-year-old Narendra Modi installed a tea stall in Janmashtami fair to collect money for the flood victims. He went there personally too.
- 1967: Passed matriculation. Took admission in Visnagar College, 20 km from Vadnagar. Went to college for a few days. Started work with the ABVP. Later, left home to become a *Sanyasi*.
- 1970: Wandered about in the Himalayas and different monasteries, and then returned home.
- 1970-71: Left home again and came to Ahmedabad. Worked on the tea stall of his uncle Babubhai on the bus station of state transport. Came into contact with the Sangh again. Stayed at the Rashtriya Swayamsevak Sangh headquarters on the request of Vakil Saheb.
- 1973: Devoted to the service of Mother India as a Sangh *Pracharak*.
- 1973: Completed Sangh training, first year at Nadiad, second year at Bajwa (Baroda) in 1975 before Emergency, and third year at Nagpur in 1978. On the advice of Vakil Saheb, restarted his studies and completed his BA in political science as an external student from Delhi University.
- 1974: Played vital roles in anti-corruption and reconstruction

movement and remained underground for 19 months (from June 75 to January 77) to fight the Central Government against its Fascist policies and revived the spirit of democracy.

- 1978: Became the *Vibhag Pracharak* of the Rashtriya Swayamsevak Sangh (Baroda gram, Panchmahal, Dahod, Anand, Kheda). Two years later became *Sambhag Pracharak* (Baroda to Dang area).
- 1981: Stayed at Dr. Hedgewar Bhavan, Gujarat state Sangh headquarters, and carried the responsibility of Ahmedabad *Vibhag Pracharak* and *Prant Sahvyavastha Pramukh.*
- 1981: Earned his postgraduate degree from Gujarat University.
- 1987: Joined the Bharatiya Janata Party and thus entered mainstream politics. Within a year, he was appointed the general secretary of Gujarat unit of the party. By this time, he was known as a skilled organizer.
- 1987: With his entry in the BJP, he got the party victory in Ahmedabad nagar palika elections. It was for the first time for the BJP.
- 1987: Planned for Nyaya Yatra, perhaps the BJP started the *yatras* from this period, and its credit goes to Narendra Modi. Gujarat suffered from drought for three consecutive years and the State Congress Government failed miserably. This *yatra* passed through 115 tehsils and 15,000 villages. Narendra Modi also organised the Footpath Sansad too, that is, he held small meetings in streets, houses, colonies and crossings.
- 1989: Organised the Lokshakti Yatra to extend the influence of the Bharatiya Janata Party. This *yatra* was organised in five stages and it created awareness in Gujarat for five months.
- 25 September 1990: Started the historical *yatra* from Somnath to Ayodhya under the leadership of Lal Krishna Advani. The *yatra* from Somnath to Mumbai was organised by Narendra Modi. This *yatra* could travel up to Bihar only.
- 3 March 1990: The alliance government of Bharatiya Janata Party and Janata Dal came to power. In this victory, Narendra Modi spread the influence of the Bharatiya Janata Party to the rural level.
- 11 December 1991: The Ekta Yatra started from Kanyakumari and completed with the hoisting of the Tricolour at Lal Chowk in Srinagar, despite the threats of terrorists. The entire *yatra* was under the charge of Narendra Modi. Its organisation was so well-

managed that his power of organisation and ability to hold programmes came into the eyes of the national leadership.

- 1991: Narendra Modi made the member of the BJP national election committee. In Gujarat, BJP won 20 out of 26 seats in elections for the Tenth Lok Sabha.
- 1993: The centenary anniversary of Swami Vivekananda's historical speech at Chicago was held in America. Narendra Modi visited there on special invitation.
- 1995: Narendra Modi made the organisation of Gujarat BJP so strong and effective that it won 121 out of 182 seats in the Vidhan Sabha elections held in this year. Keshubhai Patel became the Chief Minister on 14 March 1995.
- 1995: Shankarsinh Vaghela of BJP grew power hungry and he revolted against his own party, and Keshubhai Patel had to resign from the post of CM. On 28 September 1995, Narendra Modi resigned from the post of state general secretary. On 20 November 1995, he was made the national general secretary of the BJP. Now, his centre of work was Delhi. He was made the in-charge of Haryana, Himachal Pradesh, Chandigarh, Punjab and Jammu and Kashmir. He was given the charge of organization, which was a great achievement for any youth leader. Narendra Modi carried out this tough task devotedly and with perseverance.
- 1998: Impressed by his organizational skill, the national leadership assigned him the responsibility of national general secretary (organization). This post was held in the past by such stalwarts like Pandit Deen Dayal Upadhyay, Sundar Singh Bhandari and Keshubhau Thakre.
- 1998: Elections were held for Gujarat Vidhan Sabha. Modi was once again asked to command this election in Gujarat. With his arrival, the entire scenario underwent a change. His rapid fire propaganda destroyed the Congress there. The BJP Government was formed under the leadership of Keshubhai Patel.
- Narendra Modi returned to Delhi soon after elections. He continued with his work with devotion and hard work helping the BJP extend its image. In 1999, the NDA Government was formed at the Centre under the leadership of Atal Bihari Vajpayee.
- 2000-01: Visited Australia and Malaysia. Also travelled America

and other countries, and held discussions with prestigious leaders.

- October 2001: The party asked him to command the Gujarat Government. When on 7 October 2001, Narendra Modi was sworn in as the Chief Minister, Gujarat was passing through a critical stage due to the massive earthquake as well as other natural calamities. Narendra Modi took benefit of his national and international experiences and confronted with these problems head on.
- He was faced with the challenge of reconstruction and rehabilitation after the earthquake, as Bhuj had turned into a town of ruins and thousands of people were living in makeshift shelters without any basic amenities. Narendra Modi transformed the negative situations into opportunities for all-round development.
- Narendra Modi decided to pay attention to the social sector in order to reform the imbalance adopting suitable methods for all-round development in social and economic fronts. He laid down the Panchamrit scheme for all-round development of the state.
- A great change occurred under his leadership in the fields of education, agriculture and health. Keeping the future of the state in mind, he started the policy-based reform programmes. He reconstructed the government structure in order to bring Gujarat back on the prosperity track.
- 24 February 2002: Won election from Rajkot Vidhan Sabha constituency.
- 2002: His wish and capability was known in 100 days of his becoming the CM. With his administrative insight, foresight and character integrity, he came back to power with a massive victory, in which he won 128 of 182 seats.
- 22 December 2002: Was sworn in for the second term as the Chief Minister.
- 2007: Once again won huge majority in the Vidhan Sabha elections under the leadership of Narendra Modi. He was sworn in as the Chief Minister for the third time in a row.
- 17 September 2012: Narendra Modi completed 4000 days in the service of Gujarati people. He continued to get people's affection and support in three consecutive elections.

- 2012: Modi once again won huge majority in the Vidhan Sabha elections. The BJP won 115 seats, and on 26 December 2012, he was sworn in for the fourth time.
- Gujarat has won several honours and awards from all over the world. The UN gave him the Sasakava award for disaster management, CAPM award for creative and active administration, and UNESCO award, as well as CSI award for e-governance. For three consecutive years, Narendra Modi has won the award of best Chief Minister, which more than enough proves his achievements.
- He has done wonders by the Vibrant Gujarat programme. Now Gujarat has become a favourite place for the global investors. In 2013 Vibrant Gujarat summit, representatives from 120 countries took part, which is an achievement in itself.
- 9 June 2013: Narendra Modi became the chairman of the BJP election campaign in Goa executive council, and in September 2013, he was announced as the prime ministerial candidate of the BJP. It was announced by Rajnath Singh, the national president of the Bharatiya Janata Party.

The inauguration of the Statue of Unity, representing Sardar Vallabhbhai Patel, the national leader of integration and unity, near Sardar Sarovar Project (Kevadia), which is the tallest statue in the world.

Continuous affection and all-round success is adorned by only a few people, but Narendra Modi has achieved all this. Within a small time, he has emerged as a leader who is capable to emancipate India from her sufferings and scarcities, and can lead the country to prosperity.

26 May 2014, took the oath as 15th Prime Minister of the country after BJP-led NDA won the Lok Sabha election with an emphatic victory.

□□□